The Auerbach Will

"Has the magic word 'bestseller' written all over it . . . Birmingham's narrative drive never falters and his characters are utterly convincing."
—JOHN BARKHAM REVIEWS

"Delicious secrets—scandals, blackmail, affairs, adultery . . . the gossipy, Uptown/Downtown milieu Birmingham knows so well."
—KIRKUS REVIEWS

"An engrossing family saga."
—USA TODAY

"Colorful, riveting, bubbling like champagne."
—PHILADELPHIA INQUIRER

"Poignant and engrossing . . . has all the ingredients for a bestseller."
—PUBLISHERS WEEKLY

STEPHEN BIRMINGHAM
THE AUERBACH WILL

B

BERKLEY BOOKS, NEW YORK

The translation of the lines in Yiddish on pages 56 and 404 is by I. J. Schwartz (Foverts Publication, New York, 1918), and was kindly supplied by Dr. Herbert H. Paper, Dean of the School of Graduate Studies at Hebrew Union College.

This Berkley book contains the complete
text of the original hardcover edition.
It has been completely reset in
a typeface designed for easy
reading, and was printed from
new film.

THE AUERBACH WILL

A Berkley Book / published by arrangement with
Little, Brown & Company

PRINTING HISTORY
Little, Brown edition published 1983
Berkley edition / September 1984

ISBN: 0-425-07462-5

A BERKLEY BOOK ® TM 757,375
Berkley Books are published by The Berkley Publishing Group,
200 Madison Avenue, New York, New York, 10016.
The name "BERKLEY" and the stylized "B" with design
are trademarks belonging to Berkley Publishing Corporation.

PRINTED IN THE UNITED STATES OF AMERICA

For Ed Lahniers

CONTENTS

THE AUERBACH WILL

The
BOOK
of
ESTHER

One

———❦———

"PEOPLE used to say I was an absolute ringer for Gene Tierney," Joan is saying, standing in front of the long mirror of the entrance hall. "An absolute ringer." She fingers her throat. "Do you like this necklace, Mother? It's by Kenny Jay Lane. The stones aren't real, and neither is the gold, but I think it's an amusing fake."

"I'd be nervous about wearing real stones these days," Essie says. "Mrs. Perlman, downstairs, had a diamond and sapphire clip ripped off her jacket by a man on the street, right here on Park Avenue." Essie is thinking how well Joan has kept her figure, that extraordinary thinness. Most women, when they reach a certain age, tend to thicken around the middle like— well, like Essie Auerbach herself—but not Joan. Oh, of course Essie knows how Joan does it. She never eats. Oh, sometimes an asparagus spear, a little bit of fish, a mouthful of spinach. But otherwise she just pushes the food about on her plate, pretending to eat. She lets her wineglass be filled, but just pretends to sip at it. She helps herself to the dessert, spoons the raspberry sauce over it, but doesn't touch it. Before dinner, she always asks for a bourbon old-fashioned, but just pretends to drink it. Essie Auerbach has long since given up trying to tell her daughter that she needs to eat to stay healthy. After all, Joan is never sick.

Seeing Joan, still a perfect size four, walking toward you on a crowded street, or across a softly lighted room, you might think for a moment that this was the body of a trim teenager, her glossy reddish-brown hair—thanks to the ministrations of

3

her hairdresser—bouncing slightly. Only at close range would you discover that Joan is . . . well, that Joan is Joan. Has Joan had her face lifted? Essie would never dare to ask that question of her oldest daughter, but there was that long, unexplained trip to Argentina just before Joan married Richard, and when she came back everyone had remarked on how "rested" Joan looked. And Essie had noticed that the small mole on Joan's chin was gone. And so the answer to that question, Essie thinks, is probably.

Standing before the glass, Joan straightens the shoulder strap on her black lace dress and turns to her mother. "Before we go in, I want to ask you to do something for me, Mother. I want you to speak to Richard. He's got this idiotic idea of going to South Africa to research a book he wants to write on race relations, or some idiotic thing. I can't afford to let him go. I need him to edit the paper. I want you to tell him that this is not the time for him to go, that I need him here, that you personally oppose it."

"Richard's your husband, Joan."

"Ha! That's just the thing. He won't listen to me. *Your* word will have more weight."

"And aren't you also his—well, employer?"

"That's the rest of it. How can I threaten to fire my own husband? Think of the story the *Times* would make of that one. Besides, he has a contract. Richard's no slouch."

"Well, then that's easy. If he has a contract, he has to stay."

"Unfortunately, he doesn't. Stupidly, I agreed that he could have a six-month sabbatical every two years. He wants to exercise that option now. So please do as I ask, Mother. The paper's at a crucial point right now. He's damn good at his job, and it's crucial that I have him here."

Essie hesitates. "Joan, has that newspaper of yours ever made any money?"

Joan's dark eyes flash angrily, and Essie knows that it is not wise to trespass any further into this danger-ridden territory. Joan's temper is legendary. When, Essie thinks, did the flighty debutante turn into the strident female executive, when did thinness turn to brittleness? *Stop the presses!* she can hear Joan commanding. *Start them again!*—all in the exercising of

Joan's managerial power. Did Gene Tierney ever play Lady Macbeth? "Never mind," Essie says.

"Of course it's made money!" Joan says. "And right now it's at a *crucial* turning point, into the really big money. We have new advertisers all lined up. That's why it's so important."

Essie does not say that she has heard this sort of thing often before from Joan. New advertisers have always been "lined up." Essie envisions them in a long queue, single-file, portfolios in hand, bulging attaché cases, outside her daughter's walnut-paneled office door downtown. But the line does not move. It just stands there, blocked at the gates of power, foundering, uncertain—afraid, perhaps, to tap on the door of the thin, stylish woman who sits at her Chippendale desk inside, twirling a gold pencil. Whenever Essie has read of her daughter's enterprise it seems to have been in terms of the word "foundering": "The foundering New York *Express,* still fueled by the Auerbach millions, etc., etc."

"Don't forget you're a stockholder in the paper, too, Mother. Will you do as I ask?"

"I'll do my best," Essie says. They start together across the wide foyer and into the paneled library where Richard, looking fit in a hacking jacket, stands at the bar fixing drinks.

"Good evening, Richard," Essie says.

"Hi, Nana. Merry Christmas." He steps toward her, takes both her hands in his, and gives her a peck on the cheek.

Richard McAllister is the fourth of Joan's husbands, and perhaps the nicest. At least Essie thinks so. Of the others— well, the less said of them the better, since they are all gone now. Gone, each with a certain share of Joan's money, of course. Richard has always seemed, to Essie at least, to be less interested in the money, more interested in turning Joan's newspaper into something profitable and worthwhile and not, as it had once seemed to Essie, just another expensive hobby of Joan's. Richard, at least, had been listed ("journalist, author") in *Who's Who in America* when Joan married him, whereas the others . . . but forget about them. When Joan had told Essie that she was marrying a *goy,* that she was fed up with Jewish husbands, Essie was more than a little apprehensive. "Oil and water don't mix," as Essie's own mother used to say. Mama

had been full of little homilies like that ("Too many cooks spoil
the stew," "The early bird catches the worm"), picked up,
Essie supposed, as Mama had learned her new language. But
as far as Richard was concerned, Essie kept her own counsel,
as she usually did when it came to the things Joan wanted. And
the marriage seems to have worked out well, better than the
others, God knows. Joan and Richard have been married
now—how long?—eight years, at least, longer than the others. And as far as Essie knows Richard has never physically
abused her daughter, which was more ancient history. And he
seems to get along well with Joan's daughter, Karen. Seeing
him tonight, Essie thinks he looks very fine, distinguished
even, with his full head of sandy hair, blue eyes and that good,
straight nose. Essie has always been certain that Richard is
several years younger than Joan, but she has never brought up
that matter, either.

"I'll have my usual, darling," Joan says, sinking into one of
the deep leather chairs, all in one motion, with her thin ankles
crossed. "Bourbon old-fashioned, no cherry."

"How about you, Nana? A martini tonight, or some champagne?"

"I think my martini tonight, thank you, Richard."

Joan sits forward, looking expectant, as though about to
speak, but at that moment Mary Farrell appears at the library
door, a folder of papers in her hand. Mary has been Essie's
secretary for the last eighteen years. "Excuse me, Mrs. A,"
Mary says, "but I thought you might like to check the seating."

"Oh, yes, I'd better," Essie says. She follows Mary out of
the room, adding, "But I really don't know why, Mary. You
always do it perfectly."

The dining room is at the other end of the apartment, nearly
a full city block away. The apartment is large—too large,
Essie often thinks, for one old woman—but one grows accustomed to things, to certain familiar spaces, and one doesn't
want to make a change. She needs so much space, she has
always reminded herself, because of the art collection. At this
point in Essie's life, her paintings have become her oldest and
dearest friends, and she thinks that she could not bear to part
with one of them. As she and Mary pass through the long
central gallery where the heart of the collection hangs, she

greets them anew as they glow out from the dark walls under their museum lights—the seven Cézannes, the five Van Goghs, including her precious "L'Arlésienne," the Manets, the Monets, the Degas, the Renoirs, the Rousseau, and the magnificent Goya which the Prado has wanted to buy for years. Along the walls, too, in lighted glass cases, are the Shakespeare first folios and the collection of illuminated Bibles, and at each corner of the room the guardian sculptures—two by Rodin, two by Bourdelle. How did we have the wisdom, Essie asks herself, to find these beautiful things so long ago? The two women pass the curving staircase that leads to the upper floor, and enter the dining room where more old friends smile down from the walls.

"Oh, everything looks very pretty, Mary," Essie says. "Perfect, as usual."

"I chose anthuriums and ferns for the centerpieces," Mary says, "because I thought they looked—well, Christmassy. And I had them put in the two pink-and-green Ming bowls."

"Anthuriums. Very nice. They're an economy flower, too, you know. They last for weeks and weeks. Be sure to send them over to Mount Sinai in the morning."

"Of course. Now here's what I've done with the seating, Mrs. A." Mary takes out her seating chart, and moves along the table checking her diagram against the hand-lettered placecards in their silver stands. "On your right, I've placed the new man, Mr. Carter. First name, Daryl."

"Carter. Daryl Carter. Remind me, Mary. Who is he?"

"He's the gentleman Mrs. Schofield is bringing. She telephoned to ask if she might."

"Oh, dear."

"Should I have told her it was inconvenient?"

"Oh, no. No, it's all right. But you know what I mean."

Mary smiles discreetly. "Yes, I suppose I do."

"Another one. What will she come up with this time?"

Mrs. Schofield is Karen Schofield, Joan's daughter Karen, Essie's granddaughter Karen. "Poor Karen," Essie says.

"Well, I put him on your right so you could find out all about him first hand."

"Good girl."

"All I know about him is that he's with the Parks Department."

"Well. What kind of a job is that? He plants trees?"

Mary smiled her little smile, her secretarial smile. Mary Farrell's life is a mystery to Essie, despite all their years together. She comes and goes by subway, to and from her house in Kew Gardens where, as Essie gathers, she lives alone, arriving promptly at nine in the morning and leaving at five except, on nights like this one, when there is a party, when she stays a little later. There is much more that Mary does besides order the flowers and diagram the dinner table. She manages all the household accounts, pays the bills, pays the servants, remonstrates occasionally with Cookie—as Essie has always called her cook—for a tendency toward extravagance, particularly for ordering chocolate truffles from Maison Glass, which Cookie does simply because she knows Essie likes them. Mary is a list-maker, and in her files are lists of everything Essie owns, each filed in its separate category—the silver, the china, the jewels, the furs, the dresses, the shoes, the hats, even the gloves, the books, the stocks and bonds, and of course the paintings. Mary answers all of Essie's mail—the endless entreaties from charities, worthy and unworthy—meticulously typing the business letters at her little desk, writing the personal ones in a stylish longhand on heavy linen notepaper. Mary balances Essie's checkbook, and does all her business at the bank. She handles the telephone on Essie's private line. The only thing that Mary refuses to do is walk the poodles, Mimi and Charlemagne. That, she says, is Yoki's, the butler's, job, and probably she is right. This morning, Mary has been busy addressing—in longhand, of course—the last of some seven hundred Christmas cards, adding personal notes where appropriate, and writing out checks to each of the building's thirty-seven employees—-most of whom Essie has never seen—each in its proper amount, for their Christmas tips. In their years together, Essie thinks, Mary Farrell must have learned every secret there is to know about Essie and her family, and yet of Mary's private life—she must have been a nice-looking woman once; was there ever a lover? ever a husband?—Essie knows almost nothing at all.

Mary moves along the table with her list. "I didn't put Mrs.

Schofield next to Mr. Carter," she explains. "I gave him Mrs. Martin Auerbach on his right." Mrs. Martin Auerbach is Christina, married to Essie's oldest son, Martin, who has always been called Mogie, ever since Harvard days when he was called "The Mogul."

"And next to her I've put Mr. Klein . . ." Mr. Klein is Joe, married to Babette, the younger of Essie's two daughters. "Then Mrs. McAllister . . . then young Mr. Josh . . ." Young Mr. Josh is Joshua Auerbach, Jr., Essie's grandson, her youngest son's boy, just out of Princeton. He has joined the family business and is doing very well, and Essie is very proud of him. "Then Mrs. Schofield . . ."

"Good. As far away from her tree-planter as possible."

"And at the opposite head of the table, Mr. Wilmont . . ."

Jake's place, Essie thinks. But Jake has been dead for fifteen years.

"Now, on *your* left I've put Mr. Josh, Senior, then Miss Linda . . ." Linda Schofield is Karen's daughter, home on winter break from Bennington, and the only Auerbach great-grandchild at the party. "Then Mr. McAllister, then Mrs. Klein, then Mr. Mogie, and then Mrs. Josh, Senior, who'll be on Mr. Wilmont's right."

"Good. She'll be on the right of the Chairman of the Board and won't feel slighted. You know how Katie gets."

The secretarial smile again. "Yes. Well, that's it, Mrs. A. One reason I thought it would be all right for Mrs. Schofield to bring Mr. Carter was that otherwise it would have been thirteen."

"I'm not superstitious."

"And it does even out the sexes."

The occasion is Essie Auerbach's annual Christmas tree-trimming party. It is not, of course, the grand affair that it once was, years ago when Jake Auerbach was alive, when extra caterers' tables and gilt chairs were set up in the long gallery, and when as many as a hundred people sat down for dinner. In those days, with Jake's great influence, the Auerbachs' Christmas dinners had amounted to something like command performances for all the elite of New York's German Jewry—old Mrs. Lehman in her diamonds, and her nephew, the Governor, and old Mr. Lewisohn, who always wanted to sing the *Lieder*, and little Mrs. Loeb, so scatterbrained, who inevitably managed to get lost in the apartment trying to find the ladies' room and wound up in the butler's pantry dodging waiters with trays of food. And old Mrs. Warburg, who was hard of hearing, who shouted to compensate, and whom no one really liked, but who had to be invited because the Warburgs were—well, the closest thing to Jewish royalty New York City had ever seen, or so they seemed to think. Farther down the social scale came the Strauses, who owned stores but had "married up" into Guggenheims, and the Altmans and the Seligmans, nearly all of whom were in one way or another peculiar, but who were married to everybody who was supposed to matter. Through marriage, nearly everybody was related to everybody else—a number of them to Jake Auerbach himself—and there were double and triple cousins. Essie wishes she could say that she misses those kinds of entertainments, or any of those people— the women who wore long gowns and pearls for picnic lunches in the Adirondacks—but the fact is that she misses none of them at all. In fact, she can remember times when she actually despised—but no, it is Christmas, and she will try not to have uncharitable thoughts. But still, but still—

"I have them," she says.

"Beg pardon, Mrs. A?"

"Just thinking aloud, Mary. I mean I think I have them all memorized. Where they'll sit. Why don't you wind up, dear. You've had a long day."

"Well, then I think I'll say goodnight, Mrs. A."

"Goodnight, Mary."

Yes, Essie's Christmas parties are much smaller now, just the members of her immediate family. And Charles Wilmont, of course, who is almost like family—her children call him Uncle Charles—her husband's right-hand man at Eaton & Cromwell for all those years. Yes, Charles is just like family and, in some ways, more like family than some of the rest of them.

On her way back to the library, Essie pauses in the large sitting room where the big Norwegian spruce has been set up on its stand, and where Yoki has placed a stepladder and laid out all the boxes of ornaments from all the other Christmases. Somehow, though Essie's parties have gotten smaller, there seem to be more boxes of ornaments, and strands of lights, and tinsel, each year. There are at least thirty cartons full of ornaments and, when these are all hung, those boxes will be replaced with the gift boxes, now stacked in crowded closets. Essie sees that Yoki has laid fires in both fireplaces, at either end of the room, which will be lighted while they are having dinner. Meanwhile, to give the room a welcoming aroma, the tall scented tapers have been lighted in all the heavy silver sconces and candelabra, and the heavy récamier silk window hangings have been drawn shut. This is the largest, and most formal, room in Essie's apartment, but it is perhaps her least favorite. The other rooms are smaller, cozier, more inviting. Once upon a time this room was called the ballroom, and Essie does not need to be told that ballrooms are seldom found anymore in New York apartments. The Aubusson rug, woven for the room, can still be rolled back for dancing and, in the old days, two concert grand pianos nested back to back for music. Now there is only one piano, and the rest of the room is filled with French sofas, chairs, and tête-à-têtes originally bought for the Chicago house. Still, the room seems cavernous. But what can be done with a room two full stories high, with paneling of carved gilt boiserie, in which are set painted views of Florence, with trompe l'oeil frescoes painted on the ceiling to represent medieval tapestries, and suspended, from huge carved plaster rosettes, with a pair of Baccarat crystal chandeliers? The room, with its massive scale, has always had a way of miniaturizing, and trivializing, everything—and everyone—entering it. Essie rings for Yoki. "Let's put a small grouping of chairs around the tree," she says. "Otherwise, everybody will be all spread out."

"Yes, Madam."

From the library, now, Essie hears voices—more people have arrived. She hears Mogie's voice, and the shrill giggle of Christina, Mogie's very new, very young wife who, Joan said (could it be true?), had until meeting Mogie been a Rockette at Radio City Music Hall. Then, from the elevator entrance, there are more voices—the others seem all to have come together. The two maids are collecting coats, Yoki, changed from his white coat into gray, is passing drinks. The party has begun.

*   *   *

The young man on her right, Mr. Daryl Carter, Karen's new friend, seems pleasant enough, and is even good-looking in a pale, thin, rather washed-out way. Karen, who is in her forties, seems to be picking them younger and younger, Essie thinks. This man appears to be in his mid-twenties, and seems quite awestruck. He has been fingering the silk lace tablecloth, lifting the heavy silver three-pronged forks and pistol-handled knives, doing everything but pick up the series of service plates to examine the markings on their undersides. Essie has tried to put him at ease. But he has been so full of questions that Essie has been unable to find out much about him.

"So you're Karen's *grand*mother. Gee. Your granddaughter tells me you once had dinner at the White House," he is saying.

"Well, yes, when my late husband was alive."

"Which President was it?"

"Well, in fact, we had dinner at the White House a number of times. The first President was Mr. Wilson, who was rather stiff, and then came Mr. Harding, and then there was Mr. Coolidge, and then Mr. Hoover."

"You mean *all* of them?"

"They used to consult my husband on economic matters. Of all of them, I liked Mr. Harding the best. They said he was a crook, but I found him very down-to-earth."

"Golly!"

"When Mr. Roosevelt came along, my husband fell out of favor."

"But still—knowing all those Presidents!"

"I actually used to dread them, those White House dinners. All the formality, all the protocol—"

"Dread them? Really? I'd have given my eyeteeth."

The meat course is being passed and, from down the table, Joan leans out across her plate and, interrupting, says, "Mother, I told Richard that you had something to say to him."

"Can't it wait till after dinner, dear?" Essie says.

Eying Richard fiercely from across the table, Joan says, "Mother's position is that of a concerned stockholder, darling."

Really, Essie thinks, that is a little silly. Her interest in the *Express* is really very small—just a few hundred shares which she bought to keep Joan from badgering her to invest in it—

surely nothing compared with what Joan herself must have tied up in it.

"My son-in-law, Karen's stepfather, wants to go to Africa," Essie says rather lamely to Mr. Carter.

"Africa! Golly!"

Richard, working quietly on his veal chop, says nothing, but seems to be smiling slightly, or perhaps it is simply a chewing expression.

"We simply cannot let you go at this *point,* darling. The paper needs you now more than it ever did before. You, the most brilliant and talented journalist in the United States—"

Really, Essie thinks, this is carrying it a little far, simply because Richard is in *Who's Who in America.* Richard, looking up from his plate, says pleasantly, "I agree with Nana, Joan. After dinner. Okay?"

"She's a concerned stockholder."

At the foot of her table, Essie sees Charles Wilmont, who of course knows all about this, and who appears to be in earnest conversation with Katie, Josh's wife, but who manages, in just the briefest moment, to catch her look and to return her a quick wink. Dear Charles. What he has had to put up with with the Auerbachs. Essie decides that this is the moment to turn the conversation, and she turns to Josh, her youngest son, on her left. "Tell me, Josh," she says. "I want to know everything. I want to know how young Josh is doing with the company. . . ."

After dinner, Essie finds herself on the arm of young Mr. Carter, who has asked her to show him the rest of the apartment.

"Golly, is that a real Picasso?" he asks.

"Yes, and in fact all four of the big paintings in this room are by Picasso. We wanted one from each of his periods—the rose, the blue, the cubist . . ."

"Oh, wow."

"I call this the Picasso room," Essie says and, leading him along, ". . . and this little room I call the Gainsborough room, though the two paintings on that wall are by Romney. Both Gainsborough and Romney have gone out of fashion, I'm told, but still I'm quite fond of them.

". . . And this we called the Oriental room. As you can see, my husband also collected Chinese Export porcelains. I think it looks pretty displayed against the Coromandel screens, don't you? And these"—pointing to the locked glass bookcases—"are all incunabula."

"Incunabula?"

"Books printed before the year fifteen-oh-one. They're also called cradle books, for some reason."

"How did your husband have time to collect all these things, on top of everything else he did?"

"Well, there was a Mr. Duveen who helped us. And the Post-Impressionists were all bought when the prices were very, very low. Tell me, Mr. Carter—what do you do with the Parks Department?"

"Nothing as interesting as this," he says. Then he says, "Karen drinks too much."

"I know. What do you propose we do about it?"

He shakes his head. "She says she drinks because she's unhappy. But how can she be unhappy with all this—beauty—in her life? Golly, it's beyond me, Mrs. Auerbach. Beyond me."

"It's her mother. Joan hounds her. She hounds everybody."

He hesitates, as though wondering whether or not it would be proper to agree. "Mrs. McAllister is—a very good looking woman," he says.

"Oh, yes. When she was younger, there were some who said that she bore a resemblance to Gene Tierney, who was an actress," Essie says.

Now is it time to trim the tree and give the toasts, and everyone is gathered in the big sitting room where the tree has been set up and where Yoki has lit the fires. By tradition—how it started Essie cannot remember—each guest selects an ornament, fills a glass with champagne, and mounts the stepladder. From the ladder, he pins his ornament on the tree, and then proposes a toast. Sitting on one of the French sofas, Babette is still chattering, as she has been most of the evening, about Palm Beach, where she and Joe will soon be going to spend the rest of the winter in the Addison Mizner house they have bought there. Of her two daughters, Essie has to admit, Joan got the brains, whereas Babette—well, Babette has a mind more suited to the society type of life she chooses to live. Babette is saying, "Do you know that ever since Marjorie Post died, and now that Rose Kennedy is nothing but a shell, the Shiny Sheet is calling me one of P.B.'s leading hostesses? Isn't that extraordinary?"

Essie claps her hands. "Time to begin the toasts," she says.

As the president of Eaton & Cromwell, it is up to Josh Auerbach to make the first, and to carry the big star up and pin it to the top of the tree. It's funny, but whenever Essie sees Josh's name and photograph in the papers she has trouble reconciling this graying, good-looking "business leader," as he is usually called, in his early fifties, with the picture in her mind of the bright little boy who was her youngest son. Surely this tall man in a dark business suit who is mounting the ladder rather carefully, the star in one hand and his champagne glass in the other, cannot be the same Josh. But of course it is.

Essie finds an empty spot on a sofa next to Karen, and sits down beside her. "I very much enjoyed talking to your young man," she whispers.

Karen smiles into her glass, which Essie notices is not champagne, and is probably vodka. "Yes, he is nice, isn't he?"

"Is it serious, dear?"

"Oh, Grandma, I don't know. He's not all that smart, and he has no money. I almost didn't bring him, thinking he wouldn't be good enough for this family."

"I thought he held up very well," Essie says.

Now, from the top of the ladder, Josh has affixed his star and, with his free hand grasping the ladder, he turns, faces the room, and lifts his glass with the other. "Family, friends," he begins, "as most of us know, our mother celebrated her eighty-ninth birthday just two weeks ago. We all know that this time next year, when we all gather again, Mother will have marked an even more momentous birthday—her ninetieth. I know that all of us know, that as Mother enters her ninetieth year as head of this house, we all wish her another decade of health, happiness, and usefulness. Let's drink, then, with a special *l'chayim* greeting to Esther Auerbach."

There is a round of clapping, and cries of "Hear, hear!"

"Why, Josh, dear, how very nice," Essie says.

Now it is Mogie's turn. If Josh has turned out to be the

business head of the family, Mogie is the sensitive, artistic one. It is Mogie who plays both the cello and the violin so beautifully, and has collected four extraordinarily matched Amatis. Mogie also collects old silver, antique toys, and precious stones. He was not cut out for business, not from the very start, but that is all right. Or at least at this point there is no point in dwelling on Mogie's shortcomings as a businessman. Mogie is nine years younger than Joan, eight years younger than Babette, and ten years older than Josh, and it is sometimes difficult for Essie to realize that none of her remaining four children is in any way still a child. Far, far from it. Mogie is sometimes considered the best-looking of her children, though Essie would not agree. Her vote, if solicited, would go to Josh. But Mogie himself thinks highly of his looks, and cannot pass a mirror—or indeed a shop window—without an admiring glance, a necktie-adjusting pause, to appraise his reflected image. He is always immaculately tailored in bespoke suits from Helman, always shod in hand-made, hand-benched shoes from Lobb on St. James's Street. At home, Mogie is usually to be found in one of his large collection of silk pajamas and robes from Sulka, and Joan has wickedly suggested that even her younger brother's underwear has a designer label. The small gymnasium off his bedroom in his house in Beekman Place contains the latest in exercise equipment. His pink nails with their carefully shaped half-moons are always perfectly manicured and polished, and his crowning glory—a full head of wavy, silver hair—is dressed twice a week by Mr. Elio at Bergdorf's. There have been more women in Mogie's life than Essie could possibly count, and so she was happy to see him end his long bachelorhood, even though his pretty little blonde Christina still reminds Essie of a dance-hall hostess, despite the furs and jewels Mogie has bought her.

Mogie steps toward the tree, leaving behind him a faint waft of Guerlain Eau de Cologne Impériale as he moves. He has chosen an antique glass bell to hang on the tree, and now he turns to propose his toast. "I'd like to ask that we drink to someone who is no longer among us," he says, "a man whom we have to thank for all the blessings and good fortune and comforts which life has bestowed upon us—a pioneer in business and finance, a pioneer in philanthropy, both Christian and Jewish . . ."

Over her shoulder, Essie hears Mr. Carter whisper to Karen, "Is your family Jewish?" And she hears Karen giggle.

". . . To the warm and lasting memory of a great man, Jake Auerbach."

"Hear, hear . . ."

Essie rises, blinks a bit of mist from her eyes, and says, "Mogie, that was very nice, too. Thank you."

Mogie descends the ladder and offers his hand to Joan. Joan pins an ornament to the tree, but does not climb the ladder. Instead, she stands in front of it, smiling brightly, her glass raised. "Darlings," she begins, "darlings, all of you. I'd like to propose a toast to a man who *is* here. To a man who has just agreed to make the most extraordinary sacrifice, to give up an exciting trip to South Africa, where he has an assignment to write a brilliant book, in order to remain at the editorial helm of the New York *Express*. . . ."

Essie thinks: This is news. She looks at Richard. Richard, who has said very little all evening, merely smiles.

"My darlings, I propose a toast to the most brilliant newspaper editor in America, to the most brilliant writer in the world, to the most wonderful husband a woman could ever have—my husband, my Richard."

More applause, more voices of approval.

But Joan isn't finished. "And now," she continues, "for those of you who have a special interest in the *Express*—and particularly those of you who are stockholders, including Mother, Mogie, Josh, and Babette—as publisher and chief executive officer, I have exciting news. . . ."

Goodness, Essie thinks. She's turning my party into a business meeting.

"The point in our paper's eight-year life has been reached where it is about to become one of the great journalistic forces in the United States. I'm talking about a *national* newspaper, not just an afternoon tabloid for the city of New York. I'm not at liberty to release the full details yet, but let me just tell you that the response from the advertising community has been fantastic, unbelievable, almost overwhelming in its enthusiasm. All I can tell you now is that all of you, particularly you who are stockholders, will watch with amazement and"—she laughs—"a certain amount of pecuniary anticipation as events unfold in the next few months."

There is a brief silence, then more polite clapping.

"The name of Jacob Auerbach has come up this evening," Joan goes on. "Let me tell you just this: that great and wonderful man would be truly proud, were he with us today, of what his older daughter, a mere woman, has been able to accomplish. . . ."

The room, Essie notices, has grown a bit restless. Karen has gone to the bar to refill her drink, and Karen's daughter Linda has come to curl on the floor by Essie's feet, her elbows resting on Essie's knees. "Did you love him very much, Great-Grandma?" Linda whispers. "I was so little when he died I hardly remember him."

"What a question! Hush and let your grandmother finish what she has to say."

"I'm never going to get married," Linda says. "Everybody in this family just gets divorces, anyway. I'm going to live in sin."

"Papa," Joan goes on, "was a great philanthropist, and a great humanitarian, as the world knows. But at heart he was a great businessman, who built a little company called Eaton and Cromwell into the corporate giant it is today. He never undertook anything which wouldn't show a profit. And I, his oldest child, who knew him longer and better than anyone in this room . . ."

Except me, Essie thinks.

". . . feel that I can safely say that Papa would be proud of me today. Thank you, my darlings, and to all of you a merry Christmas, and a happy, and *profitable* New Year."

"Joan would do well on Hyde Park Corner," Josh says in an amiable voice, and Joan throws him an angry look.

"Now I want to make a toast!" Karen says somewhat loudly. She starts toward the ladder, drink in hand, weaving slightly.

"Don't forget an ornament," someone says.

"Fuck the ornaments. I want to make a toast." She starts up the ladder, misses the bottom rung. and her drink sloshes in her hand and trickles across her lower arm.

"Karen!" Joan says sharply.

"I want to make a *toast!*" She tries for the ladder again, misses again, and falls clumsily against the ladder. This time, the drink spills across the front of her pale green dress.

"Karen, you're making a fool of yourself!" Joan says.

Karen straightens up, looks down at her dress. Then she drops her glass—it rolls harmlessly on the thick carpet—bursts into tears and runs from the room.

In the silence that follows, Mr. Daryl Carter, his pale face now very red, rises and follows her out of the room.

Joan, still standing, says, "Don't pay any attention to her. That's all she does it for—attention." And Karen's daughter, still kneeling by Essie's feet, merely stares up into Essie's face.

"Actually," Joan says, changing the subject, "Josh brought up a good point a moment ago. You're not getting any younger, Mother, and I think all of us would like to know what you're planning to do with your and Papa's art collection. Let's be realistic, after all."

"I'm leaving it to the Met," Essie snaps. It is a perfectly spontaneous response. Actually, not until that very moment had she decided to leave it all to the Met, though she has certainly considered it and Mr. Hubbard has paid several polite calls. But now the decision is made, final, done.

"Mother, don't be a *fool*. If all this goes into your estate, you'd be crucified for taxes."

"Crucified? I'd be dead."

"Why, the value of the Goya *alone*—"

"Joan, this is neither the time nor the place," Josh says.

"Josh is right," Essie says.

Joan's tight, compressed body seems to gather into itself, to become tighter, more compressed. Wellsprings of resentment and old grudges are bubbling up. "'Josh is *right*,'" she mimics. "Josh is always right, isn't he? Who the hell is Josh? Who the hell is he, besides your favorite? Everyone has always known that Josh is your favorite!"

Richard McAllister is finally bestirred. He stands up. "Joan, please . . ."

"Shut up! I raise a perfectly good question, a perfectly reasonable and practical question which concerns us all, and what am I told? 'Josh is right.'"

"For Christ's sake, Joan!"

"And what about all that Eaton stock that Mother is sitting on?—three hundred thousand shares!"

"Three hundred and *twenty-five* thousand," Essie corrects.

"That's right! What's going to happen to that? I don't know—does anyone in this room know? Oh, I suppose Josh gets that, because Josh is right. Who the hell is Josh, Mother? What does he do besides tell you how to vote your proxies, which happens to be absolutely against the law?"

"Among other things, Josh is the president of the company from which we all derive a comfortable living," Essie says. "And he's your brother."

"But he's not a real Auerbach! He's not even a real member of this family."

"We're all members of this family, Joan," Josh says.

"Joan, you're ruining my party," Essie says. "I take that back. You've already ruined it."

"He's not! He's not!"

"Joan, what on earth are you talking about?"

Joan is as angry as Essie has ever seen her, but she seems nowhere close to tears. "You know exactly what I mean, Mother. Some Auerbachs are real, and some aren't. My analyst explained it all to me years ago, and I explained it all to you. We're two families, we had two different sets of parents. Does Josh remember 5269 Grand Boulevard? No, but I do! Babette and I do! Babette and I remember a little house at 5269 Grand Boulevard, Chicago, Illinois, that had only one john, and it didn't always work! And we had a mother who cooked our meals and ironed our dresses and darned our stockings and patched our underwear and walked us to the streetcar stop for school, and a father who came home at night in his shirtsleeves for dinner at the kitchen table under one bare light bulb. Oilcloth on the table. Catsup in a bottle. Boiled potatoes. And we had a mother who read us stories before we went to bed at night, holding the book in hands that smelled of onions and were red from washing dishes. Those were *our* parents, Mother. We were *their* children. Then Papa got rich. Then, when I was nine years old, along came Mogie, and ten years later came Josh. They never set foot in 5269 Grand Boulevard. *They* were brought up not by parents but by governesses and nurses and bodyguards and servants—a cook who wouldn't even let the children into the kitchen of their own house, and a big estate in Lake Forest with a guard at the gate because of kidnappings. They had a mother who had a butler and a chauffeur and a German private secretary who guarded her like a hawk and who said, 'You may go in to see your mother now, but she only five minutes has,' and a mother who, if she was home at all, was dressing to go out to some grand ball. And a father who, if he ever came home at all—if he wasn't in somewhere like Brussels or Copenhagen or Milan or the end of the world on business—if he came home at all, he came home in a tall silk hat in a private railroad car, to attend a reception for the Governor, or Henry Ford, or John D. Rockefeller. And if he came home at *all,* he was soon off again to address the League of Nations in Geneva. Those were Mogie's and Josh's parents, Mother. They weren't *my* parents, *Mother!* Babette, remember the lemonade stand? Remember our lemonade stand? Two cents a glass, and we gave the money to Mama. Did Josh ever have a lemonade stand? No, everything was handed to him on a solid silver platter. Babette—" Her eyes are streaming now, but there are no sobs. "Babette—tell them about our lemonade stand. Tell them . . . tell them . . . Oh, please tell them. . . ."

Babette fidgets nervously with her bracelets, twisting them this way and that. "I don't remember it," she says at last.

Josh rises, a little wearily, and says in a flat voice, "Would anyone like a little music? How about some Christmas carols?" He walks to the piano, sits down, and runs his fingers over the keys. He begins to play "O Little Town of Bethlehem." "C'mon. Let's sing. It's Christmas."

At first, no one responds. Then Linda quickly stands up and says, "If no one else will sing, I will." She goes to the piano and begins to sing in her clear young voice, while Josh Auerbach accompanies her:

> *O Little Town of Bethlehem,*
> *How still we see thee lie.*

Above thy deep and dreamless sleep
The timeless stars roll by. . . .

All at once Joan rushes across the room to the piano and
screams at her brother, "Josh, you little shit!" Then she bangs
down both fists hard on the upper register of the keyboard.

In the echoing, jagged silence that follows, Essie stands up
and walks out of the room, to leave them to their bickering.

The terrace of Essie's apartment wraps around two sides of
the building, the south and the west. The terrace is bare now,
the awnings down, the garden furniture stored away, the plant-
ers and the window boxes empty. But on the first of May, all
the things will come out again from their storage places, and
the men from Woodruff & Jones will come, and the freight
elevators will fill with new trees and shrubs and flowering
plants and ivies. The December night is clear and cold, and
Essie has thrown a cashmere shawl over her shoulders, but the
fresh air is tonic and the view from the twenty-ninth floor at the
corner of Seventieth Street and Park Avenue where Essie lives
has a certain splendor. Below her, the lights from the cars
along the avenue crawl silently by, then stop while the light
turns red, then crawl on again. Though there are no sounds
from the streets, the air is filled with the city's persistent hum
which never goes away. Was it always like this? she asks
herself. Was it always so awful, so much unkindness? Perhaps,
if Jake were still alive, it could have been different, but only
perhaps. If, by some magic, she could command him back, but
no, the trouble is—the shameful, awful, secret thing is—that
she doesn't want Jake back. And of course much of what Joan
said is true. Though she shouldn't have said that about Josh not
being a real member of the family, even though Josh has
always been different, special.

There would be stars on a night like this, if the lights of the city
didn't always manage to outdazzle them. Essie has often noticed
how the lights from her terrace with its two views, the south and
the west, are different, depending on which way one faces. The
two views are like two parts of a symphony. To the south,
downtown—the New York Central Building, the Empire State
Building, the Pan Am Building and, at the farthest reach, the

twin towers of the World Trade Center, none of which were there when she was a girl—the lights strike an aggressive, almost warlike chord: intense, full of furious enterprise, crackling with the fiery notes of money. To the west, across Central Park, through the bare branches of the trees, the residential lights of the West Side are softer, pinker, quieter. These strike more lyrical and modulated chords of domesticity and care and love. Oh, my city! Essie thinks, gripping at the half-wall of her terrace and looking at the contrasting rhythms of the lights.

It was not so long ago—surely not nighty-nine years ago— and not that far away, where it all began. How many miles is it from here to Norfolk Street, to a place that now lies buried somewhere deep behind that strident Midtown skyline? Essie used to know how many city blocks there were to a mile, but it is not that many blocks, and even fewer miles. It is not so far, or so long ago, to where she came from. And now they are all waiting for her to go away.

Norfolk Street—is that what a life comes round to at the end? A small circle, with the journey finished almost within sight of where it started? Essie wonders suddenly whether the ghosts of her mother and her father still linger somewhere in the walls and stairwells of the old building, the way the scent of a man's or woman's presence will hang in the air long after he or she has left the room. All at once she can smell the smell of cabbage cooking, and the chocolatey smell of her mother's fingers, and hear the sound of her father's voice:

"Outlaw. Pariah. When you defy your parents, you defy the ground under your feet, the sky over your head. He who separates himself from his people buries himself in death. This is written in the Torah."

"But I was young, Papa, and I loved him, and I wanted to marry him!"

Suddenly Essie realizes that she is not alone on the terrace.

"Mary! I thought you'd gone home hours ago."

"I had a feeling in my bones, Mrs. A, that things wouldn't go so well tonight. I'm sorry."

"Did Karen leave?"

"Mr. Carter took her home."

"He's *much* too young for her. That's the trouble."

Mary touches Essie's hand, very lightly, where it rests on

the half-wall. "Mr. Wilmont's in the library, Mrs. A, and he's alone."

The library is Essie's favorite room in the apartment, all done in warm and earthy colors, golds, browns, yellows, and deep greens, the colors of the bindings of the fine old books that line the walls behind glass casement doors. Arrayed in the cases, too, are all the awards, medals, and citations of Jake's lifetime, as well as her own, the signed photographs of Presidents, some of them a little yellowed now, and over the mantel hangs Jake Auerbach's Chandor portrait under its museum light. At night, the lamps with their dark parchment shades cast a warm glow. Essie enters the room from the terrace, and finds Charles there, sitting in one of the leather chairs, nursing his pipe.

"Well, well, old girl," he says.

"Oh, Charles," she says. "It's not *kind*, is it? None of it is kind."

Charles says, "Each of them loves you, Essie—in his own way."

"I'm not so sure," she says, taking the chair across from him beside the dying coal fire in the fireplace. "I'm not so sure at all."

"Would you like a brandy?"

"Yes, I think I would."

He rises, goes to the bar, and fills two small brandy glasses from the decanter. Returning, he hands one glass to Essie, and touches his glass to hers. "Cheers, old girl."

"Cheers, Charles."

He returns to his chair, and they sit in silence for a while, sipping their brandy. The fire smolders in the grate. Above them, in the center of the wall, over the mantelpiece, looms the portrait of Jacob Auerbach, which he sat for with Douglas Chandor in 1929. He glowers down at them, his face frozen in disapproval. Wouldn't it have been more appropriate for the great man, the great humanitarian, the great philanthropist, to have let the artist depict him with even the slightest semblance of a smile? But no, a smile had evidently not been what Mr. Chandor's subject wanted, and so instead we have Jacob Auerbach perpetually frowning from eternity. Sometimes, alone in the room, Essie talks to the frowning face, which now has no way of articulating its displeasure. She mocks it, tries to make it smile. Nothing works. His portrait dominates the room, lords it over the entire apartment, just the way he used to dominate their lives. *I want to replace little Prince. Please let me try!*

"Should I be worried, Charles?" she asks him suddenly.

"Worried? Why?"

"The things Joan was saying. About Josh."

"That was just her analyst talking," he says.

"Joan wants more money. I can smell it."

He laughs softly. "Joan always wants more money."

"But she's not getting it from me. Is she?"

"You know how I feel about that. I think you've done more than enough for her."

"So do I. But still—"

"But still what?"

"Charles," she says quickly, "do you think that Joan knows something? Something that could hurt us? Hurt us all?"

"Of course not. How could she possibly?"

"Joan can be destructive. Do you remember that kidnap letter years ago? That was Joan."

He whistles. "Really? Did Jake ever know that?"

"No. I saw to that. If he'd known, there'd have been hell to pay. But it was Joan."

"But she was just a little girl—"

"She's always been like that. Destructive."

"I wouldn't worry about her, Essie. For one thing, I think she's going to have her hands full hanging on to this latest husband."

"*And* her paper."

"And that."

Her eyes wander upward to the portrait. "Sometimes I wonder, if Jake were still alive, whether he could straighten everybody out."

"But it was usually you who straightened everybody out, Essie. Remember?"

"Or you, Charles."

"Yes. You or me. What was that Yiddish word you used to call him?"

"*Shmendrick?*" Essie laughs. "I'd call him that when I was angry, yes. But Jake wasn't a *shmendrick,* exactly. A *shmendrick* is a little man who wants to do big things. But Jake was a big man who wanted to do big things. And did."

"With a lot of help from other people."

"Oh yes. Who got no credit. Do you know—tonight—in the middle of everything—Linda asked me if I loved him?"

"What did you tell her?"

"I didn't know what to say. The question knocked me nearly off my pins."

Smiling, he says, "It would take more than that to knock you off your pins, old girl."

"I don't know. My pins aren't as steady as they used to be."

"Miracle worker."

"Yes . . . I remember that. When was that, Charles?"

"I'll tell you exactly. It was September twentieth, nineteen thirteen."

"A Saturday . . ."

"And you'd been drying dishes. The dishtowel was blue."

"Yes . . ."

"So remember the miracles, Essie."

She studies his kindly, one-of-the-family face. "I'll try. Still, I'm worried, Charles," she says.

Two

The town house residence of Mr. Mogie Auerbach on Beekman Place is always kept very dark. Even during the daytime, the heavy blackout shades and draperies are kept securely drawn on both the east and west exposures of the house, and the purpose of this, Mogie explains to guests, is to preserve the delicate hues of the Chinese silks with which the sofas and chairs are covered, the tones of the Aubusson and Oriental rugs, and the soft pastels of the antique scenic Zuber wall coverings. The darkness also serves the better to display Mogie's personal collections, the precious Amatis, the uncut gems, the silver and the seventeenth- and eighteenth-century toys, which are arranged about the downstairs double drawing room in lighted glass cases. His long years of bachelorhood have turned Mogie Auerbach into a creature of fixed and immutable habits. Nothing in his house can ever be changed from its original arrangement, and small chalk marks on the floors and shelves and walls indicate where each object must be replaced when it has to be moved for dusting. Here, Mogie likes to imagine acquaintances thinking as they enter his house, is the home of a gentleman, scholar, and esthete.

In the center of the larger of the two drawing rooms which flank the entrance, stands Mogie Auerbach's ancient rolltop desk, a Chippendale piece of considerable importance, its tambour top rolled upward to reveal a certain amount of gentlemanly clutter—a massive crystal inkwell and quill-tip pen on an ivory base, purchased by Mogie in Venice in 1949, and thought to have belonged to Felipe II of Spain; a Chinese

27

abacus from the twelfth century, with ivory bars and counters of pink jade, which Mogie actually uses to figure his accounts; a heavy pair of silver library shears with inlaid mother-of-pearl handles, which Mogie uses to cut clippings from newspapers and journals; and the clippings themselves, secured beneath *millefleur* Baccarat paperweights; a magnifying glass with a carved baleen handle; a photograph in a silver frame of Mogie and his father at the railing of a sailing vessel; a photograph by Man Ray of Mogie himself, and a great deal else.

It is at this desk that Mogie does what he calls his "serious" work, which is writing art criticism for various small and usually obscure journals. A partly written article, in longhand, on India paper, is also on Mogie's desk, conspicuously in preparation. Mogie is the first to admit that he writes slowly. Often it will take him weeks to produce a piece of criticism just a few hundred words long. At the same time, Mogie's writing displays certain mannerisms, fond as he is of such phrases as "catholicity of taste," "insightfulness," and "meaningful juxtapositions." Just this afternoon, for example, he has written, "Joan Miró's skeinlike line suggests not only the artist's catholicity of taste, but reveals his wit, insightfulness, and philosophy through meaningful juxtapositions." Mogie is rather proud of that sentence.

It is in this room, too, that Mogie now sits with his sister Joan and his young wife, also having a nightcap after his mother's party. Joan, whose husband went directly home complaining of a headache, had offered to drop Mogie and Christina off in her car, and was invited in. Now Joan would like to light a cigarette, but knows that she may not, since smoking is not permitted in Mogie's house. To emphasize this rule, the house on Beekman Place is not furnished with a single ashtray. "If you must smoke, please go out into the garden," Mogie rather irritably tells his smoker friends at the small, formal dinners for six or eight he is fond of giving.

"Well," Joan is saying, twirling the stem of her champagne glass, the contents of which she has not touched, "what did we all think of that performance tonight?"

Mogie picks a speck of lint off the shawl collar of his dinner jacket and says, with a trace of sarcasm, "Whose performance are you talking about, dear?"

"Mother's, of course. Just getting up and stalking out of the room like that."

"I can't stand that secretary of your mother's, that Mary O'Brien or whatever her name is," Christina says.

"Farrell."

"I just can't stand her. She's so snippy. She acts like she owns the place."

"*Stalking* out—right in the middle of a conversation. Such rudeness. Really."

"Weren't people singing?" Christina says. "I thought people were singing when she walked out." She kicks off her shoes. "I don't know about you, honey," she says to Mogie, "but I'm pooped."

"Christina, darling," Joan says, "if you're tired, why don't you just run upstairs to bed? There's something I want to talk to Mogie about. And alone, if you don't mind—family business."

"But Christina's family," Mogie says.

"Would you mind, Christina?"

"Oh, sure," Christina says, reaching down to pick up her shoes. "Because I'm really pooped." Slowly, she rises from the sofa, goes to Mogie, puts her arms around his shoulders, and kisses him on the top of the head. "Don't stay up too late, honey," she says.

"I won't, darling," Mogie whispers, stroking her hand and running his lips along her lower arm. "I promise."

"Good night, Joanie," Christina says, stifling a yawn. "You and Richard have got to come by and see us real soon. I'll do a little din-din."

"Good night, darling," Joan says, blowing her a kiss.

After Christina has left the room, Mogie Auerbach sits quietly, a dreamy smile on his face. "Wonderful girl," he says. "Don't you think so, Joan?"

"Oh, yes. Wonderful. Very pretty."

"I'm a lucky man. A very lucky man."

"I'm so happy for you, Mogie."

"Do you know that she's the first woman with whom I've been able to achieve a full erection?"

Joan makes a small choking sound. "Really, Mogie," she

says at last, "why did you think I'd want to know a thing like that?"

"My doctor says I should tell people. 'Extemporize your feelings,' he says. 'Act them out. Free associate, in order to get into your primary process.' It's really very helpful. He's very pleased with the way it's going."

"Of course you go to that damned Jungian," Joan says. "But what I really want to talk about is Mother. Mogie, we're going to have to do something about Mother."

"Really? What's wrong with her? She seems perfectly fine to me."

"She's becoming senile, Mogie. That's all there is to it."

"Do you really think so, Joan?"

"Oh, there's no question about it, darling. Going quite ga-ga. That business about giving her paintings to the Metropolitan—sheer insanity. If that collection went into her estate, it'd be taxed until there'd be nothing left. It's got to be sold, Mogie, and soon. We've got to do something before she—well, dies."

Mogie studies his sister across the quiet room, and carefully crosses one elegantly tailored knee atop the other. "Speaking of performances," he says at last, "I thought yours was rather spectacular tonight. Quite worthy of a Bernhardt, if you ask me."

"Well, I did get angry."

"And of course it was me you were talking about, wasn't it. Not Josh."

"Nonsense, Mogie."

"Nonsense? That business about Josh not knowing what it was like to be poor. You were looking at me when you said that. It was directed to me."

"That's not true!"

"You've always hated me, Joan. You know that. You never wanted me to be born. Miss Kroger told me that when I was little. 'Your sister never wanted you to be born,' she said, and a nanny doesn't lie."

"Well, she was lying. I always hated Miss Kroger, if you want to know the truth!"

"So you've been punishing me for being born for sixty years."

"That's your Jungian talking again."

"I only mention it because it's pivotal to this particular dynamic," Mogie says.

"But it has nothing at all to do with what I want to talk to you about. Nothing at *all*."

"Then what do you want to talk about, Joan?"

"*Mother*. And what we're going to do about her."

"Well," he says carefully, "what do you propose we do, exactly?"

Joan hesitates, setting down her glass of champagne. "I don't suppose you'd bend the rules just once, and let me have a cigarette. Just one. A quick puff."

"Now, Joan—"

"Sorry. Shouldn't have asked. Anyway—" She picks up her glass and studies it. "Anyway, you're almost ten years younger than I am, so I don't suppose you remember Uncle Abe. Mother's brother—Abe Litsky."

"Oh, I know he was somehow in the picture for a while," Mogie says.

"Yes. Very much so. He lived with us on Grand Boulevard when Babette and I were children. He helped Papa get started at Eaton's. He was important long before Charles Wilmont came along."

"Then something happened."

"Yes. And I'm not sure yet exactly what, but there was something, some kind of falling out. Papa bought Uncle Abe out, and as far as I know the two never spoke to each other again."

"This is all very ancient history," Mogie says. "We're talking about pre–World War One, before I was even a glimmer in Papa's eye, as they say."

"I know." Joan stands and begins to pace back and forth across the room, a thin, moving exclamation point in her short black dress. "Now—second question. Does the name Arthur Litton mean anything to you?"

"Vaguely. Prohibition. Bootlegging—"

"*And* extortion. *And* the rackets. *And* the longshoremen, *and* the Teamsters, *and* Las Vegas gambling. *And* prostitution, *and* drugs—probably."

"Is he still alive?"

"Very much so. Alive and well and living in Hollywood Beach, Florida, with a new wife and two Welsh corgis."

"Fine. But so what?"

"They call him Mr. Untouchable. A life spent in and around organized crime, arrested dozens of times, but never spent a night in jail. They couldn't even get him on income tax. The worst they could do to him was revoke his passport, so he can't skip the country."

"All very interesting. But again, so what?"

"I had my people at the *Express* go through all the old files, all the old newspaper clippings, asked them to find out everything they could about the early days of Eaton and Cromwell, and everything they could about Arthur Litton." She goes to the table where she has laid her handbag, opens it, and takes out a sheaf of papers secured with a rubber band. "I brought some of these things along to show you, Mogie," she says, "because what would you say if I told you that Arthur Litton *is* Abe Litsky?"

"You're not serious."

"I am *quite* serious. It's all here—photographs, news stories, everything. Arthur Litton is our Uncle Abe—Mother's long-lost baby brother!"

Mogie slips the rubber band from the sheaf of clippings and spreads them in his lap.

"Look at these two pictures," Joan points. "One of Abraham Litsky, Eaton and Cromwell partner. Another of Arthur Litton, wanted on an illegal gambling charge. It's obviously the same man."

Mogie studies the photographs. "There is a resemblance," he says at last. "But tell me, Joan—if this is true, why has no one uncovered it before?"

"Because not too many people are around who remember what Uncle Abe looked like, and I do. Because he lived with us when Babette and I were little. And because the company has conveniently forgotten that anyone named Abe Litsky was ever connected with it. At the office, I also have a copy of the company history that was published in nineteen seventy-five. I'm sure you got a copy of it too. There's a whole section in it called 'Early Struggles.' It's all about Papa, and there's a lot about Charles, but I assure you that Abe Litsky's name is not mentioned even once, even though he was Papa's first partner. And for good reason."

"An untidy branch of the family tree."

"Precisely, Mogie."

Mogie Auerbach sets the sheaf of clippings aside. "Have you mentioned any of this to Babette?" he asks her.

"No. I wanted to get your opinion first."

"Opinion? What sort of opinion? What I'd like to know is, now that you have this information, what do you intend to do with it?"

"Well, I happen to run a newspaper, and this in my opinion is news. Can you imagine the reaction in the business community if this came out? The stockholders, for instance. What would this do to Eaton's sacred image—honesty, integrity, public-spiritedness, the customer is always right? Think of what Charles's reaction would be—because he's been part of the cover-up. And dear little Josh's reaction, who I'm sure doesn't suspect a thing. And *Mother's* reaction—her own brother."

Mogie looks up at her. "Would you really do that, Joan? Use your newspaper to expose your own family?"

Joan laughs a little shrilly and sits down in the nearest silk-covered chair. "I'm not saying that I would do that," she says. "But I'm saying that I'd certainly have that option, wouldn't I? And frankly, Mogie, I keep thinking that this thing may go even deeper than what we know already. Because what I keep asking myself, as a newspaperwoman, is this—why has Arthur Litton, or Uncle Abe, kept so quiet about his Eaton connection all these years? What would he have to lose by spilling the beans?"

"Unless—"

"You're reading my mind, my darling. Exactly. Unless the company—or someone in the company—has been paying him off. Regularly. Steadily. For years and years. Paying him to keep his mouth shut."

Now it is Mogie who rises, his hands thrust deep in his trousers pockets, and walks to the lighted vitrine where some of his antique toys are displayed—fire engines, a miniature Ferris wheel with tiny passengers rocking in their seats, their faces painted in expressions of delight and awe, a regiment of tin soldiers, muskets in firing position, cannon aimed, a corporal ramming gunpowder into its cascabel, another standing ready with a torch to ignite the fuse; his have been called the finest collections of tin and lead soldiers in the world; behind the cannoneers and artillerymen are arrayed the mounted cavalry, ready to charge. Mogie Auerbach studies the frozen scene in the glass case as though for the first time. "Of course this is a very serious allegation, Joan," he says at last. "And you have absolutely nothing to prove it."

"No, but I think I know where to go to find proof if I need it."

"Yes," he says quietly. "You know, you mentioned tonight the lemonade stand that you and Babette had. Of course I have no memory of that. I wasn't even born. You're right. I don't remember the house on Grand Boulevard at all. I never lived there. I grew up at The Bluff. I don't even have a clear memory of Prince. I was only six when all that happened. . . ."

"Yes."

"But you're right. It was like having two different sets of parents. And then, after Prince . . . left us . . . you were the oldest, and I was the youngest, and I was always more than a little afraid of you. I used to feel that you were always jealous of me. And then, a few years later, when Josh came along, he was the baby, and I was very much relieved, because then you transferred your jealousy to him."

"I suppose that's true enough," Joan says easily. "I was jealous. Of both of you. Because both of you had things as children that I never had. It was as simple as that."

"Funny. Years of analysis, and I'm still trying to deal with your ability to intimidate me. Perhaps it's part of the cause of what Dr. Gold calls my too-introverted nature, why I must concentrate on immediate conflicts rather than the conflicts of childhood. Why I must think more about my will to live than my sexual drive. I remember being even more relieved when you went off to boarding school. It's good to talk about these things, Joan—to get these conflicts out in the open."

"Listen, Mogie," Joan says impatiently, "please don't misunderstand me. I don't want to do anything that would hurt Mother. Please believe that. The only thing I'm thinking of doing is using what I know to get her to think sensibly. Doesn't that make sense? What she should be doing now is disposing of some of these things—these *possessions*, these objects that are simply cluttering up her life—and turning the proceeds over to us children. For tax purposes, she should begin dividing up her estate right now. Before it's too late, and the government steps in to take a big fat slice. She's eighty-nine, Mogie. She can't last forever. What does she need with an art collection now? She hardly ever entertains anymore. What does she need that enormous apartment for—that takes five people to run it? She should be living in some smaller place. It's ridiculous—all that acreage for one old woman. What use does she have for all that Eaton stock? She can't take it with her. It should be distributed among the next generation. That means you, Mogie, and Christina, and me, and Babette, and even Josh. And her grand-children—why, you may even have children of your own soon, Mogie, now that you've got Christina. It's the sensible way to do things, don't you see? All I want to do is talk to her, and try to make her use some sense."

"I understand."

"Do you realize what three hundred and twenty-five thou-sand shares of Eaton stock are worth in the marketplace?"

"I have a fair idea."

"And the art collection? So that's my point. Imagine that amount reduced by half—at *least* —by taxes when she dies."

"Yes."

"Then do I have your support, Mogie? Can I talk to her? Try to convince her? Maybe apply a little pressure? In a nice way, of course."

"What about Babette?"

"Babette will do whatever I tell her to do. First, I need your support. All I want is to be able to say to her, 'Mogie agrees with me that if any of this came out a lot of people would be hurt.'"

Mogie smiles, still gazing at the tin militia. "Well, I do agree with that, Joan," he says.

"Then you're with me?"

"Let me think about it for a day or so," he says. "I'd like to talk it over with Dr. Gold."

"*Don't* talk it over with Dr. Gold. He'll get it all involved with childhood conflicts."

"Well, at least let me study these clippings."

"Certainly. That's why I brought them. I have Xeroxes of everything at the office."

"You know," he says, "you're my sister, but you never fail to surprise me. I don't think I've ever understood you."

"I think that may be because I'm tougher than you are, Mogie," Joan says. "And I think that's because I had a mother who used to tell me stories of what it was like being a little Russian Jewish immigrant girl growing up on the Lower East Side."

"The Litsky genes coming out," he says, still smiling at the miniature battle scene. "But, you know, you were lucky. I never had a mother at all." He pauses. "Say, I think that's a meaningful insight. I must remember to tell that to Dr. Gold."

After Joan has said good night, Mogie Auerbach, who is in his early sixties but who, thanks to the ministrations of a caring therapist, now often manages to feel much younger, juicier, more resolved in his will to live, moves about the lower floor of his town house, turning out the lighted cases one by one. I never had a mother, he thinks. Joan did. I am the one who should be jealous. The thought gives new lightness to his step, and to his mood. And now, he thinks, Joan needs me. He leaves burning only the lamp by his big desk, where he returns and picks up the sheaf of clippings and slowly thumbs through them, whistling softly to himself. Then he stops. One photograph in one of the yellowed clippings strikes him in particular, and he goes back to it, studying it intently under the light, turning it this way and that. He rises slowly from his chair, the clipping still in his hand, and takes a deep breath. Help is needed.

And so he goes to the nearest window, draws aside the heavy drapes, raises the light-proof shade, and then lifts the window sash an inch or two, pausing, his chin cupped in one hand, to give the image of his face a fond sizing-up in the dark glass. A chill December wind blows in from Beekman Place. On the street, a private guard, making his rounds, does not look up. I would have made a splendid homosexual, Mogie thinks, having come to this conclusion from several clandestine encounters in the past. He returns to his desk, opens the lowest left-hand drawer fully, and presses a finger against the back panel of the drawer, which falls open. Inside this second compartment are a small cloisonné footed box, said to have come from the Palais de Versailles, an ivory pipe, and a box of kitchen matches. He removes these objects, and opens the box. Inside is what appears to be a small cake of clear golden soap. With a penknife Mogie scrapes and pares several shreds of this amber, waxy substance, and tamps these shavings carefully and compactly into the rounded bowl of the pipe. It is pure, uncut hashish from Izmir.

Mogie picks a match carefully out of the box, strikes it across the sole of his shoe, and lights the pipe, inhaling deeply. The night outside is very still.

He sits at his desk, studying the photograph. Somewhere in all of this, he thinks, lie the seeds of a delicious little plan. There they all are, the early members of Eaton & Cromwell's board—his father, Abe Litsky, Charles Wilmont, George Eaton, Cyrus Cromwell, much younger than when he had ever known them, but still recognizable. He sits back, draws again on his pipe, waiting for the rush of insight to come, for the seeds to germinate.

Suddenly he puts the clipping down. The answer is not there, not quite, but Mogie is quite sure where the answer can be found. When Mother broke up her house at The Bluff, Mogie fell heir to several family scrapbooks and, in his informal role as family historian, he has kept them up. They repose behind locked glass doors in one of his many bookcases. He rises and goes to the bookcase now, unlocks it with a key from his watch fob, and removes two albums. He returns with them to his desk, and slowly begins turning pages. Their lives fan out in front of him, in chronology, but with a gap, since the two photo albums he has chosen are one of the oldest and one of the most recent. He studies the children's faces, his own, Joan's, Babette's, Josh's, their parents' and the faces of their parents' old friends and business associates, Charles, Daisy Stevens—everyone, of course, except Prince—watching them all grow older as the pages turn. It is not long before he has selected two clear and well-focused snapshots that will suit his purpose perfectly—one from the older album, one from the newer. Ah, he thinks, sucking deeply on his pipe, ah, dear darling Joan, Queen of Greed, what elegant fun we are going to have with you. Ah, the luxury of mischief, especially when perpetrated by Mogie Auerbach, the Renaissance Man!

Beside his elbow, a buzzer sounds and, with his free hand, he picks up the interhouse phone. "Yes, my darling?"

"Aren't you ever coming up to bed, honey?"

"Just be patient, darling," he says in a soothing voice. "Daddy's just finishing some work on his article. Then he'll be straight up." And he adds, laughing softly, "And that pun *is* intended." But first he marks the places in the albums with two white slips of paper, returns the albums to the bookcase, closes and locks the door with his little key, smiling and whistling softly to himself.

In another part of town, on West Tenth Street in Greenwich Village, where Karen Auerbach Collier Schofield has kept an apartment since her divorce, Karen lies naked across her bed with a cold washcloth folded across her forehead. Daryl Carter who sits, fully clothed, on the bed beside her, lifts the cloth gently, refolds it, and replaces it so that the cool side is down. "Feeling better now?" he asks her.

"Parks," she says. "You work for the parks. There's a statue of my grandpa in a park. Lincoln Park. That's in Chicago."

"You've just had a little too much to drink," he says, his eyes carefully averted from her nude body.

"So what. What's that got to do with parks?" Her head rolls sideways toward him. "Aren't you going to make love to me?"

"I think—not tonight."

"Or," she giggles. "Or. Or."

"Or what?"

"Or are you gay?" Giggling again, she says, "I think you are. I think Mr. Parks is gay."

"Well, I'm not."

"Not even a little bit?"

"Not."

"I had an uncle who was gay."

"Oh? What happened to him?"

Another giggle. "Family secret. Pots and pots."

"Pots and pots of what?"

"Secrets. Pots and pots of family secrets."

"I had no idea your family owned Eaton and Cromwell."

"Yup. All of it. Pots and pots of it."

"Golly. You must be really rich."

"Oh, yeah." She closes her eyes. "Especially Granny. Not my mother, though. She just spends it."

"Your mother is—quite a woman."

Her eyes flutter open. "Now you just leave my mother out of this," she says. "What's she got to do with anything?"

"Sorry. But you brought her up."

"Just leave her out of this," she says. "Besides."

After a pause, he says, "Besides what?"

"Besides," she says. "Besides, you've made me forget what I was going to say."

"And your family is—Jewish."

"Not *Jewish*," she says. "Jew-*ish*. That's different, you know. We're Jew-*ish*. Just a little bit Jew-*ish*. Just a little bish—I mean *bit*. Like a little bit south of North Carolina. Besides, my father wasn't Jewish. Just Mother."

"I see."

"But don't go bringing up my mother again. Besides, I think you're gay."

He stands, and in the same movement reaches down and pulls the coverlet up across her. "I think I'd better go now," he says. "Get some sleep."

But Karen reaches up and seizes him tightly by the wrist, her long polished fingernails digging into his flesh, and says, "No. Stay. I want to talk to you. Fix me another drink."

"I think you've had—"

"No." She pulls him down beside her again. "Listen to me. No one ever listens to me. I want to tell you everything."

He studies her pale face on the pillow, the blond hair, damp now and clinging to her temples from the cold washcloth, and the outline of her thin body under the coverlet. Tossed on a chair beside her bed is the pale green evening dress, the shoes, the underthings that he has helped her remove. For a moment or two he says nothing. Then he says, "Tell me how old you are."

"Thirty-two."

"That's not possible. You have a daughter in college."

"Thirty-four, then."

"Even so—"

"Besides, she was my husband's daughter by an earlier marriage."

"But she has your same name."

"Of course. She was my husband's *daughter*. I adopted her."

"But your mother's over seventy. She must have been . . . well on . . . when you were born."

"Right. She was."

A hesitation. Then, "I think—you're older."

Karen sits straight up in bed, the coverlet falling from her bare breasts. "There!" she says. "See? See the way you are? Always dragging my mother into it! And while you're asking all these nosy questions—how old are *you?*"

"Twenty-five. I can show you my driver's license."

Her head falls back across the pillow again. "Oh, no," she says. "I don't want to see your driver's license. Where did I meet you, anyway?"

"At P. J. Clarke's. Now I've really got to go."

From the outer corners of her eyes, two nearly identical tears flow downward toward the pillow. Her hand still grips his wrist tightly. "Oh, no," she says in a small voice. "Don't go. Lie down beside me. It's cold in here. Lie down beside me and keep me warm." With her eyes tightly closed, she says, "In the old days—when I was a girl—I was considered to have—great—charm."

With his free hand, he works as gently and yet as firmly as possible to release his wrist from her grip.

Three

"Who is that woman in the picture?" one of her grandchildren would occasionally ask when, years later, they stumbled on one of the old photograph albums with their brittle pages filled with yellowing snapshots, which used to lay about on tables at The Bluff.

"Her name was Daisy Stevens," she would say. "She was an old family friend."

Daisy Stevens's picture would begin turning up in the family albums in the year 1918. Essie remembers the year for two reasons. For one thing, it was in September of that year that Jake and Essie's second son was born. They had named the baby Martin, but by the time he got to Lawrenceville and Harvard he had permanently acquired the nickname Mogie. And it was in 1918 that Essie had first met Daisy Stevens, when she had come to a party at The Bluff, as they had named the Lake Forest estate, a party to celebrate the Armistice between Germany and the Allies that had been signed in November of that year.

This particular morning, in her apartment at 710 Park Avenue, Essie has been thinking of Daisy Stevens again, though she has heard little from her in nearly fifteen years. Not long after Jake died, she knows, she had received an announcement in the mail saying that Daisy had married a man named Burton St. George, a widower and, Essie believes, a stockbroker. Of her doings in the years since, Essie knows little, though Daisy would be a woman in her early eighties now. Still, Jake had not been particularly generous to Daisy in his will—a bequest of merely fifteen thousand dollars in cash—and, for whatever reasons Jake had for being so miserly with Daisy, Essie wonders if now is not the moment to set things to rights.

It has been a busy morning. Essie has spent it with her lawyer, Henry Coker, redrafting her own will. Jake had never trusted lawyers, and Essie supposes that she has inherited some of her distrust from him. "Make the decision, draw up the plan, and then tell the lawyers what you're going to do," he used to say. "Then, by God, if anything goes wrong, let them straighten it out. If you ask them ahead of time what you ought to do, you'll never do anything." Also, as he grew older, Jake became convinced that the lawyers were hovering around like vultures, ready to snatch up for themselves whatever crumbs there were from the estate. Still, Essie got along well with Henry Coker.

"I want a will," she told him, "that can't be broken by any disgruntled member of my family, Henry."

"That's exactly what we're going to give you, Essie," he said.

"Can we insert a clause to the effect that, if any of my legatees attempts to take action to break the will, that legatee will be automatically disinherited?"

"We most certainly can."

"Good. Now I want it made clear that immediately upon my death, or if I am taken to a hospital prior to my death, this apartment is to be locked and sealed. No one is to be admitted. The insurance company has a full inventory of everything that's here, of course, but I don't want anyone even trying to come in and snitch anything."

Scribbling notes on a pad of yellow legal cap, Henry Coker nodded.

"Then, immediately upon my death, Mr. Hubbard or his representative from the Met is to be invited in, and he will be told to pick out anything he wants for the museum. Anything he wants. What he doesn't want is all to be sold at auction. I don't want any of them quarreling over my things, you see."

"I understand."

"Now, Joan and Babette and Mogie will all be taken care of comfortably, of course, and their children and my great-granddaughter. But the major share—fifty percent—of my estate I want to go to my youngest son, Joshua. You can write it in such a way as to say this is not to be considered a case of favoritism. It is simply because Josh is the only one who's ever really given a damn about the company."

"Yes," said Henry Coker.

"And now," said Essie, "I'd like to bring up a point. I'd like to ask you a question in confidence."

"Everything we talk about today is in the strictest confidence," Henry said.

Essie hesitated. "Let me put it this way," she said. "If any member of my family should claim—should claim to have evidence, or should threaten to claim—that my son Joshua, who will be my principal heir, is not a legal member of this family, could they, using that, try to break the will?"

"I'm not sure I follow you, Essie," Henry Coker said. "What do you mean by 'not a legal member of the family'?"

"Just what I said, Henry."

"Do you mean that Joshua was adopted? Or—"

"No, no. I meant—not legal."

Henry Coker's eyebrows rose just slightly. "Oh," he said. "I think I see what you mean, Essie. You mean that Joshua is not, was not—"

"Was not Jacob Auerbach's son."

Coker cleared his throat. "Yes," he said. "Well, of course Joshua has already inherited substantially from his father—I mean from your late husband."

"I know. But I'm talking about what I want to give him. If that came out, would it make a difference?"

"Only," he said, "in the sense that someone might try to blackmail him with that knowledge. But I don't think Joshua Auerbach is the sort of man to sit back and let himself be blackmailed over something that is, after all, a private and secret matter between you and your Creator."

"And now you," she said.

"Yes."

"Will it make any *legal* difference—with the will?"

"None whatever. After all, Joshua was raised as Jacob Auerbach's legal son. Jacob Auerbach's name is on the birth certificate—even if he may have been, as you suggest, illegitimate."

"Are you absolutely certain, Henry? I want to be very clear on that point."

"Absolutely. For one thing, after your death Joshua's parentage can only be a matter of speculation. For another, your will is what it says it is—*your will*. Under the terms of *your will*, you can do whatever you *will* with your estate. You can disinherit all of them, and leave everything to a hostelry for homeless cats—if that's your *will*."

Essie sighed. "Good," she said. "I'm glad to hear that. As you can imagine, it's been something that's been weighing on my mind."

"I understand," he said.

"How much is it, Henry?" she asked him.

"How much is what?"

"My estate. How much am I worth?"

He smiled and spread his hands. "Dear Essie, I really don't know," he said. "I can't give you a firm figure. Of course I could have the office put together some figures, and get back to you in a couple of weeks."

"No, no," she said. "Don't bother. I guess I'd rather not know."

"I know this—it's vast," he said.

"Yes. That's the trouble with it, isn't it?"

Henry Coker had then cleared his throat. "But to get back to the point you brought up earlier," he said. "About Joshua's parentage. There is one small problem that you should be aware of, Essie."

She sat forward in her chair. "Yes? What's that?"

"Your late husband's trust instrument, under which Joshua and the other three children derive income."

"What about it?"

"I shouldn't have said that there *is* a problem there, but that there *might* be."

"Please explain what you mean."

"Well, unfortunately—unfortunately, the way the instrument is worded—and I know because I drafted it—"

"Please get to the point, Henry. You're upsetting me."

"Your late husband's trust is directed specifically 'To my son Joshua Auerbach, et cetera, et cetera.' Therefore, if anyone—one of the other beneficiaries of the trust, for example—

should have reason to believe that Joshua is *not* Jacob Auerbach's son, the trust could be challenged. On that technicality."

"And broken?"

"There's that possibility. I'm not saying that such a challenge *would* be successful, but that it *might* be. Similarly, it might not."

"But it would have to be proven, wouldn't it?"

"Presumably, yes."

"How could it be proven, Henry?"

He hesitated. "I don't want to ask too many questions, because I don't want to know the answers. I don't want to know who the boy's natural father is, I'm not asking you that. But just tell me this. Is the boy's father living?"

"Yes."

"Well, then, unfortunately there are ways of proving paternity. Rather recent medical procedures. A complicated series of blood tests performed on the mother, the child, and the alleged father. It is called the Human Lymphodite Antigen test. Courts have ordered it performed in cases where there was—a question of paternity."

Essie said nothing.

"I don't want to alarm you, Essie. But since you've told me this, I felt it was my duty to alert you to this possibility, however remote, that there could be a challenge—not to your will, but to Joshua's trust from his father, or rather from your late husband."

"And the trust is everything he has."

"Well, very nearly everything."

"And they could get their hands on it."

"They?"

"Joan. Mogie. Babette."

"Put it this way—they would have a legal basis on which to try to do something of the sort."

"And it would be just like them. Thank you, Henry. You've eased my mind on one score, and given me a whole new worry on another."

"Would they really be that vindictive, Essie?"

"Oh, yes. Joan would, certainly. She hates Josh. Babette—perhaps not. Babette is too interested in seeing her name in the society pages. And Mogie—well, Mogie is a loony, you know that."

"Do any of them suspect?"

"I don't know. I'm not sure."

"Surely, if any of them did, you'd have heard about it before now."

"Yes, that's a point."

"I'm sure your secret is safe, Essie," Henry Coker said. "It's certainly safe with me. What you've told me this morning will never go beyond the four walls of this room. I wouldn't worry if I were you. In fact, I urge you not to."

Then Henry had left, kissing her hand in his courtly way, as though he had told her nothing at all of importance. And though he had told her not to worry, not to worry if he were she, Essie kept thinking that she was *not* Henry Coker, and what is a greater potential cause for worry than to be told not to worry? But then she had thought of Daisy Stevens, and wondered whether she should telephone Henry at his office and ask him to insert another bequest for Daisy. Of course such a thing would probably come as a great surprise to Daisy. But it would be done in the spirit of what Essie's father used to talk about, *zedakah*—righteousness. And thinking of Daisy reminded her of something she had not told Henry Coker—something that might, in fact, be very useful, the card up the sleeve, the chip that might win the game if and when the time came for it to be played. After all, Daisy was a part of the puzzle, too. Essie had buzzed for Mary Farrell and asked her to try to locate the whereabouts of Mrs. Daisy Stevens St. George. With that project under way, Essie found herself feeling somewhat better. "*Cherchez la femme,*" she had said with a wink to Mary Farrell.

During the day, too, and for the past several days, there have been a number of telephone calls from Joan, which Essie has chosen not to take. Though nearly a week has passed, she has not yet forgiven Joan for her performance at the tree-trimming, and Mary had offered Joan various excuses—that Mrs. Auerbach was out shopping, that Mrs. Auerbach was at lunch, that Mrs. Auerbach was taking a nap, and so on. And, needless to say, in the meantime these unsuccessful telephone attempts and unreturned calls have not created an atmosphere of serenity at the South Street offices of the publisher of the New York *Express,* Joan Auerbach McAllister, or, as she calls herself professionally, Mrs. Joan Auerbach.

"I know that that bitch is lying," Joan says to her secretary after the latest failed try to reach her mother. "I know that Mother's right there in the apartment."

It is at this moment that Richard McAllister steps into her office. "Can I talk to you about South Africa?" he asks her.

Joan presses her fingertips against her temples and says, "*Please,* Richard, not now. I've got to talk to Mother first, before we make any decisions. It's important."

"Joan," he says, "I love you very much, and I admire you even more, for your spunk and determination to keep this paper going. But you know as well as everyone else that the handwriting's on the wall. I've got to think of my own career now."

"Richard, I've told you before—give me six months. Just six months. That's all I ask."

"In six months, there won't be any more New York *Express.* You know that as well as I—"

"*Please!*" Joan cries. "I've got a *plan,* I tell you—a plan!"

And, while all this is going on, Josh Auerbach is with Essie in the large sitting room of the Park Avenue apartment, pressing on her a plan of his own for which Essie really has no enthusiasm. It is five o'clock, and Essie knows she is in a cranky mood. Her meeting with Henry Coker that morning has left her feeling irritable and out of sorts.

"Oh, no, no," she is saying. "I don't want to go back to Chicago. I always hated Chicago, you know that."

"Now, Mother, I don't know that at all. I remember wonderful times growing up in Chicago."

"If I went, I know I'd want to go back to see The Bluff, and I really don't want to see it now—all developed and built up with whatchamacallit—middle-income housing? No, Josh."

"Everyone's coming—Mayor Byrne, the Governor of Illinois, Chuck Percy. It'll be a party—like the old days."

"No, no. I'm too old for that sort of thing." The occasion is to be the dedication, in the upcoming year, of the new Eaton & Cromwell Tower in Chicago.

"Just think of it, Mother. The tallest building in the world."

"Yes, and I don't like the whole idea of it. Too showy. Your father would have hated it."

"Nonsense. Dad was a real glory boy, you know that. He loved to throw it around."

"You should invite some prominent black people, too, you know, for your father's sake," she reminded him.

"All been taken care of. Jesse Jackson, Benjamin Hooks—they've all accepted. But we need you there, Mother."

"But why? Why? I never had anything to do with the business."

"Don't you see? You're the living link. You're the last living link to Dad and his work. You're Mrs. Jacob Auerbach."

"I'm not sure I fancy being thought of as a link," Essie says. "When I think of links I think of chains and prisons."

"It could be thought of as Dad's crowning achievement. I think you owe it to his memory to be there."

"Now we're invoking the dead," she says. "What do we owe the dead?"

"In this case, quite a lot, Mother," Josh says.

At this point, Mary Farrell slips quietly into the room and places a typewritten note on the table by Essie's chair. Josh glances at it and reads:

> Mrs. Burton St. George (Daisy Stevens)
> Gramercy Park Hotel
> 52 Gramercy Park North
> New York, N.Y. 10010
> 475-4320

"Now, Mother," he says with some annoyance, "why are you getting involved with her again?"

"Never mind. I have my reasons," Essie says.

"Anyway, it's important that you be there," he says. "Right up on the platform—Jake Auerbach's widow. It's a symbol."

"I don't want to be a symbol. They'd ask me to make a speech. I'm terrible at making speeches."

"Just a few words, Mother. It doesn't have to be a speech. Anyway, it's nearly a year away. Will you at least think about it?"

"A year from now—who knows? I'll probably be planted under a tree at Salem fields."

"Now, Mother, don't talk like that."

"It's true."

"Nonsense. You've never been in better health."

"Well," she says, hesitating. "What does Charles say?"

"Charles feels very strongly that you should be there, just as I do."

"Well," she says, "as you say, there's lots of time. Let me think about it, Josh." Then, trying to be less irritable, she says, "I'll try to think about it in a positive light. Now give me a kiss, dear."

It is easy to remember The Bluff in terms of the parties or, as Mr. Duveen used to call them, the grand entertainments. But when Essie Auerbach thinks of the house in Chicago, she prefers to remember the quiet times, when she was alone there. The garden—or, as some people had begun to call it, the park—had been her bailiwick. Cattle had once been fielded there, and the trails they had carved across the hillside behind the house became the pattern for her landscape design of tan-bark walks and bridle paths for the children's horses. She had left most of the standing growth—the birches, tamarisks and hemlocks—as it was, and had supervised the planting of smaller trees and shrubs—azaleas and dogwood—at points which seemed to demand a burst of spring color. She had overseen the planting of hundreds of wildflowers—trillium, arbutus, lady's slipper, jack-in-the-pulpit, anemones, ferns and mosses, columbine, yellow and purple violets. Natural rocks were rearranged, just slightly, to set off clumps of spring bulbs, tulips, daffodils, and hyacinths. The garden came to its full glory in May and early June, when a tent was often raised over the tennis court for a party, but Essie's best moments were the solitary ones, walking through her woods with one of her children by the hand, thinking: this is the forest primeval, the murmuring pines and the hemlocks. Her beautiful house might have been the creature of Joseph Duveen, but her beautiful garden was her own. "How can I have had such a vision?" she would ask herself, years later, when it was time to say good-bye to The Bluff forever. Where did it come from? From some lost ancestor in the Ukraine who had looked at a forest and imagined a wild garden? Who knew? Who knew where the notion had come from of damming a stream with a few rocks and creating a pond for carp and water lilies? Or the labyrinth of paths that led to secret grottoes and sudden surprises of open spaces? There had even been a fairy ring circled by flat stones where elves and gnomes could sit when they assembled in the moonlight. "Let's go exploring in the garden, Mother," Prince would say to her.

Exploring. That had been his word for it—their firstborn, Jacob Junior, whom they had nicknamed Prince. It is hard to remember now, after everything that happened, so many years after he was banished from the memory of all of them forever, that he was once a very real, living and breathing presence in their lives. Had they asked too much of him, expected too much of him? Had they favored him too much over the others? One year later, Joan had been born, and Babette the year after that, but somehow Prince had always seemed to occupy a special, central place, over the little girls. He had seemed while he grew up the perfect child, the perfect little boy, and to have earned the nickname. Had Essie doted on him too much, let him have his way too quickly, and let him know too early that perfection was simply all that was demanded of him? So that when the time came, when perfection was discovered to be a human impossibility, when frailty came and the sin of one tiny error, when the sentinels that his heart was supposed to post to alert him that God was watching could no longer do their duty . . .

The answer to all these questions is perhaps yes. Given hindsight, anything is possible. Such are the penalties of love.

"I want to replace our little Prince!" she had cried to her husband.

Tell me a story, Mother.

But not now, Prince. I have no time!

In 1919, Jacob Auerbach, Jr.—Prince—was eleven, and the talk was of where he should be sent to boarding school. Law-renceville had been selected. "Is the boy in any part Hebraic?" the application had asked, and Essie had watched in some amusement as her husband wrote "No," firmly, in the blank space. We are now only Jews when we want to be, she had thought—when it suits us, not when it doesn't. A bodyguard had been selected for Prince, because of the phobia about kidnappers. His name was Hans, and he had been a Chicago policeman. Now, of course, he wore civilian clothes, though the outline of a police revolver in its holster bulged beneath the jacket of his suit. His suits were invariably blue. Perhaps his years with the police force had conditioned him to that color. Hans was blond, blue-eyed, German, handsome in a rough sort of way, and muscular. Essie would see him, in bathing trunks, exercising with weights and barbells beside the swimming pool. His other duties were to teach the children swimming, tennis, and horsemanship. Essie cared little for Hans, but then there was little occasion for contact with him. In the fall, it was understood, Hans would accompany Prince to Lawrenceville. All these decisions were made by higher-ups than Essie.

But the one servant she could not abide was Spencer, the majordomo. Theirs, from the outset, had not been a meeting of the minds.

"Everyone has an English butler," her husband had said to her.

"I can't help it. I don't like him."

"Why not, for God's sake?"

"He tries to boss me around. If I say I think we'll use the green china, he'll say he thinks the blue is more appropriate. If I want white flowers on the table, he'll say pink roses would be better. I can't get along with him, Jake. I don't like his superior attitude, and I don't like his English accent. And I don't like him being taller than me."

"Essie, you are a fool."

"I don't care," she said defiantly. "I want someone smaller than I am. How about—a Japanese?"

"Very well," he had said at last, picking up his *Wall Street Journal*. "Do as you wish. See Charles about it."

And so, over the years, there had been a series of them, all with names like Taki, Suki, and Yoki. During the second war, Essie had succeeded in keeping her Yoki out of an internment camp. A telephone call to Herbert Lehman had done it.

Put something together. This is the way the orders descend

from the Auerbach High Command. Home from San Francisco, where a new distribution center is being developed, Jacob Auerbach advises: "The Danish ambassador to the United States is coming to Chicago next week. Put something together." And so it is done. The bootlegger is notified, the invitations are telephoned or mailed, the servants are advised, down through the chain of command. "I never remember the names of my servants," Mrs. Bertie McCormick once airily told Essie Auerbach. But, if pressed to do so, Essie could recite to you the names of every one.

Now it is late. The servants have retired for the night, Mary Farrell has left, the telephone has been turned off, and Essie is alone in her bedroom where a glass of warm milk and a plate of fresh fruit have been placed on her bedside table. It has been an oddly unsatisfying day, full of loose ends, full of unresolved questions, unmade decisions. Starting with Daisy, the memories have kept crowding back, pressing through unexpected openings like children at a grownups' party begging to have their presence heeded. Norfolk Street—perhaps some day she should take Josh back to see that, just to drive slowly past the building in the car to look up at the fifth-floor windows, and point—*there*. But who knew if the building still existed, or whether she would see the ghost of her father there?

What would he have made of all this?—Christmas parties. Think of it!

"Apostate!" she can hear him shouting at her from his troubled grave. "Whore of Babylon! Jezebel! You have reared up an altar to Baal to provoke the God of Israel. Can you touch pitch without being defiled? Neither can you hold on to all your money without losing your soul. Poverty becomes a Jew like a red ribbon on a white horse. But you're no longer a Jew. You're a *meshumeides*. You have earned every shred of suffering that has befallen you."

"But Papa," she cries back to him, "why did we come to America if it wasn't to find something better than what we had in Russia?"

He will not answer this.

"*Shmendrick!*" she shouts at him.

Four

"She will marry a rabbi," her father used to say, "or at least a rabbi's son. But even that would not be good enough for her."

Then he would sit her on his knee and tell her the story of Esther, in the Bible, after whom she had been named: about the disobedient queen Vashti who had refused to comply with the commands of her husband, King Ahasueris, thereby setting an example for all women to defy their husbands. And of how the king had renounced Vashti and, after viewing all the eligible virgins of the kingdom, had selected the orphan girl, Esther, who had been raised by her uncle Mordecai, a Benjamite, to be his new queen. And of how, when the wicked Haman conspired to destroy the Jews, Esther interceded with the king on the Jews' behalf, and of how she had thus saved thousands of Jewish lives, and had had her revenge in seeing Haman and his ten sons strung up on the gallows that had been prepared for Mordecai. To celebrate Esther's deed, the festival of Purim had been created. "Think of it!" her father would say.

Essie's father, Shmuel—later Samuel—Litsky claimed that he himself was a descendant of the Benjamites, that is the Tribe of Benjamin. The Benjamites were famous for the bravery of their warriors and for the beauty of their women, of whom Esther was just one shining example. Also, so pure was their faith in God that the Benjamites marched fearlessly into the parting of the Red Sea while other tribes held back, suspecting a trick, worried that the sea might close up on top of them. The Benjamites had also provided Israel with its first king, Saul, who was "swifter than eagles . . . stronger than lions." "Your ancestors," her father would say. "Think of it!" According to Sam Litsky, Essie's ancestors also included a great array of rabbis and scholar-teachers going back to the destruction of the First Temple in the sixth century B.C.—Men of the Book who, like Sam himself, spent most of their waking hours studying the Scriptures and the Midrash, and endlessly scribbling interpretations of the Talmud, when they weren't praying in the synagogue. But, as far as Essie knew, there had never been a family tree to prove, or disprove, any of this.

The earliest home that Essie could remember was the one on Norfolk Street, number 54. There had been one other, before that, on Canal Street, about which her mother had simply told her that it was "not so nice." Essie had no memory of that place. Nor could she remember anything of the little *shtetl* in Russian Poland, as it was then, where she had been born, and which she and her parents had left in 1892, when she was less than a year old, to come to the *Goldene Medina*, the Golden Country. The town was called Volna, in the Ukraine, and the nearest city of any size was Kiev—that much she knew. And on a little shelf above the stove on Norfolk Street there was kept a heavy, old-fashioned, rusted iron key. This was the key to the *alte heim*, which Minna Litsky had brought with her to America. "What was the old home like?" Essie would sometimes ask her mother, but she only got vague answers. "It was built of wood," Mama would say. "There was a river near. Sometimes, in the winter, it was so cold that there was ice on the inside of the walls."

"What was the town like, Mama?"

Her mother would shrug. "It was a nothing of a place. It is better here. We are lucky."

"Would you ever want to go back, Mama?"

"Never! Now don't ask me so many questions. Tell me what you learned in school today."

Minna Litsky always swore that she would never go back to Russia, not even after the success of the second revolution, when everyone cheered the fact that at last the Romanovs had been overthrown, and when some people actually did go back. Never would Minna consider anything of the sort for herself or her family. In fact, after that long journey across the face of Europe—first to Vienna, then north to Hamburg, then to

London, and finally across the ocean to New York, with border guards to be bribed at each frontier—Minna Litsky appeared to have lost all taste for travel, and seldom ventured farther than the limits of her own block on Norfolk Street. She was frightened of the streetcars, and certainly would not ride—when it came, with great fanfare—the subway. ("Ride in a hole in the earth?" she would say. "Never. There are dead spirits down there.") And yet, in its special place, she kept the key to the *alte heim*. It was something that Essie could never understand.

There were a few other things she had learned about the Old Country as she was growing up. Once, with tears streaming down his cheeks, her father had told her of how, as a young man, he had been forced to watch as his younger sister was disemboweled on the street by a band of Cossack soldiers. (Later, she learned that this same girl had been repeatedly raped before the soldiers cut her stomach out.) Her father had also told her about a good and pious rabbi in the little town who had been captured by the soldiers and kept prisoner in a dungeon under the church. Then, tired of this sport, the soldiers had led him out, stripped him naked, and strung him up by his feet in the shape of a cross in the public square. He hung there for a month before the Jews were given permission to cut his body down and bury him.

Once, when Essie was in the third or fourth grade, and when the Christmas holidays were approaching, Essie's teacher had read her class an editorial that had been printed a year or so earlier in the New York *Sun,* and which had since become quite famous. It began, "Virginia, your little friends are wrong . . ." And it ended, "No Santa Claus! Thank God he lives, and he lives forever. A thousand years from now, Virginia, nay ten times ten thousand years from now, he will continue to make glad the heart of childhood."

Essie had admired the words, and her teacher had suggested that she might want to memorize Mr. Church's editorial as a homework project, and recite it later to the class.

That night, when she told her father about it, he looked very sad. "Your teacher is wrong," he said. "Do not misunderstand me. Your teacher is right to want you to memorize something, but your teacher is a Yankee woman and she does not understand many things. It is wrong to ask a Jewish child to memo-

rize those lines. She does not understand that Christmas is not a
happy time for Jews. At Christmastime, in Russia, the soldiers
would be given their leaves and their spending money, and
then they would get drunk. After enough vodka, they would
decide to come into the Jewish quarter, and they would set fire
to the houses, hurt the women, kill the men, even the little
children, saying, 'You killed our Christ. Now we will kill
you.' No, a Jew does not want to honor Christmas. Ask your
teacher if you can memorize something else—one of Mr.
Shakespeare's speeches, no?"

And so she had memorized *Der shtrom fun menshenz maysim bayt zikh imer / nemstu dem rikhtigen, firt er tsu glik*. . . .

Details of the old life in that other country came out like
that—in bits and pieces, almost as if by accident. Essie
learned, for instance, that her mother's father had been a man
of position and responsibility and respect in Volna. The family
had kept a goat and—a matter of some status—a horse.
Minna's father had been in the drayage business, and it was for
this that the horse was used. Sam Litsky's father had been a
blacksmith, and it had seemed a perfect match—the blacksmith's son, and the daughter of the man who owned a horse.
Into the marriage, Minna had brought a dowry—two feather
beds, a lace tablecloth, a pair of candlesticks, a menorah, a
silver thimble, a darning egg of painted china, and a hairbrush
with a silver back and handle. All these things she had carried
with her, along with her wedding canopy and the key to the
alte heim, when she came to America.

At home on Norfolk Street, at times, they spoke in Yiddish,
but on the street they were careful not to. The important thing
was to become a good American, and good Americans did not
speak Yiddish. And as Essie's parents' mastery of the new
language improved, more and more of their conversations were
in English, even at home, for the good practice it provided.
"Say it in American," Essie's mother would remonstrate,
whenever her father lapsed into the old tongue. On the ground
floor of the Norfolk Street house, Essie's mother kept a shop
where she sold newspapers, pencils, school supplies, and
candy. It was not at all a mark of shame in the neighborhood to
have a mother who earned the living for her family, and a
father who had no livelihood at all and who busied himself

with prayer and holy texts. On the contrary, it was a mark of distinction and pride. Minna Litsky was regarded as a *berrieh*, a good and efficient woman who lifted the cares of trade from her husband's shoulders in order that he could devote his life to higher pursuits. Essie grew up thinking that she was fortunate to have such a set of parents. When she was three, her mother had presented her with a baby brother. From her earliest memories, one of Essie's principal responsibilities was caring for little Abe while her mother worked in the store downstairs. Later, when Essie was old enough to go to school, Mama would keep little Abe downstairs in the store with her. On her way home from school, Essie would collect little Abe at the store, and take him up to the fifth floor of the building where they lived. She had never wanted for a doll. It seemed that she had always had little Abe to dress, and feed, and play with.

Essie knew that the building where they lived was called a tenement, and that the apartment was something called a railroad flat. Years later, encountering descriptions of the Lower East Side, Essie would read about the squalid conditions that existed there—mounds of garbage in the halls and entryways, foul stenches everywhere, rats and cockroaches and other vermin, buildings stinking of poverty and disease. But Essie could never recall anything like that at all at 54 Norfolk Street. They had two rooms, and a toilet on the floor below which they shared with only one other family. And there was gaslight—though Essie's mother never really trusted the gas jets, and always kept a window in each room open a crack, even in the coldest weather, lest the treacherous gas escape and poison them all in their sleep. All these were counted as luxuries, and the Litskys were considered fortunate. They knew that they lived better than other people, and their good fortune flowed from Minna Litsky, who had been able to scrape together enough money from taking in sewing to open her little shop.

Behind the building, to be sure, there ran an alley, and there was often garbage there—though periodically it got hauled away—and the children were warned not to go into the alley because rats had indeed been seen there. But none of the garbage came from the Litsky household. As a *berrieh*, Minna Litsky knew how to dispose of her garbage, and it was deposited nightly, wrapped in yesterday's newspaper, in the containers on the street.

The smells of the house on Norfolk Street that Essie would always remember were pleasant ones—the smell of warm milk being heated on the stove for Little Abe's bottle, the smell of soaps and polishes—in addition to everything else, Minna was a fanatic housecleaner—and then there was Mama's own, special smell which she brought home with her from the store, the smell of candy. There was the bright, sharp smell that would fill the kitchen when her mother scattered a few cloves on a white-hot skillet and let them dance about. This was not done to sweeten the air, but to ward off evil spirits, and whether this was simply a tradition in her mother's family, or an ancient Jewish rule, Essie never knew.

This, then, was how Essie would always remember her early childhood—the mixture of her father's spirituality and her mother's benevolent witchcraft.

Even more fixed in memory are the noises. Having grown up with noise, Essie takes it in her stride. There is the noise of the pushcart vendors from the street: the knife- and scissors-sharpener's cry, the cry of the bread-man with his thick loaves of Russian rye, the chicken-soup man with his steaming vats, the old-clothes man. They hawk their wares at the tops of their voices, shouting. Buy me! Ask my price! Lady, you need this! Buy! Cheap! Buy! And they continue to try to outshout one another when they pause from their labors at the end of the day in the coffee houses. What do they shout about? Socialism! Revolution! Jobs! Working conditions! The masses! The bosses! High rents! The landlords! Strike! Too many people coming! Organize! All these shouts Essie hears from her fifth-floor window.

The day begins with the familiar *thunk* as the baled bundle of *Tageblatts* is tossed from the delivery truck onto the sidewalk in front of Minna Litsky's store, and Essie watches as her mother rushes out—one has to be fast, or the papers will be stolen—and snatches up the bundle by its balings and carries it inside. Inside, she quickly snips the baling cords with a penknife and counts her newspapers—she has occasionally been short-shipped.

All around are the sounds of people—people everywhere—
thousands upon thousands of people. And they keep coming.
The year 1901 is declared the "worst" in terms of immigrants—a record—but still more come in 1902. In 1903, the
record is broken again, with 90,000 given as the figure of new
arrivals in New York Harbor. There has been a series of terrible pogroms in Kishinev, and in 1904 still another record is
set. Where will they all go? Some of them will stay in the
Litskys' flat because, as Minna Litsky says, the Litskys are
more fortunate than others, with their two rooms. Some are
relatives, near and distant, and others are merely *landsmen,*
from Volna or the outlying districts. "They must stay somewhere," Minna Litsky says, as she takes these people in—for a
few days, or weeks, until they can find places of their own, and
Essie has grown accustomed to sharing her bed with some
small cousin who speaks not a word of English and who cries
in her sleep. It is these people's good fortune that the Litskys
are so fortunate.

And the children. Essie's school, already overcrowded, goes
into split sessions, and then the sessions split again and there
are morning, afternoon, and evening classes. And some of the
children are not even children. An eighteen-year-old boy may
be in the first grade, because he must begin by learning the
English alphabet. Meanwhile, the greedy landlords, even the
Jewish ones, grow greedier, and the more crowded the tenements become the higher climb the rents, and the slower is the
landlord to make repairs.

From Uptown, the New York *Herald* speaks of "unspeak-
able conditions" in the ghetto, and berates the mayor and City
Hall. The *Tageblatt* berates the *Tribune,* and Essie's father
berates the *Tageblatt,* slapping the newspaper with the back of
his hand as though it were an unruly child. Most of the stories
the *Tageblatt* prints, he says, are lies. If the *Tageblatt* can find
a single point of controversy, it will leap upon it and turn it into
a headline. SOMETHING MUST BE DONE! the *Tageblatt*'s
headline screams. "Headlines, headlines!" her father shouts,
slapping the paper, adding to the din. A boatload of Russian immigrants has been diverted to Galveston. "Texas!"
her father bellows. "What's there for them there? Think
of it!"

With so much crowding in the streets, one must choose one's route with care when one ventures out. One section of Delancey Street, for instance, is given over to street toughs and gamblers who run poker and crap games on the sidewalks and the stoops of houses. Here, too, there are Jewish pimps and prostitutes, young girls who sell their bodies for a dollar or two, and fulfill their contracts stretched out on a row of garbage cans in a back alley. In a way, it is horrible to think of Jewish girls doing things like this, and yet, in another, secret way, it is exciting. On Delancey Street, an interesting alliance has been formed between the Jews and the Italians, and a whole new industry has been invented. It is called Protection. Once a week, two tough-looking men come to Minna Litsky's store for their two dollars' protection money. One pays it, because one has seen what has happened to shopkeepers who refuse. Minna is philosophical. "They have to earn a living, too," she says, and figures her protection money into her overhead, part of the cost of doing business, reminding Essie that Delancey Street is to be avoided at all costs.

The Irish are the enemy. The Micks—big, thick-headed, tough, and mean—prey on the Jewish children, calling them Christ-killers, and when little Abe is old enough to go to school, Essie must take him on a circuitous route to avoid the blocks which the Micks patrol. Even so, a group of Micks may be encountered unexpectedly, looking for victims. When this happens, Essie puts her arm tightly around her brother's shoulder because even the wicked Micks have their scruples. It's the Jewish boys they're after. They will not bother Jewish girls. Minna Litsky talks of moving to the Bronx, but only in a worried, uncertain way. She dislikes, you see, the thought of travel.

From Uptown come Do-Gooders—rich women in stone marten scarves, little animals with glass eyes and their jaws clasped fiercely to each others' tails—women like Mrs. Oliver Hazzard Perry Belmont, and Mr. J. P. Morgan's sister. Their pictures are in the *Tageblatt*, which disapproves of them. They are suspected of being Christian missionaries. The Do-Gooders come down to the East Side and pass out cookies and doughnuts and apples to the children on the street. But even the hungriest children who accept these gifts are afraid to eat them because they are probably not kosher. It is humiliating to be on the receiving end of the Do-Gooders' well-meaning charity, and yet their presence is begrudgingly accepted since it must be admitted that the Do-Gooders do some good. They put on lectures, they help the teachers in the schools, they care for the sick.

SOMETHING MUST HAPPEN! the *Tageblatt*'s headline declaims. The Jews have been shipped to Texas, but Texas doesn't want them—as Sam Litsky could have told the authorities all along, he says, slapping at the aberrant daily. (If her father hates the *Tageblatt* so much, Essie wonders, why does he insist on having the first copy of the paper that comes off the pile?) There must be International Talks. In Washington, D.C., Congressmen are rattling their legislative swords and calling for quotas. President Theodore Roosevelt has declared, "We should aim to exclude absolutely not only all persons who are known to be believers in anarchistic principles, but also all persons who are of a low moral tendency or of unsavory reputation."

"Give me your tired, your poor, your huddled masses," the Statue of Liberty implores, beseeches, from New York Harbor, holding high her lamp above the golden door.

In 1904, there are rent strikes all over the city, some of them quite violent. Strikers are clubbed and knocked about. One, knocked over the head by a policeman's billy, dies in the hospital. Now there is talk of a children's strike—surely the strike-breakers would restrain themselves and not harm innocent children. Essie is thirteen, and there is much talk at home of whether or not Essie should be allowed to march with the strikers, most of whom are young girls in their early teens. At issue is the situation at the Cohen paper-box factory on the Bowery, where the girls were being paid three dollars for every thousand cigarette boxes they turned out, and where a wage cut of ten percent has just been announced. The *Tageblatt* is raising a special fund to help the strikers. Seven hundred dollars is raised by the United Hebrew Trades, there are benefit concerts, and the Do-Gooders from Uptown, led by such social workers as Jane Addams, have offered their full support.

Minna Litsky is opposed to the idea of having Essie march with the demonstrators, but Sam, who has decided that he is a

Socialist, is for it. And so Essie marches, with her father keeping close by, in case of trouble. There is none, but in the end it is hard to see what the strike has accomplished. The Cohen paper-box factory remains inflexible. But Essie Litsky's picture is in the paper.

And so, though the Lower East Side keeps growing, changing, there is much that remains the same. Within the community flourish beggars, thieves, plunderers, heroes, clowns, noisemakers, rapscallions, miracle workers, saviors, Samaritans and sinners, goldbricks, warriors, saints and bloodsuckers, ruffians, reformers, rebels and backsliders, cutthroats and comedians and revolutionaries, all held together by some common glue—America.

Now the *Tageblatt* is inveighing against Victrolas. The newfangled machines, played at full volume from open windows of the tenements, simply add to the din and chaos of East Side living. Victrolas! Think of it!

Nothing is permanent, except the fact that life goes on.

It is a world in which one grows up quickly.

In 1907, when Essie was sixteen, she realized that her school days were coming to an end. Ten years of schooling was enough for a Jewish girl—in fact, it was more than most had, her mother pointed out, reminding her again of her good fortune. Most girls were at work by age fourteen, and the time had come for Essie to begin to make some financial contribution to the household. If nothing else, she could help Minna in the store. The time was also approaching when Essie should begin thinking about finding a husband. Minna herself had been fifteen when she was married, and seventeen when Essie was born. These matters, however, would be left in the hands of Essie's father, who would find her a match in the customary way.

At P.H.S. Eleven, knowing that this was her last year, Essie was not studying very hard, nor was her mind really on the complicated business of what lay ahead for her. Most of the courses she was taking—Home Economics, Civics, Botany— were designed to teach a Jewish girl to be a practical housekeeper, to cook and to sew and to press flowers under glass, and she found them too easy to get high marks in. But that was the year she had discovered books—not the books that were the texts for her courses, but the books on the shelves of the branch of the Public Library on East Broadway near Chatham Square. All that was needed was her name and address on a little card, and all these books were hers to take home for free. There were newspapers and magazines at the library, too— magazines on art and travel and science and history—and all at once she found herself lifted up, transported, out of the constricted and quarrelsome little world of the *Tageblatt,* into the Casbah of Marakesh and onto the landscape of the moon.

She read ravenously, everything she could get her hands on, from Shakespeare's plays to the latest novel by Joseph Conrad, called *The Secret Agent,* and the more daring modern novels by Bertha M. Clay, the poems of Ethel Lynn Beers and Rose Terry Cooke. Vicariously, she rose in the ranks of the French bourgeoisie with Emma Bovary, was titillated by the erotic Kate Chopin, and suffered the humiliation of Hester Prynne. "Let men tremble to win the hand of woman, unless they win along with it the utmost passion of her heart," she read, and sighed.

Her father complained about it. "Look at her," he would cry, "her nose in a book again!"

"But you're always reading, Papa."

"Not the trash you read—novels, picture magazines."

"You wanted me to memorize Shakespeare. Remember?"

"But that was for your school," he argued. "No husband will want a wife who spends all her time with a book."

"Your papa's right," her mother said. "Men don't like bookish women. If a man ever finds out you're bookish, he'll want nothing to do with you."

Still, she continued her journey to the center of the earth with Jules Verne.

At school, meanwhile, there was one weekly lecture which she had begun to look forward to. It took place on Fridays, and the tall young man who conducted it was one of the Do-Gooders from Uptown who worked as a volunteer in the school system. The course he taught was called Living With Our City, and the topics he chose were almost uniformly boring—How Our Fire Department Does Its Job, A Day in the Life of a Sanitation Inspector, Our Mayor and His Councilmen, Why

the Policeman is Our Friend, and so on—nor was his manner
of delivery particularly inspiring, as he droned on about the
sewer system and abjured against young people's practice of
opening fire hydrants on hot days. And so, instead of listening
to what this tall young man had to say, Essie had taken to
making sketches of him in her notebook, because Essie thought
him simply the handsomest young man she had ever seen.

He must have been in his early twenties, with the darkest,
curliest hair, the bluest eyes, the strongest chin, the straightest
nose. He was also beautifully dressed, and one of her classmates had told her why—his family was in the men's clothing
business. Essie sketched him with a mustache, didn't like that,
and erased it off. Then she sketched him with a small, pointed
beard, but didn't care for that, either.

One afternoon, as she was leaving school, she encountered
him on the steps. He smiled at her, and said, "Do you live near
here?"

"On Norfolk Street," she said.

"I'll walk you home," he said. "Here, let me carry your
books," and he took her packet of books that were tied together
with a slender string. She had actually been headed for the
library. But that could wait.

Up close to him, not separated from him by rows of students
and their desks, and by the lecture platform, she saw that he
really was extraordinarily handsome.

In that memory, he still is.

It is February there, and the low late-afternoon sun is leaden
and cold. There is a damp wind coming up from the river, and
instinctively Essie draws her scarf up over her nose and mouth,
and they push forward, heads lowered, clutching their coats,
against the wind. It is too cold for conversation, and there
seems no point in trying. Warm gusts of steam blow up from
the storm sewers, the hot innards of the city that he has described in his lectures, and fling up soot and candy wrappers,
all the detritus of the city, spiraling into the air. A blowing
sheet of newspaper cuffs about his trouser legs and he does a
little dance to rid himself of it. Essie cups her hand across her
eyes to keep cinders from flying into them.

In that memory, the city is all motion, people rocking about on the pavements like passengers on a huge ship on a stormy sea, swaying to keep their balance, grasping for handholds as the vessel that is Manhattan Island pitches and tosses in the waves. But in more ways than one this short journey to Norfolk Street seems to Essie Litsky like an ocean crossing, and in the wind she and only she feels that she is walking on sheer air. Where will this journey lead? For this young man himself, in his fine clothes, with his highly polished dark brown shoes, is from the Other Side. And on the Other Side, she knows from what she has read in her books and magazines, stand open spaces, green lawns and picket fences, trees and streams and fountains, gardens where children play in swings and sand-boxes, where sunshine falls on all four sides, not just slanted narrowly through streets and airshafts. This is where she suddenly feels herself headed now, with this fine-looking young man as her escort and her guide. The trip may be full of perils, but it need not be long, and she knows immediately that this is the trip she has always dreamed of making, and it is as though, if she stood on tiptoe, she could see and greet the horizon of that shining opposite shore. Because it is as simple as this: he is taking her out of the Old World, and into America at last.

I must make him fall in love with me, she tells herself. I must make no false moves. Then, holding tight to him, I will leap to it.

They turn into Hester Street, and the wind falls, trapped behind the buildings, but there another storm assails them—a moving sea of humanity and sound. The street is lined on both sides with pushcarts topped by makeshift canopies and umbrellas as far as the eye can see, and in between are people—bearded men in heavy coats, women in long skirts and aprons and shawls, children, and everyone, it seems, is carrying some sort of bundle or basket, buying, selling, bickering, haggling: newsboys, egg-sellers, fish-peddlers, the matzoh men, the cash-for-clothes men, thrusting goods at one another. Blocking their way is a group of women arguing loudly with a yard-goods dealer over a bit of cotton cloth. People lean against each other, shout and move away. Fists shake. Threats are issued. Terrible terrors and curses are invoked. Then there is a sudden burst of laughter and from somewhere the sound of an organ-grinder's music. The crowd sways as two policemen move slowly through, fingering their long sticks.

"What's going on?" the young man shouts in Essie's ear.

"It's all right. It's always like this," she shouts back. "It's the safest place in town. You just have to push through."

And so they push forward, shouldering, elbowing, shoving and forcing themselves against the crush of human traffic that assails them, between the pushcarts and their disputatious customers, through the warm smell of charcoal fires and the cooking smells of bread, chicken broth and garlic sausage and, above all, the pungent smell of human bodies, through the seething, jostling throng.

The next block is even worse. "Hold my hand," he says. "So we don't get separated." They push on, clinging to each other, step by step through the tide.

At the corner, Essie shouts up to him, "Do you like egg creams?"

"What?"

"I said, do you like egg creams?"

He stops and laughs, and Essie sees that he has a nice laugh, much more compelling than when he is standing at a lectern in an auditorium, holding forth on water mains. "Don't think I've ever had one," he says.

"They make good ones here," she says, pointing to a little shop.

Inside the ice cream parlor, it is considerably quieter. They sit side by side at the counter and order egg creams, and Essie shows him how to spoon the runny liquid out of his glass. "This is good," he says, though from his tone she is not entirely sure he means it. Then he says, "Do you like living in this neighborhood?"

"I've lived here all my life."

He seems to consider this. Then he asks, "Are you enjoying my lectures?"

"Oh, yes. Very much."

"I've noticed that you take a lot of notes."

Essie feels her face redden. He is still holding her books, and she prays that he won't ask to see her notes and discover what they really are. "Yes," she says.

"I just wish they'd let me lecture about some of the things that really interest me," he says.

"What sort of things?"

"European history. And art."

"I was born in Europe, but I don't remember it."

"I guessed as much."

"Why won't they let you talk about that?"

He makes a face. "We must teach the new people *useful* things."

"I think art is useful."

He shakes his head.

"I'm studying botany this year," she says. "What use is that?"

"Very useful," he says. "We must interest Jews in farming—agriculture."

"Are you Jewish?"

He nods.

"Where do you go to *shul?*"

"*Shul?*" He laughs again. "I guess we don't go in much for that sort of thing, my family," he says.

Puzzled, Essie spoons up the last of her egg cream. "I'd better get home now, or Mama will worry," she says.

Outside, they push on, through more crowds, across Allen Street, then Orchard Street. The winter sky has grown darker, colder, and there is a scattering of snowflakes in the air. "Only two more blocks," Essie says.

At Norfolk Street, they turn the corner and head north, toward Grand Street, and leave the crowds behind them. "This is where I live," Essie says, and realizes that a note of pride has crept into her voice—pride that her street, at least, is not as crowded and noisy as some others. But when they stop in front of number 54, and Essie says, "This is my house," and when she sees him plant his feet on the sidewalk and gaze upward at the facade of the building—and when she lets her eyes follow his—it is as though she is seeing her building now as he is seeing it, and she feels suddenly helpless and apologetic for the narrow, ugly, soot-blackened building where she lives, its face crawling with zigzagged fire escapes, a building identical in its grimy sameness with every other on the street, with nothing special about it in the whole wide world.

"We live on the fifth floor," she says.

"Shall I walk you up?"

"Oh, no," she says with alarm, thinking of all the possibilities which her mother has warned about arrayed before her. "No, this is fine."

He hands her her books. Thus, with both her hands briefly encumbered, he kisses her lightly on the forehead.

It is a first—the first time Essie has ever been kissed by a man other than her father and her baby brother.

He smiles, steps back, gives her a little salute, says, "See you next Friday," and starts off.

"I don't even know your name!" she calls after him.

"Jake Auerbach."

Five

~~~~~~~~~

THE atmosphere in the Litskys' flat that night had been heavy with recrimination and reproach. Little Abe had been sent into the other room, with the door firmly closed behind him, since the matter under discussion, Essie's impure act, was considered too awful and momentous for a boy of his tender years, even though Abe, at thirteen, had become street-wise in ways that would have surprised his parents. He had already, though Essie would not know about it until much later, managed to filch a dollar from Minna's cash drawer and had been inducted into manhood by one of the Delancey Street girls.

"But Mama, *you didn't see what happened!*" Essie kept repeating.

"No! But I'm the only one on the street who didn't," her mother said. "Mrs. Potamkin from downstairs saw it, and Mrs. Brachfeld from across the street—all those nosy *yentes* who have nothing to do all the day long but sit in their windows and watch what goes on in the neighborhood. Mrs. Potamkin was the first one into the store to tell me. 'Guess what, Mrs. Litsky. Your daughter Esther was just now out in front on the street, carrying on with some strange man.'"

"Mama, I wasn't carrying on! He just gave me a little kiss, just a peck, like this"—she demonstrated—"I wasn't even expecting it. That's all there was. I didn't kiss him back. He just gave me the little peck, and said good night."

Sam Litsky's head was in his hands, and he rolled it back and forth as though he were experiencing a convulsion. "Who is he?" he demanded. "Who is this man, this piece of filth, who would defile my daughter and bring shame and disgrace upon my family? Who is he, that's all I want to know."

"His name is Jake Auerbach, Papa."

"Auerbach? I know no Auerbachs. How did he pick you up?"

"He *didn't* pick me up, Papa. He teaches at my school. We just happened to be going out the door together, and he offered to walk me home."

"What sort of course does this filth teach? What sort of ideas is he putting into the heads of our young people?"

"It's a course called Living With Our City."

"*What?* Living with sin?"

"No, Papa—Living With Our *City*. It's about how water starts out in a reservoir upstate and comes down in big pipes to people's houses, and things like that. He's really very nice. He bought me an egg cream at Mr. Levy's."

"*What?* You let him buy you things? Don't you know that that's how the seducer always begins? Haven't your mother and I told you often enough never to take food or candy from a stranger? How many times we've told you? A thousand, maybe? Two thousand? Three?"

"But Papa, I told you, he's not a stranger—"

Now Minna was becoming cross with her husband. "Now, Sam, enough already," she said sharply. "Let Esther tell her story. Esther—" she hesitated. "Did he try—did he try to touch you in any way, in any special place, in a woman's special places?"

"No!"

"Well, thank God for that!"

Now her father was shouting at her mother. "Do I believe what I am hearing?" he said. "Do I believe my own two ears? Do I hear you *thanking God* for a man, a man who is a teacher, a man who is hired to instruct the lives of little ones in moral ways, for a man in that position in the school, for that man to grab one of his girl students and kiss her—you thank God for that? I think you have just gone crazy! In Russia, if a man teacher did that to a girl student he would be marched into the square and shot!"

"He didn't grab me," Essie said.

"He didn't grab her," Minna echoed. "And it isn't Russia. Thank God for that, too."

"Still, you cannot say that this is the proper way for a teacher to behave in any country—and thank God for *that*. No, it is wrong. And I am going to write a letter, in English, to the proper school authorities tomorrow, first thing in the morning, explaining what has happened and what this man has done to my Esther from his school. No, I take it back. I'm not going to write a letter. I'm going to the school myself tomorrow and personally tell the authorities what this man has done. He'll have no more paycheck after tomorrow."

"Oh, Papa, please don't. A few people on the street saw him give me a little kiss. If that was so bad, do you want the whole school—the whole neighborhood to know? They will, if you do that."

"She's right, Sam," Minna said. "There are enough busybodies right on this block without bringing in the whole East Side."

"A man like that should not be working for the New York City public school system."

"He doesn't really work for the school system, Papa. He's a volunteer. He comes down from Uptown to give his lectures, once a week, on Fridays."

"So much for his paycheck, Sam," Minna said.

Essie's father looked suspicious. "Is he Jewish?"

"Yes."

"Ah," he said, "I know exactly the type. He's one of the Uptown *shtadlonim*. I know all about those types, Esther. They've turned their backs on their faith, they don't keep the Sabbath, their synagogue is even in what used to be a church. They've taken out Hebrew from the service, their women sit right beside them in the *shul*. The men don't cover their heads in God's house, and instead the women wear fancy hats. They sing Christian hymns, they're more Christian than the Christians. They're not real Jews. They don't keep the dietary laws, and they want to force good Jews like us to be like them. Did you know that one of those *shtadlonim*—right on Grand Street—took a Russian Jew into a restaurant, trying to convert him, and made him eat an oyster? Don't look so shocked! It happened. I read it in the *Tageblatt*. The poor Jew died, of course."

"Papa, you're always saying that most of the stories in the *Tageblatt* are lies."

"This one was true. On Grand Street."

Shtadlonim—it was a Yiddish term her father used somewhat indiscriminately. Technically, it meant any wealthy, influential Jew who was able to intercede on the Jews' behalf with the government. As such, it was a term of gratitude and respect. But her father also used the term sneeringly, and applied it to anyone who groveled before the feet of the Establishment, or who tried to curry favors from higher-ups. Among people like these, he included what were also known as the *Amerikanishe Deitche Yahudim,* the haughty, purse-proud, arrogant American German Jews, who lived in great brick and brownstone mansions Uptown. Though the *Deitche* were the self-appointed leaders of New York's Jewish community, and though they headed all the important Jewish hospitals and charities, they were suspected of secretly harboring no small amount of *riches,* or anti-Semitism. They claimed that they wanted the Russians to "assimilate," which meant be submissive and inconspicuous, and being inconspicuous meant shaving off sidecurls, discarding yarmulkes and phylacteries, abandoning traditions that were thousands of years old. The *Tageblatt* frequently complained about the missionary nature of the Uptown Germans' incursions on the Lower East Side.

The Germans feared the Russians, but they didn't call it fear. They called it philanthropy.

"Then I think," her father said, "that if we can't get that man out of school, where he is bothering our little children, that it is time to take Esther out of that school."

"Sam, we agreed that she could finish this year," her mother said.

"And I'm really not a little child, Papa," Essie said. "Mama was married when she was my age. You know that."

"It's true, Sam," her mother said. "Our Esther is growing into a woman. So—what's an innocent little kiss? That's all there was to it."

"I'll show you a picture of him, Papa, if you like," Essie

said, and reached for her notebook that lay on the kitchen table. "I made some drawings of him in the class."

Her father took the notebook, and flipped slowly through the pages.

"Drawing pictures!" her mother said. "When you should have been writing down everything that your teacher said."

Looking at Essie's sketches, her father muttered "*Shtadlonim*" once more. But then his face brightened somewhat. "Esther, I didn't know you could draw like this," he said. "When did you learn to do this? Who taught you this? Minna-lein, do you know that I think our Esther has talent as an artist? Think of it! Do you think an art school, maybe?"

The sketches seemed to have brought the family quarrel to an end. Minna Litsky rubbed her hands firmly across her apron front, and said, "Well, is anyone else starving to death for supper? I know I am."

Little Abe, grinning broadly—surely he had been able to hear absolutely everything that had gone on, every single word through the thin partition—was released from the back room, and everyone gathered at the kitchen table. It was the beginning of the Sabbath, and the candles were lighted. Sam said the blessings, sliced the loaf. Then Minna served her family's dinner.

Throughout the meal, the talk was small and inconsequential. But after dinner, Essie heard her mother say in a low voice to her father, "Sam, I think the time has come to look for a husband for our Hadassah." Her father gave her mother a stern and disapproving look. It was improper to discuss such matters on the Sabbath.

But Essie knew that things were serious whenever her mother used her Hebrew name.

Essie had begun to take an interest in Jake Auerbach's weekly lectures, now that she knew that the topics interested him not at all. It was a wonder that he could get up on the platform, week after week, and take such pains to illuminate a subject he cared nothing about, simply because he thought it might do some poor soul some good. Now she was listening with rapt attention as he applied himself to today's theme, which was Our Friend Electricity.

"Now you will hear many false rumors and superstitions about electricity," he was saying. "When many people think of electricity, they think of electric storms and bolts of lightning which come out of the sky and split tree trunks in half and even occasionally kill people. Domestic electricity, which is spreading rapidly into homes throughout America, is of an altogether different kind. It is not dangerous. Perhaps you have heard that if an electric light bulb is not screwed tightly into its socket, the electricity will leak out into the room, or that if an electric plug is not plugged into every outlet in your house the same thing will happen. None of this is true. The electricity goes into the light bulb only when the bulb is screwed into its socket, and the switch is turned to 'on.' On the other hand, it *is* dangerous to place your fingers in an empty socket or to place pins or other objects into an electrical outlet. You can give yourself a very nasty shock that way, which will hurt you and burn you because your body then becomes what is called the 'conductor' of the electricity . . . like any friend, we must respect Our Friend Electricity . . . electrical engineers foresee the day when not only our homes in America will all be lighted by electricity, when all our cooking will be done by electricity, when our homes will be heated by electricity, but when electricity will also be used to power locomotives, automobiles, huge ocean liners. The uses of electricity are many . . . Here is a typical incandescent lamp bulb, which was invented by Thomas Alva Edison . . . The first to recognize the potential—does the class know that word? Potential? It means power. He was a man named Benjamin Franklin. One day, while flying a kite . . ."

"That was so interesting!" Essie said to him afterward. "I didn't know any of those things."

He smiled. "Did you enjoy it? Frankly, I'm beginning to look forward to the summer recess, when I can take a holiday from all of this."

Essie did not want to think about the summer recess, which would mean the last of school for her. Their walks home to Norfolk Street had become a weekly ritual, along with the stops at Mr. Levy's for egg creams. But after the first time, she had warned him that there were to be no more kisses by the front door. He winked at her and said, "Why not?"

"Everybody gossips so on Norfolk Street. My mother heard about it before I got inside the house."

"Then I'll kiss you on Hester Street," he said, and did it again. "See? Nobody noticed."

She had shivered. "Don't be so sure. Everybody comes here."

"In this crowd, who'd pay any attention?"

In the process of their weekly walks, she had learned a bit more about young Mr. Jacob Auerbach. He was twenty-three years old, and had graduated from Columbia University, where he had studied history. He was an only child, and he lived with his parents at 14 West 53rd Street, Uptown. Essie herself had been Uptown only once or twice in her life, on school trips, and where the numbered streets and avenues began she was still confused about which way the numbers ran, and about which avenue separated East from West. He explained it to her, but she knew that if she ever went up there by herself she would certainly get lost.

His parents were German, but they were not quite top-drawer *Deitche*. His parents were not rich but, though he did not come right out and say so, she gathered that there were relatives who were. His father worked for some of these relatives, who had the men's clothing store, where—he told her with a laugh—he was able to buy his nice clothes "at family prices." His father was pressing him to go into the family business, but Jake Auerbach was resisting. He had not yet made up his mind, he said, as to what he wanted to do with his life. "Plenty of time," he said, and while he waited for his mind to be made up he did this social work. He also worked for the Henry Street and University settlement houses. And part of the weekly ritual, too, became the little kisses, stolen Essie could never predict where, but always in a crowd, and never on Norfolk Street. It became their little joke. February passed that way, and March, and in April you knew that spring was coming because there were more pushcarts than ever in the streets.

One afternoon, at Mr. Levy's, she said to him, "You were frightened when you first saw Hester Street, weren't you?"

"My first thought was—pickpockets. Believe me, when I had you on one hand I had my other on my pocketbook, all the way."

"There aren't any Jewish pickpockets," she laughed.

"Ha! Don't you wish that were true? There's a Jewish everything, and you can be sure that Jewish pickpockets are better at it than any other kind."

"That sounds like *riches* talk," she said.

"*Riches?* What does that word mean?"

"As though you didn't like the Jews."

He laughed. "How could I not like the Jews? I'm Jewish myself." Then he changed the subject. "I'm studying your face," he said. "Do you know that you're very beautiful?"

She lowered her eyes and concentrated on her egg cream. She wanted to tell him that she thought he was beautiful, too, but she said nothing, feeling him continuing to look at her.

The following week, as they started out, he said, "Instead of Mr. Levy's, why don't you let me take you out to dinner? I know a nice place, and my Uncle Sol just gave me my birthday check."

"Is today your birthday?"

"No, that was months ago, but Uncle Sol takes his time about giving out his birthday checks. So how about it? Straight home, and I'll pick you up in front of your house tonight at seven."

"Oh, but not tonight. We couldn't possibly go out tonight."

"Why not?"

"The Sabbath begins at sundown. Did you forget?"

"Oh," he said. "That's right, I did forget."

"Don't you observe the Sabbath?"

"Oh, yes—sometimes, not always. As I told you, we're not all that strict about things like that. But I try to go to temple at least twice a year—at Christmas and Easter."

"Christmas and *Easter?*"

"That's supposed to be a joke. I mean Rosh Hashanah and Yom Kippur. Haven't you heard about Reform?"

"Of course, but Papa says—" She decided not to tell him what Papa said about Reform. "Papa is very strict," she said.

"I guessed as much. But don't you see—?" He left the

question unfinished. "Well, how about Sunday, then? Sunday for lunch."

"All right," she said quickly, hoping that her shock at some of the things he had said did not show too much.

"I'll pick you up at your house at noon."

"No. Let's meet in front of Mr. Levy's."

She was about to tell a lie to her mother. "Mama," she said, "the school is having a trip on Sunday, Uptown to one of the museums."

"How much does this one cost?"

"It's free, Mama."

"Oh, they'll want something," Minna said. "Wait and see, they'll send a letter home, wanting something." Then she said, "You've been seeing him again, haven't you, the young *Deitche?* You think people don't talk? You think people don't tell me things?"

"He walks me home on Fridays, Mama."

"But no funny business?"

"Of course not, Mama. So—can I go on the trip?"

"Well, if it's free, why not?" her mother said. "As Mrs. Potamkin says, 'If it's free, take two.'"

The restaurant was called Saltzman's, on the "good" end of Delancey Street. Essie had seen Saltzman's curtained, plate-glass windows from the street, but had never been inside, and it all seemed very large and grand, with shiny china and silverware, white linen napkins, and waiters in black mess jackets with clean white tablecloths wrapped around their waists. There was even a large bouquet of fresh flowers in the center of the room. She dreaded to think what this meal was going to cost him.

"I was going to take you uptown, to Delmonico's," he said, "but then I remembered. For you it has to be kosher, right?"

"Oh, yes."

"This was the best I could find of that variety, I'm afraid."

"But Saltzman's is famous!"

A waiter handed each of them a menu. It was large and long, and contained many dishes Essie had never heard of. She had decided not to tell him that she had never been in a real restaurant before, and so she said, "Why don't you order for both of us?"

"Let's try the veal tenderloin," he said.

"Do you mean that you don't keep kosher, either?" she asked when they had ordered.

"Of course not. My favorite lunch is a ham sandwich with a thick slice of cheese—and lobster—"

"*Lobster?* You've eaten lobster, and it didn't make you sick?"

"We had lobster for dinner last night, and I'm here, aren't I? You see, Essie—" He hesitated. "You see, I don't want you to think I'm criticizing the way you were brought up, but a lot of the things you Russian Jews are taught are based on nothing but superstition. The dietary laws, for instance."

"But the Talmud—"

"The Talmud was compiled thousands of years ago by scholars who had no access to any of modern science. Don't get me wrong. There are many wonderful, beautiful things in the Talmud—what it teaches about morality, righteousness, social responsibility, caring for the needy, about love—all that is fine and wonderful, and I agree with it. But the rest of it—all the ritual—is based on circumstances that haven't existed since the Middle Ages. This is America, Essie, and it's the twentieth century—a whole new century ahead of us, new discoveries every day. Maybe, back in the fifth century B.C., when there was no such thing as pasteurization, maybe it wasn't safe to put milk and meat together in the same dish. Maybe the combination caused bacteria, or microbes, to grow, and this made people sick. But that can't happen anymore, where everything's tested, inspected, sterilized. I like what Rabbi Wise had to say on the subject—'There is a law which stands higher than all dietary laws, and that is: Be no fanatic.'"

She decided not to tell him what her father had to say about Rabbi Isaac Mayer Wise.

He laughed. "I'm sorry. I'm back on my lecture platform, aren't I? But it's just that I believe so strongly that these new Jews who have come to America, like your family, have got to adapt to this country, have got to join the mainstream of American life. They can't come to a new, modern country and carry the traditions of the old country around with them on their backs like peddlers' packs. If they do, they'll never get anywhere. They'll be stuck here forever, on the Lower East Side."

"Someday I'd love to hear you arguing with my father."

"I'd love to do that, I really would. But anyway, enough of that. Let's enjoy our kosher lunch."

Afterward—it was a bell-like clear spring day—they walked northward, hand in hand, and before they knew it they had reached Union Square. Union Square was a great oval with tall trees that were springing into bud, with acres of green grass, with an ornamental iron fence that ran around it, circled by a wide drive, and with three huge fountains splashing at the center. It was one of the city's showpieces, and nearby were Tiffany's, Stewart's, Lord & Taylor. They window-shopped the closed, expensive stores.

"I suppose your mother's store was closed yesterday, but is open today," he said.

"Of course."

"You see? That's what I mean. This is America, and Americans love to shop on Saturdays. But the Orthodox Jews refuse to do any business on a Saturday. They won't even lift a pencil or button a shirt. What's the point of it? They gain nothing. Instead, they lose. What difference does it make—in all eternity—what day of the week a man celebrates his religion on? Isn't religion supposed to come from the heart? The heart can celebrate what it believes whenever it wants to, can't it? But there I go again. Lecturing again."

"But I like it when you lecture," she said. "You teach me things. This has been one of the nicest days I've spent in my whole life."

They decided to take the streetcar back.

The following Friday, Essie hurried down the corridor to the auditorium where his lecture was to be, but when she got to the door the topic of his series, Living With Our City, had been changed to something called Putting Up Jellies and Preserves on the easel to announce the lecture. He was not there. He had sent her no word, and she had no idea—she had forgotten his Uptown address—of how to reach him. All at once she knew

that she would never see him again. She leaned against the
door, her temples pounding, and a strange visceral pain surged
upward from her stomach and into her chest and throat. She
thought she was going to be ill, that she was going to faint.
And on top of all these violent feelings was a kind of blind
rage—how could he do this to her? She leaned against the door
jamb, thinking that this is the way it must feel to die—anger,
nausea, loss, betrayal, impotence—all those things in one
final, hopeless rush. Then she realized that the thing she had
read about, the thing she and her friends had talked about and
wondered about and giggled about had actually happened to
her. She had fallen in love with him.

And the next week he was back.

"I missed you," she said, suddenly shy with him.

"At the last minute, Uncle Sol wanted me to do some work
at the store. It's inventory time. But I didn't know how to reach
you."

"And I didn't know how to reach you, either."

"Well, now we've reached each other," he said.

They started down the street toward Mr. Levy's.

"They keep trying to turn me into a businessman," he said,
"but it isn't working."

"What do you want to do, Jake," she asked him, "if it isn't
business?"

"Oh, something of the sort of thing I'm doing now, I guess.
Teaching. Social work. Some sort of public service work,
helping people, helping the poor. I want to do something
where I can help enlighten people, bring them into the twentieth century. Yes, that's it. I want to enlighten people—people like you, Essie."

"'Thy word is a lamp unto my feet, and a light unto my
path.'"

"That's it." He took her hand, and that strange, violent,
swelling, hurting, fainting feeling came back again. She took a
deep breath and quickened her pace to keep up with him.
Arched and ready, she felt her body poised for that leap with
him.

At the kitchen table, Essie sat opposite Ekiel Matoff, where they were sipping tea in glasses. Ekiel Matoff was a *landsman*, from Volna, and he was even some sort of relative—one of Papa's cousins had married one of Ekiel Matoff's mother's cousins. Ekiel was twenty-one, not tall, about Essie's height, and not bad looking, but rather angular and pale, with wide, rather frightened-looking dark eyes which looked even blacker against his too-white face, framed with dark sidecurls and the black skullcap on his head. He looked starved for sunlight. Even Essie's brother, Abe, who had learned to swim when a gang of rowdy Micks tossed him bodily into the East River, looked ruddier and healthier than this. Ekiel Matoff, Essie was certain, had never learned to swim.

Ekiel Matoff worked for his father, who was the proprietor of a shoe-repair shop on Orchard Street. Essie had passed it often, and had noticed the sign MATOFF SHOE COMPANY over a set of steps which led down to a dark basement, where Ekiel Matoff and his father had their business. In winter, she could imagine, snow blew down the steps and through the crack above the doorsill, into the shop. In Ekiel Matoff's wintry pallor, Essie felt she could read, as in one of her books, the entire story of the Lower East Side: the cobbler's son who himself would have a son who would be a cobbler, from one generation to the next of the family trade that had been theirs in Russia. The walls of the Matoff Shoe Company would be their prison, keeping the Matoff generations perpetually tilted toward the past. No light ever came into their little shop, and, because they had carried the Old World with them like a peddler's pack, they would never see the Other Side, much less yearn for it. In Ekiel Matoff's ashen, sunken face, his lips solemnly pursed as he lifted his tea glass, in his averted eyes, there was no thought of escape, no thought that the possibility of escape existed.

Of course, these were only imaginings, indignant projections on Essie's part, which made Ekiel Matoff's future seem so bleak and cheerless. She had no idea what someone like Ekiel Matoff might be dreaming. She had met Ekiel Matoff only recently. They sat across from one another at the Litskys' kitchen table like fellow prisoners let out for air in a prison yard. Neither said much because, apparently, neither could think of much to say.

Though there should have been something. Because Ekiel Matoff was the man her father had chosen to be her husband.

Six

PRIVACY had always been in short supply in the Litsky household, and so it was not a commodity to which one gave much consideration. In the one bedroom where they all slept, sheets hung from the ceiling to separate the three beds—Essie's, Abe's, and the larger one their parents shared. But beyond this prim gesture, there was only a shared intimacy. Essie no longer wondered about—or even really heard—the rhythmic creaking sounds that began from her brother's bed soon after he had pulled the covers over himself, or the long sigh that followed after a few minutes, and that was followed soon after by his soft snoring. Nor did she even really hear the infrequent sounds of her parents' lovemaking. These unnoticed sounds were all part of the familiar landscape of living, no more disturbing than the voice of the ice-man in the street, crying, "Ice today . . . Oh, lady, ice today . . . !"

But there were occasionally times, when her mother was downstairs in the store, when her father was at the synagogue, and when Abe was off at school—though he skipped it often enough, Essie knew, in order to run with his new street friends—that Essie would find herself all alone for an hour or so in her house. This was one of those times, and Essie was using it to study her reflection in her mother's hand mirror.

She held the mirror at arm's length, and tried to be as critical of what she saw as possible. The question was simply this: *Was* she beautiful?

Esther in the Bible was described as fair and beautiful, and she had much pleased the king, but Essie herself was not fair.

Her wavy hair, which fell to halfway down her back, was a dark chestnut color, and Essie decided that it was a bit too curly at the temples. She experimented, pulling her hair to the back of her neck in a small bun, but decided that this made her look too severe and schoolmarmish. Her eyes were greenish and set, perhaps, a little too far apart—though that was certainly better than having them too close together—and her skin was honey-colored. She pinched her cheeks to pinken them a bit. She drew the mirror closer to inspect her eyebrows, smoothed them with a fingertip, and decided that they were satisfactory. Her best feature, she decided, was her nose, which was straight and slender, turned up just slightly at the tip. Jews, she knew, were often sensitive about their noses, but it was the Germans who tended to have prominent ones. The Russians, generally, were better favored in that category. And her chin, she decided, though unremarkable, had nothing really wrong with it, and even contained a small suggestion of a dimple.

But her worst feature was her mouth. The lips were certainly too full, although perhaps that made her mouth look more—what was the word?—more sensual. Perhaps it was the lips that made Jake Auerbach want to kiss her. She unbuttoned her blouse and examined her throat. Passable, she decided. There was a small brown mole just above her left collarbone, but, with the high-collared dresses women wore these days, that little flaw would never be visible. With her free hand, she cupped her breasts, first one, then the other. Too large? Too small? Probably average. Some girls her age, she knew, had large brown nipples and were embarrassed by them, but hers were the same color as the rest of her, an asset. She had been told by others that she had pretty hands and nice, small feet—she kicked off her shoes and pulled off her stockings to examine them—and she had been told that she had a nice figure. But never in her life had there been a full-length looking glass to stand in front of and assess her entire body in the nude, and she had had to settle for looking at bits and pieces of herself in the hand mirror. The next best thing to a full-length glass was the imperfect reflection in the windowpane, but that required caution because someone might be looking out from across the street and see a naked woman standing at a window. Still, she slipped off her blouse, stepped as close to the window as she dared, and turned this way and that.

She picked up the hand mirror again and held it to her face. She tilted her chin upward, closed her eyes slightly, sucked in her cheeks a bit, and pursed the full lips, then studied the results for a long moment. Then, gingerly, she lifted the hem of her skirt, and lowered the mirror to look at that other intimate place, which only the man who was her husband would know. Its lips were full and pink and moist, too, as she spread them gently apart with the fingertips of her free hand. "You're very beautiful," he had said. Would he find her beautiful there as well?

Then she heard the sound of footsteps mounting the stairs. Hastily, she flung on her blouse, buttoned it up, tucked it into the waistband of her skirt, and put the little mirror back where it belonged, beside her mother's bed.

"What are you running around in your bare feet for?" her mother wanted to know. "Do you want to catch your death of cold?"

"How are you and the Matoff boy getting along?" her father asked. "Very nicely, I'm sure. He's a good boy. He wants to be a rabbi, and as soon as he gets enough money set aside he's going into the rabbinate. And Mr. Matoff has a good business, and Mrs. Matoff is a real *berrieh*. They'll make wonderful in-laws for you, Esther."

"Oh, Papa," she said, "I really don't like him. And I don't even think he likes me."

"Now, now. All that comes later, after the babies start to come. That's when the love comes, and the true happiness of a marriage and a family. Am I right, Minnalein? Your mother and I hardly knew each other when we were married—think of it! It was all arranged by the *shadchen*. And yet we've never regretted it for a single minute, have we, Minnalein? Nowadays, of course, it is all much more modern. The young people have to get to know each other a little bit. That's progress. You'll be very happy together. The Matoffs are very happy about it, and so is Ekiel."

"Papa, I don't want to marry him!"

"Now, now. I understand. Sometimes a girl is a little frightened at first of the idea—such a big step, marriage—until she gets used to it. You'll get used to it. Wait and see. In another week—"

"Mama, *must* I?" Essie cried.

Minna Litsky, bent over her dishpan, doing up the dinner dishes, did not turn but said quietly, "It is the duty of a daughter to do as her father wishes. It is written in the Book."

"It's ridiculous! It's barbaric! We're back in the Middle Ages," Jake Auerbach is saying. "It's worse than that—it's criminal. It's criminal to force a young girl to marry a man she hardly knows and doesn't even care for. That's what's wrong with these people, that's why they get nowhere. Can't they see? Can't they see that this is the way they perpetuate their poverty and misery and ignorance? What sort of future can you look forward to with this man, this cobbler, this shoemaker? Nothing more than the kind of life your mother leads—drudgery, night and day, having babies, more people to cook for, less food to go around, getting fat, growing old, losing your looks. . . ." They are sitting on a park bench under a big tree in Union Square. Essie has chosen this spot not only because it is some distance from her neighborhood, with its prying eyes, but also because it is a place where not long ago they had a happy time.

"Your papa isn't God, you know," he says, "your papa isn't the President of the United States, and he isn't even a policeman. What law does he have over you?"

"Papa's is a biblical law, Jake. It's a law that says, 'Every man should bear rule in his own house.'"

"But we aren't living in biblical times, thank God. We're in America. This is a free country, and you're a free person with a right to do whatever you want. These aren't biblical times, and this isn't Russia, where your Papa still seems to think he lives. Do you know why the Russians are so ignorant? Because the czar wanted them to be that way. He wanted to make the Jews powerless, and so he turned a whole people inward upon themselves, into a ghetto which they couldn't leave, and where they were left, for generations, to inbreed their superstitions, their rituals, their fears. Now that they're free of all that, they don't know what to do. But maybe their children will, and maybe you will, too, Essie. Maybe you'll find out what can be done in a free country, even if your papa won't. They can march you in chains to the altar with that cobbler, but they can't make you say 'I do.' Not in America, they can't!"

Essie touches his knee lightly with her fingertips. "Don't worry," she says, "I'm not going to say 'I do' to Ekiel Matoff."

"Good girl. Thank God!"

She has let him make his little speech, as she had been sure he would. Now it is time to let the bigger plan unfold, the plan that has been brewing in her mind for the past three days.

"But the thing is," she says, "if I disobey Papa, I'll have to leave."

"You mean he'd turn you out of his house? Would he be that cruel? That monstrous?"

"He might. Or he might not, I don't know. In some ways, I feel very close to Papa, and in other ways I feel I don't know him at all. The Bible doesn't say exactly what the king did to Vashti when she defied him, but it probably wasn't very pleasant. The thing is, once I disobey Papa, *I* wouldn't want to go on living in Papa's house. How could I? He's going to be very hurt and angry. He's never going to forgive me. How can I go on living in a place where, every day, someone is waiting for me to beg to be forgiven? I think that would be the worst kind of punishment of all."

"But where would you go? What would you do?"

Her eyes brighten. "I could go to work. Most of the girls my age I know are working if they aren't already married. There are new factories opening up in New York every day. I could run a sewing machine. I could make cigarette boxes in Cohen's factory."

"Work for the same Shylock you demonstrated against? Essie, you're cut out for better things than that."

"Or," she says, "there's another possibility."

"What's that? You mean walk the streets?"

She laughs. "No." She opens the purse that is in her lap and takes out several folded pieces of paper and hands them to him.

He unfolds them, looks at them a moment, and then he is laughing too. "My God," he says, "this is *me!*"

"Of course. There's more—other poses, other expressions."

"This is what you were doing when I thought you were taking notes."

"Some people think they're pretty good. The *Tageblatt* prints drawings every day. The stores that advertise in the *Tageblatt* use drawings, too, of people wearing the clothes they sell. Don't you think I'm good enough to earn some money from my drawings?"

"I think you're *very* good," he says. "But of course it would probably take some time to get yourself established."

"I know."

"They're *all* of me," he says, wonderingly, leafing through the sketches.

"And in the meantime," she says, "I could marry you."

The sheets of paper fall from his hands onto the grass, and he reaches, fumbling, to pick them up. Then he looks at her full in the face and she tries to return his gaze steadily, without blinking. "Do you really want to marry me, Essie?"

"Yes," she says quietly, and now that she has said it she hurries on. "For Papa, it would be a compromise, a way out. I wouldn't be marrying the man he's picked out for me, and of course he might not be too happy about that—at first—but at least I'd be marrying a good Jewish man. And that's what you are, Jake, a good Jewish man—the very best I've ever known. And for me—for me, it would make me the happiest I've ever been in my entire life. Because I'm in love with you, Jake."

She thinks she sees tears springing to his eyes, and he turns away from her. Then he stands up and begins pacing back and forth across the small stretch of grass in front of her. "The thing is," he begins, "—the thing is, I'm not good enough for you, either, Essie."

"Oh, yes you are. You're the best I'd ever want."

"My family thinks I'm worthless, a foolish dreamer."

"What's wrong with dreamers? But I see more in you than that. I see—what was that word you used in class? Potential?"

"I'm not so sure."

"But there's just one thing, Jake. I've just told you that I'm in love with you. I can't help that, because—because I *am*. I know you like me, Jake. But do you love me, too? That's the only important thing to me."

"I know I'm happier with you than with anyone else," he says. "And oh, yes, I love you, too, and have almost since the day I met you, I suppose. And I've thought of this, too, myself, but didn't say anything because I was afraid—"

"Afraid of what, Jake?"

"Essie, do you think that it would work?"

"I'll try. I'll try so hard."

"Oh, yes. Let's try." He sits down beside her on the bench again and covers her hands with his, but the worried look has not left his face. They sit in silence for what seems a long time, and Essie feels the pulsebeat of his hands pass through to hers, almost like an electric current, and wonders if he can feel the same throbs passing from hers to his. Finally, he says, "First, of course, you must meet my family. Yes, that's the first order of business. I'll arrange for that."

"I love you, Jake," she whispers, unable to believe that this has all happened the way she prayed it would. "I always will."

A few days later, he said to her, "It's all set. They've invited you for tea on Thursday. It won't be kosher, but I can promise you that you won't be poisoned. I'll meet you at Mr. Levy's at three o'clock, and we'll go Uptown."

"Do you remember when you shook hands with the butler?" It would become, over the years, something of a private joke between them because, indeed, in her understandable nervousness and excitement about what was happening, Essie had mounted the steps of the brownstone house at 14 West 53rd Street, and when the door had been opened by a gray-haired man in a frock coat and striped trousers, Essie had assumed the man to be either Jake's father or one of his uncles, and had immediately extended her right hand. Marks, the family butler, looking startled, had accepted her hand in his own, which wore a white glove, and shook it gingerly.

On their way Uptown in the streetcar, Jake had explained to her what he called "the cast of characters" whom she would meet. First, there were the two bachelor uncles, Uncle Sol and Uncle Mort. Solomon Rosenthal, the elder of the two, was president of Rosenthal Brothers, Inc., Purveyors of Fine Men's Suitings. Uncle Sol, Jake explained, would probably do most of the talking, as was his wont, because he was not only president of the company but also head of its sales force. But Essie was not to underestimate Uncle Mort, who was more closemouthed, because Mortimer Rosenthal, executive vice-president and the younger brother, was, as Jake put it, "the real brains behind the business." As for Jake's father, Louis Auerbach, Jake said, "Pop's title is business manager but, let's face it, Pop is essentially their accountant, their bookkeeper. Uncle Sol and Uncle Mort run the show. You see, when my mother, who was Lily Rosenthal, their only sister, married Pop, Uncle Mort and Uncle Sol felt they had an obligation to offer Pop some sort of position at Rosenthal's. He took it, and that's where he is today." All these people, the Rosenthals and the Auerbachs, lived together under the same roof.

"And so your mother keeps house for four men."

"Yes, but of course she has help."

At the time, Essie was not entirely sure what he meant by this. She also thought that Lily was an odd name for a Jewish woman. In her experience, Jewish women were never named for flowers. Unless it was Rose.

She had put on the best dress she owned, the dress she had bought for little Abe's bar mitzvah. It was of bright green bombazine, with a long, narrow, pleated skirt and a wide black patent-leather belt at the waist. Over the white shirtwaist top, there was a matching green bolero capelet, and at the collar was a big bow of white tulle. The outfit had drawn compliments at the bar mitzvah. She had pulled her long chestnut hair back loosely, and secured it at the back with a green ribbon bow.

They had dismounted from the streetcar at the corner of Fifth Avenue and 53rd Street, and walked the short distance to the house. "How do I look?" Essie whispered.

"Beautiful."

Then up the brownstone steps to the door, which was immediately opened by someone who clearly had been watching for their arrival—and the confused handshake. They were then escorted by Marks down a wide, paneled hallway where, at the end, a pair of carved doors were opened for them, and they entered the first-floor sitting room where four people sat.

The room was large and high-ceilinged, and Essie's first

impression of it was that it was done entirely in red. Dark red damask covered the walls from floor to ceiling, and the windows were framed with heavy red damask hangings, caught back by thickly twisted, tasseled gold cords. Behind these hangings hung glass curtains of intricately fashioned white lace. All the furniture in the room, and there was a great deal of it—high-backed sofas, low ottomans, chairs large and small and little footstools—was covered in the same red damask, with gilded frames, and there were many little tables with red damask tops and gilt legs. Even the lampshades were of red damask, with long gold fringe. From the walls, large, dark oil-painted landscapes gazed down somberly at the room beneath museum lights. There was a thick red carpet in an Oriental design on the floor and, overhead, from the center of the carved plaster ceiling, hung a gilded chandelier sparkling with what seemed to be thousands of crystal prisms. It was only at this point, in the midst of all this gilt and crimson splendor, that Essie realized that the entire four-story building that she had looked up at from the street must be the Auerbachs' and Rosenthals' house. They lived in it all.

The three men in the room, who were dressed in dark business suits and vests, stood up when Essie was presented to them. The woman remained seated. The men, she thought, were very formal, and somewhat curt and frosty, in their greetings to her. Only Jake's father, who was tall, plump and bespectacled, smiled when he took her hand. The uncles were both short, heavy, and bald. Jake had once described them to her as Tweedledum and Tweedledee and, indeed, they might almost have been indistinguishable, except for the fact that Uncle Mort had a handlebar mustache, and Uncle Sol was clean-shaven. Jake's mother was a tall, thin, fair-haired, nervous-seeming woman with blue eyes—years later, in Essie's own daughter Joan, Essie would see echoes of Joan's paternal grandmother, Lily Auerbach—and Essie could see why, to those who named her, she might have called to mind a lily. She wore a simple long dress of watered black moiré with long sleeves, and her only ornamentation was a triple strand of pearls at her throat and a large bright stone on her ring finger.

"Here, come sit by me," Lily Auerbach said, patting the seat of the long red damask sofa, and Essie knew instantly that she looked all wrong, in her green party dress, in that crimson room. "Jake tells me that you live on Norfolk Street," she said.

"Yes."

"Tell me—where is that?"

"Near Grand Street," she said. Surely everyone knew Grand Street. It was one of the widest streets in the neighborhood.

"Grand . . . I'm afraid I really don't know that part of town at all. What an interesting dress," she said, and then added, "Very pretty."

Jake Auerbach cleared his throat. "Mother—" he began.

His mother raised her left index finger slightly. At that moment the butler had reappeared, now wearing a white coat, carrying a large silver tea tray which held a heavy silver teapot, a silver covered pitcher of hot water, a silver creamer and sugar bowl, silver teaspoons, and teacups of the thinnest white porcelain Essie had ever seen. He placed the tray on a low table in front of Mrs. Auerbach.

"Thank you, Marks."

As she lifted the pot to pour, the polished silver cast paler reflections on Lily Auerbach's pale face.

"One lump or two, Miss Litsky?"

"One, thank you."

"Lemon or milk?"

"Lemon, please."

Lily Auerbach handed her a teacup with its spoon in the saucer and, under the saucer, a small, lace-edged napkin. Essie, whose hand shook slightly, accepted the teacup and placed it on the small table in front of her.

"I was so happy that you could come today, Miss Litsky," Lily Auerbach said. "Tomorrow, you see, we leave for a few days at the shore."

A maid appeared in a gray starched uniform with starched white collar and cuffs, a little white cap pinned in her hair, with another silver tray. She offered it to Mrs. Auerbach first, and then to Essie. The tray was arranged with a number of little sandwiches on the thinnest of white bread. Essie accepted a sandwich, saw that it contained what appeared to be a thin slice of turkey. She also noticed that both slices of trimmed bread were spread with butter. Without even looking at Jake, she took a bite of her sandwich, thereby breaking for the first time

in her life the dietary laws. Somehow this deed gave her a
sudden small burst of confidence, and she lifted her teacup in
its saucer, with the napkin underneath, lifted the spoon and,
with hands that didn't shake at all, stirred her tea, replaced the
spoon in its saucer, lifted the cup and took a sip, all the while
feeling Lily Auerbach's blue eyes upon her.

Throughout the tea, Lily Auerbach guided the conversation,
and kept it on a level of trivialities and current events. She
talked of the family's summer plans—in addition to the sea-
shore, there was to be a holiday in the Adirondacks. She spoke
of Elberon, and Saranac Lake. And wasn't it dreadful to read
about the terrible earthquake and fire in San Francisco? But
wasn't it exciting to think of the new canal that was finally
going to be dug in Panama? How did everyone feel about
President Roosevelt being the first President in history to leave
the United States during his term of office to go to Panama for
the groundbreaking? What sort of precedent might that set?
How did Essie feel about all the suffragettes who were popping
up everywhere campaigning for votes for women? What would
women *do* if they had the vote? In Lily's opinion, if women
had the vote, there would be no difference in the outcome of
elections, because women would simply vote the way their
husbands did. All it would do would add another burden to the
taxpayers, because there would be double the number of
ballots to be counted. The men answered her light questions
with grunts and monosyllables. What did they think of this
woman, Emma Goldman? Was she really for *complete* anar-
chy? How silly . . . more tea?

And in the middle of this deliberately idle chatter, Essie had
a sudden insight. It was not Uncle Sol and Uncle Mort who ran
the show. Uncle Sol might be the president of his company,
and Uncle Mort might be the vice-president, and Jake's father
might toil away in a little office wearing a green eyeshade and
going over his ledger sheets. But the person who ran the show
was Lily Auerbach. Jake was wrong.

Only once did Lily bring up the subject of marriage, even
obliquely, when she said, "Jake tells me that your father feels
that it is time for you to marry, Miss Litsky. But he tells me
that you are only sixteen. Isn't that terribly young?"

"My school is finished," Essie said. "And unless I marry, or go to work, I will become a burden."

"I see."

When tea was finished, and after the tea things had been removed by the servants, Lily Auerbach turned to her son and said, "Jake, dear, I think you will understand if we say that the rest of us would like to have a few words with Miss Litsky alone."

"Of course, Mother." He stood up and left the room through the double doors.

There was a little silence, and then Lily Auerbach leaned forward in the red damask sofa. "Miss Litsky—" she began, "let us be frank—it seems to us a very strange thing that our son wants to do." She spoke of *our son* in such a way as to imply that his uncles also shared his parentage. Clearly, in some way, there was a feeling that he belonged to all of them.

"Yes, strange," said Uncle Mort, speaking up for the first time. "Even in a lifetime of wanting to do strange things."

Lily ignored this, and continued, "There is the great difference in your backgrounds, for one thing—socially, economically, and culturally. Jake has been brought up in a world of certain privilege. Your background is—let us be frank—more humble. These vast differences—"

"If you think you're marrying him for his money, you're wrong," Uncle Sol said. "He hasn't any."

"Now, Sol," Lily said, "we agreed to take up these matters one at a time."

Somehow, knowing that her principal adversary was another woman made Essie feel emboldened, even daring. She sat forward in her chair and said, "Yes, Mrs. Auerbach, I know what you mean. By your standards, we are a poor family. I was born in Russia, in a little town I don't remember because I was less than a year old when my parents brought me to America. But by our standards, we are a very fortunate family. My father is an intellectual and a scholar of the Talmud, and my mother has worked very hard to give my brother and myself the things we have. Because of this, I have been able to have much more education than other girls my age in our neighborhood. My family sets great store by education. In my neighborhood,

other girls go to work in factories when they are twelve or
thirteen. I have never had to go to work, other than to help my
mother when she needs me. It is true that we live in a small
apartment, so small—" She looked about her. "So small that it
would not even take up one tiny corner of this big room, and
you must climb four narrow flights of stairs to reach it, and
there are only two rooms, and we share a bathroom with a
neighbor on the floor below. Our idea of luxury is—a Victrola.
You may think of us as poor, Mrs. Auerbach, but we do not
think of ourselves that way. We have always paid all our bills,
and we have never had to accept a penny's worth of charity
from anyone, as others do, all the time. You may think of me
as a humble person, Mrs. Auerbach, but I do not think of
myself that way. I think of myself as privileged—and proud."

Her eyelids lowered, Lily Auerbach nodded. "Then there is
another matter, a cultural matter. Your family practices an
Orthodox form of our religion that is still practiced in the Old
World, in countries where Jews have—let us be frank—been
held backward, and repressed. We practice what we consider a
more enlightened form, more suited to America, and we have
practiced this in this country for three generations of our family. For two young people who wish to marry, these cultural
differences can be very difficult to reconcile."

"I think," said Essie, "that in our discussions Jake and I have
already reconciled those differences."

"Perhaps."

"Get down to brass tacks, Lily!" Uncle Sol said sharply.

"Yes," she said. "Miss Litsky, has Jake told you that he has
seen an alienist?"

"An alienist?" When Essie thought of aliens, she thought of
Castle Garden and Ellis Island, and all the aliens who were
streaming into New York Harbor, day after day.

"A doctor. A specialist. A doctor who specializes in treating
diseases of the mind. In New York, we have Doctor Edmund
Bergler, who has studied in Vienna with Doctor Sigmund
Freud, of whom you may have heard. But even Doctor Bergler
is at a loss to explain our son's problems, or to find a way to
deal with them."

"What are his problems?"

Lily Auerbach studied her pale fingernails. "A certain—

indifference. A lack of motivation, a lack of direction, a lack of ambition. A habit of going from one enthusiasm, getting all involved in it, then dropping it, and going on to another. An inability to apply himself, to stick to any one thing. You mentioned the importance of hard work, which I agree with. But our son won't work." She shrugged her shoulders and threw up her hands. "What more can I say?"

It was such a Jewish gesture, the little shrug, the hands, a gesture Essie had seen her own mother make hundreds of times, that Essie almost laughed at her sudden discovery that this strange, pale woman was Jewish after all. After all! Ah, the eternal, the universal Jew!

"His current enthusiasm," said Uncle Sol, "which I might add he has only been indulging in for about the last six months, is social welfare programs. The settlement houses. Uplifting the poor. Teaching classes for the poor children of the Lower East Side. This sort of thing seems to excite him now. How long it will last, who knows? What would you say, Miss Litsky, if we told you that this idea of marrying *you*—of taking a poor girl out of the Lower East Side, and elevating her, through marriage with, if I may say so, a family of some prominence and position—that we believe that this notion of marrying you is just another expression of a passing obsession? What would you say if we told you that we believe that you are being used—cruelly used, in my opinion—as part of some sort of social-betterment experiment? That you are being used as a guinea pig in a test that has currently taken his fancy? What would you say to that?"

"If I believed that for a minute, I wouldn't marry him," Essie said. "And I don't believe that."

"And meanwhile, he has no occupation, and no income. We do not intend to feed and house and support him forever, make sure of that. How do you propose to eat? Where do you propose to live?"

"Mr. Rosenthal—"

"You can't live *here*, mind you. That's out of the question."

"Mr. Rosenthal," she said, "he may not have ambition now, but I do. I'll be his ambition. We'll work together. I'll help him. I'm young, I'm strong—"

"Now, see here young lady!"

"Sol, let her finish what she has to say," Lily said.

"I mean it. I can help him. There are some things about Jake which I know, which I think you don't. He has a brilliant mind. He has become a marvelous teacher. He has had a fine education at Columbia University. If you want my opinion, I think he has had too much privilege. Jake and I don't need privilege. All we need is each other! I'll help him and—you'll see—he'll be a great success at what he finally does, because we'll do it together—wait and see!"

"Are you saying," Lily Auerbach said carefully, "that you think you can accomplish something which even Doctor Bergler has been unable to do?"

"Yes!"

"Well," said Lily, "I suppose we should say that we'd be willing to try anything. As Jake is always saying, it's a free country. But, dear child, please give us time to think about all these things."

"Of course."

"I'll tell you one thing, young lady," said Uncle Sol. "If you marry him, you'll be getting the runt of the litter."

"Sol, what an unpleasant thing to say about our son," Lily said, but from her tone of calm reproach Essie was certain that Lily had heard this expression often before.

"The runt of the litter," Uncle Sol repeated. "The boy has absolutely no head for business."

"I wouldn't say he has no head for business, Sol," Jake's father said. "I'd say he has no head for figures, yes, but not no head for business." These were the only sentences Essie had heard Louis Auerbach utter all afternoon. He had sat there, through it all, nodding and smiling—smiling even during moments when there was nothing to smile about—and Essie had begun to wonder whether Jake's father might be simple-minded. At least, she thought, he had a tongue in his head, even though he was clearly at the bottom of their pecking order. It was he, not Jake, who struck her as the runt of the litter.

"And tell me one more thing," Lily said. "How do your parents feel about all this?"

"I haven't told them yet."

"Is that what you'll do—just tell them? Not ask?"

"Tell them. Because our minds are made up."

"Their reaction," said Lily, "will be very interesting." She rose slowly from the red sofa where she sat. "And now," she said, "would you like to refresh yourself before you leave?"

"Yes," said Essie, though she wasn't quite sure what Lily meant by the expression.

Lily moved to a smaller door at the corner of the red room, opened it, and said, "Down this little hall, the first door on your right."

Essie followed Jake's mother's directions, and turned the handle on the indicated door. It led into a bathroom, but it was like no bathroom she had ever seen, stranger than anything else she had encountered in this strange household. It was all done in shiny black marble—floor, ceiling, walls—and it was not one room, but three. In the central room was a huge marble washbasin, with golden spigots. On either side were stacks of fresh white towels, folded, monogrammed with L.R.A. in gold threads. On a golden soap dish reposed an enormous cake of fresh, sweet-smelling transparent soap. Behind the soap dish were arrayed large crystal bottles of perfumes, and over the basin hung a mirror in a golden frame. In a separate room, on one side, was the toilet with a caned seat and back and, on the other side, in the third room, was a huge bathtub set in more black marble, and placed so high above the floor that two short steps and a railing were required to reach it. She closed the outer door, and found herself facing a full-length mirror.

Looking at her reflection in the tall glass, she found herself smiling, thinking: Jake Auerbach's mother had called her "dear child." Think of it!

Seven

"THEY liked you," he said.

"Yes, I think they did."

"Uncle Sol said, 'She's got spunk.' Coming from him, that's high praise. And what did you think of them?"

She thought for a moment of how to put it. "They're dealers, aren't they," she said at last. "Traders. Merchants."

"Have been for three generations, right back to Great-Grandpa R. B. Rosenthal himself in eighteen fifty."

"And I have a feeling that some sort of deal is going to be offered," she said. "Some sort of bargain is going to have to be struck with them. You're going to be asked to give up something, in return for me—a trade."

"What makes you think that?"

"Just a feeling. And I think, when it happens, that we ought to accept it, Jake—whatever it is—even though we may not like it all that much at first."

He whistled. "Well, let's wait and see."

"Your mother dominates your father, doesn't she, Jake."

"Oh, yes. She's the *Rosenthal*, you see. The Auerbachs were considered nobodies. Years ago, when she married Pop, it was supposed to be a great *mésalliance*. Want to know a family secret—why she did it?"

"Yes."

"Can't you guess?"

"Let's see," Essie said. "She had a domineering father—like mine. She did it to show her independence."

"I wish it were as dramatic as that. No, I'm afraid it was a much more basic reason." Against the rattle of the approaching streetcar, he bent and whispered something in her ear which at first she did not hear, and asked him to repeat it. "She was pregnant—with me," he whispered.

"Really?"

The downtown streetcar was crowded at that time of day, but they managed to find two seats together. "It was quite a scandal," he said, still whispering. "I'm not supposed to know anything about it, by the way. But a nurse told me, when I was growing up. Why do she and Pop never celebrate their wedding anniversary? Because if I knew the date, I might put two and two together. I'm the product of a shameful union. Now you know it."

All at once she began to laugh, was laughing so hard she could not stop, and several passengers turned around to look at her. "Oh . . . oh . . . oh . . ." she laughed, doubling over and hugging her elbows to her sides.

"What's so funny?" he asked in a harsh whisper. "It's something that I thought my future wife should know."

"Oh . . . oh . . . Jake, I'm sorry. I can't—" Because what she couldn't tell him was that the most outrageous, wild mental picture had just flown into her head. It was of thin, cool Lily Auerbach outstretched across a row of garbage cans in an alley behind Delancey Street, fully clothed, legs outspread, and of plump little Louis Auerbach laboring on top of her to get his two dollars' worth. "Oh . . . oh . . . oh," she sobbed.

"Essie, you're making a scene! I don't see why you're treating this as some sort of joke."

"Oh," she said, struggling to control herself, "it's just . . . just a crazy thought I had . . . a shameful union. . . ."

"Essie, people are staring at us."

She whispered in his ear, "And I suppose that's the first thing they thought when you told them you wanted to marry me—that you and I—that I was—" She was still giggling, but now the picture in her mind was of herself sprawled in some dark place, and the figure above her was—but that picture was more sobering to contemplate. "Am I right?" she asked him.

His face reddened. "How did you know that?"

"Let men tremble to win the hand of woman, unless they win along with it the utmost passion of her heart."

"What in the world are you talking about? Is that from the Bible?"

She was still trying to suppress the giggling fit. "Do you know?" she said. "I've thought of it. Does that shock you? I've thought of it—a shameful union—with you. Do I have an evil mind?"

"No," he said quietly. "I've thought of it, too."

"So let's cheat them," she said. "Let's disappoint them and not be shameful—until—and let's make our marriage—not like theirs. Let's stay shameless and blameless."

"You've got to remember," he said, "that when my father was younger he was a very handsome man. Maybe not too bright, but he was considered quite a heart-breaker. To give the Rosenthals credit, they've always been very good to Pop—and to me. And though Mother pretends not to care anything about what goes on in the store, she goes over the daily figures every night with Uncle Sol and Uncle Mort. Like a hawk." They rode in silence for a while.

"We won't ever let her dominate us like that, will we, Jake?"

"Of course not. What's that your father says about the man being the king of his house? I subscribe to that."

She covered his hand with hers, and waited to feel the heat from his hand rise up to join hers. Instead, his fingers fidgeted beneath her own, and she knew that somehow she had managed to disappoint him. The streetcar lurched to a stop, and they stood up. "And speaking of that," she said, "I've got to get home. The king is in his castle now. Give me a kiss for courage." But he was still cross with her, she knew, for her reaction to his news, and when they had dismounted from the car and were on the street again, she said, "I'm sorry I got to laughing. I don't know what was the matter with me. Nerves, I guess."

"I shouldn't have told you that on a public streetcar. It was my fault."

"No, it was mine. Forgive me."

"You've got to remember that Pop used to be a very handsome man," he repeated.

"I'm sure of it. He has a very handsome son. And the quote was from *The Scarlet Letter*. My evil mind."

Then he kissed her.

There is a side to him, she thought, that is very serious and dark, and that cannot be taken for granted.

But why, in her excitement, in her foolishness, had she that afternoon been able to delude herself into believing that her apprehensions about her father's reaction to her decision had been misplaced? All Essie remembers is that, walking home from the streetcar, she had suddenly been flushed with a euphoric burst of wishful thinking. All at once she was so full of confidence and resolve that she could imagine quite a different scene taking place from the other one she had been dreading. Her father would leap from his chair in happiness at her news, crying "*Mazel tov!*" And taking her in his arms. His only daughter, whom he wanted to marry well, was going to marry this fine Jewish boy, from a fine Jewish family—a boy with a college education, and what seemed like limitless prospects and expectations. Excitedly, she would tell Papa first about the fine Uptown house—a whole house, four stories tall, with only one family living in it—about the room all done in red damask and gold tassels, the manservant, the silver tea service, the elegant mother in her pearls, the bathroom that was not one room but three, the full-length mirror, the stacks of towels with their embroidered monogram, L.R.A. "How my little Esther is improving herself!" he would say, and perhaps he would open a bottle of the special wine that was reserved for the High Holy Days, and toast her with his blessing. There would be talk of joy! Freedom! Luck! Only in America! Then Mama would join them, and produce, from the trunk underneath her bed where it lay folded, her wedding canopy which now of course would be Essie's. Then perhaps some of the neighbors would be invited in to share the happy tidings. Oh, there might be a little surprise at first, of course, a few questions and a few misgivings—Jake, after all, was a *Deitch*—but how could Papa deny her happiness? Perhaps, in her memory, if she had brought up the matter a little less abruptly, a little more delicately, it all might have turned out just that way.

Or perhaps not.

Probably not.

It is foolish now to try to guess.

*   *   *

Instead, she finds him in his familiar place, bent over at the kitchen table in the fading afternoon light, in his black skullcap, with his books, his prayer shawl and phylacteries. In another corner, her mother sits with a basket of mending in her lap.

Essie sits down opposite him and says, "Papa, I want to talk to you."

He closes his Bible and looks up at her, blinking twice, bringing himself back from the land of Judah into the world of Norfolk Street. "Yes, my child?"

"Papa, I'm not going to marry Ekiel Matoff."

"Oh, yes, Esther, it has been all arranged."

"But I'm not going to do it, Papa. I'm going to marry Jake Auerbach."

"Who?"

"Jake Auerbach. The man from my school who used to walk me home."

"That *Deitch?* No, no, that is not possible."

"But that's what I'm going to do, Papa."

"No, no. Your dowry has already been paid to Mr. Matoff."

"We hope you'll give your blessing, Papa."

"What? What are you saying?"

"I'm saying that I'm going to marry Jake Auerbach, and that we both hope we will have your blessing."

"My *blessing?* You want me to bless one of the *Deitch*—a people who have stripped their religion to a skeleton, and left it where it is nothing but a dead thing, a corpse? No, you are foolish and ignorant. You don't know what you're talking about. Now leave me alone. I am busy. I have no more time to talk of this."

"But it's what I'm going to *do*, Papa," she says, her voice rising. "And I'm going to do it with your blessing or without it."

He looks at her wearily. "This is the voice of ignorance I am hearing," he says. "No, no, I want to hear no more of this. And I want this conversation never to go beyond these four walls. Think of it—the shame, the humiliation, if it got around the neighborhood, to the others in the *shul,* the news that Sam Litsky has a daughter who has thought of disobeying her father. No, no. This is the end of it. I do not intend to become a laughingstock."

"I'm sorry, Papa, but I *am* disobeying you."

"But I will not permit it!"

"But I'm going to do it anyway—permission or no."

Suddenly he stands up, the patriarch in skullcap and prayer shawl, towering over her, and points his finger at her. "If you will not listen to me, then you will listen to the Bible, the source of all knowledge! Here, I will read to you what the Bible says—"

"I don't care what the Bible says, Papa. I'm going to marry Jake Auerbach."

"What? What? This is what this *Deitch* has taught you—not to care what is written in the Torah? This is what he has taught you—to hate the Jews? To hate the eternal knowledge of the Holy Scriptures?"

"What has all that knowledge ever done for you, Papa? While you pray and glory in your holy books, while Mama slaves downstairs—"

"What? You are saying that I should have sold my religion? You are saying that God is for sale? God comes before everything—even before a man's own flesh and blood. Are you saying that you will defy God as well as me?"

From behind her, she hears her mother's voice whisper, "Sam, please stop."

"I will *not* stop! I want an answer—does she defy her God as well as her father?"

Looking up into his angry, God-stricken face, she says, "Yes, Papa. I defy you both."

"He's rich, isn't he? That's the thing. That is why he is not a Jew. A Jew is poor, and suffers. A Jew does not live in big houses and drive motor cars. You cannot serve God and Mammon, and nothing—nothing but evil, evil and death—will come of your wicked pursuit of Mammon. What will it get you but a higher place in the Tower of Babel? What will you become? Can the Ethiopian change his skin, or the leopard his spots? Is there no balm in Gilead? Is there no physician there? You will feed your family with wormwood, and give them water of gall to drink—in your ignorance and your defiance!

You will make your heart deceitful above all things, and desperately wicked. . . . You will be buried with the burial of an ass, because you are no longer a Jew but an apostate, an enemy of your people, and Christians and Jews alike will hate you! Is that what you have chosen?"

"I am going to marry Jake Auerbach, Papa."

He throws his head back and lets out a terrible scream, a scream that seems to come from some deep and mortal wound. "Then I have no daughter!" he cries, and with one hand he clutches at the front of his shirt, ripping a gaping, triangular hole in it and exposing a pale section of his chest and undershirt. Holding the torn piece of shirt in his hand, he says, "Do you see what I have done? I have rent my garments." Now he sits down, and opens his Bible. "Now I am going to sit *shiva*, for my daughter," he says, and she hears him begin to intone the Hebrew words of the *kaddish*, the Prayer for the Dead.

With a violent sob, Essie's mother jumps from her chair and runs from the room.

Under her bed, she kept a small wicker suitcase, and now she was filling it with her things.

"Hadassah . . . Hadassah," her mother wept. "Don't do this! Tell him you're sorry. Oh, you're breaking my heart!"

"I'm sorry, Mama, but I can't stay here any longer."

"Where will you go? I'll never see you again."

"Of course you will, Mama. I'll come back to visit often."

"Where will you go?"

"Not far. For now, the rooming house in Hester Street. You know the place."

"Oh, no. That awful place!"

"Just for the time being. Until I'm married, Mama."

"Oh, don't . . . don't go . . ."

But when she had finished packing, and gave her mother a farewell kiss, Minna Litsky pressed a small wad of bills into her hand.

On her way out the door, she said to her father, deep in his prayers, "Good-bye, Papa." But there was no answer.

"We will ask Dr. Kohler to perform the ceremony," Lily Auerbach said to her four menfolk who were gathered at her dinner table at 14 West 53rd Street. "But we'll have it here at the house, and just the immediate family."

"And friends," added Uncle Mort.

"No, I think not even friends, Mort," Lily said. "We can't just have a few without inviting them all, and goodness knows there's going to be talk enough as soon as the word gets around. You know how everybody is. If we invite the Schiffs and not the Strauses, Mrs. Straus will be on the telephone to Mrs. Schiff, wanting to know what she's like, and there's no telling what Therése Schiff might tell her. No, I think just the immediate family. I suppose we've *got* to ask Aunt Julie? Anyway, I gather that the Litskys will not be coming."

"Essie's father took it very badly," Jake said.

"I was afraid that might be the case," Lily said. "Isn't it funny—the Germans and the Russians? East and West, and never the twain, et cetera. And I think we should have the wedding as soon as possible, under the circumstances?"

"And get it over with," said Uncle Sol.

Jake Auerbach looked at his plate.

"And tell me, Jake," his mother said. "Do you think Esther would like any little tips from me on what she might wear—or would she resent that? I mean, she really *is* a pretty girl, but you must admit—that green dress—"

"I don't know," Jake said. "I'll ask her."

"Do you know what day this is?" Minna Litsky asked her husband.

"The day is Thursday."

"It's the day our only daughter is getting married!"

"I have no daughter. My daughter is dead," he said returning to his studies.

"Oh, damn you!" she cried. "Oh, damn you and your Bible!" She struck his Bible with her fist. "All my life I've listened to you and your damned Bible. Is this what the Bible teaches you? Only hate and punishment? Where is love? Where is your heart? Where is forgiveness? It's not your daughter who is dead, Sam Litsky, it is you and your dead heart. Is there no kindness left in your dead heart? Oh, I hate you, Sam Litsky, and I curse your damned Bible! I tell your damned Bible to go to hell and burn in the devil's fires!"

He stood up, closed the Bible, and gave her a sad look. "I'm going to the *shul* now," he said quietly. "And I will pray for you."

"Go to hell with your prayers!"

Now Minna Litsky was like a woman possessed, tearing around her apartment at full speed, this way and that. She put on her best black dress and pinned up her hair and put on her best hat. From a little drawer she removed a pair of white lace gloves that had been her mother's, and which she had never worn. Then it was down the four flights of stairs to her shop, where she placed a CLOSED sign on the door and emptied the entire contents of the cash drawer into her patent-leather handbag. With dismay, she realized that she had never told Esther anything about marriage, what the man did, or about the laws of *niddah*, that a woman must not let a man touch her during the days of the month when she is unclean, nor for at least twelve afterward, and not until she has been immersed in the *mikveh*, the ritual bath. She had told her nothing! Then, suddenly remembering, she rushed upstairs again to her apartment and pulled out the trunk from under her bed, removed the white wedding canopy quickly, and tucked it under her arm.

While all this was going on, Essie Litsky was saying good-bye for the last time to her rented room, just a few blocks away—a room, its wooden floors slimy with rot, its smells of fish and overripe fruit. "Good-bye," she said, and closed the door, leaving the key hanging in the lock.

Had either of the two women known what the other was doing, they could have made the journey to their common destination together. But that did not happen.

Instead, for Minna, it was out—into the streets where Mrs. Potamkin had given her careful directions to a corner where she could find a taxi.

When she found the taxi, she opened its door roughly. She had never been in such a vehicle before, a motor car with an internal combustion engine, and she was suddenly so frightened that she seemed to have forgotten all her English. She could not speak, and so simply handed the driver the address which she had printed on a scrap of paper.

Then it was off through the alien, forbidding streets of the strange city where she had lived for fifteen years but never visited. As they moved Uptown, the prospect of the city grew taller, more daunting. Steeples and banks, God and Mammon, jostled each other for priority. Tall, dark, unfriendly buildings rose all around her, and the streets were filled with strangers she had never met, and would never dare to turn to, or ask help from. She remembered other cities—Vienna, Hamburg, London—but none of them she could recall being so massive, so overpowering and warlike. Next to this, those older cities seemed to have been miniatures etched in glass. This city was all stone, like a prison. They turned into a street wider than any she had ever seen, and she saw a sign—Fifth Avenue.

When they arrived at the address, and when she had paid the driver what seemed an immorally large sum of money, she got out of the automobile and hurried up the front steps. She rang the bell, and presently a tall, gray-haired man, wearing white gloves rather like her own, answered the door.

"Mr. Auerbach?"

"I'm afraid Mr. Auerbach—both Mr. Auerbachs—are not available at the moment, Madam. Would you care to leave your card?"

"I want to see Mr. Auerbach."

"Did you have an appointment, Madam?"

"I want to see Mr. Auerbach!"

"I'm afraid that's impossible, Madam. There's a family wedding going on."

"I know," said Minna. "I'm the mother of the bride."

". . . In the sight of God and this company. . . ." Minna took her seat in the red room.

When the wedding was over, Essie and Jake were invited up to Uncle Sol's oak-paneled study on the second floor, where the matter was business. How very like them, Essie thought, to save this for after their wedding, when whatever his family had to offer them she and Jake would have no choice but to accept.

"We have written you a check," Uncle Sol said, "in the amount of two thousand dollars. One half of this amount, one thousand dollars, is our wedding gift to you, from all of us."

He cleared his throat. "The second thousand we would prefer to think of as a loan, payable at an annual interest rate of four percent. With that loan, however, goes a provision. We have recently acquired a piece of property in Chicago, on LaSalle Street, which is considered to be an up and coming location in that city's business district, and where we plan to open a Midwest branch of Rosenthal Brothers. Merchandise is already being shipped. This is our first venture outside of New York, and so naturally we are very anxious that it succeed. Chicago is a young city, but it is growing rapidly. . . . It is becoming an important rail center . . . Great Lakes shipping. . . . Money being made there, and money being spent. You may remember that Uncle Mort and I visited Chicago for the Exposition. It was clear to us what was happening there. Chicago is trying to change its reputation as a roughneck, frontier town, and wants to be taken seriously as a city where there are sophisticated ladies and gentlemen, interested in the latest fashions. . . .

"It seems that many Chicago businessmen come to New York to shop for their finer clothes. We already have a number of Chicago customers, so we are not going into the Chicago market as unknowns. What we hope to do at Rosenthal's of Chicago is to offer the same high quality and workmanship men have learned to expect of Rosenthal's in New York, but right on LaSalle Street, a quality location near the best clubs, hotels, and restaurants. . . .

"What Mort and I are proposing, Jacob, is to appoint you manager of our Chicago branch. We offer you a salary of two hundred dollars a month. That may not seem to you a particularly princely figure, nor is intended to be. You are still an unproven quantity, and we are taking a considerable risk, a gamble. Naturally, if we are pleased with your performance, salary increases will reflect our pleasure accordingly. However, this entire offer is conditional, and the condition is simply this: our Chicago venture must show a profit within twelve months' time. If it does not, our interest in your business career, and in your financial future, will terminate. I want to make that point very clear. We are not in this business to lose money. And so, that's it in a nutshell, Jacob. Do you accept our offer?"

"Oh, how exciting, Jake!" his mother said. "A store of your

own!" All this seemed to come as a surprise to Lily, though Essie was sure that much of the plan had been of Lily's own devising.

Jake was smiling wryly. "You'll turn me into a retailer, won't you, Uncle Sol," he said. "Or die in the attempt."

Essie reached out and touched his hand.

"Beggars can't be choosers," said Uncle Mort.

"No," said Jake. And then, "Thank you, Uncle Sol. Thank you very much, both of you. And yes, I accept."

"A thrilling challenge," his mother said, standing up. "Now let's go downstairs and join the others for champagne."

"Chicago!" her mother said. "Oh, Hadassah, that seems so far away." She dabbed at her eyes when Essie told her.

"There are trains back and forth every day, Mama, and I'll come home whenever I can. And Mama, I'm so happy that you came."

"Mrs. Litsky," said Lily Auerbach, extending her hand. "I knew the minute you walked in that you must be dear Esther's mother."

"What's this?" Minna asked when a butler paused in front of them with a silver trayful of brimming glasses.

"Champagne, Mama."

"Champagne," she whispered, taking a glass in her white-gloved hand. She looked bewilderedly around at the red room, where perhaps a dozen other people stood. "Just think," she said, "my little Hadassah—marrying into all of *this*."

The wedding canopy was still folded and tucked under her arm.

Overnight in a railway compartment to Chicago may not have seemed much of a wedding trip, but that was what it was. The train left Grand Central at midnight, and they would be in Chicago the next morning. What neither of them said, of course, and what both knew, was that his family wanted them in Chicago so that they would be as far away from New York as possible.

Alone in their compartment, they lowered the window shade, turned off the lights, and undressed in darkness. And when Jake slipped his naked body into the narrow berth beside hers, she had begun to cry. "What am I doing? Where am I going?" she sobbed.

"With me," he said. He had run his tongue lightly around her eyelids and said, "You are so lovely. I love to taste your tears."

"Do you love me, Jake? Do you really love me?"

Why had she asked him that? Was it because, even then, she had had doubts? And what had he answered her?

If there was an answer, the memory is lost.

LADDER

Eight

———

"You've been hiding from me for five days, haven't you, Mother," Joan is saying. "I've called and called, left messages, and you haven't called me back."

"Well, I admit I was cross at you for the way you behaved at the tree-trimming," Essie says. "But it's Christmas Eve, and I've decided to bury the hatchet. I've even bought you a little peace offering." She hands Joan a gift-wrapped box from Saks.

"Oh, Mother, how sweet. Shall I open it now?"

"If you like."

Joan pulls off the ribbon, opens the box, and lifts aside the folds of tissue paper. "Oh, Mother, what a beautiful sweater. Thank you."

"I thought it was pretty," Essie says.

"It's beautiful. I didn't bring your present by tonight because I was planning to drop it off for you tomorrow."

This, Essie is certain, is a lie, since Joan has probably not bought her a Christmas gift, and will now have to hurry out and do so, but Essie says nothing. "My only thought," she says, "is for peace in the family. That's really the only gift I want now—from any of you. Just a little peace among my children. Lord knows we've had our share of troubles in the past. Can we try now for a little peace?"

"Oh, yes," Joan says, refolding the sweater in its box. "Let's try for that."

"Now tell me exactly what it is you want to talk to me about," Essie says. "And why it's so all-fired important that Richard not go to South Africa and write his book."

Joan hesitates. Then, her arms folded across the Saks box, she says, "I need him here if I'm going to save the paper."

"Save it? From what?"

"Creditors."

"But the other night you said that everything was going so well."

"That's because all the others were here. I didn't want them to know, but I'm going to be honest with you, Mother. I'm in desperate straits. I need to raise half a million dollars, and if I can't do that—" She spreads her hands; "then the paper's finished."

"I see," Essie says guardedly.

"And Richard is trying to leave the sinking ship."

"Well, half a million dollars shouldn't be hard to find, should it?"

"That's the trouble. At this point, it is," Joan says.

"But your papa left you plenty of money," Essie says. "Your share of his trust—"

Joan casts her eyes downward at her hands. "I've borrowed against the trust," she says quietly. "Borrowed all I can. They're talking now of calling in loans."

Essie stands up. "What do you mean, borrowed against your trust? How is that possible?"

"I know I wasn't supposed to. But they let me, and I did."

"This is very distressing news," Essie says, and she thinks: And in practically my last breath I was talking about having a little peace. Peace on earth, good will toward men. Well, Essie thinks, there goes that delusion out the window.

"Half a million dollars is all I need, Mother. That's all I need to get us over this present hump. With that, I know I could make the paper turn the corner. If I had that, I know I could persuade Richard to stick with it. I need him desperately, but even more desperately I need the money."

"Are you saying you're broke?"

"Overextended. Overborrowed. If I can't get hold of this little extra bit of cash, my only alternative will be to fold the paper. Sell the plant and equipment, the printing presses, everything. Everything I've worked so hard for all these years."

"I don't call half a million dollars a little bit of cash," Essie says.

"Mother, I've come to you tonight on bended knee. Will you help me out?"

"Oh, dear," Essie says, sitting down again. "Oh, I suppose I knew that it was going to be something like this. It always is with you, isn't it? No, I wasn't expecting anything different."

"I could pay you back, Mother, in just six months' time. I know I could. It would be just a loan. I'd pay you back, with interest."

"Joan, how many times have I heard that argument from you? It's always just a loan."

"On bended knee, Mother . . ."

"It was just a loan to pay off that first husband of yours, the polo man. The same thing for the second one, Karen's father, and for the third one, the queer one. How much has it all added up to? I'd hate to go back into my books and tell you. I gave you two hundred and fifty thousand to help you get your paper started—"

"You bought stock, Mother."

"Well, it's never paid a penny's worth of dividends that I know of. Joan, that paper's never made a profit, has it? I'm not saying it's your fault. Yes, it sounded like a good idea in the beginning—'A liberal voice in New York in the afternoons,' as you put it. But it's just never caught on, has it? I mean, I read the New York *Times* and the *Wall Street Journal*. I know what they've said about the New York *Express*—'The financially ailing New York *Express*,' they call it, 'fueled by the Auerbach millions.' Joan, if you want my advice I'll give it to you. Admit that you've run out of fuel. Fold the paper, as you say, and get what you can for the plant and equipment. Let Richard go off and research his book. And you—you can look for some new outlet for your energies. Yes, that's my best advice to you."

"The paper is my life!"

"Find a new life. And I'll tell you something else. I don't think it's been a good idea for you and Richard to have worked so closely together. I've noticed it in Richard. He isn't happy—"

"Now don't get into my marriage, Mother!"

"It's never good for a marriage, that sort of arrangement. It wasn't good for your father's and mine, when we used to work so closely together years ago. Oh, it worked for a while. But then—then it didn't. It just didn't. Take an old woman's advice, Joan."

"Half a million dollars would be nothing to you."

"That's not true. You've been to this well too often. The well's run dry."

"You have all that Eaton stock—"

"Yes, but I can't sell it. Not without the permission of the trustees—Henry Coker, Charles, Josh. I live on a fixed income, Joan."

"But a rather *large* fixed income."

"It's comfortable. Sufficient for my needs. But if I had to get my hands on half a million dollars in cash, I wouldn't know how to do it."

"Which brings me to the point I was trying to make with you the other night, Mother. The art collection."

"The art collection goes to the Met, as I told you."

"But it doesn't *have* to go to the Met, does it? Leaving it all to the Met is plain foolishness. It would mean its value would be taxed as part of your estate. The taxes would be staggering. The thing to do, if you want to be clever, would be to sell it, and begin making disbursals to—"

"And live with bare walls? No, I couldn't stand that."

"And that's another thing—why do you need this big apartment? Practically a whole city block. At your age. With a staff of people working for you who—well, who may not be the most reliable. If you want *my* advice, you'd sell this too, and I'd help you find a smaller place that's more practical and easier to care for."

"What's the matter with my staff? I have an excellent staff."

"Well, there are some people who think that Yoki has a few under-the-counter deals with certain tradespeople, kickbacks—"

"Nonsense. Mary's very meticulous about things like that. There's never been the slightest question—"

"But you've got to admit, Mother, that you don't really *need* all this space."

"Need it? No, I suppose I don't. But I like it. I didn't always live like this, you know. But now that I do, I like the way I live. No, I think the thing for you to do is close the paper, sell the plant, and stop sending good money after bad."

"But wouldn't that be a terrible embarrassment to you, Mother, personally—to the whole family? To have the news all over town that Joan Auerbach has failed? Wouldn't it be an embarrassment to Charles and Josh and everybody?"

"Not at all," Essie says. "All families have their share of bad luck—certainly ours has had some. I can't speak for the others, of course, but as for me I'd be considerably relieved."

Joan says nothing, merely crosses her legs and reaches for a cigarette from a cut-glass box, staring absently to space.

"Joan, fix me a martini," Essie says. "I'm ready for a little Christmas cheer. Let's try to look on the bright side of all this."

"There is no bright side," Joan says in a dead voice. She rises, goes to the bar, pours gin and ice into a silver shaker, and adds a splash of vermouth.

"Such as, if you sold the plant, how much could you get for it?"

"How many martinis do you drink a day, Mother?"

"As many as I wish, thank you!" Essie says. "Now, Joan, it's Christmas Eve. I asked you to come by because you're my daughter, and I love you, and I wanted to patch things up between us. I didn't ask you to come by to quarrel."

Handing her mother her drink, Joan says, "But you won't give me the money."

"Not won't, dear. Can't."

Joan resumes her seat, and replaces the flat Saks box on her lap. With her lacquered fingertips, she raps out a short tattoo on the polished surface of the box. It is a warning signal, and Essie braces herself for another of Joan's angry outbursts. But it doesn't come. Instead, Joan says, "Whatever became of Uncle Abe?"

The question catches Essie off her guard. "Abe?" she says. "What about him?"

"I just asked whatever became of him."

"He changed his name. He lives in Florida. I haven't seen him in over fifty years."

"He's Arthur Litton now, isn't he?"

"Yes, that's the name he goes by."

"The gangster."

Essie laughs abruptly. "Well, I think that's rather too strong a term," she says. "I've heard him described as a racketeer, but not a gangster."

"He was one of the original investors in Eaton's, wasn't he?"

"Yes. Very briefly. Fortunately, your father was able to buy him out, and that was a good thing all around."

"What did he do, Mother?"

"Do? Well, Abe was—Abe is—well, you know Arthur Litton's reputation. Not the best. I can't—I don't try to—what is the word the psychology people use? I don't try to *rationalize* Abe's behavior anymore. Oh, I used to. But now I try to think about him as little as possible. When he was a youngster, he got in with a bad crowd on the East Side. He stayed with that bad crowd. How to explain it? It was hard for me then, because once upon a time we were very close. He was my baby brother, and I loved him very much. We slept in the same room, even in the same bed when he was little. Now I try to push all that into the back of my mind because—because he was a bad boy. Every family has its black sheep, I suppose, and Abe is ours. Why are you so interested in Abe?"

"I was just wondering—was any of this ever in the papers?"

"Oh, I think so. Years ago, I think there was something. Then he changed his name, and went away."

"As a newspaper woman, I should think that might make what we call a hot story—one of the original investors in Eaton and Cromwell being Arthur Litton."

"Do you think so, Joan? It was years and years ago, and your father had the good sense to get him out of the company the minute he showed his true colors. Your father and Charles."

"What caused the split?"

"That," says Essie firmly, "is something that I do not choose to talk about. Suffice to say he did something to try to hurt us—to hurt all of us. It had nothing to do with the company. It was personal. That's all I have to say about it. Believe me, you'll be grateful that I'm not telling you more."

"I was thinking of getting in touch with him," Joan says.

Sitting forward in her chair, with her glass in her hand, Essie says, "That would be very unwise. Abe may be my brother, but he is also a very dangerous man. I don't know what purpose could be served by your getting in touch with him, but I can tell you this—if you do, you will heartily regret it. That I can promise you. The man is dangerous. He hurt me badly. He can also hurt you."

"Just an idle thought," Joan says. "Renewing old family ties."

"Don't do it. Unless you want more trouble than you can imagine."

"She knows about Arthur Litton, Charles," Essie says when she reaches him on the telephone.

"Ah. The investigative reporter, I suppose. Well, what did she say about him?"

"Vaguely threatening. Suggesting that it might make a story for the paper—her paper, of course."

"Of course."

"Would it hurt the company if something like that came out at this point?" she asks. "Could it hurt you—or Josh?"

"Mildly embarrassing, perhaps. Mildly. Even though everything important that happened at Eaton happened long after he left."

"She also says she's broke."

"Naturally."

"Do you believe her, Charles?"

"I just don't know."

"She wants half a million."

"And you told her?"

"I told her no."

"Good girl." And then, "All alone on Christmas Eve, Essie?"

"Josh and Katie are coming by a little later. Why don't you come too, Charles, if you're free?"

"I'd like that," he says.

"Good. The servants are gone for the evening, but we'll rustle up something. We'll raid the icebox. There's cold chicken. We'll have cold chicken and champagne. We'll get drunk."

While waiting for Charles and the others, Essie takes down a slim volume from a library shelf, and opens it to a page she knows by heart. The book is Prince's yearbook from Lawrenceville, and it is the only photograph of Prince that her husband did not destroy that terrible afternoon. He could not destroy this, because Essie, longing for some tangible memory, had later thought of the yearbook, and had ordered it sent to her privately from the school. In the blurred photograph, Prince's young face looks almost wistful, though the corners of his mouth are turned up as though at the beginning of a smile. And he is squinting slightly, as though the sunlight on the dormitory steps where he stands with his classmates were too strong for his eyes. Once, years ago, Josh had said to her, "Of course I never knew Prince, but I know he was the oldest, and Joan and the others told me what happened."

"Hush. Your father doesn't want us to talk of him."

"But he must have been special to you, being the first."

"Oh, yes."

"Will I ever be that special to you, Mother, being the last?"

"Oh, yes, always special to me, Josh. All of you are special, but you are the most special because you are the most like him."

"Well, how did it go?" Mogie asks her.

"I asked for half a million, and came out with a blue cashmere sweater."

"What about Arthur Litton?"

"She was rather secretive. Something she doesn't want me to know. I must say she didn't seem too concerned about what I've found out."

"That's why we've got to find out more."

"Yes. I've got to find out if there was some kind of payoff, or cover-up. If I could only get at her books. But how can I do that? Mary Farrell keeps everything guarded like a hawk."

"Well, on that score I happen to know something that you don't," he says.

"What's that?"

"Mother and Mary Farrell are going to the opera next Thursday night. You could think up some excuse for dropping by the apartment. I'm sure Yoki would let you in."

The following Friday morning, Mary Farrell says to Essie, "Somebody's been in my desk, Mrs. A."

"Why? Is something missing?"

"No. Nothing's missing. Everything's in perfect order."

"Then what makes you think—?"

"It's like a sixth sense. I sense it, Mrs. A."

"Perhaps one of the maids, dusting."

"The maids have strict instructions never to touch my desk."

"It must be your Irish imagination, Mary," Essie says.

Later, Mary Farrell says to Yoki, the little Japanese butler, "Did anyone come in to the apartment last night, Yoki?"

He shakes his head vigorously. "'Cept Miss Joan. She came by. She looking for gloves left here other night."

"How long was she here?"

He shrugged. "Don't know. I go back to kitchen. Not see her leave."

"Thank you, Yoki."

Now Mary Farrell is faced with a moral and political and tactical dilemma of considerable proportions. She knows that Mrs. A would not take kindly to the idea of Joan rummaging through her desk and files, and she knows that Joan and Mrs. A do not always see eye to eye on every matter. On the other hand, she also knows that Joan is her employer's daughter, and that in a number of battles in the past Mrs. A has wound up coming to Joan's defense, particularly when she feels Joan may have been wronged. It is a natural, motherly reaction, and a demonstration of the proverbial truth that blood is thicker than water or perhaps any other substance. The lioness will spring to defend her cub, even when it is in the wrong. And of course it is also possible that Mrs. A, on learning of Mary Farrell's suspicions, will fly into a rage at Joan. And it is certainly not Mary Farrell's wish to do anything that will aggravate the frictions that already exist between mother and daughter.

And so, after weighing the matter in her mind for most of the afternoon, whether or not to bring this up, and recalling several occasions when she has seen her employer react like a cornered lioness, Mary Farrell finally decides not to tell Mrs. A what she suspects.

Nine

‏⸻‏

YEARS later, when Jacob Auerbach would be asked, as he often was, what he considered to be the secret of his success—how, from almost nothing, he had built Eaton & Cromwell & Company into one of the largest corporations in the world, headquartered in Chicago but with sales outlets in more than two hundred cities in the United States and abroad—he would routinely answer, "Hard work, trust in God, and my faith that the customer must always be satisfied with the quality of the merchandise he or she gets. Hence, our motto: Our Customer Is Our Only Boss." Essie, of course, would recall certain other factors, including the early contribution of her brother, Abe, which was somewhat greater than the company now chooses to remember.

From the little house at 5269 Grand Boulevard which they had rented—Essie was determined not to dip into the wedding money, and that there would be enough left over at the end of each month to send Uncle Sol a check for the interest on the loan—Jake would write his letters, in careful longhand, to his uncles when he came home from the store at night.

December 2, 1907

Dear Uncle Sol:

I hope you are not disappointed with the November sales figures. We are really just getting started, and I know you cautioned me not to expect dramatic sales during our first months. Also, the heating bill ran high last month ($24.20) because of the very cold weather. It seems

*it can get much colder here than in New York in winter,
since we are more northerly . . .*

*We are looking forward to a good Christmas season,
though retailers here are hoping that there will not be too
much snow, which will keep away trade. So far, no snow,
just cold. Keep your fingers crossed.*

*Every day, it seems, a few more customers come into
the store . . .*

Esther joins me in love to all the Family.

> *Yours sincerely,*
> *Jacob*

And Essie would write her own letters home, which Minna
Litsky would save, in a packet tied with string, in a dresser
drawer.

(undated)

Dearest Mama:

*What a strange city Chicago is. It is on a huge lake so
wide that you cannot see across to the other side, and
when the wind blows there are waves, just like the sea.
But the water is fresh, and the lake provides our drinking
water. There is a big beach, and in the summer people
walk straight from the city streets onto the beach! The city
is on flat land, and so the streets are very straight, with
not so many bends as some of the streets in New York. I
am having an easy time of it, learning my way
around. . . .*

*The house Jake found for us is very nice. It is built of
brick and is in what is called the bungalow style, as are
most of the other houses on the street. On the first floor is
a living room, with a corner for a dining table at the end.
Then there is a cozy kitchen with a gas stove. Upstairs
there are two bedrooms (one small, one larger) and a
bathroom, and an attic space which could be turned into
another bedroom. There is a nice yard in front, and a
smaller one in back, where when spring comes Jake has
promised to help me start a vegetable garden. We were
very lucky to find this house for $37.50 a month. The rents*

here seem much lower than in New York, though the heating costs are high. We have not bought much furniture yet, just the essentials. . . .

The neighbors seem very nice, though I have not had time to meet too many of them yet. One lady who lives next door, Mrs. Nielsen, brought us a fruit cake when we moved in. I think there are not too many Jews here, but there are many Negroes. They work with the railroads. . . .

Jake works very hard at the store, six days a week, and sometimes until very late at night. Here it is necessary to remain open on the Sabbath, because all the competition does. I sometimes go in to help him, particularly at the end of the month when there are accounts to do and bills to be sent out.

Mama dear, it was not necessary for you to send me money, though I appreciate the thought. I miss you all, and wish I could be with you all this Hanukkah Season, but this is Jake's busiest time. . . .

Give Abe a kiss, and tell him to study hard. . . . Give Papa a kiss and tell him it is from me. . . .

She did not tell her mother that she, too, often worked at the store with Jake on Saturdays, or that she was not keeping kosher. But she had found, at the shops in her neighborhood at least, that most kosher items were simply not available.

January 3, 1908

Dear Uncle Sol:

I think we should be pleased with the December figures, considering the fact that the blizzard we had on December 15, which you may have read about, made the streets all but impassable, and four or five good Christmas-shopping days were lost. All retailers here felt it, not just me. . . .

I think we should do well with the new foulard neck scarves. . . .

Yours sincerely,
Jake

January 19, 1908

Dear Uncle Sol:

A torrential downpour yesterday washed away most of
the snow, and in half an hour I sold every umbrella in the
store! And I couldn't find a single supplier in the city who
had more stock! If I had had more stock myself, I think I
could have sold at least 50 more! But who can predict the
weather?

One of the problems here, as I see it, is the tremendous
loyalty Chicago customers have to the older established
stores—Marshall Field's and Carson's, etc., etc. A couple of typical situations are these: A customer will come in
and say, "I've looked all through Field's and can't find
what I want—let's see what you have." Or, conversely, if
a customer can't find exactly what he wants here, he'll
say, "Oh, Field's will have it certainly." Breaking down
that loyalty to Field's, etc. is turning out to be our biggest
battle. . . .

I'm hoping to do well with the seersucker and alpaca
suits for spring and summer, but when I suggested to
one customer that the suit might look well set off by one
of our white piqué vests and a straw boater, he said
it looked "too sissy." Chicago is a very He-man sort of
town.

Yours sincerely,
Jake

Putting down his pen wearily after one of these late-night
letter-writing sessions, Jake said, "I wish I could afford someone who could type these things."

"I can type," Essie said. "I learned in school. I could type
your letters for you—all I'd need is a machine. I'll be your
helper!"

The next night, he brought home a typewriter for her. He
started off by dictating his letters and orders to her, but within a
few days the dictation was no longer necessary. All he had to
do was tell her what he wished to say, and she would compose
the letters for him.

New York City
March 15, 1908

Dear Nephew:

Among the expense items for February, ult., I came across an item in the amount of $29.50 for the purchase of a typewriting machine. Are you quite sure this purchase was strictly necessary?

"Christ!" said Jake, flinging down the letter. "Doesn't he realize the bargain he's getting? A free assistant? And all the time it saves me? All for a rotten thirty dollars!"

Your Uncle Mort and I have always felt that hand-written letters provide a more personal touch in the conduct of our business. . . .

"Fine," Essie said. "From now on, all his letters will be handwritten. But only *his*."

Incidentally, I have not yet received the final figures for February, which I had expected to have in hand before this date.

Yrs., etc.
Solomon J. Rosenthal

"The figures did go out, didn't they?" he asked her.

"Yes, but they were a few days late. You got behind, because of the short month, remember?"

He folded his arms on the kitchen table and rested his head upon them. "Christ," he said, "but I hate this business."

She studied him for a moment. Then, in imitation of him, she flung her own arms across the table, sank her head onto them, and let out a long wail. "Oh, God!" she pretended to moan. "Oh, *Riboyne Shel O'lem!* The harvest is past, the summer is ended, and we are not saved! What shall become of us? *Alles ist endet!*"

He sat up abruptly. "Essie?" he said. "Are you all right?"

She sat up too, and faced him. "As my mother would say, enough already—all *right* already! So go hit your head against the wall! Why this moaning and complaining? We have a roof over our heads and food in the larder. You have a job and a salary, what else do you want? Listen," she said, jumping up from the table, "I have a bottle of Riesling in the icebox, so let's have a party. Let's celebrate our good fortune. And listen," she said, as she fetched the wine, uncorked the bottle, and filled two glasses, "don't forget that I'm a Russian Jewess, with mystic powers. I am a daughter of the Benjamites, for whom the Red Sea parted, and I can work miracles. So let's drink to miracles! To success! To health! To money! To the end of the rainbow and the pot of gold! *L'chayim!* You at least know that Jewish word, don't you?"

He was laughing now. "*L'chayim*," he said, "to you and to me," and they clinked glasses.

Later, a little heady from the wine, she was walking slowly back and forth across the kitchen linoleum, her glass held in front of her. "Something is happening to me, Jake," she said softly. "Do you know what it is? I'll tell you what it is. The Russian peasant is coming out in me. I can feel it coming out in me—the Russian peasant." Slowly she began unbuttoning her blouse. "Ah, I feel it coming, Jake dearest—can you see it coming? Can you?"

He rose and began moving toward her.

She undid the last button. Then she sat, facing him, on the edge of the wooden kitchen table, and lay back across it. "Right here," she whispered, "like the peasant girls did . . . right here on the kitchen table . . . like the girls did at home . . . in Volna . . . Ah, Jake!" she cried as his body sank across hers. "Make love to this poor peasant girl!"

On mornings when he did not need her at the store, she would rise ahead of him and prepare his lunch, a couple of hearty sandwiches and a piece of fruit, a banana or an apple, and a Dewar bottle of hot coffee, wrap everything in waxed paper and put it in a paper bag. Then she would fix his breakfast. During the mornings she would type his business letters and work on the billing and account books. The afternoons were her private times. Some of the magazines she read contained pages on the fashions of the day, and for a few cents you could send away for the patterns. But why, she asked herself, spend good money on patterns when she could sketch dresses herself, and make her own patterns? And so she began designing and stitching together her own dresses and suits. A little outfit inspired by one she had seen in *Harper's Bazaar*—and which cost forty dollars in the stores—Essie could make for less than six dollars.

Some of the books that she borrowed from the library now were books on gardening. In the small rectangle of earth behind the house, which Jake had spaded up for a garden, she set out tomato plants, and rows of carrots, radishes and lettuce. She also left space for some showy perennials—phlox, iris, and peonies. When the streetcar line that ran in front of the house was being torn up and relaid in the spring of 1907, Essie was able to salvage a few flat stones, and to build a short, winding path through her little garden. Her botany course was turning out to be useful after all! Wonder of wonders!

From the store, it seemed to Essie, the figures got gradually better as the weeks went by. Actually, she decided, Jake enjoyed the selling part of his work, and was very good at it. With his good looks and easy manner, and with his own good taste in clothes, he was a persuasive salesman. But it was the paperwork he didn't like, and so Essie did that for him.

April 7, 1908

Dear Uncle Sol:

Enclosed, please find proofs of some new advertisements we plan to run in the Chicago Tribune. If you find them as exciting as I do, you may wonder who the talented artist is who has executed them.

Well, the artist is none other than my lovely wife who, to my added delight, offers her services completely gratis. . . .

New York City
April 11, 1908

Dear Nephew:

Thank you for sending me the proofs of the adv'ts.

At first I was puzzled by the fact that the faces on the figures wearing the clothes do not have features such as eyes and noses and mouths drawn in. But then I decided that perhaps this is rather clever, in that it calls to greater attention the garments themselves, and their details, rather than to the details of the human figure. The details of the garments seem to me to be well done.

I must offer a cautionary word, however, on the use of adv'ts in general. Even the cleverest adv't cannot sell an unsalable garment. If the adv't does not sell a g'mt, be sure not to make the mistake of spending money on another adv't for the same g'mt. Instead, a sale tag should be immediately placed on said g'mt, or else it should be passed on to another retailer at the most favorable discount you can get. Do not make the mistake of buying a certain g'mt in large quantity based on the fact that you intend to run an adv't on it, for the results may be disappointing and you will be left with a large overstock.

Meanwhile, I suggest you give more attention to your accounts receivable. Looking over last month's figures, it would appear to me that Chicagoans do not apply the same meticulous care to paying their bills which New Yorkers do. Or the problem may lie in not sufficiently checking the financial status of certain customers to whom you are extending credit. . . .

April 30, 1908

Dear Uncle Sol:

Rosenthal's advertisements are becoming the talk of Chicago!

Every day, in the mail, come more letters praising our advertisements for their stylishness and originality. My artist-in-residence deserves full credit. . . .

*New York City
May 5, 1908*

Dear Nephew:

I am delighted that Rosenthal's adv'ts are "the talk of Chicago," as you put it, but do not let that fact carry you away into spending more money on adv'ts than your sales figures warrant.

While having artistic adv'ts no doubt creates "good

*will" for the store, it is always difficult to place a dollar
value on "good will."*

> *Yrs., etc.*
> *Solomon J. Rosenthal*

> *May 25, 1908*

Dear Uncle Sol:
*Well, our suspicions of the last two months have been
confirmed. I am to become a father in early September!
What do you think of that? Please tell Mother and Pop
that I hope they'll forgive me for turning them into grand-
parents at such an early age.*

*If the baby is a boy, which we both hope it will be, his
name has been chosen—Jacob Auerbach, Jr. If a girl, we
are still undecided. . . .*

*Essie is in fine health, and the doctor foresees no com-
plications. And since most of the work she does for the
store is now done at home, she is expected not to be much
inconvenienced by the pregnancy.*

We both send love to you and to the Family.

> *Yours sincerely,*
> *Jake*

"Mama's not going to be happy with the name Jacob
Junior," Essie said.

"Why not?"

"Tradition. Tradition says that you name a baby after the
relative who's died most recently. I guess that would be my
Uncle Ike."

"Doesn't that strike you as kind of morbid?"

"Or at least with the same first initial."

"Do you want our son named Ike or Isidor? At Columbia,
there was a fellow everybody called Ikey the Kikey."

"No, you're right. This is the New World. But Mama won't
be happy, just the same."

" 'I' and 'J' are close enough."

"Of course we could name him Riesling," she said, smiling.

"Riesling?"

"For the wine."

(undated)

Dearest Mama:

On Tuesday, September 10, I gave birth to the most beautiful baby boy you have ever seen, wonderfully healthy and fat at eight pounds, six ounces, and I cannot describe our happiness to you.

Jacob, Jr., as we have decided to name him—now don't be upset, this is a very American custom, and since I and J are next to each other in the alphabet he also memorializes Uncle Ike—has Jake's blue eyes and, though it is hard to tell since he has so little of it, I think my hair coloring. He has long fingers, which he uses to cling to me when he is feeding. He eats well, and there is very little crying. Dear Mama, how I wish you could come to see him, since it is now going to be so difficult for me to come to New York. . . .

Jake has worked very hard in the last few weeks to turn our smaller bedroom into a nursery, and he has even made a little crib, which I have lined with blue satin cloth because, you see, I was sure that it was a boy. . . . We call him "Prince."

There was some pain for me in giving birth, but it passes so quickly that it is forgotten.

Dear Mama, I wish so much that you would accept Jake's mother's invitations when she asks you up to tea. She only wants to be friendly, and at my wedding you discovered how very easy it really is to get from one part of town to another. I think it hurts her that you keep saying no.

I know she frightens one a little bit at first with her "ways," but when you get to know her you will find that she is a nice woman on the inside.

There is a family secret about her that no one talks about. I'll tell it to you. She got pregnant (with my Jake) before she and Jake's father were married. Whenever I think about that I giggle. It proves that she's a human being after all!

Oh, how I wish you could be here to share our joy with our little boy!

Tell Papa for me that, though he may never forgive me

for my disobedience, and may still curse me in his
prayers, I pray that he will say a special blessing in the
shul for this little child, who bears him no ill will—in fact,
who bears no ill will for anyone in this world.
My love to everyone.

Esther

"It just isn't good enough," Jake had said, when that first
year with the Chicago store came to an end, and the balance
sheets were totted up. "It isn't good enough, is it, Essie?" She
had never seen him look more discouraged.

"But the point is, it *is* a profit," Essie said.

"Seven hundred and fifty-three dollars and eighty cents," he
said. "That's all we've ended up with, after a full year."

"But it's in black ink—not red."

"They expected to do much better than this, you know that.
They expected profits at least in the thousands. Not just a few
hundred."

"But a *profit* was what he wanted to see. That's what he
said—a profit. He didn't say how much. I know what he said. I
was in the room when he said it. He said a profit, and a profit is
what you've got."

"He isn't going to be happy."

"But he's got to keep his word. We've got to hold him to his
word."

He put his head in his hands in what was becoming a familiar gesture. "I'm in a rut," he said. "I'm getting nowhere."
Then he looked up at her blankly. "You've married a failure,"
he said.

"Don't say that, Jake! I won't listen to that kind of talk!"

New York City
October 31, 1908

Dear Nephew:
    As you might well imagine, we are more than a little
disappointed with the profit picture at the close of your
first full year as manager of Rosenthal's of Chicago. I
would like to repeat to you my contention that one of the
causes for this poor performance is what I see as exces-
sive expenditures on advertising. . . .

However, since, as you point out, you have at least minimally fulfilled your end of our agreement, I will renew same for another twelve months on the same terms as before.

Incidentally, your mother requests that you have a photograph taken of Jacob, Jr., the cost of which she agrees to pay.

> *Yrs., etc.*
> *Solomon J. Rosenthal*

And so it continued, from one year to the next.

The telephone which they had installed in the house at 5269 Grand Boulevard did not ring that often, particularly during the day, and so when it rang that summer morning in 1912 while Essie was fixing lunch for herself and the three children—for by now there were the girls, Joan and little Babette—she rushed into the front hallway to answer it.

"Essie?" his voice said. "It's Abe—your brother Abe."

"Where are you?"

"In New York."

Suddenly she was sure he was calling her with some terrible piece of news. "What is it?" she cried. "What's happened? Is Mama—?"

"Everybody's fine," he said. "Mama's fine, Papa's fine. But look—I'm in a kind of a jam, and I'm hoping you can help me out, Essie."

"What's wrong?"

"It's nothing. Just a little gambling thing. But the police came, and I was arrested—I'll explain the whole thing to you when I see you."

"You're coming here?"

"Could I, Essie? I'm out on bond, but I'm going to skip it, because if there's a trial—the thing is, I've got to get out of New York State until this whole thing blows over. Could I come and stay with you and Jake for a while?"

Wildly, she tried to think where he would sleep. The children's room was already crowded. The living room? Then she remembered the little unfinished attic room.

"Essie, I'm your flesh and blood. Could you help me out? Just for a few days, till I can find a job in Chicago, and get back on my feet again."

She had no idea how Jake would feel about this—a sixth mouth to feed.

"Can you help me, Essie? You know I wouldn't ask you if I wasn't desperate."

"Of course," she said. "Come as soon as you can, Abe." She gave him directions for how to take the streetcar from Union Station to Grand Boulevard.

"Thanks, Essie." Then she heard him chuckle. "Two black sheep," he said.

"What?"

"Papa's got two black sheep now. First you, now me."

Ten

———◦———

"Is he really looking for work, do you think?" Jake asked her. It had been two months, now, since her brother had moved in with them.

"He goes through the Help Wanted ads every morning in the paper," Essie said. "And he's gone all day long."

"I should think he could find something if he was willing to get his hands dirty. There are plenty of jobs in this city. I suspect that what your brother Abe is looking for is not so much a job, as a deal."

Essie had almost not recognized Abe when he first appeared at her door—he had changed so much in the six years since she had seen him. When she had left New York, he was still a boy. Now, at eighteen, he had shot up tall—taller than either of their parents—with a thin, angular face and body, curly red hair and mustache and a quick, engaging smile. Although he had promised to explain everything about the trouble he had got into in New York, he had offered only a few, very vague details. It had something to do with gambling in Delancey Street, and the police had broken it up and arrests had been made. But, beyond that, Essie knew nothing. Abe had asked her not to tell their mother that he was here—in case the police should go to Minna and Sam and try to trace his whereabouts. Whatever the offense was, he had assured her it was very minor. The only reason why he hadn't wanted to stand trial for it was that he didn't want to involve certain of his friends.

"This blood-is-thicker-than-water business can be carried on too long," Jake said.

"Can we give him just a little more time?"

One morning not long afterward they were all sitting at the breakfast table, and Abe Litsky was studying the newspaper. Suddenly he whistled. "Listen to this," he said, and read them the headline. "'Large Rail Shipment of Marshall Field Merchandise Goes Astray.'" Then he read them the story that followed. "'Three railroad boxcars, filled with merchandise bound for the Marshall Field department store in Chicago, have vanished into thin air, an embarrassed spokesman for the giant retailer revealed today. The cars, part of a larger shipment from the East Coast on the Burlington Line, were to have been unloaded yesterday on the spur of the railroad which terminates at the Fields' Warehouse in Diversey Street. But when the train pulled up at the loading platform, three of its freight cars were mysteriously missing. The possibility of theft has not been ruled out but, said the store's spokesman, Mr. R. J. Kelley of the Shipping Department, "It's hard to see how a thief could have made off with three loaded boxcars, without attaching an engine." More likely, said Mr. Kelley, since the three missing cars were at the end of the train, they somehow became uncoupled and, through error, became rerouted to some other destination. The cars were loaded with merchandise in a variety of categories, much of it home electrical appliances. The value of the missing part of the shipment has been placed at four million dollars.'"

"Think of that!" Abe said. "The great Mr. Marshall Field losing three whole box cars! Just losing them! Three!"

"If any of them contained menswear, that won't hurt us," Jake said.

Abe jumped to his feet. "Three boxcars shouldn't be hard to find," he said, and he was out the door.

"I'd like to see Mr. Marshall Field, please."

"Your name, please?"

"Abraham Litsky."

The receptionist looked at a tablet in front of her. "Did you have an appointment, Mr. Litsky?"

"No, but I want to see him."

"I'm afraid Mr. Field cannot see anyone who is not on his regular appointment schedule."

"I think he'll see me," Abe said.

"I suggest you write a letter."

"I think he'll see me," Abe repeated, "when you tell him that I have located his three missing boxcars."

The receptionist looked up at him a moment. Then she said, "Excuse me," and rose and stepped into the inner office.

When she returned, she held the office door open. "Mr. Field will see you now," she said.

When Abe Litsky entered the big office, Mr. Marshall Field III, none other, large, ruddy-faced and handsome, stood up behind his desk and, with his hands thrust into his trouser pockets and swaying slightly on the balls of his feet, smiled faintly and said, "What is this you're saying, young man?"

"I've found your boxcars, Mr. Field."

"Indeed," said the great man. "And where, pray tell, are they located?"

"On a siding north of the railroad station in Gary, Indiana."

"And the merchandise?"

"Intact, as far as I could tell, sir. All three cars are locked and bolted, and their seals have not been broken."

"And what makes you think that these are the ones we're looking for?"

"The shipping labels are on them, sir."

"I see," Field said. He reached for the telephone. "If you'll wait outside a moment, I'd like to do some checking."

"Certainly, sir," said Abe. "Incidentally, the siding is called Track C-Nineteen."

About ten minutes later, the great man appeared at his office door himself. "Do come in," he said. He ushered Abe to a long leather sofa, and said, "Do sit down." They sat down at opposite ends of the sofa, and Field said, "Remarkable."

"Thank you, sir."

"How long did it take you to accomplish this feat?"

Abe consulted his watch. "Well, it's two o'clock in the afternoon, sir, and I started a little before nine this morning. But of course I had to go to Gary and back—that took most of the time."

Field studied his fingernails, and Abe noticed a heavy gold ring. "Of course," said Field, "the shipment would probably have been traced and located in due time."

"But in your business, sir," said Abe quickly, "I know that time is money."

"This is true," said Field. "Would you mind telling me how you did it?"

"Certainly," said Abe. "First, I went to the library and looked at a map of the Burlington's route. Then, I telephoned the line's traffic master, and asked if any of his trains had had trouble in the last two or three days. None, said he, except one train bound for Chicago two days ago which had minor brake problems outside Gary. The train was shifted to a siding, where they worked on the trouble, and in the course of this all the cars were routinely uncoupled, and then recoupled. I figured that one pair of cars might not have been recoupled properly, and so the last three cars got left behind. Then it was off to Gary and the freight yards, which was where I found them."

"Very—resourceful," said Field. "I admit that it does seem strange to me that none of our employees had the resourcefulness to come up with such a simple stratagem."

"That thought did pass through my mind, too, sir," Abe said. "Not to say that you don't have many fine employees, sir," he added.

"Yes," said Field. "How old are you, young man?"

"Twenty-one," Abe lied.

"Very resourceful, for one so young."

"Thank you, sir."

"Of course," said Field carefully, "you realize that no monetary reward has been offered for locating these cars."

"That was farthest from my mind, sir. I'm just happy I could be of some small service to you."

"Still," said Field, "one good turn deserves another, as the fellow says. What can I do for you, young man?"

Abe hesitated. "Well, sir, to be truthful, I've been looking for employment here in Chicago—interesting employment, where I can meet interesting people. All I've been offered is manual labor, sir, and I feel I'm cut out for something better than that."

"Yes," said Field. And then, "Tell me, are you interested in opera?"

"Oh, yes," said Abe glibly. "Very interested."

"And have you any experience in the art of mixology?"

"Mixology?"

"The art of mixing drinks—tending a bar."

Though Abe could see no possible connection between the two unrelated questions, he said, "Oh, yes, sir, I'm very good at that."

"I'll tell you why I ask," said Field. "Mrs. Field and I are very interested in the Chicago Opera, and I am on its board. We hope one day to have an opera company here that will rival the Metropolitan Opera in New York. But our Opera House, it seems, has suffered from one shortcoming. This is the Middle West, after all, and it seems that certain opera patrons—particularly the gentlemen—would enjoy having a bar on the premises, where opera patrons could repair to during the intervals. Up to this point, we have had no bar, and the board has decided that opera patronage would be substantially increased if there were one. So Mrs. Field and I have made a small contribution to the Opera House, with which to build one. Now we are looking for some bright person to run this as a concession."

"I see," said Abe.

"Would this sort of situation interest you?"

Abe Litsky flashed what he knew was his most winning smile. "Mr. Field," he said, "you have found your railway cars, and I think you have also found your man."

"You will be serving libations to the elite of Chicago," said Marshall Field III, with a little wink.

That evening, at the dinner table, when Abe rattled off the events of his busy day, Jake Auerbach shook his head in disbelief. "And you'll be working for my competition, on top of it all," he said.

"Only for his opera," said Abe.

And within the week, Abe had found a room for himself in walking distance of the Opera House, and had moved with his belongings out of the house at 5269 Grand Boulevard.

And now picture, if you will, Abe Litsky behind the paneled and popular new bar of the Chicago Opera House, during that particularly popular winter opera season of 1912–1913—*Parsifal, La Bohème, Carmen*—serving libations to the elite of Chicago, men in white tie and tails and tall silk hats and decorations pinned across their chests on crimson sashes, women in dresses from Worth of Paris wearing coronets of jewels in their hair, long ropes of pearls, and carrying lorgnettes carved from the tusks of elephants—tycoons who snoozed through the music, and their wives who came to the opera simply to be seen—serving this elite, and charging them more than twice as much for a drink as any other bar in town because, after all, they are the elite, and can afford it, and are literally a captive audience and patronage. And watch Abe as he inevitably shorts them a bit on the measure and, if they are obviously well into the arms of John Barleycorn, short-changing them as well and pocketing their tips. See this attractive, clever fellow water his stock before each performance, and watch as he resorts to other profitable tactics. Medicinal alcohol can be bought cheaply at any drugstore. Add to this a little real Scotch for flavor, a drop or two of caramel for color, add some Lake Michigan water, and funnel the resulting concoction into empty bottles labeled Johnnie Walker and Haig & Haig. . . .

Abe Litsky ran the bar concession at the Chicago Opera House for seven months, at which point he was summoned again to the office of Mr. Marshall Field III. This time the meeting was not so pleasant.

"Certain bookkeeping and financial irregularities," Mr. Field muttered, riffling through some papers on his desk. "But I don't need to tell you about it, do I? You know exactly what I am talking about. In light of what you did for us, I have decided not to prosecute. But of course you must have known that, too, didn't you? That if I did prosecute, I'd come out of it looking like a fool. How much did you take out of it, Litsky? No, don't tell me, I don't want to know. That's all, Litsky. Good-bye. Get out."

Of course neither Jake nor Essie would know about any of this until years later.

But in seven months Abe Litsky had made eleven thousand dollars.

It was more money than Essie had ever seen in her entire life, and Abe had spread it out, in thick stacks of bills, on her kitchen table for his sister's and her husband's inspection. It was eleven thousand and much, much more.

"What are you going to do with it?" she asked him.

"Invest it," Abe said. "Is that not the American way?"

"In what, Abe?"

"I have a couple of good ideas," he said. "But one in particular."

"What is it, Abe?"

Abe sat back in his chair, his eyes shining. It was after nine, and the children had been put to bed. A teakettle sighed and whistled on the stove. Abe turned to his brother-in-law. "Jake," he said, "how did your great-grandfather Rosenthal get started in *his* business?"

"In the usual way," Jake said. "He came over from Bavaria in eighteen forty-five, worked in a butcher shop for a few months, made a little money, and started out on his own as a peddler—on foot, all through Pennsylvania, New Jersey. Dry goods. Handkerchiefs, undershirts, cheap German watches. When he could afford it, he bought a horse and wagon, so he could carry more merchandise and extend his routes. Soon he'd made enough money to lease a building and open his first store."

"And today the Rosenthals are millionaires."

Jake shrugged. "Some of them," he said.

"But today, what's become of the country peddler? He's no more. I'm not talking about the Hester Street peddler, Jake, though his days are numbered, too, I reckon. I'm talking about the country peddler, the young Jew who went from farm to farm with his pack of goods and, if he was lucky, the farmer let him spend the night sleeping on the haymow in his barn. He's gone, because he's no longer needed. He's been replaced, and do you know what replaced him?" Abe snapped his fingers. "The year was nineteen-o-three, and what replaced the peddler was called Rural Free Delivery. The mail-order business. That's the future of the retail business in the twentieth century, I reckon—mail order. Oh, you'll always have some big stores, like Rosenthal's, in the big cities. But what about the rural population, the farmers, the small-town housewives—they can't get to the big cities to shop whenever they feel like. So now they buy by mail order."

He produced a slim volume from his pocket. "Take a look at this," he said. "Two fellows here in Chicago, George Eaton and Cyrus Cromwell, got an idea back in nineteen-o-three, when they read about Rural Free Delivery, to go into the mail-order business. This is their catalogue. Right now, they're strictly in medical items, but they want to expand—into clothing, housewares, home furnishings. In just ten years, they're already doing a business of two hundred fifty thousand dollars a year, and I've even got a slogan for them—though naturally I haven't told them what it is yet."

"What is it?" Jake asked.

"'Eliminate the Middle Man—and Save.'"

Jake flipped through the catalogue. "But the customer wouldn't really be eliminating the middle man, would he? Eaton and Cromwell *are* the middle man."

"Oh, I know that," Abe said airily. "But it sounds good, don't you think? As I said, they need cash, to expand. For a hundred thousand dollars, they're willing to cut us in for a half share of their business."

Essie studied the catalogue. The adjective "Amazing" seemed to apply to each of the remedies, potions, and lixiviums which Eaton and Cromwell had to offer. There were amazing bust developers, creams, and foods; there were amazing cures for "female complaint"; equally amazing were the baldness cures, the youth restorers, the obesity powders, the virility pills, the bowel restoratives, the liver and bile pills, the cures for consumption, morning sickness, nerves, dizziness, drunkenness and the tobacco habit. Still more amazing potions eliminated flatulence, hysteria, heart disease, cancer and the common cold. The amazing bust development machine for $1.49 looked to Essie very much like an ordinary plumber's friend. Toward the back of the catalogue were sections offering eyeglasses, ear trumpets, false teeth, hair dyes—"Amazing! Eliminates gray hair permanently!"—and, for those whose baldness was of the incurable variety, a selection of toupees, wigs, false mustaches and beards.

"Do any of these things really work, Abe?" she asked him.

He shrugged. "The point is, people are buying them. Their sales have gone up every year. So," he said, leaning forward in his chair, "what do you say, Jake? For a hundred thousand, half of this business is ours. Here's my half of the partnership right here—fifty thousand dollars."

"How did you ever get so much money?" Essie whispered.

He winked at her. "Oh, I have my little ways," he said. "A little bit here, a little bit there. So, Jake, what do you say? With another fifty thousand from you, we'll each own a quarter share in a business that's doing a quarter of a million in annual sales. Within two years, we should have our investment back—and more."

"You want *me* to go into this with you, Abe?" Jake said.

"Why not? You'd be working for yourself, not for your relatives. Think about that."

"Why don't you just buy a quarter share for yourself," Jake said, "with what you've got?"

"A half share is what these fellows have for sale. And a hundred thousand dollars is their price."

"You couldn't have made that much just tending bar," Essie said.

"I didn't say I did, did I?" he said crossly. "I didn't come to Chicago dead broke, you know. So, how about it, Jake?"

"Have you approached your friend Mr. Field?"

"Field is a fool!" Abe snapped. "No, I want you, Jake. I want someone I can trust. I told you they want to go into the clothing business. You know the clothing business. I know nothing about that. You know who the manufacturers are, the suppliers—"

"But I don't have fifty thousand dollars, Abe," Jake said. "I don't even have a tenth of that."

Abe Litsky spread the fingers of his left hand and studied them. "But," he said carefully, "you have relatives in New York who have ten times that much, don't you? Ten times ten times that much? A little loan?"

"No," Jake said, shaking his head. "I owe them money already. I can't ask them for any more. No, that's out of the question."

"Well," Abe said, slowly gathering up the piles of cash that lay about the table and stacking it in the canvas suitcase he had brought it in, "Eaton and Cromwell are not in that big a hurry. I've promised them a decision by the end of the month. Think about it, Jake. Take your time. It could be our big chance, Jake. *Your* big chance. On your own, at last—like me."

"No, it's out of the question."

*   *   *

Later, after Abe had gone, and Essie and Jake had gone to bed, they had made love, but Essie had not been able to give this matter her customary happy concentration. Her head was awhirl with other thoughts. It was not just what Abe had said; there were other thoughts racing through her head, which were connected. With what Abe had said about little towns and farmers' wives was linked something else, something she had read in the newspapers just a month or so ago. It was in all the headlines . . . a storm of controversy . . . bitter, acrimonious . . . small-town merchants in an uproar . . . petitions, protests from people who called themselves collectively "the little fellow" . . . letters to Congressmen. But, said the modernists, the past was dying, the wave of the future was at hand and, in its wake, the little one-room schoolhouse, the village grocer, the friendly corner druggist, would disappear.

She touched his shoulder to see if he was still awake. "Jake?"

"What?"

"What if—I mean, what harm would it do, just to ask your Uncle Sol and Uncle Mort? I mean, there'd be nothing to lose, would there, in just asking?"

He sat straight up in bed, suddenly very angry. "No!" he said. "Haven't I had enough? Enough humiliation? Enough degradation? Enough of thanking them day after day for the simple fact that I earn enough to feed and clothe my wife and children? Do you want me to endure even more of that? Is that what you want? You may not know it, but I still have some pride left—not much, but some!" His voice cracked and, in the dark, she wondered if he was weeping. Beside her, she felt his arm go up and thought for a moment that he was going to strike her, but he only struck the pillow. "And when I think of what I used to want to do, the work I did best, working with the poor, helping people—people like yourself—all gone, for nothing . . . no way back. And what do you think it was like for me tonight? I'm almost thirty years old, and what do you think it was like for me to see a man more than ten years younger than I am—your baby brother—come in here rich tonight, with more money made in seven months than I've been able to make in seven years? And from being a bartender! Dear God, give me *something*, Essie—a little shred of pride! No. I say no, Essie. I say it's out of the question. And I never want to hear another word from you on the subject again. Do you understand? Not another word."

The bedroom door opened a crack and, silhouetted in the night light from the hall, Little Jake, six years old, stood there rubbing his eyes and asked, "Mommy, why is Daddy crying?"

Eleven

"I HAD a letter from Mama this morning," she said to him a few days later. "She hasn't been feeling well, and I really think I should go to New York to see her. After all, it has been nearly seven years. . . ."

"How much is the train ticket?"

"I have enough. From what I've saved from the household money. Mrs. Nielsen, next door, has offered to take care of the children during the day, and she'll walk little Jake to school in the morning and meet him in the afternoon. I'll leave plenty of food in the house for your dinners. And it will only be for a few days. Can I, Jake?"

"Of course," he said. "If your mother's ill, you must go."

And so, with that small, white lie out of the way, she boarded the train for New York on a windy April day in 1913.

She had chosen to arrive on a weekday morning, when the uncles would be at the office, and she made her way from Grand Central Station, a dozen or so short blocks, to 14 West 53rd Street on foot, wearing her new gray traveling suit, to where she was certain she would find her mother-in-law at home alone. Marks, looking just slightly surprised, answered the doorbell, ushered her into the red sitting room, and said, "I'll tell Madam you're here."

"Esther, what a delightful surprise!" said Lily Auerbach when she stepped into the room a few minutes later, wearing a white silk dressing gown and white satin slippers. She gave Essie a little kiss on the cheek and then, holding her hands, held her at arm's length. "You're looking *very* well," Lily said, inspecting her. "You've changed your hair. It's very becoming. Now come sit down, and tell me all the Chicago news. But shame on you for not telling me you were coming to New York!" With her hand she gently tugged at Essie's, pulling her down into a red loveseat beside her. "Quickly—how *is* everyone?"

"Everyone is very well," Essie said.

"I feel so badly that I haven't been able to get to Chicago to at least meet my grandchildren," Lily said. "I will, one of these days, but life keeps one so busy in New York. I have all their photographs, of course, on my dressing table, in pretty silver frames."

"They all send their love, Mother Auerbach."

Still smiling, she looked Essie up and down. "Yes, you look very well, my dear. Three children, and you've kept your figure. That's the hardest thing on a woman's figure—childbearing. And that's an attractive suit. Where did you find it?"

"Actually, I designed and made it myself."

"Really? How clever you are! I couldn't edge a hanky!"

"At least I know better than to wear a green party dress for tea in a red room," Essie said.

Lily Auerbach put her head back and laughed. "You know," she said, "after I met you for the first time, I said to Jake, 'She had all the makings of a beautiful young woman.' But then I admit that I added, 'All she lacks is a sense of *style*.' But now I see that you've acquired that, too, and that pleases me. Do you mind my telling you that? Yes, I'm sure you've become a great asset to our Jake—in Chicago."

There was a slight inflection there, which Essie caught. "In *Chicago*." Chicago was where they had been assigned, and Chicago was where they were intended to remain. Only a long tenure in Chicago, an inferior city, would earn the exiles their reprieve, a commutation of their sentence, and the possibility of a return to the only world that mattered, which was New York.

"Would you like a cup of coffee, Esther? Some tea?"

"No thank you, Mother Auerbach."

"Then tell me," Lily Auerbach said, leaning forward, "I'm sure the purpose of this visit isn't entirely social. Am I right?

Tell me why you have come to see me. Tell me what it is that's on your mind."

It was one of the things that Essie liked about her mother-in-law. Lily might start a conversation obliquely, taking light and inconsequential little tangents, but it wasn't long before she got down to the business at hand.

"Well," Essie said, beginning the little speech that she had rehearsed in her mind the night before sitting up on the train, "the fact is, Mother Auerbach, that Jake has been offered what seems to us a tremendously exciting business opportunity—in Chicago. A feeling in my bones tells me that this is his chance of a lifetime, Mother Auerbach—as they say, the bird in the hand."

"Really? What is that?"

"It's a company called Eaton and Cromwell, Mother Auerbach. They sell—"

"Yes, I've heard of them. They sell cheap medicines. Through the mails, with a catalogue. Not the best reputation, you know."

"I know," Essie said quickly, "but the point is that their business is at a turning point right now, right now in nineteen thirteen. They're at a point where they're ready to branch out, into a wider variety of merchandise, of better quality, with more—"

"And they're looking for financing. Correct?"

Essie decided to ignore this and to plunge ahead. "Mother Auerbach," she continued, "Jake has told me a bit of how your grandfather, R.B. Rosenthal, started his business as a peddler in little towns and communities where there were no stores. From this little start, he built a wonderful business. Eaton and Cromwell was started just ten years ago, in nineteen-o-three, as a result of a new service offered by the United States Post Office called Rural Free Delivery. They started as peddlers, too, but with more modern methods—through the mails. It's more modern and more efficient, and already their business has a quarter of a million dollars a year in sales."

"I understand all this. Now they want to expand."

"Yes, and they've just been given—by the government, again—a wonderful new *means* to expand." She took a deep breath, and played her trump card. "Have you read in the papers, earlier this year, about still *another* new postal service called Parcel Post? Small merchants in little towns all across the country were up in arms against it, swearing that Parcel Post would drive them out of business. But they lost their fight, and Parcel Post went into effect the first of this year. Think of what that means, Mother Auerbach! Eighty-five percent of our population lives in rural areas, on farms. Up until the first of this year, if a farmer wanted to collect a package that was too big for his rural mailbox, he had to hitch up his horse and wagon and drive miles to the nearest freight depot. Now that package comes to his doorstep! Think what this will mean to the mail-order business, Mother Auerbach—to the future—"

"Of course I've read about Parcel Post," Lily said. "It doesn't prove very useful to our business. Most of our customers are here in the city, and we do our own local delivery."

"But think of what it will mean to the *mail-order* business, Mother Auerbach—what it could mean for a company like Eaton and Cromwell!"

"Yes, I see what you mean," said Lily.

"Mother Auerbach, this could be Jake's big chance—the chance to get in on the ground floor of a company where the future is practically unlimited, where he could be his own boss. Just think—your only son, with a business all his own, which is bound to grow! For fifty thousand dollars, he can buy twenty-five percent of this business. I'm here to ask you if you can loan him that much. A loan, with interest, which I swear to you will be paid. That's why I'm here, Mother Auerbach. Will you help him? Please?"

Lily Auerbach rose from the sofa and began slowly pacing about the room in her white robe.

"Esther," she said after a moment or two, "speaking of things that are in the papers, there is something I've been meaning to ask you. Last summer, in the papers, there was quite a sordid scandal on the Lower East Side, and one of the people involved was named Litsky. Would that have been any sort of relative of yours?"

"If it was in the Chicago papers, I didn't read about it," Essie said.

"The young man's name I believe was Abraham Litsky. Don't you have a brother by that name?"

"It's a very common name," Essie said. Then she added, "But my brother lives in Chicago."

"I see," Lily said. "It was all quite—sordid." She hesitated. Then she said, "Esther, I want you to understand that it's not the money. Whatever the sum was that you mentioned."

"Fifty thousand dollars."

"Whatever. It's not the money. Esther, you see, there are some things that you may not realize about our family, and there is no reason why you should. There are things which not even Jake has fully realized—yet. You mentioned the name of Richard"—she pronounced it *Reek-hard*—"Rosenthal, who was my grandfather. You could not possibly have known Richard Rosenthal, who died in eighteen seventy-five, but I remember him very well. He was a wonderful man, with the most wonderful, sparkly blue eyes, a wonderful human being. He was loved and respected by everyone, both socially and in the business community of New York. I remember Grandpa, and how proud he was of the business he founded. He had worked so hard, against so many pressures—not knowing the language when he came from Germany, and social pressures that existed at the time because there was, well, some anti-Semitism in New York in those days. And yet he overcame all that, and even Mr. J. P. Morgan was his customer and friend. I have the little thank-you notes Mr. Morgan used to write to Grandpa every time he ordered a new suit. Mr. Morgan always asked for Grandpa when he came into the store. He'd let no one else wait on him." Lily continued pacing.

"Grandpa built Rosenthal's into one of the most respected names in retailing. This was his legacy, to New York and to us. And Grandpa was so proud to have a son, my father, to carry on. Richard Rosenthal's shoes were not easy for Daddy to fill, but Daddy did it, and did it superbly, adding even greater luster to the Rosenthal name. I wish you had known my father, too, who died—too young—in 1900. But Daddy died proud that he had two strong sons, Sol and Mort, who wanted to carry it on—Richard Rosenthal's dream. You see, it was an American dream, Esther, an American dream come true—that a poor immigrant German could create something for his family which would allow his family to walk tall, and proud, and hold its head high as an equal among the Christians. It was a great achievement, given the times.

"My two brothers, unfortunately, though both brilliant men, were neither one cut out for marriage. Don't ask me why, but neither Sol nor Mort has shown, ever, the slightest interest in a woman. But both have devoted their lives to the continuation of Grandpa's dream, to reinforcing that reputation the family has gained of honesty, integrity, public service, responsibility. That mantle—that shining mantle—has been passed on from generation to generation.

"Which brings us to myself. I would have loved to have had more children. But Jake's was a difficult birth for me, and after it was over I was told that I could have no more. . . ."

The child of a shameful union, Essie thought.

"And so now there is only Jake. Jake *must* carry the torch for the family now. As I see it, he has no choice. For Jake to cast it aside would make meaningless—a mockery—of everything that has gone before. This is something rare and precious that has been passed on to him, and he must learn to recognize it as the treasure it is. Now you have a little son. Every day, I look at his photograph in its silver frame, and think that, yes, it must be he who, once the importance of this has been instilled in him by Jake, must carry on from him, continuing the dy———" She broke off.

"The dynasty," Essie said.

Lily laughed. "Dynasty—that's not a very pretty word to use, is it? It sounds as though we thought of ourselves as the Russian czars or something. No, it's not that, it's the *family*. It's an American family, created and established by one strong and idealistic man, Richard Rosenthal. This heritage cannot be flung aside. It's like a religion. You may not think us very pious Jews, Esther, but in our own way we are. The family is our religion."

She came and sat by Essie on the loveseat again, and covered Essie's hand with hers. "I'm fond of you," she said. "And I always believed that you would help Jake find himself, and see his way to doing what he has to do. I think I told you once about Doctor Bergler, the famous alienist whom we had consult with Jake—one of the finest, if not *the* finest doctor in the country. Doctor Bergler addressed himself to this problem of Jake's, and he told us that it would probably take time for Jake to realize his destiny, the importance of what earlier generations have left him with, the duty and responsibility he has inherited. He *will* realize it, Doctor Bergler told us. He has to. I remember Doctor Bergler's words exactly. He said, 'It's in his blood and in his bones and in his genes. It is only a matter of time before it is in his mind as well.' I thought that was a very wise thing he said. And so you see, dear child, that Jake is a link in a chain—a chain that cannot be broken. If Jake should break it, what will have been the point of any of it? My brothers, my father, and my grandfather might just as well have never set their footsteps on this planet."

"You're condemning him to a life he hates," Essie said.

Lily raised her eyebrows slightly. "You may think of it as a condemnation," she said. "But we see it as a gift, a heritage that he has been given to fulfill, and make even more illustrious."

"He won't—not this way."

"But Doctor Bergler has already been proven right," Lily said. "True, Jake's profits in the first year of the Chicago store were not spectacular. But each year, I've noticed, they get a little better, as he gets better at doing what's in his blood and bones and genes. Until someday—you'll see—"

"So you're saying no to the money," Essie said.

"My dear, what else can I say? I have no choice. Would you ask me to help break the link in the chain? To bring down everything that has been built up so carefully, painstakingly, over all these years? You can't ask me to do that." She fixed her clear blue eyes on Essie. "No. Absolutely. You cannot ask me to do that. Someday, perhaps when you're older, when your own son is older, you'll understand."

"I wonder if I will."

"My dear, darling child—I know I have omitted asking much about my grandchildren. You cannot think I am so remiss as not to think about them at all. You may think I've barely acknowledged them—with a few checks, on birthdays and such. Forgive me for this. But there's more to it than that—my deepest feelings. I remember so well what Dr. Bergler said when he was treating Jake. His words compel me—he said, 'Let go of your child and let it grow.' And if he's to grow, so will his children—for that I hope and pray."

Lily Auerbach stood up again. "There's only one other thing," she said. "If it's making a lot of money that you—and Jake—are thinking of, remember that if Jake continues to apply himself, then, when I am gone, and when my brothers are both gone, Jake will be a reasonably rich man. I mean, if he continues to apply himself, where else would there be for it to go except to Jake, and you, and your children? But there's more than money that he must inherit first, and that's the stewardship that was Richard Rosenthal's greatest legacy to all of us."

Lily Auerbach spread her hands. "If, at that point, after we're all gone, he chooses to break the chain and abdicate the stewardship," she said, "at least none of us will be around to see it happen, to witness the tragedy."

From the loveseat Essie looked up at her mother-in-law. She had never been sure of her feelings toward Lily—whether she hated, admired, pitied or envied her. It was probably a mixture of all these feelings, and she could still draw amusement from envisioning Lily supine across the dented lids of garbage cans, and she smiled at the picture now. "Yes," she said, "I suppose I see the logic of what you're saying. How you can speak of chains and freedom in the same breath. How you can quote Doctor Bergler about letting him go, and keep him tied down at the same time. I can see the logic of it because you don't really want him to succeed, do you? Because you've always thought of him as a mistake—your only mistake, your only embarrassment. His even being born was a mistake, wasn't it? He's a mistake that can never be corrected, in your mind. What a terrible thing he must have done to you, Mother Auerbach, just by being born. Of course you can't forgive him—or yourself—for that."

The muscles of Lily Auerbach's face stiffened and her eyes narrowed. "I don't know what you're talking about," she said, "but we don't want to turn this meeting into a quarrel, do we?"

"Certainly not," said Essie, reaching for her purse and gloves to go.

"Dear Mama," Essie said, when her mother had composed

herself from the shock of seeing her and they sat in the little store on Norfolk Street while Minna dabbed at her eyes with the corner of her apron. "You have three beautiful grand-children. Little Jake is in the first grade already, and his teacher writes that he is very well-behaved and quick to learn. The little girls are still at home with me. Joan is dark, like me, and Babette is fair, like Jake's mother. They never quarrel. Oh, Mama, how I wish you could come to Chicago to see them."

"Oh, no. Too far. Chicago is too far away. Maybe when they are older, they can come to see me."

"Of course."

"And how is Abe? Have you seen him?"

"We see him often, Mama. He is doing very well."

"Good. I had a feeling that was where he'd go."

"What did Abe *do*, Mama? I know it was something about gambling."

"Ha!" said Minna. "God knows what he did. If you believe what the cops said, there was more to it than that. But who believes what the cops said? The cops said girls—bad girls. Abe had bad friends, bad boys, that was the trouble—Italians. They got him into it. There was one boy named Corelli. He went to prison. It is better for Abe in Chicago, I think—away from those Italians."

"Yes."

"And how is Jake?"

"Working very hard, Mama. There was a chance that he might have been able to go into business on his own. It was one of the reasons I came to New York—to ask his family if they would loan us money to buy into this new business, along with Abe."

"What kind of business?"

"Medicines, drugs."

Minna nodded. "Ah, that's a good business," she said. "Doctors—God knows they charge enough."

"But his family said no."

"Ah, they're tightfisted, those *Deitch*—tightfisted, except when it's one of their charities they give to so they can get their pictures in the *Tageblatt*."

They sat in silence for a while, and then Essie said, "How's Papa?"

"Growing older, God bless him."

"Is he upstairs now?"

Minna nodded.

"Do you think I could go up and see him, Mama?"

Minna shook her head. "No, no. Save yourself the trouble."

"I thought it might make him happy to hear about his grand-children," Essie said.

"No, no. Don't you understand? He doesn't want to be made happy because he *is* happy. This is happiness for him absolutely, this misery. Leave him to his misery, his happiness, the suffering Jew."

"I see."

There was another silence, and then Minna said, "This medicine business—it would be with Abe, too?"

"Yes, but it will take a lot of money to buy into it, and we don't have it."

"Essie," Minna said, "you're taller." She pointed. "Reach up behind the cookie jar on the top shelf and get me the little book that's there."

Essie did as she was told and, from the back of the shelf, extracted a small black book, its pages secured with an elastic band. It was a passbook from the Union Savings Bank.

"Tell me how much is there," her mother said.

Essie sat down again and removed the rubber band. She opened the book and began turning the pages. They were filled with entries. Some were small—a dollar or two. Others were larger, for as much as a hundred dollars. Furthermore, there seemed to be an entry for nearly every day of the week, and the dates went back for more than twenty years. The only entries that were not deposits were interest payments which grew steadily larger as she turned the pages, year after year. There were no withdrawals.

"Mama, this bank's on Union Square," she said. "How can you have gone up there every day?"

"Mrs. Potamkin does it for me," her mother said. "Now tell me how much is there. What's on the last line?"

Essie stared, bewildered, at what she saw on the last page. "Mama," she whispered. "How did you do this?"

"Just tell me what the last line says," her mother said.

"Sixty-three thousand, one hundred and twenty-seven dollars and nineteen cents."

"Take it," her mother said. "It was to send Abe to college and medical school, to be a doctor. So what is the use of that now? What use do I have for it now? Take it. But don't give it to Abe. I don't trust him with money yet, just so long as he has a job. You take it. Take it all."

"Mama . . ."

"Take it, I tell you. Take it all." Minna held her hand up straight. "No more talking. Just take it."

On the train ride back to Chicago, Essie sat with her purseful of money clutched tightly in her lap. Every stranger in the car was a potential thief and, though she was very tired, she fought sleep, knowing that if she dozed off for a single moment her purse, and the miracle of the cash that it contained, would be snatched from her. At a station called Harmon-on-Hudson, a young man boarded the train, came down the aisle, and took the empty seat next to her. She clutched the purse even tighter against her stomach with both hands, looking at him warily out of the corner of her eye. He was a fine-looking young man with a square, clean-shaven jaw, a long, straight nose, and a shock of blond hair that fell gracefully across his forehead. He was well dressed in a tan-colored tweed suit. He didn't look like a thief, but wolves sometimes dressed in sheep's clothing, and Essie did not relax her grip on her purse. From the corner of her eye, she watched him warily as he crossed his tweed-trousered legs, lifted a pair of tortoiseshell spectacles from his jacket pocket, placed them across his nose, unfolded a copy of the New York *Times*, and began to read.

After a time, he put down his paper and said to her, "How far are you going?"

"Chicago."

"Ah, so am I," he said. And then, after a little while, "Is Chicago your home?"

"Yes."

"It'll all be new to me," he said. "I'm from Boston. I'm going to Chicago to seek my fortune in a strange land." He chuckled.

She said nothing. The fortune he sought, of course, was right in her lap.

Down the swaying aisle a Negro porter in a white coat was moving with a rolling cart full of orange and lemon drinks and sandwiches. The young man reached in his pocket and jangled some change. "Care to have something to drink?" he asked.

"No thank you."

"Sandwich?"

"No thank you."

The porter arrived at their row of seats, and the young man purchased a roast beef sandwich and a bottle of lemon pop. For the next few minutes he concentrated on his sandwich and his soda. He seemed to have very good table manners, wiping his fingers on a paper napkin after each bite. Then, finished, he turned to her and said, "If we're going to be traveling companions for the next few hours, let me introduce myself. My name's Charles Wilmont."

He extended his hand, but Essie would not release her hand from her purse. "How do you do," she said. And then, "I'm Esther Auerbach. Mrs. Jacob Auerbach."

"I see," he said. He looked at his outstretched hand, smiled, and withdrew it. "I think you're nervous," he said. "If you're nervous about rail travel, don't be. This train's as safe as—as rocking in the arms of Morpheus. Is it your first time on a train?"

"No."

"Or are you nervous about talking to strange men? If so, I'm sorry."

He did seem very pleasant and polite, and Essie decided that perhaps he was not a thief and relaxed her grip on her purse somewhat. "No, I'm not nervous," she said.

"And you've already told me you're married, so that's not what I'm interested in," he said. "I just thought it would be nice to have someone to talk to on the trip. I guess I'm a gregarious sort of fellow." He had already used two words that were unfamiliar to her. Morpheus. Gregarious. "But look, if you don't want to talk, just say so," he said. "And if you want me to move, I'll take another seat."

Perhaps, she thought, she was lucky to have had this nice

young man sit next to her. If he changed his seat, who knew what might come along next and sit down? "No, don't move," she said quickly.

"Well, then let me tell you a little about myself," he said, "so I won't seem like so much of a stranger. As I said, my name is Charles Wilmont, and I've just graduated from the Wharton School of Finance and Economics. In case you don't know, the Wharton School is where they teach you everything there is to know about business except how to get into a business yourself. I mean, I am now fully prepared to go into— even run—any kind of business in the world, but how do I find that business? That's what I'm going to Chicago to find out."

"I see."

"Now tell me a little about Chicago."

"It's a big city," she said.

"Oh, I'm prepared for that," he said. "I'm prepared for bigness. But what place will there be in all that bigness for young Charlie Wilmont? That's what I'd like to know. . . ."

And so he chatted on like that, and the more he talked the more at ease Essie felt with him. He told her about all the courses he had taken at the Wharton School, and about the courses he had taken as a Harvard undergraduate before that. He told her about his parents, whom he described as "typical, dull, suburban North Shore Boston," and about a young woman whom he hoped—though he was not yet engaged—to marry, once he had established himself in some sort of business. He had a gentle, self-mocking way about himself. "What will become of me, do you suppose, Mrs. Auerbach?" he would cry in mock despair from time to time. Listening to him talk made the long trip seem to pass more quickly, and presently she was laughing at his wry little jokes. By the time they passed the Pennsylvania–Ohio border, it was quite late, and he asked her if she minded if he slept for a while. She said no, not at all, and presently he was asleep in the chair beside her, snoring softly. Essie of course kept rigidly awake as the train sped on through the night, looking out at the lighted and mostly deserted station platforms where they stopped— Cleveland, Sandusky, Toledo, South Bend. From time to time his drowsing head nodded against her shoulder, but he always pulled himself quickly up straight again, and by the time he awoke the first light of morning was showing. He smiled, rubbed his eyes, and told her that he had dreamed he would find success in Chicago. And by the time they had reached Union Station she had decided that she had made a new friend, and he had used so many big words—Management Design, Corporate Structure, Production Potential—that she decided he might be some sort of genius.

As the train pulled into the station, he said, "This has really been very pleasant. I've talked your poor ear off, but I've thoroughly enjoyed it."

"I've enjoyed it, too," Essie said.

"Here, let me give you my card," he said. He took a card out of a small silver case, and scribbled something on the back of it. "And this is the address of the relatives I'll be staying with in Chicago, and their telephone number. Please call if I can ever be of service."

And so Essie deboarded the train in Chicago with her purse and its miraculous contents intact, still clutched against the bosom of her gray traveling suit with both hands, and with Charles Wilmont's calling card pressed between two fingers.

The Café bar at the Hotel Pierre is crowded at this hour of the evening, but Joan Auerbach quickly spots her brother sitting alone at a corner table, and makes her way across the floor to him. He rises, and Joan lets him kiss her gloved hand, one of those little Old World gestures he is fond of making. Then she settles herself at the table beside him, throws back the shoulders of her black mink coat, and removes her gloves. "Well, Mogie," she says. Then, to the waiter who appears, she says, "A bourbon old-fashioned, please—no cherry," which, of course, she will not drink. Mogie is sipping a frozen daiquiri. Then, rather defiantly, Joan lights a cigarette. Mogie Auerbach does not like people to smoke, even in public places.

"I mustn't be too late," Mogie says. "Tina's expecting me home by seven."

"This," Joan says, "will not take more than a few minutes, when I tell you what I have to say. Thank you," she says to the waiter, when her drink arrives. Then she cocks her head, just slightly, for she has just heard someone at a nearby table say to his companion, "That's Joan Auerbach, the publisher."

"Well?" Mogie says.

"We must keep our voices down, Mogie," she says. "I've just been recognized."

"Very well," he says.

"Well," she says in a low voice, "you won't believe what I've found out. I did as you suggested, went to the apartment last night, and went through Mary's files. Checkbooks. Statements. Everything. And it's just as I suspected. She's been paying him off."

"Who?"

"Arthur Litton."

"Oh, God," Mogie says, cupping one hand across his eyes.

"Every month. And—get this, Mogie. She's been paying him off at the rate of *ten thousand dollars* a month! That's a *hundred and twenty thousand* a year!"

"Oh, dear God," Mogie moans, rocking his head back and forth as though about to undergo some sort of emotional collapse.

"Even for Mother, that's a lot of money. Of course I didn't dare remove the canceled checks to have them Xeroxed—but they're *there*. We know they're *there*. Bank records will back us up—"

"Oh, Joan . . . Joan . . . it's so awful."

"Now all we need to know is what she's paying him off *for*. But you can bet it's something pretty big. You don't pay an estranged brother a hundred and twenty thousand dollars a year for nothing. He's being paid to keep his trap shut about something pretty damned important, if you ask me. That's what we've got to find out now, and the only one who can possibly tell us is Arthur Litton himself. Maybe he won't tell us, but we've got to try. I'm going to contact him, and try to find out what all that money's going to him *for*."

"Oh, Joan, don't. It's too awful."

"What are you talking about, Mogie? What's so awful? It's what I suspected all along."

"Don't, Joan. . . ."

"Here's my plan. I go to Arthur Litton—Uncle Abe—and I tell him, 'Look, Mother's old, she's going to die.' I mean—ha-ha—we're all going to die some day, aren't we? And I tell him that I know about these payments, and I'd like to continue them after Mother's gone—but the thing I need to know if I'm going to do this, is what are the payments for? How's that for strategy? Logical, isn't it?"

"But Joan, listen to me. You've got to think twice about this. Because now that you've told me about the payments, I know exactly what they're for."

"You do?"

"Just tell me one thing—how far back do these payments go?"

"Years and years. Back to the late nineteen twenties, at least."

Mogie nods. "Yes, that would be right. Yes, it's exactly what I was afraid of."

"Mogie, please tell me what you're talking about."

"I want to show you something," he says. He reaches in the breast pocket of his jacket and pulls out one of the old clippings from Joan's files. He spreads the clipping on the table and, covering the picture caption with one hand, he says, "Joan, who is this a picture of?"

"Why, it's a picture of Arthur Litton, taken sometime in the twenties. I gave it to you the other night. From my files."

"Look more closely."

"I know it's a picture of Arthur Litton, Mogie. I—"

"Look more closely. Don't you see—someone else?"

"Else?"

"It's a picture of our brother, Josh, the way he looks today."

Joan studies the picture. "Well, there is a resemblance. But—"

"It's identical."

"But after all, Arthur Litton is Mother's brother, Josh's uncle—"

"But *this* close? Did you ever wonder, Joan, why Josh never looked a bit like Papa? I always did. There wasn't a trace of Papa in Josh, and then, the other night, when I saw this photo—I had the answer."

"Mogie, are you saying—?"

"And did you ever wonder—as I often did—how Josh ever got conceived? Josh was born in nineteen twenty-eight, when I was ten. Mother and Papa were barely speaking to each other, except on social occasions when they'd put on a show of

getting along, much less *sleeping* together. I used to ask myself, how could Josh have been conceived, unless—"

"Mogie, what are you saying?"

"Unless his father was someone else. Now we know."

"You mean Mother and—you mean *incest?*" Heads turn
from several tables, and Joan covers her mouth and says, "Oh,
forgive me. Oh, Mogie this can't be true," she whispers. "This
is just preposterous, Mogie."

"Incest occurs more often than you might think. It occurs, in
fact, in one out of ten families in the United States. Those are
the statistics. I got them from Doctor Gold."

"But not Mother!"

"Didn't you say that Uncle Abe used to live in the same
house with them on Grand Boulevard? The proximity—"

"Yes, but—a brother and a sister—"

"That's not all that uncommon, either. Why, I used to have
incestuous fantasies about you when I was growing up. Did
you know that? Do you remember the pool house at The Bluff?
I used to stand on a garden chair behind the back window of the
girls' dressing room, and watch you taking a shower, and I'd
masturbate."

"I can't believe I'm listening to this at the Pierre."

"It's one of the things I've had to work out with Doctor
Gold. But it's true. When I was eleven or twelve, and you were
nine years older, I was head over heels in love with you. I
thought that you were the most exciting, most beautiful girl in
the world. And you were!" He smiles at her, and covers her
hand with his. "And in many ways, you still are."

Flustered, Joan giggles nervously, and says, "Well, thank
you, Mogie," and lets her hand rest for a moment under his,
before withdrawing it. "People did use to say I looked like
Gene Tierney. I always thought more Joan Bennett."

"You can't imagine what a thrill it is for me to watch you
come into a restaurant like this, and see people recognize you."

"But what you're saying—"

"And I can say all this even though I know how much
you've always hated me, Joan—for being the first of the second litter of Auerbach children, as we say. But just lately
Doctor Gold has given me some new insights about that problem, too."

"What's that?"

"You always wanted to be the oldest male in the family, didn't you? You always wanted to be what I've become. You always wanted to be the dominant male figure among the Auerbach sibs. You unconsciously wanted to castrate me, and turn me into a younger sister."

"That's nonsense, Mogie."

"Of course it's been unconscious on your part. But it finally helps me understand you. It's a classic case of penis envy. You wanted a cock. I had one, so you wanted mine."

"Mogie—for heaven's *sake!*" Joan says. "Please get back to what you were saying about Mother."

"Well, a tendency toward incestuous longings does tend to run in certain families. Doctor Gold told me this, too. And it's particularly prevalent among families of Eastern European origin. Jewish families—"

"Like Mother's—"

"Who were ghettoized for so long—"

"Do you really think—?"

"And here's another interesting thing. What color are Josh's eyes?"

"Blue."

"And Mother's?"

"Also blue."

"And Papa's?"

"Dark brown. Glaring at us from the portrait in the library."

"And yours, and mine, and Babette's?"

"Brown. But that doesn't prove—"

"And Prince's eyes? I've been trying to remember. There are no photographs—"

"All destroyed. But they were brown, too—I remember very well."

"Well, then," Mogie says. "What about Uncle Abe?"

"I don't remember."

"Try very hard. From this newspaper picture, it's impossible to tell."

"I'm sorry, Mogie. It was so long ago, and I was just a little girl."

"But if it should turn out that Uncle Abe's—or Arthur Litton's—eyes were blue, that would tell us something, wouldn't it?"

Joan considers this a moment. "But no, not really," she says at last. "Two blue-eyed parents can't have a brown, but two browns or one brown and one blue can have either-or."

"True enough," Mogie says. "But the chances are three out of four that brown will dominate, because blue is recessive. That's Mendel. That's the Mendelian Ratio. We need to know what color Uncle Abe's eyes were. Or are. That's the meaning of this dynamic. If they're blue, like Mother's, we could draw some conclusions, don't you think?"

"Now wait a minute," Joan says. "Uncle Abe left the company in nineteen seventeen. I know, because it was the year America went into the war. The family had no association with him after that. Josh wasn't born until nineteen twenty-eight. So how could he possibly—?"

"Ah," Mogie says, lifting his glass and looking at her over its rim with half-closed eyes. "But I know something that you don't, my darling sister."

"What's that?"

"I was coming to that. Our Uncle Abe came back."

"Came back? When?"

"It was about ten years later. I was eight or nine. You, I believe, were off on one of your—marital adventures. I never saw him, but I know he came back, because I remember Mother and Papa having a terrible row about it. I remember Papa shouting, 'Now what's that damned brother of yours trying to pull?' And I remember Papa saying, 'He's a crook and a liar, and he's not going to get anything from me.' I remember, because I didn't understand that expression, 'trying to pull.' And because I'd never even known that Mother had a brother."

"What was it he wanted?"

"I don't know. But I know when I asked Mother what it meant, and asked her who her brother was, she just said, 'It's grown-up business,' and wouldn't talk about it. So whatever Abe wanted, I gather he didn't get."

"But still, Mogie," Joan says, twirling the plastic stirrer in her drink. "Do you really think our mother would—I mean, she's always been so proper."

Mogie's eyes narrow still further. "Which brings me to my final point," he says. "I'm not sure that *she* did anything at all. In her case, I'm quite certain it was—" he lowers his voice to a whisper, and leans closer to his sister—"rape."

"Oh, Mogie. No," Joan gasps.

"Why not? Considering the man's character? Considering the amount of money she's been paying him to keep the facts from coming out? Why, it would be worth almost anything to keep the family from knowing something like that."

"Why wouldn't she have had an abortion?"

"Hard to do in those days. Illegal, and risky. And how would she have explained it to Papa? Don't you remember when she was pregnant with Josh, how strange she was—irritable and moody?"

"I always supposed she was worrying about having another baby at that age. She was thirty-six, thirty-seven—"

"Nonsense. Women didn't worry about *that* in those days. Nobody'd ever heard of Down's syndrome in nineteen twenty-eight."

Joan stares at the pale pink tablecloth in front of her. "Sometimes I wish Josh *had* been born a Mongolian idiot," she says, "instead of—as Mother keeps reminding us—so *smart*." But even as she says these words, against the pale pink surface of the tablecloth unexpected pieces of the puzzle begin to fall into place, and out of a meaningless cryptogram clues appear and gather to form clear English sentences. "Oh, dear God, Mogie," she says softly. "Because she did say—"

"Say what?"

"Said that Uncle Abe had done something terrible to her years ago. Something that hurt her. Used the word hurt. And she said it was *personal*. Nothing to do with the company."

"There. You see?"

"Something so awful she couldn't tell me."

"There. You see?"

"And she said that when they were growing up they slept in the same room. Even in the same bed."

"There. You see? It all fits." His eyes are slits now. "It's a classic case. Think of it. Picture it. Uncle Abe—driven to fury, having been denied whatever he wanted from Papa. Determined to have his revenge, against Papa and the family. In his rage, the childhood fantasies come back, intensified in middle age. Out of control, he turns on the family's most vulnerable member—Mother. And finally, irrationally, he acts those fantasies out."

"Dear God, I think you may be right."

"I know I am."

"And Josh is—"

"Arthur Litton's son."

"A gangster—"

"The result of an incestuous rape."

"We've got to get to Litton."

"There was a woman, Daisy Something, who was close to all of them—"

"Stevens. Daisy Stevens. She'd know, yes."

"The color of his eyes, at least."

"But if this ever got out, it could ruin all of us," Joan says.

"It would certainly put an end to dear little Josh's career with the company," Mogie says with a small smile.

"But what else could it do?"

"It's a can of worms, all right," Mogie says. Then he says slowly and carefully, "There is one other thing, at least, that it could do. You see, I've given this some thought. If Josh is not Papa's real son, I see no reason why he should be entitled to any share of Papa's trust."

Joan Auerbach stares across the table at her brother. Then she does an uncharacteristic thing, and takes a swallow of her bourbon old-fashioned.

"I see no reason at all," her brother says. He glances at his gold Cartier tank watch. "I've got to run. I promised Tina. We're trying to get pregnant ourselves. My sperm count is fine, and Tina's ovulating this week." He signals the waiter for his check.

Outside the hotel entrance, Mogie's car and driver are waiting, and the driver gives Mogie a crisp salute and holds open the door. "You're looking very chipper, Mr. Auerbach," he says. "You must have had a pleasant meeting."

"As a matter of fact, Warrington, I have," Mogie says as he slides into the wide back seat of the Rolls. "Extremely pleasant. Back to Beekman, please." As the car pulls away from the curb, Mogie pulls down the writing table that is set into the back of the front seat, lights the goose-necked reading lamp, and removes writing utensils—a sheet of his crested stationery and a gold pen—from the special pockets where they are kept in the car. Ah, darling Joan, he thinks. Darling, darling Joan. Phase One of his little plan, his elegant little plan, has gone more splendidly than he had ever dared to hope it would, and now is the moment to embark upon Phase Two. Mogie's orderly mind likes to do things in this fashion, in carefully timed and organized phases, and after Phase Two, in due course, will follow Phase Three.

One of the many facets of Mogie Auerbach, as a Renaissance Man, which even his family is not aware of, is that among his many talents he is also a better-than-passable sonnet-maker. He has been composing this particular sonnet in his head for several days, and now he is ready to set the lines to paper. He has chosen, for this sonnet, the Shakespearean mode, and, with a flourish, he writes its title across the top of the page—"*J'Accuse!*" He continues writing rapidly—a Coleridge uninterrupted by a gentleman on business from Porlock—and, by the time his car has traveled the short distance between Sixty-first Street and Beekman Place, it is finished, and he reads:

> *Whose pictures these, we might gently inquire?*
> *Though one is recent, one from years ago,*
> *Which is the noble son and which the sire?*
> *What is it that the wisely child must know?*
> *How scant apart, in simple years, they seem!*
> *And yet full thirty years apart be they!*
> *Has it yet dawned, all clear, as in a dream,*
> *What these two images do seem to say?*
> *Father, or not? Whose stern but kindly gaze*
> *Stares down from high upon a paneled wall?*
> *Did he suspect throughout his final days*
> *That son he called a son was not a son at all?*
> *Whose faces, these, both whom you know so well?*
> *If walls could talk! If pictures, too, could tell!*

Not bad, he thinks. Not bad at all. Too good, in fact, for the rather private use to which the lines must be put. Good enough, indeed, to satisfy the wrong-headed editors of *The Georgia Review*, for whom Mogie occasionally writes under the *nom de plume* of "Lycidas," and who have turned down three of his most recent efforts. But no, not yet. "*J'Accuse!*" must serve another purpose first. A pity, but there it is. He folds the sheet of paper, slips it in the breast pocket of his Weatherell suit, raises the writing table and snaps it into place. "I won't need you again tonight, Warrington," he says as he steps out of the car.

"Have a pleasant evening, sir!"

"I will, Warrington, I will."

Once inside his house, however, Mogie does not immediately go upstairs to Tina. First, he must go to his desk and copy his sonnet in a hand that will not be instantly recognizable. His own Italianate Chancery script is too distinctive. To copy his verses, he chooses plain block printing, of the sort taught to every schoolboy in the first and second grade. This chore completed, he opens his secret drawer, takes out his pipe, fills and lights it, and soon he is suffused with even higher spirits. An erection begins to swell in his trousers as he admires his handiwork and contemplates the excruciating pleasures that are to come. Elated, he moves quickly now. He goes to the bookcase, unlocks it with his key, and removes the two scrapbooks with their pages carefully marked with white strips of paper. Using his silver library shears with their mother-of-pearl handles, he then neatly excises the two pertinent photographs. He prints a date on each, then places them, along with the sonnet, in an ordinary white envelope, seals it, addresses it in the same schoolboy printing, and stamps it. "Farewell, my lovely," he says, and takes another long, deep draw on his pipe. Invictus!

He starts to ring for his butler to mail the letter, but then decides: too risky. Instead, he rises and, with one hand deep in his pocket to control the violent erection which seems about to burst through every seam in his clothing, he hurries out of the house again and, limping slightly because of his extraordinary condition, makes his way to the mailbox on the Fifty-second Street corner. To lift the lid of the mail chute and drop the letter in requires two hands, and for a moment he is terrified that one of his neighbors—walking a dog, perhaps—will see him in this state, but the street is empty. He lifts the lid, drops the letter in the box, and lets the lid fall closed with a gloriously satisfying slam. Darling Joan! He does another slam for good measure.

Phase Two is complete.

And now, just two blocks from his house, Mogie Auerbach floats—yes, floats!—homeward, Mogie Auerbach the Invincible, along Beekman Place, floats up his front steps, through the door, and up the curved stairway, calling ahead of him, "Daddy's home, darling child!"

Twelve

"DAISY . . . dear," Essie says, rising to greet her as Yoki ushers her into the library. "I'm so happy you could come."

The two women embrace, and then, holding each other at arms's length, appraise each other and the inevitable changes that have occurred since 1965. "Well, all things considered," Essie says, "I think we've both held up very well." Daisy is, of course, some ten years younger than she. "Naturally, you don't have to agree with me."

"But I do," Daisy says. "At least we're both still here."

Yoki reappears with tea things on a silver tray and sets them down.

"Or would you prefer a serious drink?"

"No, tea will be lovely."

"Now, sit down, Daisy, and tell me all your news."

"Well, the biggest news was my surprise at hearing from you."

The two women sit down side by side on the loveseat, and Essie pours the tea. "Is it still lemon and no sugar?"

"You have a wonderful memory, Essie."

"I know I've been remiss," Essie says. "I don't know what happens, but there always seems to be something going on. But I've thought of you often, I really have."

"I've thought of you, too."

Now suddenly an odd silence falls between them, and Lord knows what either of the two women is thinking. But isn't it always this way, when two old friends who have been parted for a space of years, who think that they have so much to say to one another, find, upon meeting, that they are at a loss for words? Preoccupied, they sip their tea with seriousness. Then both begin to speak at once.

"I thought—"

"There was—"

"Did you—?"

Then both laugh. "Who's going to begin?" Essie asks.

"You," says Daisy. "I want to hear all about the children."

"Well, where to start? I have a pet grandchild, Josh, Junior—my new toy. I have lunch with him perhaps once a month. He likes wine lists. He likes to select the wine. He's twenty-three, honors at Princeton, and he's joined the company. Handsome. And his father—working very hard, traveling all over the countryside, just as Jake did. And Mogie—well, you know Mogie. He's never believed in working very hard, and so he doesn't. He has his collections, and now and then he writes about art in one of those little magazines. He shows them to me. I thought I knew something about art, but when I read Mogie's articles I haven't the foggiest idea what Mogie is talking about. He writes about 'catholicity of taste,' and I haven't a clue what he means. He's still in analysis, of course. He'll always be. The problem, he once told me, was impotence. Why did he tell me that? It wasn't something I wanted to know about. Anyway, maybe he's making headway with his doctor because he just got married. Finally. To a woman who's at least forty years younger than he. Maybe that's the cure for impotence, who knows? And Babette . . . what month is this? January? Babette is in Palm Beach if it's January, we're not that close, with a new husband. Joe Klein. He's all right. In summer, they go to Southampton. Babette likes the society life. And Joan—well, Joan has her newspaper. She still struggles along with it, I don't know why. Joan is so—well, you know how Joan is. *Her* husband seems to want to take some sort of marital leave of absence. And Karen— Karen is still trying to get out from under Joan's thumb. One romantic disaster after another. And Linda—do you remember Linda? She's still my only great-grandchild. She's nineteen now. Pretty. At Bennington. I love her very much. Let's see, have I left anyone out? They still talk about having two sets of parents. You know, Babette and Joan, born when Jake and I didn't have much. And Mogie and Josh, born—later. When they get together here, they all quarrel a great deal. I dislike family reunions with a passion."

"And Charles?"

"Oh, Charles is fine. Going great guns. He's board chairman now, but still very active in the company. I call him the elder statesman."

"Ah . . ."

"Yes."

There is a little silence, and then Daisy, her eyes wandering upward to the Douglas Chandor portrait above the mantel, says, "And there he is."

"Yes. Wearing his famous frown. I wonder why Mr. Chandor couldn't have painted him with just a *trace* of a smile. The famous philanthropist. But who knows? Maybe Jake wanted it that way. I argue with him now and then, when I'm alone in the room. I like to, because now he can't talk back. Mary Farrell caught me doing it once, and probably thought I was losing my mind."

"Whenever he was rehearsing to make a speech, he'd frown at himself in front of a mirror," Daisy says.

"Yes. You know, it's funny. The children talk about having two different sets of parents. But it sometimes seems to me as though I had two different husbands. The one I married was gentle, idealistic, romantic—dreamy, even. Then, little by little, he turned into"—she cocks her head in the direction of the portrait—"that. What changed him, do you suppose?"

Daisy hesitates. Then she says, "Well, I always assumed it was Charles."

"Charles? *Really?* Whyever do you say that?"

"Well, Charles was the gentleman. The diplomat. The peacemaker. Those were Charles's talents, but he couldn't have built Eaton and Cromwell on just that. He needed a strongman, someone tough, someone who could knock heads together. That had to be Jake, so Charles saw to it that Jake turned into that sort of person. I always saw Charles as kind of a benevolent Svengali."

"But how? How could he do that? I mean, I always knew that Charles was smarter than Jake, but—"

"Exactly. That's it. When Jake began to realize that, it put him on the defensive. It brought out Jake's tough side. He reacted like a fighter who knows he's being outsmarted in the ring, which was how Charles wanted him to react. Or at least that's always been my theory—why they made a perfect team."

"Interesting," Essie says thoughtfully. "But I never thought of Charles as being devious."

"No. Not devious. He didn't have to be. But Charles was intuitive. It was all intuition. It created that special chemistry between them."

"Positive and negative electric charges."

"Exactly. Or that's my theory."

"Funny. I always thought it might have had something to do with my brother. The way he was forced out of the company."

"But who engineered that? Charles."

"Or with me. Simply because Abe *was* my brother. That Jake could never get over that. That my brother and I came as a package, as it were."

"But it was Charles who figured out how to break up the package. And gave the job to Jake. Cracking the heads together."

"Or then, I sometimes used to think that it had something to do with a lie I told Jake once. A white lie, but a lie I know he never believed. It may not even have been a necessary lie, but at the time it seemed so."

Daisy is smiling. "Do you mean that was the *only* lie you ever told him?"

Essie laughs and slaps her thigh. "Oh, *Lord* no! One doesn't stay married to a man for fifty-eight years with just one lie!"

Daisy studies her teacup for a moment, then says, "Did you love him, Essie?"

"What a question! Linda asked me that same question the other night at the tree-trimming. It nearly knocked me off my pins."

"But seriously, Essie. I want to know."

Love him? It is a question Essie has not asked herself in years, but now, since Daisy is asking her to be serious, it is perhaps necessary to come up with a serious answer. Love him? Instead, she thinks, *I want to replace my little Prince! Tell me a story, Mother.*

But not now, Prince. I have no time!

Tell me about the little girl who fell down the rabbit-hole.

Alice in Wonderland? Ask Fräulein Kroger to read it to you. It's good for her. It helps her English. I've got to go now. Your Papa's waiting. . . .

At last she says, "Well, oh, yes. In the beginning, quite passionately. When I first met him I thought he was the handsomest man I'd ever seen. And that woman wouldn't fall in love with the handsomest man she's ever seen, when she's the age I was then, which was just sixteen? To me, he was the Other Side. Another world. Little did I know . . ."

"And later?"

"Later, when it stopped—I was hurt, yes. But not any more. One of the nice things about getting older is that things stop hurting."

"He was always a little afraid of you, you know."

"Afraid? Jake afraid of me?"

"Oh, yes. There was always something about you that he couldn't control, that he couldn't quite understand or deal with. An independence. With me, being essentially a lazy woman, it was easier. But with you—it was as though he never could be quite sure you wouldn't do something, or say something, that would overturn his applecart. Puncture his balloon."

Essie considers this. "Well, in the very beginning, I was an experiment," she says. "In those days, he was interested in uplifting people. And I suppose when a chemist mixes two alien substances in his retort as an experiment, he's never sure whether or not there'll be an explosion. Later, of course, Jake had—other interests." She laughs. "Come to think of it," she says, "he was probably a little bit afraid of both of us."

"Women."

"Yes."

Now Daisy laughs. "You're probably right. Remember when his mother died? He sat down and cried like a baby. Whether out of grief or relief I never knew."

Now they are both laughing. "Out of relief, more than likely," Essie says.

"Funny, how we can sit here like this and talk of him as though he were—just another person. Not the great Jacob

Auerbach. Or John Jacob Auerbach, as he sometimes called himself."

"But that's all he was, of course. Just another person."

Thinking of this, another little silence falls between them. Essie rises and turns on the two lamps that flank the loveseat. "Getting dark. . . ." And then, "We've talked enough about me, Daisy. Tell me about you."

"Well, after Jake died, I was at loose ends for a while. I couldn't afford the Pierre, of course, so I moved to the Village. I thought I was too old to marry, but then I was lucky. I met a wonderful man—Burton St. George—a widower, a stockbroker. I think I sent you the announcement of my wedding—"

"Yes."

"He was very good to me. He died two years ago, and left me quite comfortable."

"Good."

"And my daughter lives in Columbus. I visit her about twice a year."

Essie studies her old friend's face, thinking, Isn't it strange, after all these years, that only now would she speak of her daughter.

"Jenny married a lawyer, who's been very successful, and they have two children, a boy and a girl, and now I'm a great-grandmother, too, Essie."

"Ah."

"So, in the end, life is fair, isn't it? A fair enough deal. I have Jenny, and you have Josh."

Closing her eyes, Essie can only remember: *But I want to replace my little Prince! Please let me replace my little Prince! Please let me try!*

The room is silent for a while as the afternoon shadows lengthen across the floor.

Looking around the room, Daisy says, "The apartment is beautiful, Essie. I see you've brought back many beautiful things from The Bluff. But you always lived surrounded by beautiful things."

"Not always. But we didn't know each other then," she says. And then, "Yes, this is home for me now. Sold the place in Seagirt. Sold Saranac Lake. Sold The Bluff. The Bluff is gone—to a developer. I came back here. I was always a New York girl, you know, at heart. I was born in Russia, but New York was the only city I ever really knew."

"Do you ever see your brother?"

"Hardly ever. Much as I used to love Abe, I can hardly bear to think of him now. After what he did. But you know all about that."

"I see him from time to time. Not being part of the family, it's easier for me to forgive him, I guess. Besides, in a sense, I feel I owe him. If it hadn't been for him, I wouldn't have met you and Jake."

"Well, when you see him, give him my—no, don't give him anything. I've given him enough already."

"Arthur is—forgive me, but he was Arthur by the time I knew him—is just . . . Arthur. I accept him. My lazy nature. And not being part of the family."

"You're the closest thing to family, Daisy."

"And it was so strange. This week, when I had the note from you, I also had a telephone call from Joan. It was as though all the little threads were coming together."

"Oh? What did Joan want?"

"A lot of questions about Arthur. She thinks she's on to something."

"What sort of questions?"

"Funny questions. What color were his eyes, for instance. I told her I couldn't remember. Then she wanted his unpublished number."

"Did you give it to her?"

"I wasn't sure whether I should or not. But then I thought— why not? Because—" And Daisy reaches out and touches Essie's knee, "Because I know that Arthur will never talk to her, Essie. I'm sure of that. I know Arthur very well. Arthur may be a lot of things, but he's also a man of his word. There's no way Arthur will ever see her, or talk to her, or tell her anything."

"His unpublished number."

"She can dial it as often as she wants, he won't come to the phone. He won't even come to the phone for *me*. I have to leave elaborate messages. Then he calls me back." She laughs. "From pay phones. His pockets are always full of quarters."

Then she leans closer. "But I wanted you to know about this because, you know, Joan has always been a troublemaker. You've had enough trouble, Essie. I don't want you to have any more. So watch out for Joan."

"Thank you, Daisy. And if she calls you again—"

"She's learned all she's going to learn from me. But now, tell me why *you* wanted to see me."

Essie rises, a little stiffly, from the loveseat, and, addressing the Douglas Chandor portrait, says, "He wasn't very generous to you."

"No, he wasn't. That hurt, too, at the time. But it doesn't anymore. I understand it now. He felt I'd let him down."

"I was going over my will with my lawyer the other day, and I thought perhaps I could remedy that situation, in my new will."

Behind her, Daisy's eyes grow pensive for a moment. Then she says, "No. It's a kind thought, Essie, and thank you, but no. I'd rather you didn't."

"Please. I want to."

"No," Daisy says, shaking her head. "No, I have everything I want. A nice apartment at the Gramercy Park. Full hotel service. Really quite luxurious. Not this, of course," she adds, gesturing around her at the room, "but all the luxury and comfort I'll ever need. So, no."

"For your daughter, then."

"No. She'd wonder why. It would raise too many questions that at this point I don't feel like answering. Let the dead past bury its dead. It's best."

Essie turns slowly to face her. Having been rebuffed, Essie feels a brief moment of resentment, which she knows is quite unworthy. Then she has a better idea. "Still, I want you to have something, Daisy," she says. "Stay here. I'll be right back."

She leaves the room and goes down the long central corridor, past the paintings in their lighted frames, to her dressing room where there is a wall safe. She twirls the dial to the combination that will open it and, from the various drawers, compartments and trays that compose her jewelry case, she removes the long rope of pearls.

"I want you to have this, Daisy," she says when she returns to the library, and she places the necklace in Daisy's lap.

"These were the first pearls Jake ever bought me. I used to wear them in four loops. If you wear them as a single strand, they touch the floor."

"Oh, Essie."

"They're real pearls. They were very expensive when Jake bought them, but today, now that everything is cultured, they're only worth a fraction of what they cost."

"They're very beautiful."

"It's appropriate, isn't it?" Essie says. "That I should give you something that Jake gave me—which was very costly—and that has since declined in value? From a man who has declined in value to both of us? I think so, yes."

"Yes," says Daisy, holding the pearls in her lap, lifting them with her fingers. "Sometimes I used to wonder what all that money was really for." Essie sits beside her again on the loveseat.

Suddenly Essie laughs. "Do you remember Paris?" she says. "Remember—that afternoon?"

"Oh, Lord—yes!"

"Look at you—you're blushing!"

"I can still blush! Look at *you!* You're blushing, too!"

"I can, too—"

"We were so *naughty!*"

"Isn't it funny?" Daisy says. "Isn't it *nice*—to sit here on a winter afternoon, two old ladies, and talk about the past, and the people we both knew and loved, and remember how young and naughty we both were?" The two women clasp hands. The pearls slide, like a river of light, from Daisy's lap to the floor.

What was all the money for? Well, it was for the seven Cézannes, the five Van Goghs, the precious *L'Arlésienne,* the Manets, the Monets, the Degas, the Renoirs, the Rousseau, and the splendid Goya which the Prado had tried to buy for years so that it could be returned to Spain. It was for the Picasso room, and the Gainsborough room, and the Oriental room with the Chinese Export porcelains, and the Coromandel screens, and the collection of incunabula, and for indulgences. And it had been for the children in a day when children themselves had been indulgences, and for old friends who, when they were offered money, had the temerity and wisdom to say no.

Thirteen

———◦◦◦———

SOMEHOW, she had felt that it was essential that she lie to him. Looking back, perhaps it wasn't, and perhaps the lie had not been a very clever one, though it had been the best she had been able to come up with at the time—a sweepstakes. The newspapers were full of sweepstakes winners, ordinary people who had been elevated out of poverty to great wealth through the good fortune of holding a lucky number. It was the era of the great circulation wars, and every newspaper seemed to offer a sweepstakes of one kind or another. Suppose, she had asked herself, she simply told him the truth about her mother's miraculous savings passbook. If he was too proud to accept money from his Rosenthal relatives, who were rich, surely he would never take money from Minna Litsky, who sold *Tageblatts* on the Lower East Side. She had seen the indulgent expression, often enough, that came across his face whenever she spoke of her mother and her father. They were the Eastern European poor, whom he had once spoken of wanting to uplift, but who had resisted the Uptowners' efforts, preferring to carry their Old World ways into the New World, refusing to join the twentieth century and America. These were the people he had called ignorant, superstitious, "Medieval." No, she had been married to Jake long enough, knew him well enough, to know that it would be too humiliating to him to know that the money had come from the life's savings of a Minna Litsky.

And she could hear him asking her, "How did your mother know that I needed money? Do you mean you discussed my business affairs with *her?*" That was the German in him. He would have insisted that she return the money, that it was money tainted by the sweat of the ignorant East Side poor. And besides, she had reasoned, the whole purpose of her journey to New York had been a lie to begin with. It seemed logical to carry the deception to its conclusion.

"Now tell me again how you got all this money," Jake said, looking skeptically at the packet of large bills.

"I told you. I was coming out of Grand Central, and a man was selling tickets for a sweepstakes, and suddenly I had this very strange, strong feeling—like a vision, almost—that if I bought a ticket I would win. It was the strangest sensation, Jake. The ticket was only a dollar, and when I looked at the numbers on it—1891–1884—I realized that it was the combination of our two birthdays, and that made me even surer. The next day, in the paper, I read that I had won."

"There's something fishy about this," he said. "Are you sure you didn't wheedle this out of Uncle Sol? Because if you did, it's going right back to him today."

"I didn't see either of your uncles when I was in New York," she said, relieved to be able to tell him something that was the truth. "Should I have? I thought of going by, just to pay a call—but I didn't see or speak to either of them while I was there."

"I can easily check on this, you know."

"Go right ahead! Check all you want, if you don't believe me! Write them, pick up the telephone and call them. They'll think you've lost your mind, of course, but go ahead. I can just see their reactions when you ask them—'Did you give Esther fifty thousand dollars?' They'll think you're crazy, but go ahead, make a fool of yourself, I dare you to." Suddenly she scooped up the pile of money from the table and began stuffing it back into the envelope it had come from. "And if you don't want to use this to buy into that company that Abe wants to buy, then *I* will!" she said.

"No, no," he said. "I believe you. Don't be angry. I'm sorry."

The brief, near-quarrel had left her feeling flushed, befuddled. You've done it, she told herself; you've convinced him, don't push him any further. She put down the envelope. He was sitting in his favorite armchair, and she crossed the room to where he sat, moved behind the chair, and put her arms around him. "Ah, Jake, dear Jake, I'm sorry, too." She kissed the top of his head. "But just think, just think what this could mean—for us, but for you mostly. A business of your own. Not having to write to *them* every month, apologizing for the sales figures. Apologizing for running out of umbrellas. You know I have funny instincts, Jake. Don't forget that I'm a Russian girl—a believer in dybbuks and charms and miracles. The minute I heard about Eaton and Cromwell, my instinct told me that this could be your big chance. It can be, I'm sure of it. And now a little miracle has happened."

She came around and sat on the arm of his chair. "Because I also believe in you, Jake," she said. "Have I ever told you that? It's true. From the first day I went to your lectures. I said to myself, What is so special about this man? So different from all the other boys I knew. And then I knew the answer. It was *quality*. I said to myself, this man has quality. But I also saw something else. I've never told you this, but I also saw that there was something about you that was strained, trapped, bottled up, like the genie inside Aladdin's lamp. Rub this lamp the right way, I thought, and that genie will be released, and more miracles will happen."

"My family."

"You said that, not I."

"They won't make it easy for me, you know."

"I know. Your mother—I like her, you know that. But she has this obsession that Rosenthal's, Purveyors of Fine Men's Suitings, is something that must be passed along from generation to generation like a kind of Holy Grail. She doesn't realize that you're a man who needs to create something of his own. And here it is—little Eaton and Cromwell, waiting for you to apply your creative touch. Your personal touch." She took his hand and placed it against her bosom.

"Forgive me, but it's taking me a little while to get used to the whole idea," he said. "You know, a famous doctor once told me that I lacked—ambition."

"I know all about that."

"You do?"

"Doctor Bergler. Forget about him. There's nothing the matter with your mind. When I think about Doctor Bergler I think about a little man in a black mask carrying a satchel, crawling across rooftops to break into people's houses. When they told me about that, I said, 'I'll be his ambition.' I said I'd be your ambition until all the ambition they've bottled up inside you finds a means to escape."

He laughed and touched her hand. "You know, you amaze me, Essie," he said. "Nearly every day, it seems, you do something that amazes me."

"I've thought a lot about this," she said. "And I have just one more thought."

"What's that?"

She stood up. "Abe is—well, Abe is a jack-in-the-box. He jumps from one thing to another. He's smart, but he's always been impulsive. As for you, everybody knows that you can run a men's clothing store, but this mail-order business is going to be so different."

"I know. Neither Abe nor I knows a damn thing about it."

"So I was thinking, before you plunge into it, maybe you should get someone else's opinion—from outside."

"Whose, for instance?"

"Coming home on the train, I was sitting next to a young man—twenty-two, twenty-three perhaps. Very nice, good manners—quality. In fact he made me think of you. We got to talking. He's just graduated from the Wharton School. I think he's very bright, and just before we got off the train, he said to me, 'Let me know if I can ever be of service.' What if you asked him to look over this Eaton and Cromwell business before you finally decide to go ahead with it? I have a feeling he could be helpful. He gave me his card."

Jake studied the card. "Charles Wilmont. Well, he's certainly staying at a good address—Lake Shore Drive. No, I guess an outside opinion wouldn't hurt."

"You'll like him," Essie said.

April 17, 1913

Personal and Confidential

Dear Uncle Sol:

    Thursday last my wife came home from a visit to her mother in New York, bringing with her a substantial amount of cash which she says she won in a sweepstakes.

What I want to know is whether you or Uncle Mort either gave or loaned her this. It is important for my personal peace of mind that I have your honest answer.

Sincerely,
Jake

"Where on earth do you suppose she got it?" Lily Auerbach asked.

"Do you know anything about this, Lily?"

"Certainly not." All at once she laughed shrilly and clapped her hands. "Do you suppose the little Kike robbed a bank? I'll bet she's capable of it!"

"For our sake, let's hope she didn't," said Uncle Sol. "The important thing is, if he's come into some money, that he not be allowed to squander it foolishly, as would be his wont." He gave his sister a stern look.

"Of course," said Lily, composing herself. "Of course."

New York City
April 20, 1913

Dear Nephew:

Y'rs of the 17th inst. quite mystifies me.

Certainly none of us gave your wife any money, nor would we had she asked. The terms of our arrangement with you remain as agreed upon, with no change in the financial stipulations.

Our immediate concern, of course, is, since your family has experienced some sort of financial windfall, that the money not be squandered in some fruitless enterprise. It occurs to us, for example, that you might wish to invest this money in Rosenthal stock, which we would make available to you. As you know, our stock is sound as the dollar, and in becoming a shareholder you would not only have a financial equity in our business but would have greater personal incentive to improve our profit picture.

The book value of our stock is presently $325 per share, and we would offer this to you at a discount of fifteen per centum.

Let me know your decision as quickly as possible.

Y'rs, etc.
Solomon J. Rosenthal

"Well, first of all," said Charles Wilmont, as the four of them sat around the living room of 5269 Grand Boulevard, "Jake— may I call you Jake?—and Abe, may I call you Abe? First of all, the brains of the business is George Eaton. Cromwell's just a cipher—an ex–watch salesman who put some money into Eaton's idea. Do you know that Eaton writes every single word of that catalogue? And Eaton's got a business philosophy that I rather like. He said to me as he was taking me around the place, 'I know that honesty is supposed to be the best policy, but I like to try it both ways.' He's certainly been doing that."

He spread some notes and charts about in front of him on the table. "Now, Eaton admits that his company has some problems—people returning the merchandise, asking for refunds, dealing with complaints from customers who say the product didn't do what it was supposed to do. Let's face it, most of the stuff he's been peddling through the mails is worthless snake oil—water with a little sulfur added to give it a medicinal taste, and that sort of thing. All that would be easy enough to fix— just stick to products that are known to have at least *some* curative powers. It would be easy enough to make this company turn legitimate, and to build up customer trust.

"That isn't the problem, as I see it. The problem, as I see it, is gross inefficiency. Eaton's got about twenty girls working for him, and they're all running around doing everything at once—sending out the catalogues, opening orders, trying to fill orders. Orders get lost or misplaced. The wrong merchandise gets sent out, gets returned, has to be reshipped, and so on. There's absolutely no organization to it. Some customers pay with checks, some with money orders, some with cash, and some even with stamps. The cash and the stamps have had a way of disappearing—into the pockets, I imagine, of some of those girls. Merchandise is sent out before checks have cleared, and checks bounce, and there's no way to get the merchandise back. Also, he often puts merchandise in his catalogue that he hasn't even bought. For instance, he'll advertise a pair of reading glasses for a dollar and a half. A thousand orders come in. Then Eaton has to run around town and try to find somebody who'll make a thousand pairs of reading glasses for seventy cents a pair. It's chaotic. Now, Abe and Jake, are you familiar with what Mr. Henry Ford has been doing in Detroit, with his assembly line?"

The two nodded.

Wilmont took out a pencil and began drawing straight lines across a blank sheet of paper. "Now, what I visualize is something like that, but on a smaller scale," he said. "A simple conveyor belt system, which wouldn't be expensive to install. An order comes in, goes onto the belt. The first girl slits open the envelope. The second girl removes the order and the money, puts the money on a belt headed straight for the till, checks to see that the money and the figures on the order match, then directs the order to the appropriate department. At the end of the day, if the figures on the orders don't equal the money in the till, who's pinching it? Second girl, of course, and out she goes. Also, I can see the whole operation being done by seven or eight girls, not twenty.

"And so," he said, putting down his pencil, "that's the way I see it, gentlemen—a twofold task. Offering honest merchandise from an honestly warehoused stock, and efficiency."

Jake was the first to speak. "Very interesting," he said.

"And I think, furthermore," said Charles, "that you have a great opportunity here—to turn a fly-by-night little company into something that will provide a real service. And I think it can be done quickly and inexpensively, and that if it works within two or three years you could both be millionaires."

Abe Litsky cleared his throat. "Mr. Wilmont—Charles— would you be willing to come to work for us? As our plant manager?"

"As a matter of fact," he said, "I'd like nothing better. I happen to be a fellow who enjoys a challenge."

Essie had said nothing, but now she spoke up. "I have one idea," she said.

"Out with it, young lady."

"Most of the merchandise goes out to people in little towns—farmers and their wives?"

"Correct."

"Well, I was thinking of something that farmers and their

wives might like—just a little something different that could
be added to the catalogue."

"Essie, what do you know about farmers and their wives?"
her brother said. "You've never met a farmer, and you've
never set foot on a farm."

"Hold on," said Charles, "let's see what she has to say."

"Well, going to New York and back on the train, and passing all those little farms—Ohio, Indiana—they looked so
lonely. Acres and acres of empty fields between each farm-
house—each one so isolated. I tried to imagine what each little
house was like inside. I saw plain little rooms, bare walls. I
thought of art."

"Art?" said Abe. "Essie, you're talking nonsense."

Charles Wilmont held up his hand. "Hold on, let her finish,"
he said.

"I thought that if a farmer and his wife could have a really
beautiful picture to hang on their walls—not just cheap calen-
dar art, but a really beautiful, famous work of art by an Old
Master—a reproduction, of course—"

"Like Leonardo's 'The Last Supper'?"

"Yes," she said eagerly. "Suppose, on the last page of each
catalogue, you offered a reproduction of Leonardo Da Vinci's
'The Last Supper'—it would come as such a surprise after all
the medicines that it would certainly be noticed. Offer it, in a
pretty frame, for a few dollars—a copy of a painting that
they'd have to travel to some great museum in Europe to see—
would that give the farmer and his wife a sense of importance,
a sense of belonging to something bigger than a little farm?"

"Rubbish, Essie!" said Abe.

"Now wait . . . now wait," Charles said. He hooked his
thumbs in his vest, frowned, and lowered his chin to his chest.
"Do you know," he said, "that I like it? I like it because it has
class. That's something your company is going to need a lot
of, gentlemen—class. Lord knows it doesn't have much now.
Jake, I suggest that you make your wife vice-president in
charge of class."

April 27, 1913

Dear Uncle Sol:
   This letter is to inform you that I have decided to leave

*your employ and embark upon a new business venture of
my own as a general partner in the firm of Eaton &
Cromwell & Company here in Chicago.*

*This decision was a painful one for me to make, be-
cause it means that I will be leaving the family business.
But I am sure you know that I have never really felt "cut
out for" the men's retailing business. Though I do not
expect you to greet this decision with pleasure, it is irrev-
ocable, and I humbly ask that you give my new venture
your blessing, however reluctantly. . . .*

*I plan to depart from Rosenthal's six weeks from this
date, in order to give you time to locate a suitable re-
placement. Once you have found him, I will gladly spend
whatever time is necessary to break him in, and if I can
aid you in this search please let me know. . . .*

Esther and the children join me in love to all the family.

> *Sincerely,*
> *Jacob*

"Well, that does it," said Uncle Sol, crumpling Jake's letter
into the little ball on the dinner table. "We've squandered
enough on his foolishness, and this is the end of it. We call in
his loan, and he goes out of the will."

"Out of the will," repeated Uncle Mort.

"And yours, too, Lily?" said Uncle Sol.

Lily Auerbach said nothing.

"Lily?"

"Oh, I suppose so," Lily said, and got up and left the table.

And now it was a month later, and Jake Auerbach and
Charles Wilmont were in the small waiting room outside
George Eaton's office. The final partnership-agreement docu-
ments were stacked on a small table in front of them, ready for
signatures. The two had been a few minutes early for the
meeting, and now Abe Litsky was a few minutes late, and Jake
had begun pacing the floor, his hands folded behind his back.
"Tell me something, Charles," he said. "Do you really think I
can make something of this?"

Charles smiled. "Last-minute doubts?"

"Not exactly. But tell me something—what was that business school you went to?"

"Wharton."

"And before that?"

"Harvard."

"In any of those courses that you took, didn't they tell you that it was important to know where an investor's money came from?"

Charles made a steeple of his fingers. "When that can be ascertained, yes, it's a good idea."

"Well, you know where my share came from."

"Yes."

"From Essie. But where did *she* get the money? That's what I'd like to know."

"At this point, I'd suggest not looking a gift horse in the mouth."

"She's lying to me. I know she is. She says she won it in a sweepstakes. That's got to be a lie."

"It might help your peace of mind, Jake, if you took her word for it. After all, what difference does it make? The money's here."

"But the point is, she's lying. God knows I've wanted to get out of the haberdashery business, and God knows the money's useful. But *where did she get it?* And why is she lying to me?"

"She may have her reasons. If she *is* lying."

"But you don't know my wife the way I do. She comes from—nothing. She's a simple, immigrant Russian girl I plucked out of the Lower East Side. From absolute nothing. Pretty, yes. And clever. But where would a girl like Essie find fifty thousand dollars? She talks about a miracle. That's rubbish, Charles. Fifty thousand dollars doesn't land in the lap of a woman like Essie through a miracle. She's ambitious, yes—"

"Ambitious for you, I think."

Jake turned angrily on his heel. "Yes, and I'm getting a little sick and tired of her being ambitious for me. Trying to run me, trying to run my life. Interfering. Making suggestions like art reproductions. I'm sick of it. If anyone's going to run this business, it's going to be me. Not her. That's got to be made clear to her. Can that be made clear to her?"

"I'm sure it is," Charles said quietly. "Already."

"But now she feels she has to lie to me. Why? What does she want now?"

"Perhaps just your happiness and success. Why not leave it at that?"

"Do you think—whoring? Do you think she got the money whoring with some rich man?"

"No, I do not think that."

"Neither do I. She's a simple immigrant girl. She doesn't know any rich men, and where would she meet one? She was only in New York for a week. How would someone like Essie meet a rich man?"

"Jake, I think you should trust your wife."

"She's clever with her pen. She does sketches. Do you think—art forgery? I was reading about a man who forged Old Masters, and palmed them off as the real thing. But he did it for years. How could she forge fifty thousand dollars' worth of Old Masters in a week?"

"I agree," Charles said dryly. "She couldn't have."

"But it's got to have been something like that. Something illegal."

Charles Wilmont was smiling again. "You know," he said carefully, "I haven't known you very long, and I've known your wife only a little longer. But I've just made an interesting discovery about Jake Auerbach. It's not *how* your wife got the money that's upsetting you. It's that she got it at all. You're upset because the money came from a woman."

"I'm upset because she's never lied to me before. And now she is!"

"I also think that if you and I are going to work together, Jake, we should not be having this sort of conversation."

But at that moment Abe Litsky burst into the waiting room, all enthusiasm, rubbing his hands. "Just think," he whispered, "in half an hour we're going to own half of this company!"

From the Eaton & Cromwell 1913 Fall Catalogue:

PROBABLY THE WORLD'S GREATEST
ART MASTERPIECE
LEONARDO DA VINCI'S "THE LAST SUPPER"
Perfectly Reproduced
in color on heavy-duty board
to hang in your home

36 by 60 inches   just $4.95
(includes genuine walnut frame)

During the first few months with the new business, Jake
Auerbach was almost never home. He worked late into the
night, and through weekends, and often slept at the office.
Charles Wilmont kept the same long hours, and that was why,
one September afternoon, Essie was surprised to answer her
doorbell on Grand Boulevard and find Charles standing there.
It was a Saturday, and Essie had been drying the children's
lunch dishes, and still carried the blue dishtowel in her hand.
"Would you believe it?" he cried. "More than forty thousand
orders for 'The Last Supper,' and they're still coming in! Don't
tell Jake I told you, but I wanted you to be the first to know—"
Seizing the dishtowel, he swung it around her waist, and,
holding both ends, began propelling her in a kind of impromptu gypsy dance on the front doorstep, in full view of the
busy street. "Miracle worker!"

"Charles," she laughed, struggling in his grip, "the neighbors—"

"To hell with the neighbors. You're going to be rich!"

Sometimes, even all these years later, Essie Auerbach can
still experience the dizzy feeling of being twirled about in that
wild dance.

Fourteen

EARLY in the year 1915, most of the talk in the newspapers was of the growing intensity of the Great War in Europe. German U-boats had begun their blockade of Great Britain, and the British navy had attacked the Dardanelles to prevent the Germans, who had seized control of Turkey, from blocking supplies to Russia by way of the Bosporus and the Black Sea. In April of that year, in the second battle of Ypres, the Germans introduced poisonous chlorine gas to modern warfare, and left the French colonial troops choking and fleeing in disarray. In May, the Cunard passenger liner *Lusitania* was torpedoed by a German submarine off the coast of Ireland, and sank in less than twenty minutes, with great loss of life—1,198 souls, including many prominent Americans, among them Mr. Alfred Gwynne Vanderbilt. America, committed to a policy of nonintervention, watched all these grim events on the other side of the Atlantic with increasing nervousness, assured by President Wilson that "There is such a thing as being too proud to fight."

It was in the summer of 1915 that the two little girls—Joan, who was six years old, and Babette, who was five—set up a lemonade stand constructed of two orange crates on the sidewalk outside the house on Grand Boulevard. Essie made them their lemonade, suggested a price of two cents a glass and, at the end of the afternoon, the girls dutifully turned over their receipts—forty-two cents—to their mother.

It was in 1915, too, as Essie remembers it, that she began to notice the change that was taking place in her husband. She knew that his business was taking up much of his time, and she didn't resent that. Even at home, he spent much of his time on the telephone, often talking late into the night long after she and the children had gone to bed. She knew that the business was expanding rapidly, and that this expansion demanded his full attention. She also knew that certain differences had arisen between Jake and George Eaton, and that these differences weighed heavily on his mind. It had been Charles Wilmont's suggestion, for example, that an independent chemist be given the assignment of checking on the efficacy of some of Eaton & Cromwell's remedies, and now there was even talk of Eaton & Cromwell building a laboratory of its own. As Charles had expected, many of Mr. Eaton's cures had been tested and found quite worthless.

"The trouble is," said Jake, "that Eaton not only invented these things, but he *named* them. He feels about them as though they were his own children. When we try to explain to him that his French Arsenic Complexion Wafers won't do a thing to cure acne, that his Vegetable Cure for Female Weakness is nothing but watered-down tomato juice, that his Great Hay Fever Remedy could actually cause kidney disease, and that his Ten-Day Miracle Cure for gout has killed rats in the lab, he can't bear the idea of having to drop these things from the line. He argues, argues all the time. He says things like, 'Well, if this Ten-Day Miracle Cure won't work, let the lab come up with a Ten-Day Miracle Cure that will.' We have to keep repeating to him, 'George, there *is* no ten-day miracle cure, dammit!' He argues back, 'But you've got to admit it's one hell of a good name!' It's an uphill battle with him, every day, trying to turn this into a company our customers will trust."

All these exigencies of the new business were, Essie knew, very trying to Jake. And all this was understandable. But it was a subtle difference in tone that she had begun to notice—the tone of voice in which he spoke to her, the tone in which he dealt with his family—a certain abruptness, peremptoriness.

"Your little daughters have retailing talents, too, it seems," she said to him. "Look—forty-two cents which Joan and Babette made from their lemonade stand this afternoon."

"I don't want them doing that."

"Doing what?"

"Running a lemonade stand."

"Why not?"

"It's not dignified," he said. "And it's also dangerous. I'm getting to be well known in this town. Haven't you heard of kidnappers?"

"Kidnappers? In this nice neighborhood?"

"And that's another thing," he said, changing the subject. "It's high time we started looking for a house in a better part of town."

And another time, he had come home from the office and presented her with a small box. She opened it, and in it were a pair of diamond earrings. "Oh, Jake," she said. "How beautiful!"

She had been about to throw her arms around him and kiss him when he said, "And incidentally, run down to Field's tomorrow and get yourself some decent outfits."

Trying not to show her hurt, she said, "I don't need any new outfits, Jake."

"The woman to ask for there is Miss Marguerite. In the French Room. Just tell her who you are."

It had been in 1915, too, that he had bought his first automobile, a long black Pierce-Arrow, and, because he could not afford the time to learn to drive, he had engaged a young chauffeur named McKay to drive him. And it was true, now, that his name was often in the newspapers. In fact, she found herself increasingly relying on the newspapers to inform her of Eaton & Cromwell's fiscal progress. On October 17, 1915, for example, the following story appeared in the Chicago *Tribune:*

EATON & CROMWELL NOW NATION'S LARGEST PARCEL POST CUSTOMER

Within two years of the inauguration of Parcel Post service, the Chicago-based mail-order house of Eaton & Cromwell, Inc. has become its single biggest user, U.S. Post Office Department sources revealed today. Eaton & Cromwell floods the Chicago Post Office with an average of 20,000 pieces a day, and these figures are expected to climb as the annual Christmas shopping season approaches.

Ordinary retailers, meanwhile, complain that the Post Office is, in effect, subsidizing the growing mail-order houses, since their catalogues have been given the category of second-class "educational matter," the same as books and periodicals, and can therefore be mailed out to customers at considerably lower costs. George Smiley, for example, a local retailer, says, "What they're sending out is nothing but advertising. And yet they're given the same break as the publishers of fine literary magazines such as *Harper's*. You tell me if that's fair."

Mr. Jacob Auerbach, however, who with advertising head George Eaton pilots Eaton & Cromwell, counters this by saying, "Our postal bill runs as high as $6,000 a day, and this money is going directly into the coffers of the United States Government. If anyone thinks we're getting a bargain from the Post Office, all he needs to do is multiply this figure by roughly three hundred mailing days, and see what our outlay is."

Eaton & Cromwell, founded in 1903 by Mr. Eaton and Cyrus Cromwell, started out solely as a purveyor of patent medicines. Since Mr. Auerbach joined the firm two years ago, the company has been steadily expanding into other kinds of merchandise, including men's and women's apparel, housewares, furniture, small appliances, and gift items. Next year, the company plans to introduce its own line of automobile accessories. . . .

"Why isn't Abe's name ever mentioned in these stories?" Essie asked him.

"Abe prefers the silent partner role," he said. "Something to do with the trouble he got himself into in New York, I imagine. He and I don't talk too much about that."

At the next board meeting, Charles Wilmont brought up a matter of business. "Rothman Brothers is for sale," he said. Rothman Brothers was one of their chief suppliers of apparel. "And I propose we buy it."

"You mean get into manufacturing?" Jake asked.

"Exactly. If we became our own manufacturers in this area, the savings would be tremendous, and if we can modernize

Rothman's operations the way we have our shipping, the savings would be even more. This seems to me the next logical step, and I think we should make this sort of thing one of our long-range goals. As manufacturers become available, we should snap them up. If we could become our own jobbers and wholesalers, nobody in the country could undersell us."

"I like that as an ad slogan," said George Eaton. "'Nobody Undersells Us!'"

"As a matter of fact, so do I," Charles said.

"I can see it on the cover of our next catalogue," Jake said. "'Nobody Undersells Us.'"

Thus it was that a new slogan was born, and that the cloak-and-suit-making firm of Rothman Brothers was absorbed by Eaton & Cromwell, the first of many such acquisitions.

. Some of the newspaper stories of the era were not entirely complimentary:

EATON & CROMWELL WORKERS AMONG LOWEST PAID IN CITY; MUST TURN TO VICE TO MAKE ENDS MEET, COMMISSION SAYS

In a report issued today, the Chicago Vice Commission, as part of its continuing effort to rid the Windy City of its reputation as a hotbed of vice and crime, revealed that more than $15 million a year is derived from vice in Chicago, and that at least 5,000 women practice prostitution full or part time. How, the report asked, is it possible for a single woman who does not live at home to eke out a living on what the Commission found to be the average woman's salary of $6 a week?

"It is impossible to figure it out on a mathematical basis," the report stated. "If the wage were eight dollars per week, and the girl paid two and a half dollars for her room, one dollar for laundry, and sixty cents for carfare, she would have less than fifty cents left at the end of the week. This is provided she ate ten-cent breakfasts, fifteen-cent lunches, and twenty-five cent dinners." Her only solution, the report implied, was to turn to prostitution in her after-work hours.

Cited as an example was Eaton & Cromwell, the emerging mail-order giant, which in recent years has become one of the largest employers in the city. Eaton & Cromwell currently employs more than 2,200 people, most of these young women in its assembly-line operations, for an average weekly wage of $9.12, with the lowest wages, $5 weekly, paid to girls under sixteen and raised to $5.50 if they have lasted three months. . . .

Mr. Jacob Auerbach, Eaton & Cromwell's chief executive officer, could not be reached for comment. The Governor's office in Springfield, meanwhile, has promised a full investigation of the Commission's findings.

Reading stories like these gave Essie a very uneasy feeling, remembering, as she did, how she had marched in the Children's Strike at Cohen's paper-box factory in 1904.

"I'm certain none of our young ladies are walking the streets at night, Jake," Charles Wilmont said, putting down the paper. "That's just yellow journalism—sensationalism to sell papers. On the other hand, we can't have stories like this appearing. We've got to do something."

"Issue a blanket denial?"

"I've got a better idea," Charles said.

"What is it?"

"It's called profit sharing," he said. Carefully, he outlined his proposal to him.

". . . And you'd be the first employer to do it," Charles said when he had finished. "And one of the first in the country. Instead of appearing to be a Scrooge or a Simon Legree, or—pardon an allusion to your religion, Jake—a Shylock, you'd emerge as—"

"As what?"

Charles smiled. "The word I'm thinking of is 'humanitarian,'" he said.

CHICAGOAN ANNOUNCES REVOLUTIONARY NEW PLAN TO SHARE PROFITS WITH EMPLOYEES

In a press conference called today at the Chicago headquarters of Eaton & Cromwell & Co., Mr. Jacob Auerbach, executive head of the mail-order giant, announced a bold and revolutionary plan whereby the company's employees will share directly in its profits.

Mr. Auerbach explained that he was acting swiftly to dispel published reports that his employees, most of whom are young females, were being ill-used or ill-paid, and were forced to turn to vice in their after-hours in order to support themselves. Mr. Auerbach added that since the majority of his energies have been expended overseeing the company's rapid expansion, he himself had left the matter of payroll in the hands of his Personnel Department, and was "just as shocked as anyone else" when he read in the *Tribune* of how little his employees were being paid.

Under the new plan, five percent of the company's net earnings will be turned over to a special fund, to be shared by employees. This deduction, furthermore, will be made before stockholders' dividends are paid. The company currently employs more than two thousand workers, and already more than ninety percent of these have voted to join the plan. In less than three years, under Auerbach's stewardship, Eaton & Cromwell has expanded from annual sales of $250,000 to a figure estimated to be over $20,000,000. Since the company is privately owned by members of the Eaton, Cromwell and Auerbach families, no firm profit figures are available, but are assumed to be considerable.

"This seems to me both a humanitarian and practical move," Auerbach said. "In letting employees share the profits, we are giving each individual a personal stake in how well we all do our jobs. Each will have a stake in our growing reputation for delivering fine merchandise at an honest price. It will be interesting to see how many other employers follow our lead," he added.

"Now that you're getting to be so important," Essie said, "why don't you change the name to Auerbach and Company?"

She had been only half-serious, but he had taken it very seriously. "Don't be absurd," he snapped. "The company's

Christian names are two of our biggest assets. We don't want to be known as a Jewish firm. Most of our customers are Christian, and wouldn't like dealing with Jews. And I might add that it's not a particularly good time to have a German name, what with what's going on over there. A lot of people are changing their names, you know."

"But you wouldn't do that!"

"The Ickelheimers have changed to Isles."

"But Ickelheimer was such a funny-sounding name to begin with," she laughed.

"I was thinking of perhaps Ayer, or Ayers."

"Oh, no," she said. "No, Jake. I'm proud of being Mrs. Jacob Auerbach!"

And on a balmy autumn Saturday, he had ordered McKay, his driver, to take them all out to see the piece of property he had bought on the North Shore, outside Lake Forest. It consisted of a hundred and ninety acres of rolling, timbered land. The land rose—unusual for the area—from the lakefront and beach to a high bluff overlooking the lake, where the house would stand, and fell behind into a wide, wooded ravine. He and Essie climbed the bluff, with the three children clambering excitedly behind them, to the top where the view spilled out before them in all directions—endless pearly water to the east, where the sun would rise across the lake, and forest to the west as far as the eye could see, a magnificent panorama. Essie would always hold the picture of the five of them in her mind, standing there in the wind on that high, exposed plateau, overcoats flapping, because it would be one of the last outings they would ever take together as a family. "There's where we'll put the tennis courts," Jake said, pointing, "and over there, the swimming pool—"

"Can I have a playhouse, Papa?" Joan asked.

"Of course," he said, tousling her hair.

Climbing down the bluff to where the car waited, Essie said quietly to him, "Now that we're so rich, could I have some money to send to Mama—now that she's getting old?"

He gave her a quick look. "You'd like your original investment back? Is that it? Yes, I think that would be a good idea. See Charles about it. He'll write out the check."

And she had been a little startled, even hurt, at how quickly he had acquiesced to that. It was almost as though he wanted to forget, now, that she had ever been a help to him. But that was how it happened. Just like that.

(undated)

Dearest Mama:

Enclosed is a check for the amount you let me borrow, plus interest in the amount you would have been paid if you had kept it in the bank, plus a little more to make it come out to an even figure. You see, I don't want Jake ever to know that the money came from you—he's so proud!

Dear Mama, I wish you would take this money and buy a nice house for yourself in the Bronx, where so many of your friends are moving. Will you think of it, please? But something tells me that you won't do this, though I wish you would.

I hope now to be able to send you more money from time to time, and really, Mama, you could retire and not have to work so hard. But something tells me you will not do that, either. . . .

Really, Jake is becoming so successful! It is wonderful, of course, but still a little bit bewildering to me. . . . Jake is going to build us a big house. What will that be like for me?

The Uptown Jewish ladies of New York each had their own particular visiting days, when they placed lacquered and engraved calling cards, corners turned down, on silver trays, and amused themselves over cups of tea. Thursday was Thérése Schiff's day, and six ladies, most of whom were related to each other in various ways, had gathered in her parlor at 932 Fifth Avenue.

"Can you believe your ears?" Mrs. Schiff was saying. "Little Jakie Auerbach, of all people? None of us thought he had a business brain in his head, and now it sounds as though he's going to be richer than all of us put together—and in the mail-order business, of all things. Will wonders never cease?"

"I heard something even more delicious," said her sister-in-law Mrs. Loeb.

"What's that?" The ladies leaned forward intently.

"Lily Auerbach had a chance to invest in his business. But she turned him down, so now she's out on a limb."

The ladies laughed pleasantly at this prospect. "Whoever told you that?" asked one.

"A little bird. Actually, her butler is sweet on my cook."

"Lily Auerbach, with all her airs," said another. "All her grand Rosenthal airs. Who are the Rosenthals, but little shop-keepers?"

"Old R. B. Rosenthal was a crook. Kept his mistress under the same roof with his wife for years."

"Mr. Schiff bought a suit at Rosenthal's," said Mrs. Schiff. "The first time he bent over in it, the seat seam popped open."

The ladies laughed even more at this slightly naughty picture of Mr. Jacob H. Schiff's undertrousers exploding into view.

"Thank goodness he was at home, and not at the office."

"I wonder how Jakie's little wife is taking it all?" someone asked. "He married a little Kikey girl, you know, from Grand Street, or something like that. Lily tried to keep it very quiet, but everyone knew. He'd got her pregnant."

"Oh, I *know*. Well, from all reports, she's a fish out of water, poor thing. A babe in the woods with it all. But then, what could one expect?"

They were posing for what would become their annual Christmas card picture, which would be sent out to each of the company's employees. Its purpose, Jake explained, was to reinforce the Christian, the Good Samaritan, aspect of Eaton & Cromwell that he wanted to project.

"Now, Mr. Auerbach, if you'll just stand there, in the center, behind the chair," the photographer said. "Mrs. Auerbach, I'd like you seated in the chair. Young Jake, if you'll stand there, at your father's right, and Mr. Auerbach, if you'll rest your right hand on your son's shoulder . . . yes, like that. And if the little girls will sit here, on the floor in front of the chair, by their mother's feet. Yes, I like that . . . that's very nice." He crouched under a black cloth, behind his camera, and held up his flash lamp. "Now, smiles, everyone. . . ."

And in December, Jacob Auerbach was invited to be Hon-

ored Speaker at the annual Christmas meeting of the Chicago
Chamber of Commerce. He spent hours composing and rehearsing his speech, and then fussed endlessly over what his
wife would wear. Finally, he took her with him to Field's
French Room, where the advice of Miss Marguerite was
sought. In the end, after hundreds of dresses had been shown
and modeled, he chose a gown of pale green silk, which Miss
Marguerite said complemented Essie's auburn hair. It was a
design by Worth of Paris, and was trimmed with frills and sash
and a girdle of the same material, and its bosom was appliquéd
with hundreds of tiny, hand-made white silk roses. A green-
and-white silk headband, and a white silk fan completed the
ensemble. It cost seven hundred and fifty dollars.

At the dinner, after the last dessert plates had been cleared
away and the waiters had retired behind the swinging doors of
the Hotel Blackstone ballroom, the guest of honor was introduced and rose to the podium. "Ladies and gentlemen," he
began, "I have often been asked to account for the success of
our business here in Chicago, where I am not a native, though
where I have been made to feel like one. I could offer standard
answers, such as hard work, good merchandise, a belief in
honest pricing, and a belief that the customer is always right.
But to all these I would like to add another ingredient—good
luck.

"As I have watched our catalogue grow thicker, our range of
merchandise grow greater, our profits larger and our profit-
sharing plan accordingly grow more generous, I have always
paused to remind myself how much of this is due to intuition—
intuition in little things. Let me give you just one or two
examples. As you know, our customers for the most part are in
the modest to average income range—those hardworking people who make America great. And so the idea of a waterproof
apron came to me, made of coated cloth, which would not have
to be placed in the laundry, but could be just wiped clean. We
offered these little items in a variety of prints and colors. The
idea was an immediate success, gratifying to me because I
believed I was helping to ease the American housewife's busy
day. We sold tens of thousands of these items, and still receive
as many as a thousand orders for them a day.

"Another example. Around the time I joined Eaton and

Cromwell, I happened to make a journey on a train, and as I passed through the isolated little farm communities of Indiana, Ohio, and Pennsylvania, I was struck by how lonely these little farms seemed, so far apart from each other. What would bring the light of happiness into the lives of these hardworking country people, I asked myself? And the answer came to me—Art. The universal language of great Art. That fall, in our catalogue, against the advice of colleagues more experienced than I, I offered what was to be the first in a series of Eaton and Cromwell's Great Masterpieces—a reproduction of Da Vinci's 'The Last Supper.' To everyone's surprise, that item—at the other end of the spectrum from an apron—was also an immediate success. Since then, from this lucky start, each of our catalogues has offered a new Great Art Masterpiece—by Titian, Rembrandt, Rubens, Tintoretto—and I have had the satisfaction of knowing that I have been able to bring the joy of owning great art into hundreds of thousands of humble homes across the length and breadth of America. . . ."

Charles Wilmont, seated beside Essie at the speaker's table, reached out and touched her hand.

Now it is February, and Essie is surprised to hear from Mary Farrell that Babette is calling Long Distance from Palm Beach. It is now the height of the winter social season, and Babette is customarily much too preoccupied with her activities in that southern resort to give any time to family matters. Sensing a possible emergency, Essie picks up the phone promptly, and says, "Yes, Babette, dear. How is everything?"

"Oh, everything is fine, Mother," Babette says, "but something very peculiar is happening."

"What's that?"

"Well, I don't want you to think I'm extravagant, but I was in Cartier's the other day—"

An emergency, Essie thinks. Some emergency. An emergency involving Cartier's, of all places.

"—and I saw the loveliest pair of emerald earrings, which would be perfect with this new Dior I've ordered."

"Yes, dear."

"And, well, to buy them, I thought I'd sell a little of my Eaton stock."

"Yes, dear. . . ."

"But when I called my man at Hutton's, it suddenly seems that I don't have any."

"Don't have any what?"

"Eaton stock. It's all being held in some kind of escrow. I'm something called a 'subordinated debt holder,' whatever that means, and I can't get at my stock."

There is a long pause, and then Essie says, "Well, how did you get yourself in that kind of pickle? Where'd your stock go?"

"Well, Mother, I think Joan has it."

"Joan? How could that be?"

"Because—oh, about six months ago, Joan gave me some papers to sign. I didn't pay too much attention. She told me that it was a very complicated deal, involving several different banks, and that it would all work out—you know, to my benefit—my monetary benefit—in the end. You know, with interest and all."

"And so you signed these papers."

There is a nervous giggle from the other end of the line. "Well, yes—I did."

"I see."

"What should I do, Mother?"

"Have you spoken to Joan about this?"

"I've tried to reach her, but she won't return my calls."

"Have you talked to Josh?"

"No. Should I, Mother?"

"No," Essie says quickly. "I'll speak to him, and find out what I can."

"Thank you, Mother."

"And I'll get back to you. How've you been? How's Joe?"

"Oh, we're both fine—"

"And how's the weather down there?"

"Oh, the weather's fine—except. Except I'm a little upset, Mother. I really want those emeralds—" Her daughter's voice is now almost a whine. "I really do, Mother."

"Well, I'll find out what I can," Essie says briskly. "Good-bye, dear." She replaces the telephone quickly in its cradle, and buzzes for Mary Farrell.

And in another part of the city, in their apartment at 161 East

Sixty-eighth Street, Joan and Richard McAllister are having a rather heated argument.

"It could be the news story of the year," Joan is saying.

"But you don't have a shred of evidence. It's nothing but speculation. If we printed that, Josh and all the rest of your family could sue the *Express* for libel, and we'd really be out of business."

"That's why I've got to get to Arthur Litton, to get the proof we need."

"But you haven't been able to get to him."

"But I'm making headway, darling! I've got his unpublished number, and I've been calling every day—"

"And getting nowhere."

"No, not getting nowhere! I get a woman's voice—it must be the wife. I've left a number of messages, trying to make it clear that it may be to his advantage—his financial advantage—to see me. I think I'm little by little getting that point across."

Richard McAllister spreads his hands. "And so," he says, "what if you find out—unlikely though it seems to me—that this theory of yours and Mogie's is true? What will you do with that information? Zap the company? Zap the hands that feed you? Zap your entire family? You amaze me, Joan, you really do."

"Not *necessarily*," Joan says. "Don't you see? Once we have the proof we need, we can perhaps—sort of present that information to Mother—"

"*Threaten* her with publishing, you mean. My God, Joan. Shades of Colonel Mann."

"Who's he?"

"Colonel Mann. *Town Topics*. It was a scandal sheet years ago. He'd dig up dirty secrets about people, and threaten to publish them if the parties involved didn't pay up. I never thought I'd get involved in that kind of journalism."

Joan slams her fist down hard on the marble surface of the coffee table. "But what other options do we have?" she cries. "Don't we want to save the paper? You said yourself—"

"But to do this to your own family. Your own mother. Your own brothers and sister. Their children. Your own flesh and blood—"

"But Mother has so *much,* darling. So much more than she needs. And we need so little of what she has. What do you think?"

He is silent for a long time. Then he says, "You want to know what I think? I think it's execrable. I think it's monstrous. I think it's shitty. I think you and Mogie are both crazy. But I know you're going to do it anyway."

"And if she won't pay up, we publish the story anyway!"

"Don't say 'we,' Joan."

"It'll be the story of the year. Why, I think that even if, in the end, we have to print the story, it could get the Pulitzer Prize! Think of it! Why, we'd be hailed for journalistic bravery! Would the *Times* ever have the guts to print a story like that about the Sulzbergers? I'd be front-page news myself for having the courage to expose the corruption and the cover-up in my own family. You see, either way it works out, we win!"

"Well," he says wearily, "it's your family, not mine. You're the boss. You're the publisher. And, knowing you, I know you're going to do it anyway. But I think it's shitty, and I wash my hands of it. Do what you want. Just leave me out of it."

"Ah, darling," Joan says, covering his hand with hers. "It's good to have your support, even if it's—passive, and not active." Then she says, "Yes, I'm going to get to Arthur Litton—wait and see."

"Joan," he says, "I don't think you understand what I'm saying. You can do this if you want, but if you do it's the end of you and me."

"What do you mean?"

"Exactly what I said."

"Richard," she cries, "you wouldn't dare!"

Looking up at her from his chair, he says, "Wouldn't I? Try me."

"No, Mother," Josh is saying on the telephone, "it's not illegal. But it was very foolish of Babette. Our papa certainly would not have approved."

"But what has she done, exactly?"

"From what I can gather, Babette has signed over to Joan an instrument which gives her the power to place Babette's Eaton stock as security for secured loans—"

"For the Goddamned newspaper of hers, of course."

"I suppose. Anyway, the Morgan Guaranty Trust now has possession of Babette's stock, and Joan has a secured loan against it, and God knows when or whether Babette will ever get it back."

"And Babette is talking emeralds! Would it help if you spoke to Joan?"

"God knows. You know how she feels about me, Mother. Always has. I don't mean to sound neurotic, but Joan hates me, Mother."

All at once, Essie is close to tears. How has it all come to this? "Oh, my babies!" she cries. "Why?"

"It seems to me that it's something that Joan and Babette will have to work out between each other."

"Babette's a ninny! Emeralds!"

"And I'll tell you something else," he says. "I ran into Karen on the street yesterday. She happened to mention that Joan is planning a trip to Florida."

"To Palm Beach?"

"No. Hollywood Beach."

Essie gasps. "To see your uncle Abe!"

From his end of the connection, Josh says nothing.

"Josh," Essie says quickly. "Tell Charles to come and see me right away. I don't want to talk to him on the phone about this. Tell him to come to the apartment, just as soon as he possibly can. . . ."

Our

FATHER'S

HOUSE

Fifteen

FROM the notebooks of Mr. Horace Temple Strong, a dilettante and diarist of the city, who hoped one day—but never did—to weave his jottings into a book to be called, perhaps, "The Many Faces of Chicago"; instead, the Strong manuscripts were presented to the Chicago Public Library many years later, and they repose there to this day:

There is a beautiful young woman of modish dress, appearing to be in her middle twenties, who lately I have begun to notice from my front window on the Drive. She appears in the mornings, at about ten o'clock, more or less, walking northward, toward the Park, and perhaps an hour later she makes the return journey southward. In clement weather, I will occasionally see her pause at a bench and sit for a while, gazing out at the Lake. She is always alone. At first I supposed her to be a common streetwalker, though I wondered why she would choose such an uncommon hour to ply that ancient trade. And the more I observed her, the more I realized that there is nothing in her mien or behavior to suggest invitation, or even to encourage conversation. She does not cast glances at passing strangers, but instead keeps completely to herself, as though wrapped up in solitary revery. She seems, for all her beauty and modishness, utterly friendless in the city. . . .

Today, I decided to follow my Mystery Woman on her southward journey, to track her to her destination. Keeping a discreet distance behind her, I followed her to the entrance of one of our more fashionable hotels. The doorman, obviously

recognizing her, smiled, tipped his cap, and held the door open
for her, and she disappeared inside.

I approached the doorman and, feigning a lost acquaintance,
inquired of him, "Was that Miss So-and-So?"

No, I was informed, and was told that my Beautiful Stranger
was none other than Mrs. Jacob Auerbach, the wife of the man
the newspapers are calling "The Mail-Order King."

Jake had decided that the family should move to a suite of
rooms at the Palmer House while the new house in Lake Forest
was being built, and this was accomplished early in 1916. This
temporary move, he explained, would put him within easy
distance from the new Eaton & Cromwell offices on Michigan
Avenue, and he also felt that the hotel's staff would provide
additional security for the children, about whom he continued
to worry. It had seemed strange to Essie—simply to walk away
from the Grand Boulevard house, leaving behind all the furniture, everything they had chosen so carefully eight years ago,
but none of it would be needed in the new house. And in the
meantime, until new things were chosen, the luxury and ano-
nymity of hotel furniture would suffice. But just before leaving, for memory's sake, Essie had slipped the key to the front
door of 5269 Grand Boulevard into her purse, as her mother
had done with the key to the *alte heim*.

The move to the hotel had left Essie with very little to do,
particularly during the day. The family meals were now
wheeled up on trolleys or on trays from the hotel kitchen, and
the cleaning and bed-making and laundry were performed by
maids. The children had been enrolled in private schools,
where little Jake—or Prince—was in the third grade, Joan in
the first, and Babette in a morning kindergarten class. It had
been arranged for Miss Marguerite of Field's to come to the
hotel once a month with her sketches and her samples, to keep
Essie's expanding wardrobe up to date. During her quiet mornings, Essie had taken to walking down to the lakefront, and
strolling along the wide drive that ran along the shore, then
home again to the hotel. When the weather prevented this, she
sat alone in the suite and read. Her library of books on gardening was growing.

At least there was something to occupy her in the afternoons, when the children came home from school. They had reached a quarrelsome stage—particularly Jake Junior and Joan—and it fell to Essie to try to referee their squabbles. Jake had asked his father if, when they moved to the new house in the country, he could have a pony, and his father had told him yes. Now Joan wanted a pony, too. "It isn't fair," she said. "Jake gets everything he asks for because he's a boy. Why can't I have a pony?"

"The pony will be for all three to share," Essie said. "It wouldn't make sense to have three ponies, would it? When we get the pony, you can all take turns."

"But it will still be *his* pony," Joan said. "He'll just want to ride it all the time. He'll never give either of us a turn."

"Yes he will," Essie said firmly. "I'll see to it that he does."

"Everybody knows that Jake is Papa's favorite."

"No he isn't. Your papa loves each of you just the same."

When she mentioned their disputes to her husband, he said, "What they need is *discipline*. Good German discipline." And a few days later, a governess, Fräulein Kroger, was engaged, and Essie's duties in this category were removed.

But not long after that, Joan had brought up the matter of the pony again, and Essie had tried to deal with the subject humorously. "Joan, dear," she had said, "there's no reason why three children can't share one pony. I mean, suppose you should have a new little baby brother or a sister. That would mean *four* ponies. And suppose there were still another baby brother or a sister—that would make *five*. Think of it—we'd be overrun by ponies!"

Joan's eyes had grown very wide. "I don't want another brother or a sister!" she had cried. "I just want the brother and the sister that I have!" She had flung herself on the floor of the hotel sitting-room, beating the carpet with her fists, screaming, "*I don't want a baby brother! I don't want a baby sister! I don't want—*"

Helplessly, Essie had rung for Fräulein Kroger. "Please see what you can do with her," she said, and Fräulein Kroger had lifted the girl by her armpits and carried her, still kicking and screaming, away.

And still later, when Joan had mentioned the pony yet again—this time with her father—Essie had heard Jake say,

"Well, I see no reason why each of you shouldn't have a pony, Joan."

Today, at least, she had company, and Charles Wilmont was sitting with Essie in the drawing room of the suite, and spread out in front of them were plans—sheaf after sheaf of blueprint plans. "Most of these won't interest you at all, I'm sure," Charles said, thumbing through them. "Wiring specifications . . . plumbing diagrams . . . how the ground will be excavated . . . the construction of the foundation. Let's get to the actual floor plans and elevations. Jake wants to be sure that absolutely everything is to your liking."

Essie wondered briefly about this. Things seemed to have progressed very far before she had even been consulted. She studied the plans. The house would be in the Palladian style, of white marble, rising three stories from the top of the bluff, and along the gabled rooftop ran a marble balustrade. Turning to the floor plans she saw such notations as Vestibule . . . Reception Room . . . Library . . . Sun Room . . . Music Room . . . Ladies' Cloak Room . . . Gentlemen's Cloak Room . . . West Loggia . . . Tea Room . . . Gallery Hall . . . Orangerie . . . East Belvedere. "Oh, my goodness," she said weakly, "I had no idea . . . no idea."

"It's going to be, as they say, quite a showplace," he said.

On the plans for the second floor, she saw the designation, "Mr. Auerbach's Suite . . . Mr. Auerbach's Bath . . . Mr. Auerbach's Dressing Room." And then, across the central corridor, "Mrs. Auerbach's Suite . . . Mrs. Auerbach's Dressing Room," and so on. She saw a room set aside as Children's Nursery, and a bedroom, bath, and dressing room for each of the children.

"The architect is very excited about it," Charles said.

"How am I possibly going to take care of such a large house?"

"I suggest that we find you a good chief steward, or majordomo," he said, "who can supervise the staff. Because you're going to need staff, Essie."

"Tell me, Charles," she said, "—if you know—how much is this all going to cost?"

He hesitated. "In the neighborhood of two million dollars," he said.

"And he can afford it?"

Charles looked at her, his handsome blue-eyed face smiling slightly. "He can," he said.

She shook her head. "How am I possibly going to fill all these rooms with furniture, Charles?" she asked him.

"Well, I have one suggestion," he said. "Your architect, Mr. Trumbauer, has worked very successfully in the past, on other large houses, with a Mr. Joseph Duveen. Mr. Duveen deals in antique furniture, art, rugs and other decorative objects. If you turn it over to Duveen, everything will be beautifully done, Essie."

Returning to the plans, which included a long, winding drive leading up from the lakefront entrance, she said, "What's this little building here?"

"A guardhouse, for a sentry at the gate. The entire property will be walled."

"A guardhouse . . ."

"You know how Jake feels about kidnappers, Essie. It's a real worry to him. And for someone in his present position, I really think it is a good idea to have the entrance guarded." Picking up the sheaf of plans, he said, "Now is there anything here that you disapprove of, anything you want changed?"

It seemed to her fruitless to suggest changes on plans as elaborate as these, and so she shook her head. "No. But I'll tell you one thing, Charles. This may be Jake's house, and it's his money, and these may be Mr. Trumbauer's plans. But I'm going to be in charge of the gardens and the landscaping, and you can make that very clear to Jake for me. I happen to like that bluff, and the ravine behind it, and you can tell him that I'm going to treat the land *my* way." The words came out quickly, almost faster than her thoughts. "I've seen pictures of some of the country places of some of Jake's relatives and their friends, and my house is *not* going to be like theirs. I mean I'm not going to have statues and fountains and topiary and formal rose gardens and marble walks. The land around this house is going to stay natural and woodsy, with little paths—paths scattered with bark—winding between the trees, with ferns and wildflowers, with everything as natural as possible. No marble benches. Just old mossy rocks, or the trunks of fallen trees to sit on. No gazebos. Tell him, for me, no gazebos. I want the woods around my house to be as God made the woods to be. That will be my garden, tell him that for me."

His eyes were shining as though there were tears in them. "It sounds perfectly lovely, Essie," he said. And then, "This is what you wanted, isn't it?"

"What do you mean?"

"For him to be successful?"

"Oh, yes. Yes, I suppose so. It's just that it's all seemed to have happened so fast that it's taking me time to get used to it."

"It *has* happened fast," he said. "Faster than I ever dreamed it would. Three years ago, I would have given this company ten years to get to where it's got today. But, as Jake says, we've been very lucky—Parcel Post, reduced mailing rates. We got in at the ground floor of a little business just at the turning point when it almost *had* to become a big business. And it's going to become much, much bigger, Essie. With the momentum we have now, it's inevitable."

"Rich," she said. "Getting rich."

"And with the war coming—and it will come—Eaton and Cromwell will play an important part. I foresee—" He broke off. "Never mind what I foresee. What about you, Essie?"

"Me?"

"Are you ready for all this?"

She laughed. "I guess I'd better be, if it's inevitable."

"Essie, pardon me for saying this," he said, "but your husband is not only becoming a very rich man. He's becoming a very powerful and influential man. But you—you seem to have made very few friends here in Chicago."

"Mrs. Nielsen, next door on Grand Boulevard. But I haven't seen her since we moved up here. I guess I've been too busy raising the children and helping Jake to think about making friends."

"Jake no longer needs the kind of help you used to give him," he said. "But you can still help him."

"How?"

"Get out into the community, do things. Get involved in something. You can't let your own life fall by the wayside, just because your husband has become a rich and influential man. Of course, when the house is finished, and you start to do some entertaining, everyone in Chicago will flock to your doorstep—just to see the house, if for no other reason. But for now—if you could involve yourself in something. To establish yourself as a force of your own."

"Jake put you up to this conversation, didn't he?"

He smiled. "Let's just say that he would be very pleased if you did. He's aware that you now have time on your hands."

"Aware." She stood up, irritated. "That's just the thing," she said. "Why can't *he* tell *me* what he wants anymore? Why does he have to have *you* tell me?"

"Jake's a very busy man, Essie. Right now he's—"

"Yes, where is he right now?"

He checked his watch. "Right now, he's on a train coming back from Cleveland. He also asked me to tell you he'd be late for dinner."

"His right-hand man. That's what he calls you, doesn't he— his right-hand man."

"It's not a bad job, you know, being Jake Auerbach's right-hand man. I've done all right, too."

"I'm sorry, Charles," she said quickly, and sat down again. "I didn't mean any of that. All right, I'm to get busy. Busy with what?"

"Well, there's the opera. The museum. The hospitals. Any charity in town would be delighted to have Mrs. Jacob Auerbach on its board. And it's a wonderful way to make new friends, Essie. You'd go sailing into society, Essie. After all, you're young, you're beautiful, and, now, you're rich."

"Very well. Now how do I go about getting on these boards?"

"If you'd like, I could speak to Mrs. Harold McCormick about it. I know she'd be delighted to hear that you were interested in doing something. Would you like me to speak to her?"

She nodded. "All right. But—again—why can't Jake make these suggestions to me *himself*?"

"To be frank with you," he said, "Jake doesn't know Mrs. Harold McCormick. I do. You see, Essie, Jake wants you to be the toast of the town, but he doesn't know how to do it. I do."

She laughed suddenly. "Dear Charles," she said, "you really are the most extraordinary man—you really are!"

"*Right-hand* man, of course," he said with a wink. "And I'll be happy to be yours, too." He stood up. "Meanwhile, down-stairs in the lobby, I have someone waiting who would very much like to be your friend. Can I bring her up?"

"Of course. Who is it, Charles?"

"Her name is Cecilia Richardson. And she's the woman I'm going to marry."

"Oh, Charles!" she cried. "You never mentioned—"

"I'll go fetch her," he said. "I think you'll like her."

It was totally irrational, there was no reason, no explanation for it, but after he had left the apartment to fetch this Cecilia Richardson, Essie's heart was pounding with—what was it?—a kind of rage, almost, a kind of fury. It made no sense, she told herself. Charles had every right—every right in the world—to marry any woman he wanted. And yet he had no right. She felt betrayed. How could he commit this sort of treachery? Charles belonged to her, to them, she told herself, even though she knew, in the sense of a sane and ordinary world, that he did not. But she had discovered him. If she had not happened to be seated next to him on a train in 1913, none of what had come about would be. How could he do this to her, to Jake—bring this woman into the established pattern of their lives? And with another flush of anger she realized that, no doubt, Jake already knew about Cecilia Richardson, this unin-vited intruder. She sat, arms pressed tightly to her sides, on the sofa in her elegant suite at the Palmer House, dumbfounded at the extent of her feelings, appalled and ashamed of herself for the feelings at the same time, trying to control herself, to bring the world that seemed to have toppled down upon her back into some sort of sane and rational perspective.

When Charles ushered Cecilia Richardson into the room, Essie felt her face still hot with anger, and she rose a little unsteadily from the sofa to greet his fiancée.

"Mrs. Auerbach," the young woman said, extending her hand. "I've heard so much about you from Charles. It's so nice to meet you."

"Yes," Essie said awkwardly, disliking Cecilia Richardson instantly, and for no good reason, but knowing that she must at least be civil.

"We wanted you to be among the first to know," Cecilia

Richardson said. "To Charles, you and your husband are like a second family."

"Yes," said Essie again, and she could not avoid noticing how bright and proud and happy Charles was looking, watching Cecilia's every move with an expression that was—well, quite obviously, adoring. Cecilia Richardson reminded Essie of a younger version of Lily Auerbach—tall, slender, blonde and cool.

"What a lovely apartment," Cecilia Richardson said.

"Well," said Essie, "would you like a cup of tea?"

"I'd adore that," said Cecilia Richardson.

It was in the summer of 1916 that Jake Auerbach's worst fears were realized, and the apartment swarmed with uniformed policemen and plainclothesmen. The note had been delivered in the mail that morning:

Mr. Jacob Auerbach:
   You a big rich man, but I think you like your little son a lot. You not want him bad hurt or killed, I think. But that he will be if you don't give us $$ we ask.
   Do not call police and wait for next instructone.

"The writer of the note has deliberately written it in a childish handwriting, in order to disguise it," said the brisk young lieutenant in charge of the case. "The postmark is Chicago, but of course we don't know what part of town. Mr. Auerbach, we'd like to place a plainclothes detective here in the apartment, to monitor any incoming telephone calls and wait for the kidnapper's next message. Meanwhile, we'll take the note back to the lab, dust it for fingerprints, and see if we can trace where the paper was purchased. . . ."

"Prince is to be taken out of his school," Jake said. "From now on he will be tutored here. He is not to leave this apartment for any reason. . . ."

New dead-bolt locks and chains were placed on both the front and back doors of the apartment. Though the weather was hot, all the windows were ordered locked and bolted, on the unlikely chance that the kidnapper could scale the walls of the hotel to the eighth floor. A very blurred fingerprint was found on the letter, but it could not be identified. A detective, changed on eight-hour shifts, remained in the apartment for three weeks, but there were no further communications from the would-be kidnapper.

"Of course we must face the possibility that this was a hoax," the young lieutenant said at last.

And it was not until several weeks after the detectives had been dismissed that Essie Auerbach, who had been just as frightened and shaken as her husband, had a sudden insight. She stepped into Joan's bedroom, where Fräulein Kroger was reading to her. "Fräulein, I'd like to speak to Joan alone," she said, and when Fräulein had left, Essie closed the door and leaned against it, trembling. "Joan, did you write that note?" she asked.

Joan burst into tears. "Please don't tell Papa!" she cried.

"What a wicked, wicked thing to do!"

"Don't tell Papa!"

"I certainly shall!" Essie said. Then she immediately reversed herself. "No, I certainly won't. And don't *you* ever tell him, either! Do you realize how *furious* he'd be if he knew what a fool you'd made of all of us? Don't you dare tell him. You are a wicked, wicked little girl." She pulled open the door. "Fräulein!" she called. "Joan is to remain locked in her room, alone, for the rest of the afternoon. And she is to have no supper. She has been a very, very naughty girl."

Then, it was in December of that year when so much seemed to be happening in fast succession, that the invitation had come from President and Mrs. Wilson for dinner at the White House. The date coincided with the date Charles and Cecilia had planned for their wedding, and so the wedding was postponed a week so that Jake and Essie could attend. For days, Jake rehearsed her on the etiquette of the White House dinner.

"The President is to be addressed as 'Mr. President,'" Jake said. "When you meet him, merely shake his hand. Do not bow or curtsy. Mrs. Wilson is to be addressed as 'Mrs. Wilson,' and again, a simple handshake. The dinner, I gather, will be kept quite small because of the situation in Europe. There will be the President and Mrs. Wilson, the President's three daughters, Eleanor, Margaret, and Jessie—who, you remember, are the President's daughters by his first marriage, and therefore not Mrs. Wilson's daughters—General and Mrs. John Pershing, and yourself and me."

At the dinner, Edith Wilson had complimented Essie on her jewels, which Jake had bought for the occasion. "Those are very pretty emeralds," Mrs. Wilson said. "I imagine green is your color—with your eyes."

"All except once," Essie said. "When I wore a green dress to meet my future mother-in-law, whose parlor is all done in red damask."

"I know good stones," Mrs. Wilson said. "My first husband, Mr. Galt, had a jewelry store here in Washington."

"My mother runs a little store," Essie said. "Newspapers and candy—on the Lower East Side."

"Really?" Edith Wilson said with a warm smile. "How charming. We're just a nation of shopkeepers, aren't we, under it all?"

President Wilson had turned his attention to Jake Auerbach. "Mr. Auerbach," he said, "I've read with much interest of how you've utilized Mr. Henry Ford's production-line techniques in the manufacture of dry goods and other merchandise."

"It works as well for dry goods as for automobiles, Mr. President," Jake said.

"Tell me something," said the President. "A year ago, I was being praised for keeping this country out of the European war. Now I'm being criticized, by the same people, for not getting us into it fast enough. In a matter of weeks, we may have no choice. We have reason to believe that Germany may soon announce unrestricted submarine warfare in the Atlantic. We can't have U-boats steaming into New York harbor. If that happens, war is the only course. And so my question to you is this: in the event of war, how quickly could you turn your plants into, say, the manufacture of military uniforms and other war materiel? Soldiers' mess kits, cots for military barracks, blankets, that sort of thing."

"Mr. President," said Jacob Auerbach, "it would not take us so much as twenty-four hours."

President Wilson nodded approvingly.

"Do you realize what this means?" Jake asked her in the

limousine that was taking them back to their Washington hotel. "This means wartime contracts. This means not just millions of dollars. It means *tens* of millions of dollars, hundreds of millions!"

"Oh, Jake—but it means war."

"Hundreds of millions," he repeated. Then, quickly, "From now on, we drink and order no more German wines. From now on, Fräulein Kroger will be *Miss* Kroger. Do you understand?"

In the darkness beside him in the car, Essie nodded, and the car turned into Connecticut Avenue.

"And Essie, why, for sweet God's sake, did you have to tell Mrs. Wilson about your mother running a candy store? For sweet God's sake—*why?*"

Despite herself, tears sprang to her eyes. "She told me it was—charming," she said at last. "She didn't say *you* were charming!"

They continued toward the hotel in silence.

Sixteen

CRUSTY little George Eaton, whose field of expertise was advertising, had always been given a fairly free rein in that department, with the only restraints being applied to Eaton's tendency, from time to time, to exaggerate the splendor and value of certain products. Usually these curbs were applied good-naturedly. "George," Jake or Charles might tell him, "you just can't say that these coats for oversize women will make them look 'thin as a reed.' A fat woman in a heavy coat is just going to look fatter." But now, at the April meeting of the board in 1917—two weeks after the United States had formally declared war on Germany—the discussion had taken a more serious turn. At issue was the advertising budget. Traditionally, the company had always spent between nine and thirteen percent of sales on advertising and promotion. Now, for the coming fiscal year, George Eaton wanted to raise the figure to seventeen percent. "Hell, we've got all these government contracts," Eaton said. "We'd only be spending the government's money."

"I disagree," Charles said, "on two counts. First of all, seventeen percent is just too much to make sense from a business standpoint. Second—and even more important—is the public-relations factor. All the talk in the papers is of shortages, of belt-tightening until the Allies win the war. I think Eaton and Cromwell's first wartime catalogue should reflect this. Instead of an even fatter catalogue, I think we should present one that's noticeably slimmed down. We want to say to the American public—maybe even say it on the cover—some-

221

thing to the effect of, 'Look, we're in this too. We know there are shortages, and that's why this year's catalogue is thinner than it's been in years. Eaton and Cromwell is doing its part for the war effort, too.' Or something like that. It would give us prestige in the public's eyes."

"I agree with Charles," Jake said.

"Abe—how about you?"

"Agree," said Abe Litsky.

"That leaves you, Cy," said Charles.

Cyrus Cromwell, who never had much to say at these meetings, fidgeted in his chair. Finally, he said, "Damnit, seventeen percent is just too much. We stand to make a lot of money on this war. Why not keep the profits for ourselves? Why squander it on advertising? Yes, I agree."

"Then," said George Eaton, "I take it I am outvoted?"

"Afraid so, George."

"Very well," he said, rising a little stiffly from his chair, "in that case, I resign." He turned and walked out of the room.

"How much will it take to buy him out?" Jake asked when he and Charles were alone again.

Charles scribbled some figures on a piece of paper. "Roughly, I'd say something in the neighborhood of ten million dollars," he said.

"Christ. Where do we come up with that kind of money?"

Charles was smiling. "Actually," he said, "this is a moment I've been waiting for. We raise the money by going public—a public offering of Eaton and Cromwell stock. We're ready for it, Jake."

"You think so?"

"Absolutely. And I don't need to remind you, Jake, that with twenty-five percent of the stock in public hands, with another twenty-five percent in Cy Cromwell's, you and Abe would own half the company. You'd be the dominant stockholders. You'd be absolutely in complete control."

"That's true," said Jake, steepling his fingers and gazing far into space.

"As for me, I have only one request."

"What's that?"

"When the offering's made, I'd like to buy a few hundred

shares, at a discount from whatever the initial offering price may be. As a nest egg for Cecilia and me."

"That's not unreasonable, Charles," Jake said. "That's not unreasonable at all."

"Good. Then, if you approve, I'll handle the details."

Jake nodded. "I approve."

From the *Wall Street Journal:*

Chicago, May 5. Eaton & Cromwell & Co., the large mail-order retail-manufacturing firm, announced today its first public offering of stock. The offering will be underwritten by Goldman, Sachs, New York. The company, according to a Goldman, Sachs spokesman, posted pretax profits of $20,000,000 in fiscal 1916, and, as a result of recent Government contracts for the production of war-related goods, is expected to show an even brighter profit picture for fiscal 1917. The initial offering, of 500,000 shares, has not yet been priced but, according to Goldman, Sachs is expected to be offered in the $18 to $20 price-per-share range.

In a not unrelated development, Mr. George Eaton, one of the founders of the company, has announced his resignation as vice-president and Director of Advertising. It is expected that some of Mr. Eaton's holdings in the company will go into the public offer.

Up until now, the company has been closely held by only four individuals: Mr. Eaton, co-founder Cyrus Cromwell, Jacob Auerbach, a member of New York's retailing Rosenthal family, and Abraham Litsky. Mr. Litsky is Mr. Auerbach's brother-in-law.

After reading this item, Mr. Marshall Field put down his newspaper and buzzed for his secretary. "Get me Robert McCormick of the *Tribune* on the phone," he said.

"Bertie," he said when the publisher came on the line, "I want to ask a favor of you. Did you by any chance see the item in today's *Journal* about Eaton and Cromwell?"

"S-sure did," said Bertie McCormick, who had a slight stammering problem.

"I'm interested in this Abraham Litsky, who seems to be a large shareholder," Field said, "I'd like you to assign a reporter to find out everything he can about Litsky—his background, his education, where he came from, everything."

"B-but why, Marsh?" Bertie McCormick said. "Th-they're not considered competitors of yours, are they? I m-mean they sell just ch-cheap stuff, don't they? They're not in a class with F-Field's."

"I know, Bertie. Let's just say it's personal. I've got an old score I'd like to settle. As a favor, Bertie. Everything you can find out about Litsky."

Mr. Joseph Duveen was a small, immaculate, elegantly groomed man with a pencil-thin mustache, bright eyes, impeccable manners, wondrous enthusiasm, and a British accent that seemed as though it had been cultivated at Oxbridge, though his actual origins were somewhat more humble. Though he had not yet become Baron Duveen of Milbank, he seemed already in anticipation of the title, and he much preferred working with women than with their usually oafish husbands. Women, he had found, were much more susceptible to his impish charm and flattery, which were at the cornerstone of his extraordinary international career of selling art and other precious objects to the very rich.

"A magnificent dwelling," he said to Essie as he accompanied her through the nearly finished rooms, "Designed for magnificent entertainments, on the grandest scale, by a hostess of magnificent accomplishment—as, Mrs. Auerbach, I can see you are. This house must be filled with magnificent objects, beautiful things, for a life cannot be beautiful unless it is surrounded by beauty, don't you agree? Now here, in this room, I have recently acquired a number of Venetian pieces, which I think would be more than suitable. And on that wall, I think perhaps—yes, a Titian. As luck would have it, I have just come upon a magnificent example which the owner, a French duke, is willing to sell at a ridiculously low price in order to pay off a bothersome mistress. . . ."

"I want to keep within some sort of budget, Mr. Duveen," she said.

"Budget? Ah, dear lady, do not talk of money. Money is of

no interest to me. Beauty cannot be bought by mere money. Beauty has no price. Beauty can be purchased for a farthing, or for a million dollars. The cost of beauty is of no consequence, and should not for one little moment be considered. Besides, dear lady, Mr. Auerbach has given us—you and me—carte blanche. We will create our beauty—your beauty, the beauty which will surround your life—together, with no thought of mundane matters. Beauty, of course, is in the eye of the beholder, but what is in the eye that the beholder beholds? If that be beauty too, then the union is complete—complete and harmonious and eternal as perfect marriage, the union between great art and a great collector, an indestructible union. Now here, in this room, I happen to have some fine Louis Quinze pieces. . . ."

"I don't want the house to look pompous or formal."

"Pompous? Formal? You have not yet seen what I have in mind, dear lady. These pieces were all especially designed for a château on the Loire, and here—here, instead of the Loire, you have your magnificent lake. No, definitely not pompous or formal. These pieces are light, airy, in a way whimsical, they are like soft chords of music—dainty and elegant. They will seem to sing to you in this room, in this wonderful north light. I will order them shipped to you tomorrow, for your inspection and approval, and you will see what I mean. And against that large wall—I think not a painting. I think, instead, a Gobelin tapestry which I have just chanced upon. A magnificent specimen. Its only rival hangs in Versailles, and that, *entre nous*, dear lady, I suspect of being a forgery. The one I have in mind, and will be shipping to you for your approval, has been completely authenticated. And now, for this little sitting room, this I want to be *your* special room, and I propose covering the walls with a watered green Chinese silk I have come across, very rare, and which perfectly matches the color of your eyes."

"Mr. Duveen," Essie said, "there are a few things about me that you ought to know, if we are going to be working, as you say, together. For one thing, I was born in Russia, in a little *shtetl* which probably doesn't exist anymore, and I grew up in New York on the Lower East Side, where I learned the value of a dollar. I also learned everything there is to know about dealing with a Jewish peddler."

The future baron threw his head back, laughed and clapped his hands. "Ah, dear lady!" he cried. "I can see we are going to get along very, *very* well!"

The young newspaper reporter whom Bertie McCormick had assigned to investigate Abe Litsky for his friend Marshall Field was named William O'Malley, and at the end of a month, moving back and forth between New York and Chicago, O'Malley had learned a good deal. He had typed up his story, and was about to present it to his publisher, when he—clever and hard-working and ill-paid fellow that he was—had a better idea. Now he was sitting in Jacob Auerbach's office, and Jacob Auerbach was reading what William O'Malley had written:

EATON & CROMWELL PARTNER IS EX-NEW YORK CRIME FIGURE

Abraham Litsky, a partner and substantial shareholder in the burgeoning Eaton & Cromwell mail-order empire, has been a fugitive from the New York Police Department since June, 1912, *Tribune* sources learned today.

Mr. Litsky and an associate, Frankie ("The Thumb") Corelli, were arrested on May 31 of that year, NYPD records show, and charged with operating a large-scale rackets enterprise, which included illegal gambling, extortion, and prostitution. Released on $5,000 bond, Litsky skipped bail, and up to now his whereabouts have been unknown. Corelli was tried and sentenced to ten years imprisonment, and is currently serving this sentence at Sing Sing, the state penal institution in Ossining, N.Y. Litsky's presence in Chicago came to light last month as a result of accounts in the financial press, announcing the first public offering of Eaton & Cromwell stock, and listing Litsky as a major shareholder in the corporation.

Litsky's position with Eaton & Cromwell appears to be no coincidence. Litsky's sister, the former Esther Litsky, is married to Jacob Auerbach, the company president and, for the past four years, its guiding light. Auerbach, a member of a prominent New York family, met his wife when he was doing volunteer social work among the poor of the Lower East Side. Mrs. Auerbach's mother, Mrs. Minna Litsky, still operates a small shop in the well-known slum neighborhood. When questioned, Mrs. Litsky claimed to have no knowledge of her son's whereabouts.

Prior to his association with Eaton & Cromwell, Mr. Litsky's only known employment in Chicago was a brief stint as bartender at the Chicago Opera House.

The revelation of Litsky's "wanted" status in New York would appear to come at a particularly awkward moment for the mail-order firm. The company has recently sought, and been granted, substantial military contracts from the United States Government, for the production of uniforms, mess kits, and blankets.

Asked to comment on his brother-in-law's status with the company, Mr. Jacob Auerbach replied:

"That's what I'm here for. Your comment," William O'Malley said with a wink.

"This is simple blackmail, isn't it?" Jake said.

"Let's call it a case of wartime shortages," said O'Malley. "I'm on the short side of cash."

"And you'd even drag my wife into it. You scum. I should call the police."

"But I don't think you will, will you? The publicity?"

"How much do you want?"

O'Malley twirled his fingers in the air. "Oh—ten thousand dollars," he said. The minute he had said it, he knew the figure was too small. The story was worth more than that. But it was too late now.

"Wait right here," Jake said. "I have to confer with an associate."

"Pay it," Charles snapped. "If this story got out, it could ruin us."

"But what's to prevent him from coming back for more?"

"Stale news is never as good as fresh news. By the time he comes back for more, your brother-in-law will be stale news."

"You mean—"

"There's no alternative, Jake. Abe has got to go. Now. Today."

"Of course."

"And I think you can handle that better than I can," Charles said.

Back in his office, Jake wrote out the check. "Here," he said. "Here's your blackmail money." Then he took O'Malley's story and tore it into tiny pieces. It was an angry, futile gesture. The reporter undoubtedly had other copies and, besides, all the facts were in his head. "Now get out of here. You scum," he said. Then he sent for his brother-in-law.

"One million, two hundred and fifty thousand dollars," Jake said. "That's what I'm offering you."

"But Eaton got ten million, and his share was the same as mine," Abe said.

"Very well, a million and a half. My God, Abe, you came into this with only fifty thousand. You'll be going out with thirty times that figure—not a bad return on your investment. You'll be a rich man. You can start another business of your own."

"It's not enough."

"A million and a half. That's my final offer."

"And what if I don't accept?"

"Then I notify the New York police of your whereabouts."

"You drive a hard bargain, don't you, Jake?"

"Yes," said Jake. "I think I do."

From the *Wall Street Journal:*

CORRECTION

A spokesman from the Eaton & Cromwell Company in Chicago has advised the Journal that Mr. Abraham Litsky is not associated in any way with that concern, as reported earlier in these pages.

Reading this, Mr. Marshall Field III put down the paper in disgust.

The ladies of the Chicago Opera Guild were meeting, and

Mrs. Harold McCormick had the floor. "It's come to my attention," she said, "that Mrs. Jacob Auerbach would be interested in working for the Guild. Her husband, as you probably know, is the head of Eaton and Cromwell."

"New money," someone sniffed.

"Yes, but there is quite a bit of it, and we can't afford to pass by potential contributors. Also, I'm told that she's quite attractive."

"Well, Edith, I'm just not sure," said Mrs. Bertie McCormick, who was married to a cousin of Harold McCormick's. "There was something Bertie said about her the other day, something about her brother. No one knows what it is, exactly, but there's something a little *off* there. And of course you know they're Jewish."

"Yes," said Edith McCormick. "Well, for the time being, why don't we just put a little question mark beside her name. . . ."

At first, Essie was given no explanation for what was privately referred to as her brother's "decision" to leave the company. It was Charles who, almost apologetically, told her the reasons, and of course Essie could see the logic of it, the necessity of it. She had never really understood Abe. Sometimes she wondered if she really understood the male sex itself . . . her father, her husband, her oldest son. At times Prince seemed to her so quiet and withdrawn. Though he said that he enjoyed his school, and earned good marks in everything, there were times when a look of sadness seemed to settle on his face, a look she couldn't penetrate. Alone, in his room, he worked on model airplanes, where his tools were single-edged razor blades, scissors, pots of watercolor paint, and tubes of glue. He worked on these with great concentration.

"Is there any way you could manage to spend a little more time with Prince?" she had asked Jake in the autumn of 1917.

"Hardly. Not at this point." He was packing for a trip.

"He's ten now. All those changes are beginning to take place. I'm fine with the girls, because I know what it's like. But what boys go through? I don't know anything at all."

"Nonsense. Nature simply takes its course."

"Sometimes I think that was what was the matter with Abe.

My father paid no attention to him. He was raised by Mama and me."

He stared at her. "Are you saying that my son is in danger of turning into someone like your brother? A common crook?"

She took a deep breath. "No," she said. "Of course not. I'm just saying that if you could spend a little time with him. Talk to him. Be a father to him."

"He has Hans to teach him sports."

"But that's not the same thing. Don't you see? Hans can't be a father . . ."

"Well, I certainly don't have the time to spend with him now. Nor will I in the next few weeks. We're in the process of going public, or haven't you been reading the papers, Essie?"

"I know all that," she said. "But I simply thought—"

"I have a six o'clock train to catch for Pittsburgh," he said. "I don't have time for this argument."

"I'm not arguing! I'm asking you to spend a few minutes being a father. Even Charles manages to spend more time with him than you do—riding with him on Sunday afternoons—"

His eyes flashed angrily. "Charles does not carry the responsibilities in this company that I do," he said. And then, "That brother of yours is never to set foot in this house again, do you understand? Talk about harmful influences. I intend to maintain my reputation as a respectable member of this community."

She looked at him evenly. "But the subject," she said, "was our son."

"I'm off," he said, snapping his suitcase shut. "I'll be home a week from Thursday." He did not even offer to kiss her goodbye. When he had gone, she lifted a small Dresden figurine, a girl with a parasol, an object Mr. Duveen had assured her had great value, and considered hurling it against the wall, saw herself hurling it, heard it shatter, saw it smashed into thousands of worthless little chips and flakes of china dust. But she did not hurl the Dresden lady, whose smile was too innocent for such a fate, and, instead, simply replaced it carefully on the table where it belonged.

In the parlor car on the train to Pittsburgh, Charles said to him, "You know, Jake, with all that's happened in the past few days, I've gotten to thinking. The thing I realize is that Chicago is really still a pretty small town, where everybody knows pretty much what everyone else is up to, and where everybody gossips. It's hard to be inconspicuous in Chicago, and for you it's becoming impossible. You've become a very conspicuous figure in that town, and when you move into your new house, and start entertaining, you'll be even more conspicuous. There'll be jealousies, there'll be resentments. You'll be criticized for every false step, and everyone will be looking for false steps—for chinks in the armor, for places where gossips can stick thin little knives through. For the rest of your life you'll be walking on eggs in Chicago. Unless—"

"Unless what, Charles?"

"I think the solution may be so obvious that we've overlooked it, Jake."

"What is it?"

"It's called philanthropy."

Seventeen

∞

EATON & CROMWELL & CO. INC.

Interoffice Memorandum

From: C.W.   June 2, 1917
To: J.A.

PERSONAL AND CONFIDENTIAL

I hope you'll forgive my Christian temerity, Jake, in attempting to explain matters pertaining to your religion, but the twelfth-century Jewish philosopher, Moses Ben Maimon (Maimonides) had a good deal to say on the subject of Charity, and as he outlined it there are eight degrees, each successive degree more worthy than the last. These are:

To give (1) but sadly; (2) too little, but with good humor; (3) only after being asked; (4) before being asked; (5) so that the donor does not know who the recipient is; (6) so that the recipient does not know who the donor is; (7) so that neither donor nor recipient knows the other's identity; (8) help to the unfortunate not in the form of a gift but rather a loan or a job or whatever means are necessary for him to help himself and so maintain his self-respect.

In your new career as a philanthropist, Jake, I'm suggesting that you keep your eye on number 8.

It also seems to me that whatever focus you should choose for your philanthropy should be something utterly original, something about which no one else in the city is doing any-

thing. I am not saying that you should ignore Chicago's pet causes—the opera, the art museum, the hospitals. All these should certainly get your generous support. But I also think that the main thrust of your giving should be toward a social cause which is both deserving, and has been heretofore overlooked. When that cause becomes identified with Jacob Auerbach, there will be no one in the city who will dare to challenge your integrity.

What might that cause be?

Well, I have a suggestion for you. You may have noticed recent items in the press concerning the great influx of Negroes that the War and War-related industry has been attracting to Chicago. These people are coming for the most part from the rural South. They are unused to our colder climate. They are unused to city life. They are poor, ignorant, and uneducated. They are clustering together in a ghetto of poverty on the South Side. The conditions in which these Negroes live are deplorable. They lack sanitation, electricity, in some cases even heat. They are being exploited as cheap labor by the railroads, etc. And, beyond blaming them for the increasing rate of crime, these people are being totally ignored.

I think your thrust might be in the area of helping these people with loans, jobs, training, education, etc. We might even consider a job-training program at E & C, for Negroes.

Of course this is only a suggestion, Jake, but I think it is worth your giving it some thought.

On another matter: Did I tell you how pleased I was with our Pittsburgh performance. I believe they are close to meeting our price, and we may soon have a manufacturer of washing machines in our pocket.

Incidentally, on the trip home you mentioned your worry that Essie may have trouble coping with her new life. I would have no worries about Essie, Jake. Once she is given the room to grow, i.e., the new house, I think you will be surprised to see the bright blooms and foliage that will appear. . . .

The little town of Elberon, on the New Jersey shore, had become the favored summer watering-place of New York's Uptown German Jewish bourgeoisie. Nearby, the town of Deal was a resort for wealthy Protestants and, farther up the coast, Sea Bright had a more Roman Catholic tone. No one seemed to know, exactly, how these ethnic frontiers had been originally defined, but they were very rigid and, one summer, when a hotel in Allenhurst which did not admit Jews caught fire, a group of children from the wealthy Jewish families stood by and cheered as it burned to the ground. Elberon was also the demesne of those who supported the acknowledged, but unofficial, sovereignty of Mr. Jacob H. Schiff as Leader of the American Jewish Community, for Mr. Schiff was a great believer in the health-giving properties of sea air which Elberon, facing the open Atlantic—with nothing between it and the coast of Portugal—possessed in full measure. It was not that everyone liked or admired Mr. Schiff, exactly. But supporting Mr. Schiff's leadership was often useful. He had made himself something of an American equivalent to the Court Jew of Europe. He had the ear of municipal and federal officialdom. His services were invaluable when something was wanted from City Hall. Also, at Elberon, many of the summer residents— Loebs, Warburgs, Seligmans, Guggenheims—were not only supporters, but also in various ways relatives of Mr. Schiff.

Besides the ocean, Elberon did not offer much in the way of scenic beauty. The countryside was flat, and the saline soil did not support foliage-bearing trees, and the only plants that flourished with any reliability were nasturtiums and blue hydrangeas. Still, summer mansions of considerable magnificence had been built across this inhospitable terrain, on Rumson Road and its side streets, earning Elberon its name as "The Jewish Newport." One Guggenheim house was an exact copy of the Petit Trianon at Versailles. The Samuel Sachs house was a white stucco adaptation of an Italian palazzo with red-tiled roofs and foundations and formal gardens adapted from the Tuilleries. One Elberon house was a replica of the Alhambra in Granada, and still another was an Italian country villa with Pompeian inner courtyards paved with marble, grottoes and sunken gardens. The majority of the houses in Elberon, however, were like the one on Rumson Road owned by Lily and Louis Auerbach, and her Rosenthal brothers—of the late-nineteenth-century era when they had been built: huge, Victorian shingled affairs, hectic with gingerbread, millwork, and decorative cupolas, surrounded on all sides by open porches covered with high-backed rocking chairs that rocked back and forth all day by themselves in the offshore breezes. To restless youngsters who complained that there was nothing to do at Elberon, their parents explained that there was surf-bathing in the ocean, tennis at the Club, and horseback riding. During the weekdays, the ladies of Elberon amused themselves with lunches and teas, followed by postprandial strolls designed to work up an appetite for the next meal. Dinner parties were reserved for weekends, when the menfolk came down from the city aboard the ferryboat *Asbury Park,* on which private staterooms could be rented by the season for the journey.

It was to Elberon that Essie had been invited by her in-laws to spend the month of July that first wartime summer while, under the hovering attentions of Joseph Duveen, her house in Lake Forest was being fitted for occupancy. Jake would join her there later. The invitation to Elberon, Jake had explained, amounted to a command performance. It was a signal from Lily Auerbach, it seemed, that Essie had been sufficiently groomed and prepared to be taken officially into the family, and to meet the members of the Jewish upper crust whom her in-laws counted as their friends.

Many of the Elberon houses, she had soon noticed, were marked by the same decorative details. There were many walnut-paneled dining rooms, many parlors with plush-covered ottomans. There was inevitably a vitrine in a corner displaying a collection of Dresden figurines; a gold-fringed lamp supported by a ring-a-rosy of bronze cherubs; there was a marble-topped table crowded with silver-framed photographs of family activities—sailing, canoeing, riding, picnicking, sitting in gardens under parasols; there was a palm tree in a Sèvres pot. And at the cornerstone of every Elberon house was the collection of family portraits, relatives gazing down solemnly from heavy gilt frames suspended by golden rópes, relatives painted both as adults and as children: the little girls in dresses of black or purple velvet with white lace collars, posed with birds, Bibles, or hoops in their hands; the little boys in short trousers, Eton jackets, and patent-leather buckle shoes. As Essie was invited to luncheon after luncheon in Elberon—to undergo inspection by her mother-in-law's friends—she was struck by these recurring details.

In Lily Auerbach's drawing room in Elberon there was a portrait of Jake, painted when he was six or seven, still in long dark curls, looking pensive, with a collie dog lying at his feet. "What was the dog's name?" she asked her mother-in-law.

"He didn't have a dog," Lily Auerbach said. "The artist just added it."

It was hard to imagine Jake growing up in this stylized, mannered world of luncheons and tea parties, of tomatoes stuffed with caviar and anchovies, of Irish linen sheets, of rooms that smelled of lavender sachet, rose-petal pot-pourris, and sea air.

"He was a frail child, you know," Lily said, as though reading her thoughts. "Frail, and rather sickly. That's why he couldn't have a dog. The doctor was worried that a dog might bring in germs. Every childhood illness there was Jake seemed to get twice. Terrible bouts of whooping cough. And he was also a very shy child—with that terrible, traumatic experience when he was in the second grade. But of course he's told you all about that."

"No," Essie said. "What was that?"

"Doctor Bergler felt it helped account for a number of things. It was at the Browning School, where we first sent him. Each of the children was given a locker—you know, for their books and coats and galoshes. One day a schoolmate, we never knew who, wrote a vile thing in chalk on Jakey's locker door."

"What was it?"

"I believe it was 'Dirty Jew,' or something like that. That night—I'll never forget—he came home and asked me, 'Mother, what is a Jew?'"

Essie hesitated. "And what did you tell him?" she said at last.

"I sat him down and tried to tell him very carefully. I explained to him that Judaism was a very proud and ancient religion, and that he should be very proud to be a Jew. I explained to him that Judaism was really no different from Christianity, except that Judaism did not accept the divinity of Christ. I also told him that, at the same time, there were some Christians who did not care for Jews, and who blamed the Jews for the killing of their Christ, even though it was not the Jews who killed Christ, but the Roman soldiers, and even though Christ himself was a Jew. I explained to him that it was very important for a Jew living in a Christian world not to push himself forward, not to be conspicuous about being Jewish, not to get into arguments with Christians about religion, not to be noisy or a show-off. I told him that it was perfectly all right, even desirable, to have Christian friends. But that if any Christian appeared not to want to be friendly, he should ignore it."

Essie wondered what her father would say to Lily Auerbach's definition of Judaism.

"You know," Essie said, "I never thought you'd forgive Jake for leaving Rosenthal's, Mother Auerbach."

"It was hard, at first, to accept it," Lily said. "It was hardest, perhaps, for me, as his mother. Breaking the chain. But now that's he's become so successful, I see that Doctor Bergler's prophecy has come true. The retailing genius that was always in his genes has finally come through, but in a different way—alas, not for us. In fact, *entre nous*, my brothers and I are thinking of putting Rosenthal's up for sale, if we can find the right sort of buyer."

In a sudden insight, Essie thought: She wants Jake to buy it. At the same time, she knew that Jake would never buy it, no matter how low the price.

"Of course, one could wish—"

"Wish what?" Essie said.

"For Jake's sake, one might wish that Eaton and Cromwell—well, it *is* mass market, you see, and for Jake's sake one might wish that his company had more prestige. I mean, it isn't Saks or Altman's or Rosenthal's—or even Macy's, is it?"

"It's getting more prestige every day," Essie said.

"Yes, but you know how people talk," Lily said vaguely. "You know how people are. Now tell me about this young man who works with Jake."

"Charles Wilmont. He's a wonderful man, Mother Auerbach. Jake's very lucky to have him."

"Jewish?"

"No. Just a marvelous human being, and very smart."

"And tell me another thing, now that we're getting to be friends. Were you in love with Jake when you married him?"

"Why, Mother Auerbach, what a question!"

"I'm not trying to pry. After all, women have been doing that for years—for centuries—using marriage to get out of one situation and into another. There's absolutely nothing wrong with it. I wouldn't hold it against you if that were the case."

"Of course I was in love with him," Essie said, wondering whether she would ever be comfortable enough with her mother-in-law to ask Lily the same question, about the shameful union.

"Good. I'm glad," Lily said. "Because I'm not unaware of the help you've been to him, helping him to find himself at last. Of course, love is endurance, isn't it? It is a race against time. Sometimes I think it is fortunate that it only happens to the young." On that inexplicable note, she changed the subject. "Now tell me what you're planning to wear for Mrs. Schiff's luncheon tomorrow," she said.

Mrs. Schiff's luncheon, Essie had been given to understand, was a key event of the Elberon social season. In terms of Essie's acceptance by the little community, it was to be a crucial test, where her appearance and demeanor, and how she comported herself, would be subjected to the most exacting scrutiny. Mrs. Schiff's standards were high, and her judgments were invariably final. In fact, Lily Auerbach was so nervous about Mrs. Schiff's luncheon that Essie had decided not to contribute to this with any additional nervousness of her own. Lily, for example, had no objection to Essie's manner of addressing her as "Mother Auerbach," but she was not sure how Mrs. Schiff would feel about it. It was not, it seemed, in the customary mode of the little group. The term "Belle mère" was proposed, then rejected as too pretentious. Finally it was decided that, for the purpose of the Schiff luncheon at least, Essie would simply call her mother-in-law "Lily."

The luncheon, as expected, was a very grand and formal affair for thirty-six ladies, and was held in Mrs. Schiff's walnut-paneled dining room hung with family portraits. Over a baronial fireplace at one end of the room hung the Schiff family crest, which featured, not surprisingly, a ship in full sail. Mrs. Schiff had not one, but two butlers, the function of one of which was simply to stand at the head of the room throughout the meal and direct the service of the other who, in turn, directed the waitresses, and who announced the courses to the hostess as they appeared, in French. Mrs. Schiff herself was a tiny and, to Essie, not particularly intimidating woman, though she did have a habit of asking direct questions.

"You were born in Russia, is that correct?" she asked.

"Yes," Essie said.

"You know, my husband, Mr. Schiff, has had the greatest interest and concern for his Russian—co-religionists."

"Oh, yes. Mr. Schiff's work with the settlement houses is well known." And she added, "And much admired."

"Admired? Sometimes I wonder," Mrs. Schiff said. "He's given so much time and money on behalf of those people. Sometimes I wonder if they really appreciate it. Do you think they really do?"

"Yes," said Essie carefully, feeling her mother-in-law's anxious eyes on her from across the table, "I think that in their hearts of hearts they do. It was help, after all, that was desperately needed, and that was coming from no other source, and the people on the Lower East Side realized this, and appreciated this."

"Then couldn't even one of them have come forth—one of those hundreds of thousands who came here with no more than the clothes on their backs—come forth with a simple 'Thank you'? Even the Yiddish language press has criticized my husband. Someday, Mrs. Auerbach, you must explain the Russian mind to me."

"I don't think it's the Russian mind," Essie said. "I think it's human nature, Mrs. Schiff. Gratitude is a very difficult emotion for people to express, and it's never pleasant being on the receiving end of charity. People who need charity accept it and resent it at the same time because they hate being needy. For people who've never been needy, this is sometimes hard to understand, but I think that's where the trouble and the misunderstanding lie. The Jews on the Lower East Side are too proud to say, 'Thank you, Mr. Schiff.' But they thank Jacob Schiff in their hearts."

"Interesting," said Mrs. Schiff. "But sometimes I think I shall never understand those people."

After luncheon, the ladies removed themselves to Mrs.

Schiff's drawing room for coffee and, variously, repaired to the powder room. Returning from this natural mission, Essie paused for a moment, on impulse, just outside the drawing room door.

"Well, she certainly doesn't look like a Russian peasant," she heard one voice say.

"She doesn't talk like one, either."

"But still. Those earrings. Emeralds for lunch? I would have thought pearls would be more appropriate. . . ."

"Did Jake Auerbach—well, *have* to marry her?"

Essie stepped into the room. "Excuse me," she said. "And forgive my emeralds. I have some lovely pearls, but I forgot to pack them. And my oldest child was born eleven months after I married my husband."

Mrs. Schiff's eyes sparkled, and she threw Essie a little wink.

But this was all too much for Lily Auerbach, who cried out much too loudly, "Yes, the children! You must bring the children with you the next time you come, Esther!"

Later, in the car, being driven home by Marks, Lily Auerbach said, "It was my fault. I should have noticed the emeralds. You could have borrowed a strand of my pearls."

By October, the Palladian house on the bluff above the lake was ready to be opened. Mr. Duveen had supervised every last detail, and was already hinting that the Auerbachs should consider a second home, a summer place, on the coast of Maine, perhaps, or in the Adirondacks, for which he would have all the right furnishings. The party to open the house, because of wartime austerity, was not to be like the lavish affairs that would follow in the years to come—strolling musicians, fortune-tellers set up in little tents, thousands of Chinese lanterns lighted in the trees, circus animals for children's parties, a concert by the Chicago Symphony, and Joan's coming-out party which, because of circumstances beyond anyone's control, had to be canceled at the last minute. All those parties would come later, in the 1920s. This first house-warming was billed as a simple reception, with a hundred of Chicago's business leaders and their wives invited. Spencer, the new majordomo, had filled all the rooms with arrangements of fall foliage and flowers.

"It's perfectly beautiful," Mrs. Bertie McCormick said to Essie. "Every room a gem." McCormicks, Fields, Palmers and more McCormicks pressed her hand and congratulated her on the new house.

"Tell me," said Mrs. Harold McCormick, "would you be interested in serving on the board of our Opera Guild?"

"I would love to do something for the opera," Essie said.

"Good. Come to my house for lunch on Thursday, and we'll talk about it."

"Isn't she beautiful? . . . Extraordinary eyes," she heard people all around her saying.

"I seem to be doing better with the Christians of Chicago than I did with the Jews of Elberon," Essie whispered to Charles when he arrived.

The only difficult guest was Cecilia Wilmont, who, at one point, when the other guests were beginning to leave, accosted Essie in the entrance foyer and said, "You think you own my husband, don't you?"

Shocked, Essie said, "I don't think anything of the sort, Cecilia."

"You think you own him, both of you—you and Jake. I know all about how you found him. I know all about that little train ride."

"I don't know what you're talking about, Cecilia."

"Well, you don't own him. I own him," Cecilia said.

It was then she realized that Cecilia had had too much to drink. She had never seen a woman intoxicated before, and had no idea of how to deal with one.

"You don't own him," Cecilia repeated. "And don't go trying to steal him away from me, because *he's mine!*"

"Certainly—"

"Trash!" Cecilia said.

"Excuse me," Essie said helplessly. "My other guests—" And she moved away.

"Mrs. Rich Jew Trash!"

Eighteen

———⦿———

"JOAN, why won't you be nicer to your baby brother?" Essie asked her.

"Because everybody spoils him. Miss Kroger spoils him. You and Papa spoil him. Even Jake spoils him. Babette and I have made a pact in blood that we're not going to spoil him."

"What do you mean—a pact in blood?"

"We pricked each other's arms with a needle, and wrote it in blood: 'We will not spoil Martin Auerbach.'"

"I don't want you pricking your arms with needles, Joan. You could get blood poisoning."

"Well, we did."

"And aren't you getting a little old for this sort of thing— nine years old? Martin's just a little baby. When I was your age, I helped my mother take care of my little brother."

"I never wanted any baby brother anyway. Neither did Babette."

"It's the parents who decide whether there'll be another baby, Joan—not the other children. Just the way we decided to have you."

"We're too old to have a baby brother! Besides, *you* don't even take care of *us*, do you? Miss Kroger does that. She's more like a real mother than you are. You're never here. You're going somewhere now, aren't you? Where are you going now?"

Essie fastened a strand of pearls at her throat. "There's a dinner for your father at the Drake. It's very important. Mr. Lloyd George, of England, will be there."

"You see? You're always going somewhere. You're never home with us anymore."

Essie sat down on the bed and patted the coverlet. "Come here," she said. "Sit down beside me, Joan." She put her arm around her daughter's narrow shoulders. "I try to spend as much time with all of you children as I can," she said. "But you've got to understand, your father's a very busy man. He works very hard to give us all the nice things that we have. And I have to do what I can to help him. Like tonight. Tonight is a dinner in his honor, and he must go, and I must go with him. We have to do these things to help you children have all the nice things you have. Can you remember when you didn't have such nice things?"

"I guess so," Joan said glumly.

"Well there—you see? All these are because your papa's worked so hard. All these things—your pony. Is there anything in the world that you want that you can't have?"

"Yes," said Joan.

"What would that be, Joan?"

"Tennis balls."

"What do you mean—tennis balls?"

"Papa told Hans we couldn't have any more tennis balls."

"Joan, I'm sure he didn't."

"He did! He did!"

"Well," Essie said. "I'll speak to your papa about it—I'm sure there's a misunderstanding. Now give me a kiss, and run along. I've got to go. I'll stop by your room and tuck you in when I get home."

On their way to the Drake, Essie rolled up the glass between McKay, in the front seat, and herself and Jake, in the back. "Joan told me that you had told Hans that the children couldn't have any more tennis balls," she said.

"That is correct," he said.

"But why?" she asked. "What's the point of the tennis court if the children have no balls to play with?"

"Why? I'll tell you why. Because they are constantly losing them, that's why. They let them roll off the court into the grass, and don't bother to chase them. The gardeners pick them up in the woods weeks later, all covered with rot and mildew.

The children have got to be taught the material value of things. They've got to be taught that tennis balls cost money. They've got to be taught that money doesn't grow on trees. They think I'm made of money, but, by God, I'm not! Until they learn that, no more tennis balls."

"I see," she said.

"You may not know it," he said in that irritable tone that he now used so frequently, "we're going through a reorganization process right now—refinancing, getting ready to go back into peacetime production. The war will be over in a matter of weeks. This isn't the easiest time for the business. The children can make some sacrifices, too, damnit."

"I didn't know," she said. She reached out and touched his knee. "You used to talk to me about how things were going with the company, once upon a time—remember? You don't anymore."

"What do you mean? I just have."

She scratched the tip of his knee with her gloved fingertip. "You used to tell me things like—like how I look tonight," she said.

"You look fine," he said.

From the New York *Times:*

BOLD NEW PHILANTHROPIC PROGRAM ANNOUNCED BY CHICAGO MILLIONAIRE

At a dinner at the Drake Hotel last evening, the chief speaker, Mr. Jacob Auerbach, brought his audience to its feet with a standing ovation when he announced a new program of philanthropy, of which the mail-order magnate will be both the chief underwriter and the engineer.

That something other than the ordinary afterdinner speech was under way was apparent from Auerbach's opening question: "Why is nothing being done for the Negroes of America?"

Mr. Auerbach continued: "A vast change is taking place in American society as we approach the quartermark of this century. The war and related industry have brought hundreds of thousands of colored citizens out of the rural South into our major cities in search of employment. Where this has been found, however, it has been at the lowest level of manual labor. Here in Chicago, thousands of decent, hardworking colored folk have come to find their hopes dashed. To find the bare, unheated shanty of Georgia and Alabama replaced by the bare, unheated, rat-infested tenement of the South Side. To find a white-dominated public school system that is overworked and uncaring. To find a judicial system that is suspicious and unfriendly, and is quick to blame the influx of Negroes for a rising crime rate. And to find an affluent white majority which prefers to look the other way and to leave the Negro to his plight."

Mr. Auerbach then proceeded to announce a three-point program which his Auerbach Fund will underwrite: A program to improve the quality of education in schools in Negro neighborhoods; a program to provide training in industry for Negro adults; and a program to provide better housing for colored people.

The occasion for last night's dinner was a meeting of the Rotary Clubs of Greater Illinois.

In a hastily called press conference after his remarks, Mr. Auerbach described his newly created Fund as "unique, and uniquely needed." His initial contribution, he revealed, will be $2,000,000.

"Hans," she said, "I want to give you the afternoon and evening off. You've been working very hard." Working, she thought to herself, primarily on his muscle-building equipment.

"Thank you, Ma'am."

"And before you come back tomorrow, pick up a few cans of tennis balls, will you?"

The pale eyebrows on his normally blank, blond German face came together in a frown. He stood there, solidly and sullenly, the outline of his service revolver bulging beneath his jacket. "Sorry, Ma'am," he said finally, "but Mr. Auerbach gave orders—no more tennis balls."

"Well, Mr. Auerbach is leaving for California tomorrow, and he'll never know the difference. The children can't very well play tennis without balls, and if he wants to teach them the value of money, let him pick some sensible way to do it."

"I don't know, Ma'am—"

She smiled her best smile at him. "You take care of the tennis balls, and I'll take care of my husband. In the meantime, it'll be our little secret. All right, Hans? Hans—I think of you as Hans for Handsome. This is for you to take your best girl out for a night on the town." She reached for his hand and pressed a folded bill into it. "And for new tennis balls," she said.

One of the most popular men in Reno was a young fellow named Arthur Litton. Good-looking and glib and always well turned out, it was said that he was the young scion of some vaguely defined Eastern fortune. At Harold's Club, the croupiers liked him because, when he won, he always tipped them generously. He had been known to win as much as forty thousand dollars during an evening at the tables, and he had also been known to lose as much. He accepted his losses and his winnings with equal, gentlemanly good sportsmanship and aplomb. He had, as the gamblers say, heart, and on his arm, most evenings, there was a good-looking young woman, for whom he always bought a tall stack of chips. Lately, Arthur Litton's escort had been a pretty girl named Daisy Stevens. Daisy Stevens was then eighteen.

Daisy Stevens's story was, perhaps, a familiar one of the era when the whole world, it seemed, was determined to go off on a prolonged debauch, or toot, the minute the great guns in Europe ceased firing. The daughter of a Columbus, Ohio electrician, Daisy had been told in high school that she was pretty enough to be in movies. And pretty she was, with ash blond hair that she wore short and coiffed in a kind of helmet shape around her face, and a figure that lent itself to the fashion craze for rising hemlines. But she was not technically beautiful, with a nose that tipped up at the end and gave her a saucy, rather than a sultry look. During the war, when the motion picture companies began moving to Southern California, Daisy had followed them there, looking for work as an actress.

Her success had been mixed—a couple of roles in low-budget films, some work as an "extra," some modeling in fashion shows for Bullock's and Robinson's. To help her out, her parents sent her a small monthly check, convinced that at any moment Daisy would become a great star—she tended to exaggerate the importance of the few small parts in her letters home to them—and that their retirement worries would be ended forever. But Daisy herself was not stupid, and she knew that her acting career was turning out to be considerably less than meteoric. At the time that we meet her in Reno, she had just been dropped by her agent.

Also, Daisy Stevens considered herself a good girl. She would not, as some of her sisters in Hollywood had done, accept money from men for her favors. On the other hand, she was not above, when someone like Arthur Litton came along, accepting little gifts and little trips, and when he had proposed an extended holiday in Reno, she had quickly agreed to go along. He had taken her to Magnin's, bought her a few fashionable frocks, and they were off.

Tonight had been a good night for Arthur. A fat stack of cash lay on the dresser in their suite at the Hotel Nevada, and Daisy, too, had been lucky with the chips he had given her. They had quit about one in the morning, gone back to the hotel, ordered champagne, and now, after a very happy bout of lovemaking, they lay together in the big bed where Daisy smoked a Murad cigarette.

"You must be very rich, Arthur," she said.

"Well, I guess I've done all right."

"It must be wonderful to have all that money. Where is it from—your family?"

"The company's called Eaton and Cromwell. I'm sure you've heard of it."

"Oh, my goodness yes. You own that?"

"Used to. At least part of it. I sold out a couple of years ago. Now my brother-in-law, who owns the company—he's *really* rich."

"What's his name?"

"Jacob Auerbach."

"*The* Jacob Auerbach?"

"One and the same. He's married to my sister Essie."

"Where does he live?"

"In Chicago."

Daisy Stevens twirled the end of her cigarette ash against the rim of the ashtray she had propped on her stomach, shaping the end of the ash carefully. "I'd love to meet Jacob Auerbach, Arthur," she said idly. "I really would."

The burnished black face of the agent at the Eastern Airlines ticket counter is of a tone that might almost be described as blueberry, and with her high cheekbones, perfectly formed eyebrows, and full lips shining with blood-red lipstick, she has a Nefertiti beauty, and one senses that she knows it as her slender fingers, long nails painted the same blood-red, move rapidly about the keyboard of her computer console. Now she frowns slightly, says, "Excuse me," and repeats some process of her keyboard ritual. She frowns again. Finally, she looks up and says, "I'm sorry, Mrs. Auerbach, but the computer declines your American Express card." Her voice is low, cool and sympathetic, each syllable carefully correct.

"I beg your pardon," Joan says. "What do you mean?"

"Has your card been lost or stolen recently?" She returns the green-and-white plastic card to Joan.

"Certainly not."

"I'm getting a non-okay on this account."

"Look. Professionally, I'm known as Mrs. Joan Auerbach. In private life, I'm Mrs. Richard McAllister. Perhaps that's the mixup."

"Well, for some reason American Express is declining this credit card."

"What do you mean 'declining'?"

"Will not accept—"

"Ridiculous. Call American Express."

"Our computers are stocked with American Express data, Mrs. Auerbach."

"Do you mean Eastern Airlines won't accept my credit card?"

"It's not Eastern, Mrs. Auerbach. It's American Express which is declining."

"Well, obviously your computer isn't working. Frank Borman is a personal friend of mine. Get him on the phone."

"I'm sorry, Mrs. Auerbach. Perhaps you have another credit card. Visa or Mastercard?"

"Well," Joan says, fishing in her alligator bag, "I do think I have a Visa. But honestly, this is too annoying. This is the first time that this has ever happened. Here," she says, producing the Visa card.

"Ah," the beautiful black woman says, smiling radiantly and showing perfect white teeth. "Thank you, that's all I need." Once more her long fingers dance over the keys of her machine, and Joan adjusts the collar of her black mink coat about her shoulders. She is wearing large, wrap-around sunglasses so as not to be recognized, and to avoid repetition of an unpleasant episode that occurred on her trip out of LaGuardia, when her cab driver kept studying her through his rearview mirror and insisting that she was Rose Kennedy. And as she waits, the black woman's smile fades, and now her expression is one of utter sadness, as though she is about to break the news of a death of a close relative to a dear friend. "I'm sorry," she says softly, "but Visa also declines."

"This is nonsense," Joan says crossly. "It's important that I get to Miami this afternoon. Get me Mr. Borman."

"I'm sorry, Mrs. Auerbach—"

"Let me speak to your supervisor."

"I am a supervisor of ticket sales, Mrs. Auerbach."

From behind her, Joan hears a man with an unpleasant voice mutter something about having a plane to catch and, behind him, another young man seizes his briefcase and moves to the end of another line.

"This is preposterous. What am I supposed to do?"

"Perhaps cash, Mrs. Auerbach?" the black woman suggests.

"Oh, very well," Joan says, and reaches in her bag again, extracting her checkbook.

"Ah, I'm sorry," the girl says, holding up her hand, her expression sad again. "But I can't accept a personal check, Mrs. Auerbach."

"What do you *mean?*" Joan cries. "Do you realize who I am?"

"I'm sorry, Mrs. Auerbach, it's company policy. Not without some form of credit verification."

"I am Joan Auerbach, president and publisher of the New York *Express.*" Behind her, she hears the unpleasant-voiced man say distinctly, "Fuck this shit," and he too moves to another line.

"I could make you and your airline look very foolish in my newspaper."

"I'm sorry, Mrs. Auerbach. It's not me, it's company policy. All the carriers have the same policy, I'm afraid. Not without credit verification. Perhaps—"

"I'm astonished at you. You seem totally unaware of who I am."

"Can you pay for this ticket in cash, Mrs. Auerbach?"

"Well, how much is it? I rarely carry cash."

"Did you still wish to travel first class?"

"How much is whatchamacallit—economy?"

"The round trip coach fare is two hundred and seventy dollars."

In her open bag, Joan finds her wallet, and produces three hundred-dollar bills. "Well, you and your airline are very fortunate," she says. "I don't usually carry this much cash."

"Ah," the black woman says, and the extraordinary smile reappears. She accepts the cash, and begins again the fingerwork at her machine that will produce the ticket.

"And I must say this is all very inconvenient," Joan says. "This will leave me very short of cash until I can get to a bank."

The relentless smile continues as the crimson fingertips glide across the keyboard as a weaver might move a shuttle across a loom.

"I'm astonished that Eastern Airlines would question my credit. My credit is good everywhere. I can show you Saks, Bergdorf's, Bonwit's—"

"Eastern Airlines does not accept credit cards from department stores, Mrs. Auerbach. Nor do any of the other carriers."

"And I'm astonished that you don't know who I am. Have you ever heard of my father, the late Jacob Auerbach? He did a great deal for your people, you may recall."

The smile is unchanging. "I can give you a center seat in the nonsmoking section of the aircraft."

"I prefer smoking, please, and on the aisle."

"I'm sorry, Mrs. Auerbach, but I only show one seat remaining, a center seat, in the nonsmoking section of the cabin."

"This is absolutely preposterous," Joan says.

"Perhaps, as you board your aircraft, if you speak to one of the flight attendants, he or she may be able to change your seat assignment."

"Mr. Borman is definitely going to hear about this!"

Still smiling, the young woman hands Joan a ticket envelope and three ten-dollar bills. "Flight number two-seven-five to Miami will be departing from gate thirty-three at four twenty-five. Please be in the gate area at least fifteen minutes before departure time. Thank you for choosing Eastern, and have a nice day."

Outside, the March night is very cold, so cold that icy patterns have formed on the windowpanes of Essie's apartment on Park Avenue, but Yoki has drawn the heavy drapes snugly closed, and built a fire in the library fireplace, where the Chandor portrait of Jacob Auerbach stares sternly down at Essie and Charles Wilmont. Charles rises to refill their glasses from the decanter at the bar.

"I hope you're right," Essie says.

"I'm sure I am. I trust Abe."

"I've never trusted him!"

"It's an honor-among-thieves thing with him, Essie. He made a deal with you years ago. It may have been a dishonorable deal, but it was a deal, and he'll have the honor to stick to it."

"But Abe's an old man now, Charles. Suppose he gets weak in the knees? The way I sometimes get weak in the knees these days."

He hands her her glass. "It used to be me who got weak in the knees—remember?"

"But never for long," she says.

"You helped me then."

"Ah. . . ."

A distant siren from a police car or an ambulance whines from the street below. Some day soon, Essie thinks, an ambulance will come whining through the night for her. The Life Squad. It is a term that has come into use rather recently, it seems, and Essie dislikes it very much. It has a military ring, it sounds obscene. It shouldn't require a squad to save a life. A life isn't worth a squad in the end. It reminds her of a Riot

Squad, soldiers with nightsticks and teargas come to put down a violent rebellion. A life, at the end, shouldn't be defended with nightsticks and bombs. "It isn't so much me," she says. "I don't care—at this point—how I get judged. That really doesn't matter. But it's the other children. And the grand-children. Young Josh. And Linda. I don't want to see them hurt. Difficult as some of them may be, I just don't want to see them hurt."

"Essie, I assure you Abe will tell Joan nothing—if, in fact, he'll even see her. She's on a wild-goose chase. All the secrets are safe."

"Again, I hope you're right." A silence. Then she says, "Two. Two of them. Joan and Abe. It takes two people to make trouble. One person can't make trouble by himself. It was something Jake used to say."

"Look," Charles says, "I've dealt with Abe before. Do you want me to try to deal with him now? Call him? I will, if you want me to."

Essie consults her watch. "It's late now. I don't think we should call him this late at night. He'll think we've panicked. Never let them know you're running scared. 'If they smell your fear, they'll attack, just like a dog.'" She looks up at the portrait. "Another great piece of wisdom from the late, great Jacob Auerbach. Maybe call him—very casually—in the morning."

"Whatever you say."

She rises, a little stiffly, from her chair, drink in hand and goes to the window and parts the curtains. Outside, a flurry of tiny snowflakes blows in the wind. *Der shtrom fun menshenz maysim bayt zikh fmer.* . . .

"Charles," she says, "it's horrid out. Why don't you spend the night here? Will you spend the night with me?"

"Of course," he says.

The affair with Daisy Stevens ended, as these things usually did for the newly styled Arthur Litton, when he gave her a return ticket to Los Angeles, and announced that he would be staying on in Reno for an indefinite period. Daisy converted her ticket to a ticket to Chicago, on the theory that, if nothing worked out there, she would only be a short hop from Columbus, and home. On the train, she read with interest of Jacob Auerbach's benefactions.

"There's a Miss Stevens on the telephone," Jake's secretary said to him.

"Miss Stevens? Who is she?"

"She says she's a friend of your brother-in-law's."

Jake hesitated. "Very well. I'll talk to her," he said. He picked up the phone and answered it with a guarded "Yes?"

"Oh, Mr. Auerbach," Daisy said in her brightest voice. "How nice to talk to you. I'm a friend of your brother-in-law, Arthur Litton, and he asked me to call you when I got to town."

"My brother-in-law is not named Arthur Litton," he said.

She laughed. "He is now," she said. "He changed it. He told me you'd know him as Abe Litsky."

"What does he want? Is he in some kind of trouble?"

Daisy had not been prepared for this sort of question, and yet she was somehow not surprised by it, and knew intuitively how to answer it. "I must see you," she said.

"Very well," he said, and looked at his watch. "Come to my office at three o'clock."

At three o'clock, Daisy Stevens was in the great philanthropist's office, looking her best. He rose to greet her, but did not immediately ask her to sit down, nor did he offer her his hand.

"Tell me what this is all about," he said. "What's he up to now?"

"It's not that he's in trouble—yet," she said carefully. "It's just that I'm afraid that he will be before long."

"What about?"

"He's become a very heavy gambler. When I left him, he was in Reno. Reno is not very nice to people who don't pay their gambling debts. There could be trouble—with the authorities."

"Sit down," he said, and when she had, he asked, "How well do you know my wife's brother?"

"Very well, Mr. Auerbach."

"Are you—romantically involved with him?"

"Certainly not."

"You may get the impression that I am not overly fond of my wife's brother. This is true, I'm not. He has at times threatened to be a considerable embarrassment to us, to myself and my company. Tell me—can you control him?"

"Yes, I think I can."

"I mean, specifically, can you keep him out of Chicago? Can you keep him out of our hair?"

"I think I can, Mr. Auerbach."

"He's like the bad penny, you know, who always turns up. I never want to see or hear from him again, do you understand?"

"You need a buffer zone," she said.

"Correct."

"And you can't trust your wife to be that buffer zone."

He threw her a sharp look.

"I could provide that buffer zone, if I worked for you," she said. "Because I know how Arthur—or Abe—operates."

He riffled through some papers on his desk. "You seem to be an intelligent young woman," he said at last.

"I can type, and I can take shorthand," she said.

"And you're also a very attractive woman."

"I've worked as a model. I could model clothes for your catalogue!" She stood up and twirled around. "I have a nice figure, I think."

"Yes," he said quietly. "But it would also be very like that brother-in-law of mine to send an attractive woman to my office as part of a scheme to get something out of me."

"Oh, no, Mr. Auerbach!"

"How can I be sure of that?"

"I have a very low opinion of Arthur Litton, Mr. Auerbach. Please take my word for that."

"Well, if this is part of some scheme, out you go, young lady."

"Do you mean you'll give me a job, Mr. Auerbach?"

"I think we can find a place for you in this company," he said. "And I also think that you have some reason for wanting to even a score with this man who calls himself Arthur Litton."

Daisy smiled. "That's true," she said.

"So do I," he said. "In which case, we ought to get on very well."

And so Daisy Stevens came into the lives of the little family, in the role of one of Jacob Auerbach's secretaries.

*   *   *

Essie had never inquired much about what other women there might have been in Jake's life before he and she had met, though she was certain there had been several. His expertise on their wedding night had been demonstration enough of that. It was not that she wasn't curious about who these women might have been, and what they looked like. And she occasionally tried to picture Jake in bed with another woman, or a series of faceless creatures. It was an era, after all, of a double standard, where young women were expected to be chaste and virginal, and where young men were expected to be just the opposite. It was also an era when things that happened at night were never discussed in daylight. Essie's own grasp of the facts of life, learned from her mother and from other girls her age, had been, until her marriage, very sketchy and vague. All she had really known was that terrible, crippling diseases came from intimate relations with a man who was not your husband. And yet young men, after being given the same lectures about venereal diseases, were routinely taken by their fathers to visit prostitutes, to be taught by experts in the ancient art of sex.

Jake's mother had alluded, obliquely, to earlier romantic attachments of Jake's. They had been, Essie gathered, intense, but rather short-lived. It had all been a part of what Lily Auerbach—and her son's alienist—had seen as her son's tendency toward indecisiveness, his inability to stick to any one thing, to follow through. "He had a pattern of starts and stops," Lily had once said. "He'd be terribly enthusiastic about something, or some person, one minute, and then completely lose interest in the next. He was always coming home saying, 'I've met the girl I'm going to marry!' Two weeks later, we'd ask about her, and he'd have forgotten her name. I really began to wonder whether he'd ever marry. When he said he wanted to marry you, I confess that I assumed that this was just another of his passing fancies. Well, I was wrong.

"I must say this for you, Essie," Lily had said. "You've made him reverse that pattern. You made him grow up at last."

"Bear in Garia," Babette kept repeating, sitting on the blue chaise longue in her mother's bedroom, dressing and undressing one of her dolls. "Bear in Garia. There is a bear in Garia."

"The *Berengeria*," Essie said. "That's the boat your papa and I are taking to Europe next month."

"Why are you going?"

"Because the war is over, and people are traveling again. And because I was so little when I left Europe that I can't remember it. And because your papa hasn't been since he was a little boy, and there are all sorts of places we want to visit." She sat in front of her mirror, pinning up her hair.

"Why can't I go too, Mama?"

"Because you're too little, and because you and Joan are going to a wonderful camp in Maine for the summer, where there'll be canoes and sailboats and horses and hikes, and where you'll have a wonderful time."

"Will Jake get to go on the Bear in Garia?"

"Hans is taking Jake to a ranch in Wyoming, where he'll learn all about pioneering days in the West."

"I suppose that brat Martin gets to go."

"No, silly. He's much too little. He'll stay right here with Miss Kroger. Don't worry, when you're all older you'll all have trips to Europe."

"Are you going to Russia, where you were born?"

"No. They've had a revolution there. The Reds run Russia now, and they want to take over the whole world, which Americans don't want them to do."

"Where will you go, then?"

"Let's see. England, Holland, Belgium, France, Germany, Austria, and Italy—I think that's the way your papa's planned it. I'll send you letters from every place, and tell you all about it."

"Bear in Garia," Babette repeated. "I want to go on the Bear in Garia."

From the society columns:

Mr. and Mrs. Robert Rutherford McCormick entertained at a small dinner dance last night in honor of their friends Mr. and Mrs. John Jacob Auerbach, who will soon depart for New York to sail to Europe for the summer. For the occasion, the dancing tent, set up on the lawn of the McCormicks' Lake Forest estate, was decked out in a nautical theme, with sailing burgees, papier-mâché life preservers, and a bandstand built to resemble a ship's prow. . . . Mrs. John Jacob Auerbach, whose green eyes are almost as famous in Chicago as her big green emeralds, wore a gown of palest blue moire, with a chiffon overskirt. A pair of white orchids in her russet hair completed the ensemble. . . .

"Oh, dear, they got your name wrong," Essie said, putting down the paper. "They call you John Jacob Auerbach all through the story. How silly."

"No," Jake said carefully. "That is the appellation I have chosen for myself. I've always missed having a middle name, and so, by taking John as a first name, Jacob will become my middle name."

"What? Am I to start calling you John?"

"If you wish," he said.

"*John*," she said. "Is that because it's a *Christian* name? Is this part of your campaign to make people forget you're a Jew? Saint John the Divine?" Suddenly she laughed. "Or are you trying to confuse yourself with John Jacob Astor?"

"I hardly think any of this talk is appropriate," he said. "When are you going to grow up and stop acting like a stupid schoolgirl?"

All at once she was very angry. She flung the newspaper to the floor and stood up to face him. "Hypocrite!" she said. "You hypocrite! For the last six years I've watched you turning into a hypocrite, and I'm disgusted with the sight I see! John Jacob Auerbach, you are a hypocrite and a fake!"

"Essie, please control yourself. The servants—"

"You—the great philanthropist, the great humanitarian. Don't you think I see through that? It's nothing but sham and show and courting the public and the newspapers. You don't care about the Negroes any more than you care about the Italians or the Jews, except that you'd like them to have enough money to be Eaton customers. Don't you think I saw through that from the beginning?"

"Essie, that is an out-and-out lie."

"John Jacob Auerbach. All over this city, people must be laughing at you behind your back."

"That's another lie."

"Oh, they wouldn't dare let you know, of course. You're much too rich—much too powerful. They'll fuss over you, invite you to their parties, but they'll sneer at you the moment your back is turned. And what is it you want, I ask myself? Is it to prove to your mother and your uncles, who for years tried to convince you that you were a weakling—the runt of the litter, that's what they told me you were—that you're more powerful than any of them, the great John Jacob Auerbach, friend of Presidents? Is that it?"

"Essie, you're crazy."

"For the last six years I've watched your ego grow, being fed in all directions by the toadies and the yes-men telling you how great you are. I've watched your ego grow and fatten, and it hasn't been a pretty sight. And while we're on the subject, Mr. John Jacob Auerbach, have you stood in front of a mirror lately or stepped on the bathroom scales? You must have put on at least forty pounds since the day I met you, and it's not a bit becoming. It makes you look even more pompous than you are—if that's possible."

"I will not dignify these remarks with comment."

"No, of course not, because nobody will ever tell you anything you don't want to hear—they wouldn't dare—except me. And what about me? You seem to have conveniently forgotten that I was the one who came up with the money you needed to buy into this business. Charles remembers it, but you've managed to forget. Where would you be if it hadn't been for me, I wonder? Still on Grand Boulevard. I think I'll call one of your famous press conferences, and tell them the whole story."

"Essie, you wouldn't dare."

"That's what you're afraid of, isn't it? That someone will find out the truth. About you. About Abe. About me."

"Essie, I am going to endeavor to forget this hysterical outburst," he said.

"Of course. Of course you'll forget it. Just as you've forgotten everything else that was our lives. Hypocrite."

He slapped her hard across the face.

She stood there, staring at him, her eyes clear. "That didn't hurt," she said. "Do it again."

He turned away from her, muttering, "Crazy Russian . . . crazy Kike. That's what they told me I'd be getting. I should have listened to them."

"Yes," she said. "You should have listened to them. And so should I."

Yet another gala in the festive round of parties to wish "Bon Voyage" to Mr. and Mrs. John Jacob Auerbach, who sail for Europe on the 14th, took place yesterday evening. This time, the venue of the occasion was the North Shore residence of Mr. and Mrs. Levi Leiter, where some 200 bedizened invitees gaily gathered to bid "Adieu" and "A bientôt" to the happy and popular pair. . . .

Accompanying the Auerbachs aboard the S.S. *Berengeria* will be Mrs. Auerbach's personal maid, Mr. Auerbach's valet, and Miss Stevens, a private secretary, who will form their retinue during the European sojourn.

Nineteen

"WHAT has happened to you is what happens to all women," her mother said to her when she went down to Norfolk Street to see her the day before the sailing. "The loves goes. It doesn't last—the love part. It's just as well. The love part just gets in the way of seeing things as they really are. It's not to worry about. A good marriage doesn't need all that love—you'll see. I found it out a long time ago, and you'll find it out too before too long."

"You wouldn't—divorce him, Mama?"

Minna shrugged. "Divorce? What's the point of that? What does that get you besides a lot of heartaches? You make a life. He gave you four fine children—two boys, two girls, that's perfect. He gives you everything you want. He's a big success, and you can have anything you want—a big house, big cars. How can you complain? He doesn't hit you. I read all about Jacob Auerbach in the newspapers. Even the *Tageblatt* writes about him. He's a big man, a *makher*. So don't talk divorce— that's *narishkeit*, foolishness. So what you do is, you make a life."

"I'm so unhappy, Mama."

"So—happy? Who's happy? Show me a woman in this life who's happy, and I'll show you a woman without a brain. You've got a brain, Esther, so use it to make a life for yourself. If you complain, all that will happen is he'll find himself another woman who doesn't complain. Forget the love part, and you'll find that once it's gone it's like a blessing. And you've got your new little son, Martin. You should be giving yourself to him."

"Didn't you love Papa, Mama?"

"Love him? Ha. I hardly knew him. But oh, yes, I loved him for a while. He was never bad to me."

"I mean—passionately?"

"Passion? Well, I gave him two children, if that's what you mean by passion."

"With me—in the beginning—it felt like a kind of passion," Essie said.

"Well, that's the first thing to go, even before the love part," her mother said.

"I feel I've lost everything."

"So sit around and feel sorry for yourself—what will that get you beside gray hairs? Have you heard anything I've just said to you, Esther? I've said you've got to make a life—for yourself. Get out. Get busy. Do something. Get to work. Then your troubles will blow over like a thunderstorm."

"But I can't run a business, Mama. He'd never let me go to work like that."

"Listen," her mother said, "there are plenty of ways for a woman to get to work without running a candy store. Look— you're the high society lady now, not me. Don't turn to me and ask what sort of things a high society lady can do—all I know is what I read about them in the papers. Just look around you, find something for yourself to do, and start doing it. That's the way to make a life."

Essie looked around her at the little shop, which seemed so much tinier and more crowded than she had remembered it, even though, she realized, it was just the same. "Mama, I wish you'd let us move you out to a nice house in the country—in Westchester, maybe, or Long Island."

"No, no," her mother said. "What would I do in the country? Listen to the birds? No, this is my place. I know the neighborhood is changing—the *shwartzes* have come. But they don't give me any trouble. They only make trouble with each other."

Essie paused. "How is Papa?" she asked.

"The same. He never changes."

"Please give him my love."

Her mother nodded. "You see," she said, "I made a life for myself—here. My life is here."

It had to be admitted that Daisy Stevens was good company. It soon became clear that Jake Auerbach's reasons for the European tour were business ones—to establish markets and distribution points for Eaton & Cromwell products in postwar Europe. This meant that Essie and Daisy had most of their days to themselves, and many of their evenings as well, and they enjoyed each other's company from the beginning. Essie had never really had a close woman friend before, and she found the experience refreshing and stimulating. It cleared the air of her life in ways that she had never imagined. Daisy, who had had four years of high school French, was determined to practice the language, and was equally determined to pass on her knowledge to Essie, and one of their purchases in Paris had been an English-French dictionary and phrase book.

Also, though Daisy had never been outside the continental United States before, she knew a good deal about Paris. During her Hollywood days, it seemed, she had picked up stray bits of information about the city, and had made mental notes of all of them. She was also clever at extracting interesting tips from hotel clerks, doormen, and taxi drivers. She had heard, for example, of a young French peasant woman named Gabrielle Chanel who had come to Paris and was revolutionizing fashion. She insisted that she and Essie visit Chanel's atelier on the rue Cambon, where they both bought a number of outfits designed to be worn with ropes of pears and golden chains. She had heard of a group of young artists who were exhibiting on the Left Bank and who called themselves, variously, Post-Impressionists and Expressionists. Their names were Matisse, Braque, Derain, Léger, and a young Spaniard named Pablo Picasso, and their work, too, was considered daring and controversial.

"But do you think—for Chicago?" Essie asked her.

"Definitely," said Daisy. "Chicago won't understand any of it, of course. But if you start hanging these painters on your walls, you'll be the talk of the town. And they're so cheap. I'd buy as many as you can afford."

And so, as they toured the exhibitions, Essie bought—not indiscriminately, as Daisy would have preferred her to do, but selectively. "I want to get my 'eye in' first," Essie kept reminding her. They toured galleries and museums, went to the opera and the ballet, and in between sat in restaurants or in cafés over glasses of wine and sparkling water, practicing their French.

Not all their pursuits in Paris were strictly cultural.

One afternoon Daisy tapped on the door of Essie's suite at the Ritz, where the Auerbach party was staying. "Today," Daisy said in a whisper when Essie let her in, "we are going to have an adventure."

"What is it?"

"You'll see. But we must go in heavy disguise. Here," she said, "I've bought us both sunglasses. Tie your hair up in a scarf, and put on your plainest, simplest dress. We mustn't be recognized. We mustn't look like rich Americans—just ordinary tourists. And don't bring much money."

Then, armed with a street map of the city, Daisy led them a few blocks away to the rue Ste. Anne, and to a little alleyway where a doorway led to a flight of stairs. "This is the place," Daisy whispered, and checked her watch, "and we're right on time."

At the top of the stairway, there was an attendant who collected a few francs from each of them, opened a curtain, and ushered them into a very dark room where he showed them to two hard chairs. When her eyes became accustomed to the dark, Essie realized that she was in a smallish auditorium with a curtained stage in front, and that all around them sat other people, most of whom seemed to be men.

"What's going on?" Essie whispered.

"Ssh. Wait and see."

And after a little time, the curtain parted and the proscenium lights went up. The stage was bare. Then, from either side of the stage, a figure appeared. The first was a naked woman, and the second was a naked young man in a state of violent erection.

Essie gasped and seized Daisy's arm.

"Ssh!" Daisy giggled. "I told you it was an adventure."

The two figures approached each other, met at the center of the stage, and proceeded to dance about while the young man fondled the woman's breasts and the woman caressed the young man's erect member. Then, while he held her hips and arched her body backward, he penetrated her.

For perhaps the first twenty minutes of the performance, the couple onstage demonstrated a bewildering array of sexual poses, positions and pleasures, while the audience watched in rapt silence, and while Essie tried not to look about her to see the faces of the others in the room. Somewhere behind her there was the sound of a man's heavy breathing. Then other members of the cast—male and female, all similarly unclad—began appearing, one by one, and then what did Essie's astonished eyes behold but men who were doing things with other men, women making love to other women, until the entire stage was filled with perhaps two dozen people, writhing in groupings and combinations, leaping from partner to partner in a violent orgy of sexual congress. Then, as if by a common signal—the performance had obviously had some sort of rehearsal—came the finale. While the women lay spent and squirming on the floor of the stage, the young men rose, faced the audience, and masturbated to climax.

The lights went out and, seizing each other's hands, the two women rushed blindly to the door and down the stairs to the street, where they leaned against the building, flushed and gasping, and suddenly giggling like two schoolgirls who had just shared a cigarette behind a fence in a vacant lot.

"Don't you ever . . . ever . . ." Essie said, when she was finally able to speak, "tell Jake Auerbach that I went to a place like that."

"And don't ever tell him that I took you," Daisy said.

And suddenly both were laughing so hard again that they had to lean into each other's arms for support. But it was also at that precise moment that Essie realized that Daisy Stevens was something other than a private secretary to her husband.

And how had this new knowledge affected her? It would be easy to say that she had reacted with dismay, with hurt and anger, with a feeling of bitterness and betrayal. With quiet resignation? But these were not her actual feelings at all. What should we say they were? It was more like a sense of relief and release. Years later, she would try to explain it to her son Joshua, who could never quite understand how his mother had been able to tolerate Daisy's presence in her life for so long. "Well, to begin with, she was fun to be with," she had told him. "We laughed at the same things, including your father. He was not the easiest man in the world to live with, you know, nor was I the easiest woman. She—well, she *deflected* him from me in some ways. He could be terribly autocratic. And it was difficult for me, at times, to accept his pronouncements, to bow to his wishes the way he expected to be bowed to—to take his orders, or to cope, later on, with his fits of temper. But all this was easy for her to do, you see, because she had no commitment. She could walk out whenever she wished, and he knew it. I didn't want to divorce him because I *had* made a commitment, but until she came along I thought I might have to. I suppose a psychologist might say she ran emotional interference between him and me. It was like he and I had made a kind of sandwich of our lives, only I was dark Jewish rye and he was a slice of white bread, and she was the filling that held the two slices together. That's it. She was the glue in our marriage. She made it possible for me to be myself. She made the air of his house easier to breathe."

"I'll never understand it," Josh had said.

"Ah, dear lady, dear lady," Joseph Duveen had said as he paced about among the twenty-odd canvases she had spread out for his inspection, and which she had brought home, rolled up in her luggage, from Europe. "I see I cannot trust you to be out on your own."

"You don't approve of them?"

"Ah, I am making a joke," he said. "No, you have bought beautiful things . . . beautiful things. It's just that I didn't think you were this adventuresome."

"I particularly like this Braque, don't you?"

"Very fine. But how could I have misjudged your character so? I had planned for you—traditional things. Conventional things. Safe things. How could I have been so wrong? Now all these other things must go. Out! Out with them! Out with the Renaissance and Italian Old Masters! Out with the Barbizons! For what we can sell these other paintings for, we can buy hundreds of modernists. You must also have Gauguin, Van Gogh, Cézanne, Modigliani. We will turn your house into a temple for your Fauve painters. It is now September. Give me two months, and it will be done. Then, of course, you must—must put on an extraordinary entertainment, and introduce Chicago—which will have its breath absolutely taken away—to your collection of modern art. . . ."

"Well, I certainly have no intention of throwing everything out, Mr. Duveen," Essie said firmly. "Nor do I intend to sell anything. I happen to be fond of *all* my paintings. But follow me, and I'll show you what I have in mind." She led him into the carved-ceilinged room called the West Loggia, where the walls and the window hangings were of pale green watered silk. "I'm tired of all this heavy French furniture," she said. "I'd like to get rid of it."

Joseph Duveen looked sad, "Ah, dear lady," he said. "The market is very poor for Louis Quatorze today, I'm afraid."

"Then we can warehouse it."

"Ah," he said, "I know just the place! A little expensive, but your furniture will be given superior care."

"My husband's company has plenty of warehouses, Mr. Duveen," she reminded him. "And I'd like to do the whole room in white. The room faces the sunset, and my new pictures have nice sunset colors. I'd like to turn this room into a separate gallery for my Fauves."

"Ah," he said, closing his eyes in ecstasy at his vision. "All white—white silk. I know just the house, in Paris. And the window hangings—"

"Please check with my husband's domestic suppliers first, before dashing off to Paris."

He made a face. "Of course, but nothing exists in this country comparable to what I have in mind. Ah, but it will be beautiful, dear lady—a whole gallery of modern painting! A wonderful room for a party!"

And that was how, really, the tradition of the annual Auerbach Christmas tree-trimming party began in Chicago, and later in New York, with the tall Norway spruce set up in the entrance foyer, and the tables set up in the gallery, and the stepladder, and the toasts. And it was the Christmas of 1919 that marked the emergence of Esther Auerbach as what the newspapers were soon calling "the noted Chicago hostess and art patron."

*   *   *

At the meeting, in January, of the Chicago Opera Guild, the topic under discussion was the selling of advertising space in the opera programs, always a thorny matter. In time, Essie would learn that the penalty for speaking up, or offering a suggestion, at any meeting was inevitably to be made the chairman of a committee in charge of whatever the problem was. But in those days she had been more outspoken, and at this meeting she said, "I know I'm a relatively new member of the Guild, but I have a suggestion. I think our programs look a little dull—both in appearance and content. I used to design advertising for my husband's business, you know, and it seems to me that if the programs had colorful covers, had some interesting illustrations inside—maybe a few interesting articles on the operas, on what's planned for the next season, and so on—then people would take them home to read, and keep as souvenirs. The programs would have a longer 'shelf life,' as they say in retailing. And that would make them more attractive to advertisers."

"I think that is an *excellent* idea," said Mrs. Bertie McCormick. "And I propose that we nominate Mrs. Auerbach as chairman of a committee to design and develop new programs. All in favor . . ."

And in that capacity Essie had served the Opera Guild for the next fifteen years, until the time came for her to be made President of the Guild.

"Tell me a story, Mother."

"But not now, Prince. I have no time."

"Tell me about the little girl who fell down the rabbit-hole."

"Alice in Wonderland? Ask Fräulein Kroger to read it to you. It's good for her. It helps her English. I've got to go now. Your papa's waiting." All that was years ago. The memories go every-which-way.

Your papa's waiting. That had been the excuse she had often used—used Jake as an excuse for not spending more time with their oldest son. Looking back, that had perhaps been at the heart of the trouble—without wishing to, she had turned her son against his father, made him afraid of Jake.

"Why is the boy crying?"

"I don't know, Jake."

"It seems as though every time I enter the room he begins to whimper. He's too old for that." He was eleven then.

"He scares me," Prince would say softly.

"What about him scares you?"

"His voice scares me. . . ."

At twelve or thirteen, he had seemed too old to have stories read to him, but why was it up to Essie to decide that? Each child is different, each has its own needs. She had chastised Jake for not spending enough time with the boys, but she was just as guilty, too, dashing off to meetings of the Opera Guild, the Field Museum board, the Symphony, when she could have been reading stories to Prince. Too busy . . . your papa's waiting. But her own mother had been busy, far busier than she, and yet had always found time for her children, particularly in the evenings, when it surely counted most. "Our lives are different now," she used to remind herself, but of course that was just another excuse, an excuse to neglect her children, to keep herself from their secret lives and longings. Secrets. Some of them, perhaps, they would have been willing to share with her, if only she had been more attentive at the time. Instead of leaving them with nurses, surrogates, bodyguards.

"Isn't Jake funny?" Daisy had said to her as they lay, side by side, on two of the cushioned chaises, shaded by umbrellas, beside the pool. It was an era when women set great store by the whiteness of their skin, when exposure to the sun was avoided, and when women still snapped open parasols to get them between shady places. Between Essie and Daisy, a glass-topped table held an ashtray crowded with Daisy's lipsticked cigarette butts, their empty iced-tea glasses perspiring on moist linen napkins, a pair of Daisy's gold earrings which she had removed because they pinched her ears, a glossy magazine splayed open, face down, the relics of a summer Sunday afternoon.

"Funny?" Essie said.

"Everything's not just a challenge to him," she said in her indolent, smoky voice. "Everything's a threat. And he makes a metaphor of everything."

"Metaphor?"

"Look at him. Listen to him."

Jake and Prince were at the opposite, the shallow, end of the pool—Prince was nearly twelve—and Jake was saying to him, "Why don't you ever swim from here down to the deep end?"

"I don't like to swim to the deep end, Daddy."

It was funny: the younger children all called their father Papa. Only Prince called him Daddy.

"You're a fine swimmer, Prince. But I've been watching you. You dive off from the deep end, swim to the shallow end, get out of the pool, walk back to the deep end, dive in again, and swim to the shallow end. You do it again and again. Why?"

"That's the way I *like* to swim, Daddy," Prince said.

"It's perfectly safe to dive in from this end."

"I know. But this is what I *like* to do."

"It doesn't make sense, Princey."

"I like to swim *from* the deep end. I don't like to swim *to* the deep end."

"But what's the point of having a pool with a deep end and a shallow end if you won't dive in from either end?" his father asked with a kind of relentless logic.

"I don't know."

"Perhaps I should have this whole pool filled in, since you don't seem to like the way it's built—with a deep end and a shallow end."

"It's not that, Daddy."

"Don't you like this pool?"

"Sure I do, Daddy."

"Then why don't you use it the way it's meant to be used? Swim your lengths back and forth, back and forth, from one end to the other, the way other people do?"

"I don't know. It's just—"

"Let me put it to you this way, Prince," his father said. "When you were little, and I was just starting out in business, working for Rosenthal's, I wasn't happy. And you know why? It was because I was swimming at the shallow end of the pool, where the little fish swim. But when I took the big step, and took over Eaton and Cromwell, I began swimming toward the deep end, toward the big fish. That was when life began to get exciting, to get challenging. I still have to deal with little fish now, but I also deal with big fish. And so that's why my business has been successful, I swim back and forth. The little fish are our customers. The big ones are our manufacturers. I swim back and forth, from the deep end to the shallow, and back again—back and forth. See what I mean, Prince?"

"See what *I* mean?" Daisy whispered in her husky voice.

But what Prince could not tell his father, what he did not dare to tell him—what he was ashamed to tell him—was that there was something at the deep end of the pool that he knew could not really be there, even though he had seen it—sometimes dimly, sometimes clearly—several times. If he dove from the deep end, he could swim quickly away from it with his eyes closed, out of its reach, and when it was time to open his eyes to look for the pool's opposite wall he was safely in the shallow water, out of danger. But if he swam toward the deep end, he would have to open his eyes, and there, in the dark blue depths, he would see the creature. It seemed to live below the grating of the main drain, though the hollow of the drain was too small to contain it, and it was able to spread out, reach out and upward from the bottom of the pool. Sometimes it was only a vague, dark, greenish-brown shape. At other times it seemed to gaze up at him with baleful, silver-mirror eyes. Sometimes it showed the black gash of a mouth with white teeth, and at times it showed the amorphous outlines of moving arms and legs, and a curling, snaky tail. At times, the arms and legs showed claws, and the tail showed spikes and scales. Sometimes the creature would bunch itself together like a ball, squirming just slightly. But at other times he had seen its waving appendages and tail uncoil and spread out and across the entire bottom of the pool's deep end. The creature had a name. It was called the Undersucker. If he didn't open his eyes, it didn't appear. But when he did, it did. The Undersucker wanted him to swim toward it, and waited until he opened his eyes.

Prince knew that there were no such things as monsters, and that eleven years old, going on twelve, was too old to be afraid of creatures in the water of the swimming pool. But still he knew that the Undersucker was there, waiting for him, daring him to swim toward it with open eyes. And he also knew that if he told his father about the Undersucker, his father would

*think that he was crazy, or that he was going crazy. The boys
at his school often talked about going crazy. Sometimes,
wrapped in their towels from the showers, they would stagger
about the corridors of the dorm before lights-out, eyes crossed,
tongues lolling out of the sides of their mouths, grunting, making gagging noises, flailing their arms—"going crazy." Going
crazy was what happened if you played with yourself; that
spurt that came at the end drained spinal fluid directly from
your brain. Still, that did not prevent the older boys from
showing the younger first-formers how to do it, how to make
yourself go crazy. That was one of the things Prince thought
about most that summer: that he was probably going crazy.*

Still, there were times with his father that his mother never
knew about, never suspected happened. Sometimes, when he
was alone in his room at The Bluff, working at his work table,
when Prince would hear a tap on his door, and his father's
voice asking, "Are you decent?"

Yes, Daddy. Decent, but going crazy.

Then his father would slip into his room, close the door
behind him, and sit on his bed, and Prince would put down his
thin strips of balsa wood and his tube of paint or glue.

"What are you making this time, Prince?"

"This is a model of *Flyer I*—the Wright brothers' first airplane that they flew at Kitty Hawk in nineteen-o-three. This
paper is for the wings. These are the struts."

"Very good," his father said. "That takes careful work."

"Uh-huh."

"Prince," his father said, "have you ever thought about what
kind of work you'd like to do when you grow up?"

He hesitated. "I think I'd like to be an airplane pilot," he
said finally.

"Really, Prince? Why does that appeal to you?"

"I think it'd be fun to fly people all over the country,
Daddy."

"Hmm. Well, I think it's good that you're thinking of something that will be serving people," his father said. "A service
business. Of course that's the kind of business we're in at
Eaton's. Service. Service to our customers."

"Uh-huh."

"You know, before I took over Eaton's it was a pretty shabby business. It was a dishonest business. They sold things that were no good—medicines that wouldn't cure anything. Machines that didn't work. People who bought them were pretty unhappy."

"Uh-huh."

"But I changed all that. I saw to it that our customers got what they were paying for. That made them happy. That's why we've been so successful."

"Uh-huh."

"A service business. And—you know—now that you're getting to be a young man, and beginning to think about your future, I hope you'll also think about coming into Eaton's with me. It would be a good feeling to know that you're at least thinking about it. Will you at least think about it, Prince?"

"All right, Daddy."

"Thirteen is a good age to begin thinking about things like this."

"Fourteen."

"Right. It's funny, when I was your age and even older, I didn't think that way at all. I didn't think that it was important to go into a business that was a family business. Of course, my circumstances were a little different. My father didn't own the family business, he just worked for them—his wife's family. I was always under somebody's thumb."

"Uh-huh."

"But to go into a family business which your own father heads—that can be a wonderful advantage for a young man. It can be a wonderful opportunity."

"Uh-huh."

"And it would give me a wonderful feeling if you did, Prince."

"Uh-huh."

"And I'll tell you this. From the way things look right now, in nineteen twenty-two, our possibilities for expansion seem downright limitless. For instance, we've been following very closely what Mr. Woolworth has been doing. On our drawing boards right now are plans to move out of mail-order and into stores all over the country, all over the world. Same honest merchandise, same honest prices, but in a chain of stores. It's the coming thing. Does that sound exciting, Prince?"

"Yes, Daddy."

"After all, an airplane pilot can only serve a few people at a time. We serve hundreds of thousands, millions of people every day."

"Uh-huh."

"I'll tell you what. Would you like me to take you down to one of our plants and give you a little tour—give you an idea of how our operation works? Would you like that?"

"Sure, Daddy." It was an offer that had been made often in the past, and it was always postponed.

"Good. Maybe next week, when I get back from Washington. When I get back from telling President Harding what he's doing wrong." His father laughed. "How do you like that, Prince? Your dad going down to Washington to tell President Harding what he's doing wrong."

"Yeah, that's pretty funny."

"Anyway," his father said, "think about what I've been saying. No need to make a big decision now. Plenty of time. But it's good to be able to talk to you about things like this because, you see, my own father—" He hesitated, clearing his throat. "I could never really talk to my own father because he wasn't—successful.Oh, he was perfectly nice to me. But we all lived together, in one big house—my mother, my father, and my two uncles, and nobody ever listened to anything my father said. They had no respect for his judgments, and so finally he sort of just stopped talking. Can you imagine what that was like, Prince, when I was your age—to realize you had a father nobody paid any attention to? Not even my mother. Oh, he was very good looking, quite the blade, when he was a young man, and I suppose that was why my mother—I suppose that was what she saw in him. But he seemed to lack basic intelligence—in the business sense, that is. He was a disappointment to the family, and I knew that from the time I was a little boy."

"Basic intelligence?" *Crazy.*

"Not clever in a business sense. They all criticized him behind his back. Or maybe it was because they refused to give him any real responsibility. And my uncles—they just didn't believe in talking to children. And when I was growing up, with a father nobody listened to, and with nobody to listen to me, I got the impression that nobody thought I had much basic intelligence, either, that I was rather worthless, too, like my father. And it was rather lonely for me, even in a house that was filled with people. Nobody ever thought I'd be successful, but I guess I've managed to prove to them that I could be. Do you see why I'm telling you this, Prince? I grew up with a father who I thought had nothing to teach me. I want you to grow up with a father you believe has something to teach you, from my own success. And I want—I hope—you'll grow up with a father you can respect. Do you mind me talking to you like this?"

"No, Daddy."

"And so I grew up feeling that I was some kind of accident. Why didn't I have brothers or sisters? It must mean that I was an accident, a baby they didn't want. And then I found out that—in fact—I was an accident."

"An accident?"

"A son they didn't really want is one way to put it, Prince. But you weren't an accident. Your mother and I wanted you very much. There's a big difference. And then, a few years ago—" He broke off.

"What happened a few years ago, Daddy?"

"A few years ago, when he was in his fifties, my father became—well, the doctors diagnosed it as a kind of premature senility."

"What's that?"

"He became—funny in the head, I guess you'd say."

Crazy!

"He had to be watched all the time because he did—terrible things. To keep an eye on him they—"

"What things?"

"Children. Little boys and girls. He'd try to touch them, and hurt them. But I don't want to talk about that."

But there it was again, with its coiling and outreaching arms and thorny tail in the deep water: the Undersucker.

"But do you know they still keep him in the office?" He laughed. "For appearances sake—can you imagine that? But that's why you've never met your grandfather. He's become the secret family shame. To keep an eye on him, they keep him at the office. But it's taken my mother and her brothers—how my mother does it, I'll never know. But she's very strong—" He broke off once more. "Funny, but from a distance, it's made me love him even more, but in a pitying way. And it's funny, but I've never told anyone about this—not your mother, not Uncle Charles, not my doctor, not even Aunt Daisy. Only you. Because still, when I get to feeling low in my mind—even with the success I've had, Prince, I still sometimes feel that there's something shameful about the Auerbach name. I wanted to change it once, but now it's too late. And I wanted you to know all this because I never want you to be ashamed of your name, or to have a father you mostly pity. I want you to make the name proud." Tears seemed to glisten in his father's eyes.

"Aren't you proud, Daddy?" It embarrassed him to think that his father might be going to cry. Whenever his father talked intimately to him like this, he felt vaguely uneasy; it was as though, whenever small cracks appeared in the mask, it was a black reminder that there was a mask. The cracks revealed uncharted territory, and he was on safer ground when the mask was intact and in place.

"How can an accident be really proud? But I've taught myself pride, trained myself, by trying to forget the past. Some days, I actually believe there wasn't any past. That's why I'm telling you this, Prince. You have no past to hide. You only have a future. You're going to be my pride. Do you understand?"

"Uh-huh." But no, sometimes when his father talked to him like this, he did not completely understand. From where he sat on the edge of Prince's bed, his father reached out a little awkwardly and tousled Prince's dark hair with his big hand and said in his gruff voice, "You know, Prince, I love you very much. I really do."

"Thank you, Daddy."

Then his father stood up, cleared his throat once more, and the mask fell into place again. "Well, I'll leave you to whats-its-name, the Wright brothers' plane. Anything you need?"

"Daddy—"

"Yes?"

"Daddy, could I have a lock put on my door?"

His father looked down at him, frowning slightly. "A lock on your door? Which door? This one?"

"Uh-huh."

"Doesn't this door have a lock? There's a key—"

"Yes, but I mean a lock that I can lock from inside, and that can't be opened with just a house key."

"Why would you want that, son?"

"I don't know. At school, they don't let us have locks on any of our doors. Guys are always barging in and out. And they have these surprise inspections. I just thought—"

"Well, at school I suppose there are a lot of reasons," his father said, still frowning. "Such as fire, and—" Then he smiled. "Still, I see no reason why a young man your age shouldn't be able to have a certain amount of privacy in his own home. I'll get somebody to take care of it in the morning. I'll speak to Hans."

"Thank you, Daddy," Prince said, and his face flushed, for he had just had the sensation of having driven a small stake into his father's heart.

Because there is a monster in this house. It has a name. Its name is Auerbach, Undersucker Auerbach.

Of such scenes, as has been noted, Essie Auerbach had no awareness. But there must have been other scenes, which, given hindsight, occurred that same year or thereabouts. Hans. Hans the bodybuilder, the bodyguard, the keyholder. Here, for example, is a scene which Essie only imagines happened. It happened—where? Who knows? But it happened. Perhaps it was at Lawrenceville. Perhaps it was at the horse ranch in Wyoming, during that first European summer. Hans—Hans and young Jake are alone somewhere, somewhere in a room. Hans—Hans for Handsome—has been playing his mandolin. Have we mentioned that Hans plays the mandolin? Because he does, he plays the mandolin not badly and smokes many black cigarettes, so put in the mandolin, for music and for magic, and paint the colors dusk.

"You're a beautiful boy," Hans says, laying down his instrument. Which is true. Young Jake—Prince—is beautiful—too beautiful, some might say. With large dark blue eyes, smooth skin—no adolescent acne for our Prince—dark, curly hair, what used to be called a Roman nose.

"A very beautiful boy," Hans says, perhaps touching his knee, perhaps running his hand softly along his thigh, perhaps covering the boy's bare foot with his own, while Prince—who knows what Prince is thinking, feeling? One can only guess.

"A beautiful boy," Hans repeats in that lazy, hypnotic way, smiling that crooked, lazy smile, moving closer until their knees touch, saying, "Look here, Princey, I want to show you something. . . ."

Who knows whether this scene actually occurred? Essie was not there to see it, and the two principals involved in the scene are no longer here. But something of the sort did. And given foresight—but none of us is ever given that.

Here, on the other hand, is a scene Essie remembers very well. That extravagant decade—the Era of Wonderful Nonsense that was the 1920s—is under way, and Essie has come home late at night from an Opera Guild benefit. It is spring, and Jake is in New York on business. Prince is home from Lawrenceville for the spring holidays. The servants have retired for the night, and Essie goes directly to her room, where the coverlet has been turned down and where a glass of warm milk has been placed for her on her bedside table.

Some time later, she is awakened from a deep sleep by the sounds of some sort of commotion in the hallway outside her room. She turns on her lamp and tries to identify the scratching, scuffling sounds. She rises, goes to her door, opens it, and there, in the weak light from her open doorway, she sees her son, fifteen, in the dark hallway, struggling to open his bedroom door just down the hall. His dark hair is tousled, his necktie is loosened, and his shirt front is unbuttoned. Half-leaning against the door jamb, he is twisting nosily at the knob, which seems to resist him.

"Prince," she cries, "what is it? What's the matter?"

"Party," he mumbles. "Kids from school . . . drove me home . . . can't get . . ."

"Is your door locked?"

He mutters something she cannot understand. Then, as she watches, he leans back against the closed door and slides slowly to the floor, where he lands in a kneeling position. Then, falling forward on his hands, he vomits noisily onto the carpet.

"Prince, what's the matter with you?" Essie cries, running to him. Dimly, from the far end of the long corridor, she sees a pale shape approaching. It is Hans, wearing only a white terry cloth robe, carrying his heavy ring of keys.

"Hans—what's *wrong* with him?"

Hans bends over her son. "Nothing," he says. "He's just drunk." Saying, "Come on, Prince, old boy," he lifts him by the arms and swings him over his shoulder in a football-player's half-carry. "You go back to bed, Ma'am," Hans says. "I'll clean him up and get him to bed. Don't worry—he'll be fine. I'll clean up the mess." With his free hand, he quickly unlocks the door to Prince's bedroom and carries him inside.

Twenty

THE Florida night is warm and moist and, from the terrace of his penthouse condominium where Arthur Litton stands, the only sounds are the susurrous rustle of the Atlantic surf on the beach below, the gnatlike buzz of small planes in the distant sky, and the occasional, jarring sound of an ambulance siren making its way southward toward Miami General on Route One. Florida, after all, is where old people come to die, and the sounds of the vehicles that minister to their needs are never far away. The night is clear, but moonless, and on nights like these there is more than the usual small-aircraft traffic heading toward the Everglades. These planes invariably fly low, out of radar range, and without lights, for they are almost always involved in drug traffic. Their activities amuse Arthur Litton in a grim way, because this is a business in which he has chosen not to involve himself, though he has been offered numerous opportunities. That is a business, he thinks, only for human beings who are little better than animals, the dregs of the world, traffickers in misery and death. No, that is not at all his cup of tea, and he is proud to have kept it firmly at arm's length. Except for once. But that had been as a favor to Essie.

Inside the apartment, he has kissed his sleeping Angelique good night, where she has dozed off with her reading light still on, with her copies of *Vogue, Harper's Bazaar*, and *Town & Country* spread out about her, her pale arms and yellow hair loose across the white satin sheets and many tiny lace-edged pillows. Angelique, he thinks, has been well-named. She is an angelic woman, and it is a wondrous thing to him that a new love such as this one should have been offered to him in old age, a kind of miracle. How could he have faced old age without her?

Arthur Litton has been in retirement for some years, and his principal activities are playing golf with his old friend and sometime partner, Frankie Corelli, fishing in the waterway from the pier, and sunning himself here on the terrace or downstairs by the building's pool. In the evenings, he and Angelique often read to one another, and occasionally they go into Lauderdale or Miami Beach for dinner, or have a few friends over—Frankie Corelli and his wife, a few others—for a gettogether. It is a quiet life. And it also amuses Arthur Litton that this quiet life is so much in contrast with the kind of life the newspapers try to depict for him from time to time—the mastermind of the Underworld, genius of the Mob. The Mob, if it can be called a Mob, hasn't solicited his opinion, advice, or help in years, and their concerns are no longer his. It is true that he will sometimes notice an FBI agent tailing him when he walks his dog—Arthur Litton will usually recognize the fellow and throw him a jaunty salute—or he will see someone from the State Prosecutor's office making notes of license plates of certain friends who come to visit him, but he is used to this. These are minor nuisances. And it is true that he assumes that his telephone line is still tapped, and so he simply makes his important calls from pay booths. His trouser pockets always jingle with dimes and quarters, telephone change. Aside from these little inconveniences, it is an easy life.

Mastermind of the Underworld. To Arthur Litton, this is funny, too. Of all the state and federal charges that have been leveled against him over the years, not a single one has been made to stick and, each year, he has smiled as the statute of limitations on one or another unproven allegation has run out. In the meantime, he has educated two fine sons, one at Stanford and one at Amherst, seen them launched in fine careers—one in real estate, the other a dentist—seen them marry and have fine children of their own. It is a good life, and he and Angelique have everything they want. Arthur Litton has only one serious complaint. Washington, as though in a fit of pique or frustration, has denied him a passport. It is as though, unable to prove any actual wrongdoing on the part of the

Mastermind of the Underworld, Washington has decided to keep America's public enemy securely on America's shores. America, love it—or stay, seems to be their motto, and Arthur Litton is bitter that he cannot go with Angelique to Rome and Paris when she goes to shop for clothes.

Oh, Arthur Litton will not deny that he made a lot of money during Prohibition; he did, and so did a lot of other people. When people talk of his "debt to society," he thinks wryly that society's heaviest debt is to itself—for the millions of dollars that it lost to its Volstead Act, that monstrous example of mass self-delusion. American society, in his opinion, is still paying for that, and may go on doing so for generations. Prohibition made a great many people rich, including men who are now regarded as the pillars of American business. Well, Arthur Litton could tell you a thing or two about these men and they would not be described in lapidary terms, unless as extremely rough diamonds. These were men who had people killed to get what they wanted, and, despite claims to the contrary, Arthur Litton has never killed anyone, nor has he ordered the killing of anyone. He ran his business like any other business, and when his people turned in poor performances, or failed to follow orders or do their jobs, they were reprimanded or dismissed—punished, just as cheats, liars and malingerers are punished in any business. He is proud of his record on that score. His record is clean on that score, it has been a clean life.

If you asked him, Arthur Litton would tell you that he has always viewed his business as just one of several avenues out of the ghetto, out of the poverty of Norfolk, Rivington, Hester, Orchard and Delancey Streets. Many others chose the same route, he was by no means unique. It was a route that worked, that brought him to where he is today, to an oceanfront condominum that would probably fetch $750,000 if he were ever to put it on the market, which he does not plan to do. His route has made him several times a millionaire, though he is not as rich as some published reports would have him be. No matter. It is enough to give him and Angelique an easy life.

His sister Essie simply chose another route, marriage, and the fact that her marriage to that piss-pious Jake Auerbach made her a woman worth *hundreds* of millions and was thanks to Arthur Litton is something that he never forgets to remind himself. It was thanks to *him*, not Jake, that the Auerbachs got in on the ground floor at Eaton & Cromwell. It was he, not Jake, who heard about George Eaton and Cyrus Cromwell and their crummy little mail-order shop—a fact that the piss-pious Jake very quickly managed to forget. Piss-pious. That is a term he reserves for his late brother-in-law. Where would you be, Esther Auerbach, he often asks himself, if it hadn't been for me? Still scrubbing linoleum on Grand Boulevard, still trying to grow cabbage in the backyard. If Arthur Litton ever decided to write a book about his life—which, of course, he will never do—he would have quite a juicy little tale to tell. But he is no longer really bitter—or so he tells himself—about being forced out of what could have been his own company. He has led his life without it. Essie has paid her debt. Still, when he thinks of her millions in the hundreds, compared with his five or six, it rankles.

Just as Arthur Litton has always thought of his as a life without regrets, he has also thought of his life in retirement as one without cares—no cares more pressing than deciding which filly to put a nickel on next Saturday at Hialeah. Until about three weeks ago, that is. That was when his niece began telephoning Angelique from New York, asking to speak to him, and leaving messages. He has not laid eyes on Joan since she was a snot-nosed little kid. He hadn't liked Joan then, and he is sure he doesn't like her now—particularly with this latest development. Now Joan is in Miami, demanding to see him, leaving a message that what she has to tell him is important for his future. He has not spoken to her, but these are the messages Angelique has relayed, and now Joan is just a few miles down the beach, checked in at the Omni.

Why should he see her? Just because she is Essie's daughter? That, to him, is not reason enough. Arthur Litton knows how to deal with federal and state prosecutors and their bureaucratic toadies, for their moves are always predictable. A family's moves are not. In fact, they are often dangerously the opposite. Joan, furthermore, runs a newspaper—he knows all about that—and if there is any group for whom Arthur Litton has less respect than federal prosecutors it is newspaper people, who will make up any kind of story, tell any kind of lie, to make a headline. No, he is certain that Joan is here on some kind of fishing expedition, wanting to pump him for some kind of information. She has told Angelique that she has some sort of message for him from Essie, but that story makes no sense. If Essie needs to reach him, she knows exactly how to do it, and so does Charles. No, a fishing expedition is what it is.

But should he see her? That is what is worrying him now. That is what is keeping him up after his normal bedtime, unable to sleep, prowling about the terrace of his penthouse, smoking cigarette after cigarette, listening to the night noises. Of course he will tell her nothing. Essie has kept up her end of the deal, and so will he. Unlike her late husband, Essie is a straight-shooter, and so, in any deal, is Arthur Litton. There is no question on that score, in which case there is no reason not to see her. But still, but still. She is a newspaper person, and a woman, and if he has no use for newspaper people as a breed, he has even less use for newspaper *women*. Newshens, *Time* magazine used to call them. Hedda Hopper, Louella Parsons, Dorothy Kilgallen, Adela Rogers St. Johns—always grubbing around in the dirt like chickens for pieces of old corn. Or old porn. It was all the same. Perhaps all she wants to write about is his "life-style," or how Arthur Litton looks today. But he has had enough publicity to fill a lifetime, and isn't looking for any more today. He has also had his share of aggravation, and doesn't need any more from a long-lost niece.

Should he see her? What does she want? He has to admit to a certain amount of curiosity. How did she find his unpublished number? From Daisy? It is not fair, he thinks almost petulantly, to be handed these questions and worries at this time of his life, when life should be easy, quiet, good. He decides to postpone any decisions until tomorrow.

From behind the shadow of his building, a half-moon appears, and Arthur Litton's wide terrace is bathed in a gentle, restful light, and he thinks he will sit for just a moment longer to enjoy it, and moves to a garden bench near the clump of blue hydrangea bushes. His terrace is his great pride. It is lushly planted, and it has a secret. Every climbing vine, every shrub and tree, every bloom is artificial, made of plastic, but fashioned so cleverly that most people, seeing it for the first time, do not realize it. Even the water lilies blossoming in the basin of the central fountain are not real. His terrace garden was

created, at no small expense, by an outfit called Fabulous
Fakes in Bal Harbour, and few people who have visited Arthur
Litton's apartment have stopped to wonder how he gets tulips
and chrysanthemums to blossom in the same season, or why
the blue hydrangea bushes, more indigenous to the New England coast, do so well in southern Florida. The reasons for the
artificial garden are threefold. First, it requires no maintenance. Second, in the hurricane season, the garden can be
quickly packed up and stored out of harm's way. And third,
having planter boxes and tubs that require no watering keeps
Arthur Litton free from complaints of neighbors on the floors
below that his water is coming through their dining room ceilings. If their ceilings leak, it is only from rain, not from Arthur
Litton. He knows that, when the identity of the anonymous
purchaser of his condo—for whom his lawyer was acting as
agent—became known, there was some displeasure expressed
by other tenants in the building. For this reason, he has always
tried scrupulously to be a good neighbor. And in the seventeen
years he has lived in this apartment there has never been a
single complaint involving the tenancy of Mr. and Mrs. Arthur
Litton. In fact, he has even heard himself and Angelique described as "model neighbors."

So I do not deserve this latest aggravation, he thinks, sitting
on his garden bench, admiring his luxuriant, man-made
garden, where palms and cacti from the desert sprout up among
sweet Williams, primroses, phlox and columbine, and where
Alberta spruce grows in a ground-cover of California ice-plant.
I do not deserve this worry at the end of a long and for the most
part satisfying life. At this time of life, a man deserves peace.
He is tired, but not yet sleepy. His head aches slightly, and
there is a small pain in his right shoulder. In his shirt pocket, he
fishes for a digitalis pill, and places it under his tongue. It is
angina pain, for his ticker has been giving him a bit of trouble
lately, which his doctor tells him is normal for his time of life,
particularly for a man who refuses to quit smoking. He waits
for the pill to do its work.

But suddenly, instead, the pain grows sharper. He starts to
rise, then decides to sit still until the pain, as it must, passes.
But there is something different now, and he thinks he should
cry out to Angelique for help, but he suddenly cannot find the

breath. He seizes the trunk of a hydrangea bush for support, to pull himself to his feet, but the slender metal rod that provides the armature for the shrub is no match for his weight and, instead, the bush is easily uprooted from its planter tub of Sim-U-Soil. At this point, the pain becomes massive, and Arthur Litton falls sideways into the hydrangeas.

The plastic boughs sag with his weight, and in the half-moon-light the vivid blooms seem to embower his fallen body with the pale blue clusters of their lifeless blooms.

On the telephone, Charles is saying to Essie, "I don't know whether I have good news for you or bad, old girl."

"What is it, Charles?"

"Your brother Abe is dead. He was found this morning in his garden."

"Ah," she says softly. She cannot help feeling a sudden, deep pang of grief.

"There's been talk of a gangland-style killing, because he was holding a bunch of flowers in one hand, but the Dade County Coroner's Office has ruled a simple coronary."

"Ah."

"I wouldn't be surprised if Joan's imminent arrival on his doorstep didn't bring it on."

"She didn't see him, then."

"No."

"Ah," she says again.

"Anyway, I wanted you to know it before you read it in the papers."

"Thank you, Charles."

"I had a call from the *Times,* from the reporter who's writing his obituary. They've made the Litsky connection, and asked whether he was related to you."

"What did you tell them?"

"I fudged it. I said, 'Possibly. It's a common Jewish name.' They may try to call you, but I hope not. I told them you were very old and ill, and couldn't be reached for questions."

"Thank you for making me old and ill!"

"The *Times* is usually pretty gentlemanly about things like that. But you might want to alert Mary, in case there's a call, so she and I can have our stories straight."

"I understand," she says. "Though actually I don't mind if they say he was my brother."

"Neither do I," says Charles. "Because he was. But think of Josh."

"You're right," she says. "I understand."

"Good-bye, Essie."

"Good-bye, dear Charles. And thank you."

Upon hanging up, she goes directly to Mary Farrell's office. "Mary," she says, "has this month's check gone out to Arthur Litton?"

"Not until the thirty-first, Mrs. A."

"Good. There'll be no more checks, Mary. He is dead."

Mary looks quickly at her employer, then back at her type-writer keyboard. "I see," she says.

"And if any newspaper reporters call for me, I am very old and very ill, and cannot come to the telephone."

"I see," says Mary Farrell.

Outside the funeral home, two heavyset men in dark suits and white neckties block Joan's entrance at the door. "Sorry, Ma'am, but your name's not on the list."

"My professional name is Joan Auerbach, but in private life I'm Mrs. Richard McAllister."

"Neither name's on the list, Ma'am. These services are strictly private and invitational, by the widow of the deceased."

"I'm with the New York *Express*."

"You ain't on the list, Ma'am. Sorry."

"Listen, the deceased is my uncle. I'm his niece."

"Sorry," the dark-suited man says, tapping his sheet of paper with a pudgy finger. "You gotta be on this list. Otherwise, my orders is you can't go in."

"Just tell me one thing," Joan says, "is it an open casket?"

"Yeah, it's open."

"Are his eyes open?"

"*What?*" the heavy man says. "Are you crazy? What do you mean are his eyes open? The guy is fuckin' dead."

"I need to know the color of his eyes."

"Wait a minute," the man says. Turning away from Joan, he

mutters to his cohort, "Al, can you take my place at the door for a sec? I got a crazy lady to get rid of. . . ."

"Yes?" Mogie Auerbach says into the telephone in a somewhat impatient tone. "Who is this?"

"Mogie—it's me. Mogie—I've got terrible news."

"Joan, can you call me back in half an hour?" he says. "Tina and I are having intercourse."

Twenty-one

ESTHER Auerbach, having donated the Auerbach Pavilion, is treated very much as a V.I.P. at Mount Sinai Hospital, and as her limousine pulls up in front of the main entrance on Upper Fifth Avenue, four people, who have been waiting just inside the glass doors, step out onto the sidewalk to escort her inside—the executive director of the hospital, the chief physician, and two senior members of the nursing staff in crisp white uniforms. The doctor offers Essie his arm as she gets out of the car, they cross the sidewalk, and one of the nurses holds open the door for them.

"She's going to be all right," Doctor Roth assures her. "We were worried about possible brain damage, but she's conscious now, and seems clear-headed. We still have her in Intensive Care, of course."

Essie nods, and they cross the foyer to where an elevator is waiting for them.

"The thing is, we're still not sure when it happened," he continues, as the doors close. "Her maid found her early this morning. It may have been only a few hours, in which case she's very lucky. . . ."

Essie nods again.

"I wouldn't recommend spending too much time with her today, Mrs. Auerbach," he continues. "No more than fifteen minutes. She's a mighty uncomfortable lady."

Essie nods her assent to all these instructions as they leave the elevator and start down the corridor.

The Intensive Care Unit is dark and shadowy, the better to

read the screens of all the computerized monitoring equipment, and its only sounds are the various little beeps from the machines and the rustle of the nurses' skirts. The head nurse leads the way now to a pale figure on a hospital bed, and Essie hears her whisper, "Your mother is here to see you, Mrs. McAllister," and lightly touches Joan's wrist, into which an I.V. tube runs. Then she closes the screens around them, and leaves them alone. Essie, who has promised herself to be brave about all this, still feels tears welling in her eyes when she bends to kiss Joan on the forehead and to squeeze her hand. "Joan . . . Joan, darling . . ."

"Hello, Mother," Joan says in a hoarse voice.

"Joan . . . Joan, why did you do this?"

"Simple . . . nothing to live for . . . lost everything . . . lost the newspaper . . . lost Richard . . . and now look. I'm still here."

"Oh, Joan. Why didn't you come to me?"

Joan looks up at her with dead eyes. "Tried," she says in that terrible rattling voice. "Stupid secretary . . . Mary . . . always said you were busy . . . out to lunch . . . Besides, you already turned me down."

"But Joan, I had no idea things were as bad as that."

"Were . . . only worse . . . still are . . . Sixty million dollars, Mother . . . your investment, too."

"That doesn't matter to me, Joan. You know I'll always take care of you. All I want is for you to be happy."

"I want to die," Joan says.

"Oh, don't! Don't say that."

Joan does not reply, and turns her head away from Essie, into the sheet, and now Essie can think of nothing to say. The wall of years behind them is too thick and sturdy. When Joan was little, back at 5269 Grand Boulevard, and had the measles, and had to lie in a dark room like this one, Essie would sit beside her bed and read to her by the light of a flashlight. In those days, she used to read to all the children, the three of them, Prince, Joan, and Babette, all snuggled together under the covers of one narrow bed—*Alice in Wonderland, Through the Looking-Glass,* and all the Beatrix Potter books which Essie almost knew by heart. But what is there to read to her now? What is there even to talk to her about? A nurse enters the screened enclosure and quietly and quickly checks Joan's vital signs, makes a notation on her chart, and leaves.

"Your poor newspaper, you worked so hard on it," Essie says at last.

Joan says nothing.

"Has Richard been to see you?"

"'Course not . . . bastard."

"Joan, I'm sorry."

"Just tell me one thing, Mother. What color were Uncle Abe's eyes?"

"He had dark eyes. Dark brown. He had my father's eyes. Why?"

Joan closes her own dark eyes. "Nothing . . . stupid Mogie . . . Mother, I don't want to talk anymore. Terrible sore throat. . . ."

"I understand," Essie says. "Good night, darling." She kisses her again. "I'll be by again tomorrow. . . ."

"We have no idea how many she took," Doctor Roth says as he escorts her out to her car. "There was an empty bottle by the bed. But the point is she didn't take enough to do the trick. Maybe twenty Seconals. That's not enough to do the trick. I suspect that this was an angry act. She wants to punish someone."

"Oh, me, of course!" Essie says. "Isn't that what the psychiatrists always say? It's always the mother's fault." And she suddenly has an ugly, irrational, unworthy and totally unmotherly thought: for the briefest moment she wishes that Joan had taken enough, as Jim Roth rather crassly puts it, "to do the trick."

"Either tomorrow or the next day, she'll start seeing Doctor Weizman, head of Psychiatry. That's routine in these cases."

"And there'll—there'll be nothing given to the newspapers about this, will there, Jim?"

"Absolutely not, Mrs. Auerbach. We'll see to that."

"What's she trying to *do,* Mother?" Babette's voice screams at her over the telephone from Palm Beach. "First she pirates a third of my trust—and now *this!*"

"Well, be grateful you still have two thirds left," Essie says.

"And don't yell at me about this. I didn't let her do it. You did."

"But I didn't *know!* I'm going to sue her, Mother!"

"Good idea. And good luck, because it doesn't sound as though she's got much left to sue for. Babette, I have more important things to think about."

"More important *things?* What's more important than my money and my social position in Palm Beach?"

"I can think of several. Such as my dinner, which is about to be served, and which I intend to eat. Good-bye."

Joan. What had ever made her happy? Essie never had been sure. The year was 1927, when Joan was eighteen, and when Joan was to have her coming-out party. It was for that party that Essie had first found it necessary to hire a private secretary, Agnes Lauterbach, because it was the largest and most elaborate party Essie had ever given and required months of preparation. It was true that Agnes Lauterbach was a little dictatorial, requiring—among other things—that the children make appointments to see their mother. But there was no doubt that she was efficient, and efficiency was required for a party of this scale.

The date was June sixteenth, and fifteen hundred guests had been invited. Not one but two tents had been set up outside the house—in pink and green and gold—one for dining and one for dancing, and Meyer Davis and his orchestra had been engaged from New York, at a cost, Essie would always remember, of $4000 plus travel and expenses. One hundred and twenty-five cases of champagne had been ordered from the bootlegger. The menu—tomato bisque, shrimp in lobster sauce, wild rice, *petit-pois, pêche* Melba—had been worked out with the caterer, the tables and chairs had been set up, the flowers, in the same pink, green and gold scheme, had been arranged, the placecards all hand-lettered, the pink, green and gold balloons released to the top of the tents with colored ribbons trailing down, the ice sculptures of swans with bowls of caviar nested between their wings, the waiters in uniforms especially made to conform with the color scheme. . . . It was an era when prosperity was the only thing one talked about, when money was no object, when Jake Auerbach was being

hailed as one of the richest men in America, not far behind the
Rockefellers, when the country seemed to run itself. President
and Mrs. Coolidge had sent their regrets, but had also sent an
immense floral arrangement which had been placed in the front
entrance hall. A special train had been hired to bring guests in
from New York. Essie had helped Joan select her long white
taffeta ball gown, the flowers she would carry, the flowers she
would wear as a coronet in her hair.

The party was to start at eight o'clock, and by three o'clock,
when it was time for everyone to start getting ready, when the
maids had laid out the women's dresses, when the hairdresser
had arrived to apply the final touches to Joan's, her mother's,
and her younger sister's hair, Joan was nowhere to be found.

The house and premises were searched. Ransacked. The
search became frantic. Kidnappers! Jake Auerbach cried, and
the police were called, and blue-and-white squad cars lined the
long front drive. A special telephone line was run in to deal
with the ransom demands.

Then, at five o'clock, a telegram arrived from Milwaukee. It
said:

> JUST MARRIED MOST WONDERFUL MAN
> JEAN-CLAUDE DE LUCY. WISH ME
> HAPPINESS. JOAN.

Crumpling the telegram in his hand, Jake Auerbach shouted,
"Russian craziness!" Then he marched upstairs, locked himself
in his bedroom and would not come out. When any of his
children displeased him, he now blamed their "Russian genes."

Under the supervision of Agnes Lauterbach, hundreds of
telephone calls and telegrams went out, canceling the party
"due to unforeseen circumstances." The train from New York
was stopped outside Detroit, and turned around, with no explanation given to its bewildered passengers until they were home
again.

Of course a hundred or so guests showed up anyway, whom
Miss Lauterbach had simply been unable to reach. They were
given drinks, and stood about chattering nervously, not knowing whether to congratulate the absent bride or to offer con-
dolences for the collapsed party. Essie did her best to put them

at their ease. "Will someone please invent a restraining harness for headstrong daughters?" she joked. "I promise you we'll put it in the Eaton catalogue." But the laughter was uncomfortable, and the guests soon departed.

The men in the orchestra, who had just finished unpacking their instruments, began packing them up again. The food that had been unloaded from the caterers' trucks was packed back into them once more. The waiters changed their clothes, collected their paychecks, and went home. The tents would be dismantled, and the tables and chairs taken away, in the morning. By midnight, Essie and her butler, Taki, were the only ones left downstairs in her house.

"Shall I turn out the lights, Madam?"

"No, leave them on for a while," she said. "I'll do it before I go up."

"Then good night, Madam," he said. "It is—so sorry a thing."

"Yes. Good night, Taki."

Then she wandered into the first of the two tents, where a hundred and fifty tables for ten were still set up for dinner, each with its long white tablecloth to the floor, each with its floral centerpiece, each set with china and silverware and crystal, each ringed with ivory-colored placecards. In the brightly lit, empty tent, hundreds of unlit candles in candelabra waited to be set ablaze for a party. But already the flowers on the tables seemed to be wilting and losing their color in the warm night air. The bright balloons, with their trailing ribbons, which were still gathered at the top of the tent, had already begun to shrink and wither. The frozen swans, their bowls of caviar gone, were dripping quietly, as though weeping, into dark puddles on the floor, and would soon be melted into unrecognizable lumps. A large moth batted noisily among the hot bulbs of an overhead chandelier. In this bright light—which would have been dimmed, of course, before the guests were ushered in—all the excited preparations for Joan's coming-out party seemed to be translated into garishness and artificiality, and from the fading flowers there was the odor of impermanence and decay. Outside, the star-filled summer sky was uncaring. Essie walked slowly to the main switch and extinguished the lights in the tent.

Then she crossed the short strip of grass to the second tent, where the bar and dance floor had been set up. On the bar, dozens of clean glasses stood in neat rows, and, behind them, the heads of champagne bottles stuck up from silver coolers; on the bandstand, empty chairs and music stands; at the top of the tent, more shriveling balloons.

"Looks kind of spooky, doesn't it?" a man's voice said.

She turned, and there was the tall figure of Charles, in his tuxedo, a champagne glass in his hand.

"Charles!" she said. "I didn't realize you were still here."

"Well," he said, "I thought I'd say good-bye to the party with a glass of champagne. I opened a bottle. I hope you don't mind."

"Of course not. Is Cecilia here too?"

"She's not feeling well. I wasn't going to come, either, when I heard what happened. But then I thought there might be something I could do to help. Thanks to the efficient Miss Lauterbach, I guess there wasn't."

"Thank God for Agnes."

"So. Will you join me in a glass?"

"Yes," she said. "Yes, I will."

He held up the bottle that dangled from one hand and grinned. "I'm rather afraid I've finished this one," he said. "Shall I open another?"

"Well, I certainly think we have enough, don't you?"

He went to the bar, took another bottle from the cooler, deftly popped the cork, and filled a glass for Essie. He carried it to one of the little cocktail tables that had been set up around the perimeter of the tent. Then he pulled up two gilt ballroom chairs, placed the bottle in the center of the table, and they settled themselves opposite each other. "I have no idea what we're drinking to," he said, "but cheers, anyway."

"Yes." They clinked glasses.

"How is Jake taking it?"

"Can't you imagine? At this point I'm sure he wishes she *had* been kidnapped."

"And you, Essie?"

"Numb. I think I'm still in a state of shock."

"Do you know anything at all about this Frenchman?"

"Nothing. I've never heard her mention him."

"What are you going to do?"

She sipped her champagne. "I haven't even thought about that," she said.

Charles stretched his long, black-trousered legs out in front of him and studied the patent-leather toes of his evening shoes. "How could she *do* this to you, that's what I don't understand," he said at last.

"I think sometimes children enjoy punishing their parents," she said.

"Punish? But for what?"

"For being born, I guess."

"And after everything you've been through, Essie. It just seems like the rottenest of rotten tricks."

He was alluding, she knew, to Prince, even though she also knew that he would never mention Prince by name. By now, Prince was a turned page, an ended chapter, a closed book, and had been for three years.

"Now don't give me a lecture on what you'd do if she were *your* daughter," she said. "In fact, I'd rather not talk about this at all, if you don't mind, Charles. Let's talk about something else. And I'm ready for more champagne."

He refilled her glass. "Well, what shall we talk about?" he said.

"You," she said brightly. "Let's talk about you. It seems as though you and I haven't had a good talk in ages."

"Fine," he said with a smile. "First off, I'll say that there are times when I'm glad Cecilia and I don't have children."

She laughed. "As my mother used to say, if you don't have children, what do you do for aggravation?"

"Well, I have your husband," he said.

"Yes!" she said, taking another sip of champagne. "Yes, that's something I've wanted to ask you about for years—yes. What's it been like, Charles, for you—you who've always given him his best ideas—to sit back and watch him collecting all the praise? Getting all the glory."

He was still grinning. "Funny, I thought you'd never ask," he said. "It's a question my wife asks me almost every day. Actually, the answer's pretty simple—it's in the kind of guy I am, and the kind of guy Jake is."

"Explain, please."

"Jake has always been cut out to be a figurehead. When I first met him—remember that day in your little house on Grand Boulevard?—I remember thinking to myself: this is a frustrated figurehead. That's why he was miserable at Rosenthal's—he wasn't a figurehead. I said to myself: inside that fellow's body is an embryo figurehead trying to get out. But me, I'm a different sort of person. I realized that about myself way back at Harvard. I'm a behind-the-scenes man—that's where I work best, and that's where I'm happiest. Behind the scenes. I'm not comfortable in the limelight, Essie. I hate publicity because I know that all the publicity in the world won't get you a free ride on the trolley. I couldn't stand having to do the things Jake does—make speeches, accept awards, honorary degrees, having his picture in the papers all the time. But Jake loves all that stuff, and he's very good at it. He literally eats it up. Each new en—en—*encomium* is the word, and how's that after a bottle of champagne?—seems to puff him up a little bit more."

Essie swirled the wine in her glass. "In more ways than one," she said. "I've given up trying to speak to him about his weight. He used to have such a nice trim figure. He just gets heavier . . . heavier."

"But you don't understand. He thinks the weight becomes him. I'm sure of that. The more there is of him, the bigger a figurehead there is for the world to admire."

Essie suppressed a giggle, and Charles reached for the bottle and refilled their glasses. "But don't you—sometimes—just hate him?" she said.

"Uh-uh. *Au contraire,* since we're drinking French wine. *Au contraire.* A company like ours needs a good figurehead, and a good figurehead needs a good behind-the-scenes man. That's why we're all—rich. Hey," he said suddenly, "I've got an idea." He jumped up, walked out of the tent, and returned carrying one of the six-branched candelabra from the dining tables and set it in the center of their smaller one. He produced a pack of matches, and lighted the candles one by one. "Now how do we turn out the Chicago Gas and Electric Company?"

"Over there—by the bandstand—there's a switch."

With the lights out, the big tent was plunged into shadows and silvery reflections from the candles on the canvas overhead. "There," he said, returning to the table. "That's more like it." He refilled their glasses once more. "Oops," he said, looking at the bottle. "Another dead soldier. I'll get some more—"

Returning with a freshly opened bottle and sitting down again, he said, "Ah, this is perfect. Story-book setting. Champagne by candlelight. May I say, Mrs. Auerbach, that this is one of the most beautiful parties you have ever given?" He raised his glass to her in a salute, and Essie laughed softly.

Something was happening to her—perhaps it was the champagne—but she could feel the color rising to her cheeks which, of course, he couldn't see, a flushed feeling of guilty excitement that was . . . that was a little like that feeling as she watched, with a prurient and nasty thrill . . . and yet had been unable to take her eyes off . . . that performance on a bare stage in Paris.

"And now let me ask you the same question," he said. "You've had some pretty good ideas for Jake in your time. What's it been like for you to see him take credit for them? Are you like me? Content to be a behind-the-scenes man?"

"No, it was hard at first," she said quietly. "For a while, I thought I was married to a man I didn't know. But now . . . now I'm used to it. I've put it out of my mind. My father had an expression he used constantly—'Think of it!' But thinking of unpleasant things made him an unpleasant man. I haven't seen or spoken to him in years, my father. So—what were we talking about?"

"You and Jake."

"Oh. Yes, well, I try to keep busy with other things. Opera Guild. The children. Working on the art collection. My garden. Entertaining . . ."

"And it's enough for you?"

"I make it be enough."

"And—Daisy?"

"Now don't say a word against Daisy. Daisy's on my side, believe it or not. Daisy's my friend. But I miss—"

"Miss what?"

Tears welled in her eyes. "I miss . . . my little Prince."

Quickly he covered her hand with his. "Now, no sad

thoughts!" he said sharply. "This is a party, remember?" He refilled their glasses once more.

"You're right," she said. "Can't turn back . . . the clock."

They sat in silence for a moment or two. A quieter mood seemed to have settled over them in the uncertain light of the slowly lowering candles, and Essie wondered whether his thoughts were racing as confusedly as her own.

"Babette," she said at last, clearing her throat. "Babette is . . . the more stable of the two girls. Don't you think? Joan has always been so . . . headstrong . . ."

"Fourteen years . . ."

"Hm?"

"Fourteen years. I've been with Eaton and Cromwell fourteen years." He reached out to refill her glass.

"Ah," she said. There was another silence. Then she said, "The front of her dress was stitched with hundreds of little seed pearls. . . ."

"Dress?"

"The dress she was to wear tonight—Joan."

"Ah," he said. And then, "So still out here tonight."

"But not hot."

"Not hot. Just right."

"I saw a deer in the woods this morning."

"A deer." Another silence. Then he said suddenly, "I have a rotten marriage."

She had hoped he would not bring up Cecilia, whom she had never really liked. Cecilia did not belong with them here in this party tent tonight. There was no room for her, but Essie said softly, "Do you, Charles? I'm sorry."

"She calls me a . . . a . . . a *sycophant*. Sycophant is what she calls me. She resents the fact that I don't want to be a Jake Auerbach. She doesn't understand that I enjoy being a behind-the-scenes man."

"Well, then she—" But Essie couldn't remember the rest of the sentence she had composed in her mind to say.

"And when she's drinking—but wait. I forgot the rules. No sad thoughts. No sad talk." He reached for the bottle again, and the candles guttered in a light breeze that made the sides of the tent heave inward and outward like gentle breathing.

"I hear music," he said.

"Music?"

"Listen—" He gestured toward the empty bandstand. "Hear it? They're playing that new song. 'Someone to Watch Over Me,' from that new Broadway show. *Oh, Kay.* Can't you hear it?"

"Oh, yes . . ."

"May I have the pleasure of this dance? Or is your dance card filled?"

"Let me see," she said, studying an imaginary dance card in her hand. "No, as a matter of fact . . . believe it or not . . . I have an empty space right here. . . ."

He led her, carrying her champagne glass, out onto the empty dance floor, where they began to dance to the phantom music, while he part-whispered, part-hummed the lyric. "'There's a somebody I'm longin' to see . . .'" whirling her, spinning her, dipping her around the floor. Then he held her more closely and said, "April tenth, nineteen thirteen."

"What's that?" she asked him dreamily.

"Don't you remember? Don't you remember April tenth, nineteen thirteen?"

"Should I, Charles?"

"That was the date I met a lovely woman on a train going west, and fell in love with her."

She said nothing, but let her forehead fall against his shoulder.

"But you've known that—haven't you? Always? I thought I could force you out of my thoughts with Cecilia. It didn't work. You know that's why I've stayed with Jake, don't you? Not to be a behind-the-scenes man. To be near you."

"Fourteen years . . ."

His persuasive body began to move in the exquisite falling arcs, the slow recoveries, the erotic pauses of the tango. And now they danced more slowly to the silent music of whatever song it was now—a slow tune—that the orchestra had segued into, and as though she was in a dream she felt her partner lead her in a dance, out across the floor, out through the entrance of the tent, out into the darkness of the late night, across the damp grass, down along the shadowed pathways of Essie's wild garden.

Later, as they lay together on the impromptu bedding they

had made of their discarded clothes, he said, "This is what we both wanted. Always. Isn't it?"

"Yes," she said.

"And of course you're right. I have hated him. Because he had you. And I didn't."

"But you do now," she whispered. "You do now."

The aborted coming-out party was given rather lurid treatment by some of the press, under such headlines as "DEB DISAPPEARS," and "HEIRESS HIGHTAILS IT."

Jean-Claude de Lucy was rather vaguely described as "a ten-goal polo player." He was forty-two, and had had three previous marriages, one of them to a Pittsburgh Scaife, who was related to the Mellons.

Jake Auerbach announced that he intended to do absolutely nothing to try to get his daughter back, nor would he send her a cent of money.

But six weeks later Joan was home again anyway, with a broken collarbone, asking for a divorce, charging "extreme cruelty."

Twenty-two

TODAY, Essie is having lunch with her only grandson, and as usual he has chosen the restaurant. He prefers the fashionable and expensive places, which is fine with Essie, since she is happy to see him develop taste and discernment. For the past few years, they have been having these little lunches together every three or four weeks, and Essie always looks forward to them. Sometimes they go to "21," sometimes to La Caravelle, sometimes to Côte Basque, sometimes to the Four Seasons. Today, young Josh has chosen Le Perigord Park, just a few blocks down the street from Essie's apartment building. Joshua Auerbach, Jr., who is just twenty-three, derives obvious pleasure from using his credit cards, making suggestions from menus, ordering cocktails, selecting wines, tipping waiters and captains. And Essie derives pleasure from imagining that the other patrons of the restaurants they visit look at the two of them and assume that the old lady in her sable cape has purchased for herself a handsome young gigolo.

Considering what some of her friends have for grandchildren—shuffling, shaggy things in beards, Fu Manchu mustaches, patched jeans and horrible sneakers—young Josh is a blessing. Not that he looks like a gigolo, however. He is tall, well-built, clean-cut and clean-shaven, a tennis and lacrosse player, a skier. His sandy-colored hair tends to have a rather wind-blown look but, with the rest of him so well put together, from his scent to his well-clipped fingernails, Essie finds this one detail attractive. Today he is wearing a neat blue pinstriped business suit, a white shirt, and a blue-and-red striped tie. As usual, he has arrived at the restaurant a few minutes ahead of her, and rises to greet her when she enters the room. One thing must be said for Katie, his mother: she taught her son manners. He squeezes her hand and kisses her lightly on the cheek—"Hi, Nana"—and no sooner has Essie seated herself than a waiter arrives with a dry martini, on the stem with an olive, just as Essie likes it. He always does this.

"Well, then," Essie says, removing her gloves. "So how's by you?" It is one of their little jokes, talking in Jewishisms, though young Josh looks about as Jewish as Robert Redford.

"Okay by me, so how's by you?"

"You like my new dress?"

"On you it looks good. You should live to a hundred and twenty."

"I should have such luck. It's a nothing of a dress."

"Well, so long as you got your health," he says. And then, lifting his glass, "*L'chayim.*"

"*L'chayim*, Joshie. It's nice to see you."

Essie loves him very much. It is wrong to have favorites, of course, but of her grandchildren Josh is hers.

"Seriously," he says, "how's Aunt Joan?"

"She's fine. She's home. She's still pretty depressed, but she's seeing this new doctor. I'm hoping—"

"What actually happened, Nana, do you know?"

Essie hesitates. "I like to think she had an accident," she says finally. "You know how doctors ladle out these pills. I think that she was pretty upset, and—well, couldn't sleep, and forgot she'd taken some pills, and then took some more. She's always been so—highstrung."

"I blame that rotten story in the *Times* about the *Express*," he says. "That story even upset me, and I didn't have anything to do with her paper."

"Well, when a newspaper goes under, the *Times* has got to print the news."

"I meant all that rotten stuff about how she couldn't control her staff, and how that meant she couldn't build a solid enough advertising base. All that was personal, and gossip, and rotten."

"Well, what can you expect from the competition? As your grandfather used to say."

"The *Times* made it sound as though she was a candidate for Welfare. She's not, is she?"

"Are you kidding *me?*" Essie says. "Her father left her ten million in an unbreakable trust. And if the income from ten million dollars isn't enough to live comfortably on, she should have her head examined. Anyway," Essie adds, "she *is* having her head examined. This new doctor—I forget his name—not that I have all that much faith in shrinks, as your generation calls them. How long has your Uncle Mogie been going to a shrink? Forty years?"

Josh laughed. "Ah, but look at him—look at that dishy new wife he's got!"

"She's—dishy, all right. Was she really a Rockette, Joshie?"

"She told me she was a dancer. But I don't think she ever made it to the Music Hall, Nana. I think it was Roseland, more like it."

"You're teasing me, of course. Actually, I like her. Not a brain in her head, of course. But a girl like that doesn't need brains. At the tree-trimming, did you notice how Mogie hovers over her? Hovers! All her brains are below the waist, if you ask me."

"The Women's Libbers would scalp you for that kind of talk, Nana," he says. "And what about Richard? Has he left for good, or—"

"Who knows? I could ask you the same question. He's in—in South America, or South Africa, I forget just where, and Joan hasn't heard a word from him."

"I bet he'll be back, Nana."

"Well, for her sake, I *hope* so. Or that she can find some new outlet for her—energies."

"How many divorces have there been in this family?"

"*Don't ask!*" Essie says, slipping back into the Jewish accent. "Enough already."

They bantered like this, back and forth, as they always did, for about half an hour, before picking up their menus. Their lunches never had any specific direction, there was never any specific reason for them, no business to discuss, no agenda. They gossiped about the family, about friends, about what Josh was doing at the office. After graduating from Princeton, with

honors, a business major, young Josh had joined Eaton &
Cromwell in the company's training program, moving from
department to department. Right now he was working in the
Advertising Department. One day, Essie knew, he would be
president of the company. Already, they were calling him the
Fair-Haired Boy. "Let's see," Essie says, studying the menu,
"do you think the shad roe would be fresh?"

"I . . . think . . . not," he says carefully. "Too early. But I
know their Dover sole is flown in fresh every day. . . ."

"I'll have that, then."

Later, during lunch, she asks him suddenly, "Joshie, when
you were in school and college, did you ever get involved in
what they call this—drug scene?"

He rolls his eyes. "Oh, heavy, Nana. Heavy, heavy." Then
he winks at her. "But I won't deny I've smoked a little marijuana."

"Now that strikes me as perfectly harmless," Essie says,
"from everything I read. Sometimes I think that Joan should
take up marijuana—something that would *relax* her a little
bit."

"Somehow, I can't picture Aunt Joan rolling a joint."

"I wouldn't even mind trying it myself," Essie says.

"Well," he says with another wink, "some Saturday afternoon I'll come by your house and we'll go tripping together."

"I'd like that," she says. "I really would. I like the sound of
it. Tripping." Then she says, "But you know, Joshie, you've
always been an exceptionally *good* boy. I thought that the very
first time you were put in my arms, as a tiny baby. I thought to
myself: this little baby is going to grow up to be an exceptionally *good* boy."

"Well, thanks, Nana."

"That's why I'm so happy you've gone into the business.
Besides you and your father, no one else in the family seems to
give a Chinaman's damn about it."

"I find the business fascinating."

"It's good. It's nice to think of the third generation still
caring about it. It gives a nice—continuity." She realizes that,
years ago, when her own mother-in-law expressed these sentiments, she didn't agree with them at all. She adds, "I didn't

use to feel this way, but now I do. It comes with old age, I guess. Anyway, your grandpa would be pleased."

"He must have been quite a guy, Grandpa."

"Oh, yes. Yes indeed. Quite a guy."

"I was pretty little when he died. I don't remember too much about him. I just remember him giving me holy hell one day for putting my galoshes on the wrong feet."

"Oh, yes. That was his way. He gave a lot of people holy hell when they didn't do things just his way. That was his nature."

"Speaking of which," he says, "I do have one small piece of business to discuss with you."

"What's that?"

"The dedication of the new building in Chicago. Will you be coming out for that? Uncle Charles asked me to ask you whether or not you've made up your mind."

"I haven't."

"We'd fly you out on a company plane. Put you up in style at the Ritz."

"Tell Charles I haven't decided yet."

"For some reason, he gets real sentimental about wanting you there. Continuity—what you were talking about."

"Well, for various reasons I don't have the happiest association with Chicago."

"Really, Nana? Why?"

"Reasons not to be gone into here."

"Of course Uncle Charles is getting pretty old," he says.

"Now see here," she says, putting down her fork and placing her napkin on the table. "Charles may be getting old, as you say—though he's two years younger than me—but he still knows more about this business than you or I or any other living soul. You must always listen very carefully to everything he says. *Very* carefully, Joshie."

From across the table he smiles at her. "What he says is that he wants you to go."

"Ah," Essie says, returning the smile, "but what I said was that *you* must listen to what he says. Not that *I* must."

"*Touché,*" he says.

As they leave the restaurant, Essie's car and driver are waiting at the curb. The driver hops out and opens the door for her. The late February wind is cold, and Essie clutches the folds of her sable cape about her. Josh takes her elbow to help her into the car and kisses her good-bye all in one motion. "So long, Nana. Enjoyed the lunch."

"So did I. Thank you, Joshie. Tell Charles I'll try to have a decision for him before too long."

"'Bye, Nana. . . ."

From the back seat, she waves to him as the door closes. As the car pulls out into the traffic, she turns and watches him as he strides purposefully down Park Avenue, coat collar turned up, shoulders hunched against the wind, his hair blowing. Watching him walk away from her she cannot help but be reminded of another beautiful young man, years ago.

The driver lowers the window between them for instructions.

"Home," she says.

Jake's company had kept the apartment at the Palmer House, and used it to put up out-of-town salesmen and plant managers whenever they came through. But it stood empty much of the time, and it was here that Essie and Charles would meet, usually in the middle of the day, at lunchtime. The hotel staff, he was certain, would be discreet, particularly in matters pertaining to one of their highest-paying tenants, and he had been correct. The only stipulation which Charles and Essie made to each other was that they should always arrive and leave separately, with their own keys.

Those years had a very special quality for them both—hard to define. They were years with bright edges framed around them that were definite and in place. Her own feelings were so different from that youthful, almost schoolgirlish love she had once felt for Jake, a love that seemed to spring from some visceral point in her belly rather than from her heart. Perhaps this was what people meant when they talked of *mature* love, because after all Essie was thirty-six when the affair began and, in those days, thirty-six was considered middle-aged. It was an affair, for instance, that did not involve much kissing. Oh, they kissed, of course, but the thing was that kissing was not the *point*. Years later, Essie would ask herself if Charles had ever said to her the words, "I love you," or whether she had ever actually uttered the words to him. Oh, they probably both had but, again, hearing these vocalized assurances was not the *point* of what they had together, was not what gave those years their strong framework and their sense of wonder and surprise. That was part of it—surprise, surprise that each could derive so much pleasure from the other. Surprise at their luck—because luck seemed an important ingredient in it all. How lucky she had been to be seated in a certain car on a certain train when he got on board at Harmon on that certain day, how lucky it had been for them that Joan had skipped out on her debut party to marry an unlucky Frenchman. And how lucky they both were to have reached points in their marriages where neither attached any guilt or remorse to the passionate happiness, the passionate affection they found they were able to offer to each other. That was it. It was not love in the love-story sense. Passionate affection described it best. They had become lovers, of course, and they were in love, and they made love, but the usual baggage and burdens that come with love did not exist, had been stripped away, and left behind somewhere in time. It was an unmortgaged love—debt-free. Essie had been astonished to find that this sort of love existed and so, she was sure, was Charles.

As a result, whenever they met, she could not wait to hear him tell her how he had spent his day, or week, and he could not wait to hear her latest news. When they met, they would talk furiously, eagerly, for twenty minutes or so. Then they would order a light lunch from Room Service, and talk some more. Then they made love. When they parted, there were never tears, and when they could not meet there were never recriminations. Though the years have blurred details, that is what Essie remembers most vividly—that bright framework that supported a tall structure of talk, laughter, passion and affection, solid as a city skyscraper.

Also, we must remember—Essie must remember—that those years helped her forget the loss of Prince. Not forget. But put it in the only perspective it could be put, which was in the perspective of the over and the past. Now, perhaps, is the moment to deal with that.

Picture a late-afternoon room, long shadows, curtains blowing in from a breeze off the lake. All this must be imaginary, of course, because Essie was not there. And fix the time at some point earlier than the beginning of her affair with Charles—make it 1923. Yes, somewhere in 1923 must have been when our imaginary scene occurred, because that was the year Prince was fifteen, and was given his first shares of Eaton & Cromwell stock and, as we shall see, there was a connection.

Imagine, then, Hans standing naked beside the bed, smiling slightly, and saying, "Princey, what do you figure your daddy would say if he knew about what you and I like to do?"

Prince pulls the bedclothes up across his knees, and says, "What do you mean?"

"I mean," says Hans, "I think he'd be pretty fairly well upset by it, if he found out. About you and me. Don't you by it, if he found out. About you and me. Don't you figure?"

"Yeah, I guess so," Prince says.

"I figure your daddy would be pretty fairly mad. If somehow he found out." He reaches down for Prince's toe under the sheet and wiggles it and says, almost in a whine, "You know, old Hans here doesn't get paid much money for the job he does. Don't you think old Hans is worth a little extra? For the little extra things he does for Princey? For making sure that Princey's daddy doesn't find out what Princey likes to do with Hans? Your daddy's a rich man. The papers say he gives away millions of dollars to people he doesn't even know. Don't you think you could work out a way for old Hans to get a little more money?"

Prince says nothing.

Hans wiggles his toe again. "You're your daddy's fair-haired boy," he says. "You can do it, I think, for old Hans."

As has been said, who knows whether this little exchange took place as written? What difference does truth make about a thing like that? Does truth bring back anything?

What is certain is that in that summer of Prince's fifteenth year, 1923, there was a discussion between Prince and his parents on the subject of his finances, and Prince had asked that his allowance be increased.

"Your grades haven't been exactly spectacular at school," his father said.

"I'm going to work real hard next year, Daddy, to bring them up. . . ."

In the end, Jake Auerbach had hit upon a better idea than increasing his son's allowance. He would sign over to Prince a certain number of shares of Eaton & Cromwell stock, enough to yield him an income for about four hundred dollars a month. Prince would open a bank account. This would give him a personal stake in the family business which he would one day head. It would teach him the value of money. It would teach him how American Capitalism worked.

Still, all might have been well if, in the following year, 1924, there had not been a ghastly scandal in Chicago. A fourteen-year-old boy named Bobby Franks had been abducted from his schoolyard and brutally murdered, his mutilated body found near a drainage ditch. Within hours, the two chief subjects were two youths not much older than Prince himself, Nathan Leopold and Richard Loeb. The suspects and the victim were all members of prominent Chicago Jewish families. The Frankses, Loebs, and Leopolds had all been to parties at The Bluff. As more details emerged, the Bobby Franks kidnap-murder became even more lurid and spread to newspaper headlines across the country. Loeb and Leopold, it seemed, had had Nietzschean visions of being supermen, of committing the perfect crime. The two were homosexual lovers, and had killed Bobby Franks to achieve the ultimate homosexual thrill. The newspapers were filled with words like "pederasty," which anyone who could read could look up in a dictionary and figure out what was meant.

These were very bad days at The Bluff—after the murder, and during the sensational trial that followed. Jacob Auerbach felt personally assaulted by the murder, and felt that it befouled the reputations of all Jews, particularly Jews such as himself who had worked to establish themselves as productive and responsible American citizens. The case was helping to fan, he felt—and with certain justification—the flames of anti-Semitism that were billowing across America in the 1920s. The case brought back ancient canards about Jewish ritual slaughtering of young children. Henry Ford, an outspoken anti-Semite, had caused to be published in his Dearborn newspaper the spurious *Protocols of the Learned Elders of Zion,* which alleged to portray an international conspiracy of Jews to take over the world's money. In Germany, a young man named Adolf Hitler had founded his National Socialist German Workers' party and, the previous November, had staged his Beer Hall Putsch in Munich.

Jacob Auerbach could not seem to shake the case from his mind, and railed about it nightly from the head of his dinner table. "Filth . . . scum . . . perverts. A disgrace to their parents, a disgrace to their religion, a disgrace to America . . . vile creatures. The worst crime a son could ever commit against his father—against his God! Fairies . . . queers . . . they should be castrated in public, strung up by their heels. We can never have the Loebs or the Leopolds in this house again. No, perhaps we should write or try to call them, Essie, and tell them how we share their suffering over this terrible thing. What do you think? Which should we do? Their monsters of sons have made them the most miserable human beings on this earth. Should we hold them responsible for what their sons did?"

"Well, if you're talking about appearances—" Essie began.

"Appearances!" he shouted. "How can you mention appearances, after the way those perverts have made us all appear? They've made Jews appear to be fiends and madmen. Discipline—the right discipline—must have been lacking in their homes. There must have been some clue their parents were too blind to see. How can you have a son that's a monster and a queer besides and not notice something? There are ways of finding out about perverts—supervision . . . discipline . . . punishment. Miserable perverts must be stopped before they get to *this!*"

During this period, Hans, who was not unaware of these dinner-table fulminations, began upping his demands.

And so, late one October afternoon when the leaves had begun to turn and there was a chilly whiff of winter in the air, the older of Jacob Auerbach's two sons took out a pen and a piece of letter paper, sat at his desk and wrote:

Dear Mother and Daddy—

I know that you have always wanted me to be a good son, and I have tried to be a good son, but I have failed, and that is why I am going to do what I am going to do.

You see, Daddy, I am a pervert, too, like Nate Leopold and Dickie Loeb. I am a pervert, like them (and I even knew about them long before this happened), and Hans and I have been perverts together for about three years.

I know you would not want to live with a son who is a pervert, and would not want to live with a monster. I don't want to live as one, either, which is why I am going to do what I am going to do. I'm sorry. I love you. So long.

Prince

He folded the letter and placed it carefully on the center of his desk. Then he walked quietly down to Hans's room, where Hans lay sprawled on his bed asleep. Hans's service revolver, in its holster, lay slung across the back of a chair with Hans's clothes. Prince lifted the pistol from the holster, put it in his pocket, left the room and closed the door behind him, making no noise at all.

Then he went downstairs and into the garden, past the swimming pool, down the wooded pathways until the house was no longer visible. There he sat down on a jutting outcropping of rock. He took the gun out of his pocket, and studied it for a moment or two. He released the safety catch, as Hans had taught him to do. Then, as though there were nothing else in the world to do, he placed the barrel in his mouth and pulled the trigger. *I'm sorry, Daddy!* The Undersucker had come at last.

One of the gardeners, whose name was Giovanni, heard the shot, hurried to the place, and found him there. He went running to the house for help.

Jake read the note, and now the revolver was in his hand.

"Stop it, Jake!" she screamed. "Put that thing down!"

But he was already heading down the long corridor toward Hans's room.

Running after him, she cried, "Stop! Stop this!"

The door to Hans's room was flung open, and Hans sat there

naked in his bed, rubbing his eyes. Jake pointed the gun at him.

Essie threw herself across her husband's back, wrestling his arm down, screaming, "Stop this! *Do you want to be a murderer too!*"

Finally, she felt her husband's arm relax, and she heard him say to Hans, "You came into this house with nothing but the clothes on your back. That's all you're leaving with."

Then, for the next hour or so Jake Auerbach went on a rampage of fury and grief, or both, which Essie, numb, could only watch. He strode from room to room of the house, and wherever a picture of Prince stood on a table it was snatched up, hurled to the floor, smashed and trampled on. From photograph albums going back sixteen years, whole pages of family pictures which contained Prince's image were ripped from their bindings and hurled into the huge baronial fireplace in the library where, soon, a bonfire raged. Then it was up the stairs to Prince's room, where the contents of his desk were dumped on the floor, gathered up, and consigned to the flames. Next came the contents of his closets and dresser drawers—shirts, sweaters, suits, socks, underwear, even shoes and toilet articles and pieces of jewelry were flung into the fire. Into the fire went Prince's stamp collection, his books, his chess set, his collection of phonograph records, the model airplanes he had made of rice paper and balsa wood. "Oh, stop . . ." Essie moaned, when she saw the airplanes go up in flames. But he would not stop, and from the central chimney of The Bluff, oily black smoke, as though from some bizarre cremation, belched upward into the clear October sky. Within an hour, or so it seemed—for who, after all, was keeping track of time?— every trace and vestige of their son's life was burning or in ashes. Through it all, Jake kept roaring, "His name is never to be mentioned in this house again!" while the servants did the prudent thing, and kept their distance.

The death of young Jacob Auerbach, Jr. was listed in the papers as accidental.

Only later, when it was necessary to go over Prince's financial affairs with an officer at the bank, and all the checks that had been written to Hans came to light, did Essie wish that she had let her husband pull the trigger.

"Was there some clue, some signal that I should have got, but didn't?" she said to Charles when he came to pay a condolence visit. "Was there something I should have noticed—some warning—that I didn't see? For instance, he was always so . . . neat. Not just about his clothes and person, but about his room. Was that it? I mean, you know how messy most young boys are about their rooms. But with him, everything had to be in its place, just so. I can see him building those little model airplanes—all those little pieces laid out in order, just so, just as the instructions said. Picking up those tiny pieces with a tweezers, applying a little thread of glue. Everything perfect. And there was such a sensitivity about him. I'd be sketching out a design for an opera program—I can see him, standing over my shoulder, making a suggestion every now and then—'Don't you think that would be better in a lighter blue?' So sensitive to little things like that. Or didn't I spend enough time with him later on? His stamp collection. He asked me once if I could paint the flags of the various countries at the head of each . . . section . . . of the album. I told him I was too busy then, I'd do it later. I forgot about it. I never did it. He never asked again, and I forgot about it—that's all! And he was so gentle. He loved his pony so. I'd hear him, in the stable brushing and currying his pony, talking to it. Not talking like he was talking to a horse, you know, but as though he was talking to a *person*. I can hear him talking to his pony. I can't remember what—or—or—or was he so unhappy in this family, in this house, that he couldn't bear it any longer, and was there some way I could have known this, or sensed this, and helped him somehow, and come to him and said—what? Where were the little signals that I missed, Charles? Or were they there—or what? Why didn't I see the danger that was living in my house, under my nose? Where was it, why was it—that I couldn't even see it? Where? Or were there signals that I didn't *want* to see, was afraid to see?"

Charles was studying, very hard, the changeless pattern of the square of carpet between his feet. At last he said, "There are no answers to any of these questions, Essie. You mustn't keep asking them of yourself."

The
BOOK
of
REVELATIONS

Twenty-three

It is April, and Linda Schofield, Essie's great-granddaughter, is finishing her Winter Work Period for Bennington, and will soon be going back to Vermont. Linda is interested in a career in television broadcasting, and has spent the winter term working as a "gofer" for the *Today* show at NBC. ("I gofer coffee, I gofer sandwiches, I gofer the makeup man's cigarettes, but I learn a lot about what goes on.") Today she has stopped by the apartment, on her way home, for tea. Sometimes, Linda calls Essie "Great-Grandma," and sometimes it is "Gee-Gee." Today it is Gee-Gee.

"Did you know that Mother's going to marry that man, Gee-Gee?" Linda says as Essie pours the tea. "That Daryl Carter?"

"No, I didn't," Essie says. "Well, I suppose I should say I hope she'll be very happy."

"He's a wimp," Linda says, "but he's a nice enough wimp. Of course he's closer to my age than to hers."

"Well, if he loves her—"

"I'm not so sure about the love bit," Linda says. "But I'll say this for him. He's gotten on Mother's case about the drinking, and she's been looking a lot better."

Essie glances at Linda out of the corner of her eye. "Good," she says. "Good, because I did think Karen was drinking a bit too much."

"She's an alcoholic, Gee-Gee—face it."

"Well, dear, everything is relative."

"He's gotten her to go to A.A. meetings. He goes with her."

"Well, good," Essie says.

"Of course I think it's a purely sexual thing with Mother. For her, Daryl is just a sex object."

Essie hesitates. "Well, as long as he's kind to her," she says.

Linda lifts her teacup to her lips and, in this little gesture, Essie sees another young girl lifting a teacup in a crimson parlor years ago. Yes, in Linda, there is something of the girl she had once scrutinized in her mother's hand mirror years ago, a definite resemblance. Funny that it would have skipped not just one but two generations, for Essie has never been able to see much of herself in any of her own children.

"I'm in a sexual relationship myself right now, Gee-Gee," Linda says.

"Really?" Essie says. "Well, I suppose that's very common these days for girls your age, Linda. It wasn't in my day. We waited for marriage, but I'm willing to admit that times have changed. I suppose you're—as they say—on the pill."

"Oh, naturally," Linda says. "It's a boy in my class at Bennington."

"Jewish?"

"Gosh, I don't have any idea. I've never asked him."

"Well, even that doesn't make much difference anymore, does it? At least not in this family. If my father knew what's gone on in this family, he'd be spinning in his grave."

"What was he like, Gee-Gee?"

Essie thinks to find the right words. "Stern. Pious. Scholarly. Rigid. Unforgiving."

"Unforgiving? What was there to forgive?"

"Oh, plenty." She nods towards Jake's portrait. "He didn't approve of my marriage, for one thing. He had another man all picked out."

"Hmm. Well, frankly, I don't think it's all it's cracked up to be, Gee-Gee."

"What isn't?"

"Sex. This sex business. I mean, what's there to it? I find it all kind of a big bore."

"Ah," Essie says. "I'm sorry to hear that, Linda."

"Sorry? Why?"

"It shouldn't be a big bore. That's all."

"What should it be?"

"Well," Essie says, again choosing her words carefully, for

this is not the kind of conversation she had been prepared to have this particular afternoon, and thinking that Linda must have some motive for the direction their talk is taking, and wondering whether—perhaps—her great-granddaughter has come to her as some sort of oracle possessed of the great wisdom that is supposed to come, but rarely does, with old age. "I can only speak of my own case," she says. "I've always felt that when you love someone, sex can be a very beautiful part of life. When you're really close to someone, when you're like—well, like one soul, not two. The beautiful thing about it is that there are no words for it. When it's over, there's not much that you and your lover can say about it. You laugh a little. You touch each other a little. Then you get up and go about your day as usual, but just feeling a little better. There's nothing to discuss, because there are no words, no language for it. I've always thought of sex as a kind of love poetry without words."

"Hmm," Linda says, frowning into her teacup.

"And so I suspect that you are not very much in love with this young man."

"That's true. I'm not."

"Then sex won't mean much, and what's the point of it? At least that's what I say." *I want to replace my little Prince,* she thinks. "I had another son," she says.

"What?"

"Never mind. Woolgathering. Anyway, that's what I say."

"But I suppose it goes away in time, doesn't it—sex?"

Essie laughs. "Oh, no. It doesn't go away. It just gets—lovelier."

"But not at your age, Gee-Gee!"

"Oh, yes. Why not? As you get older, it gets lovelier—softer, more tender—because there are less distractions. Like worrying about getting pregnant, for example. It becomes more concentrated, less—cluttered up, I guess is the expression. No, I have as much sexual drive, as they say, at eighty-nine as I did at eighteen."

"That's incredible, Gee-Gee!"

"Incredible, but true. Remember you heard it here. More tea?"

Linda offers her empty teacup and changes the subject.

"Grandma says that that Arthur Litton, who died, was some sort of relative of ours."

"He was my brother."

"Ah, Gee-Gee, I'm sorry."

"Don't be. He was not a nice man."

"What did he do?"

"I don't want to talk about it. Tell me, how is Joan getting along?"

"She's talking about reorganizing the newspaper."

"Honestly," Essie says, setting down her teacup. "I simply do not understand your grandmother. She's my own daughter, and I cannot understand her. Can you explain her to me? She talks about going broke, and owing money all over town—and she and her sister aren't speaking because she owes money to Babette. But she still drives around town in a chauffeur-driven car, still has her butler, her cook—how do you explain that?"

"We think she's found a new angel."

"Well, she'd better pay back some of the old angels first," Essie says.

"I know she's hired a fancy new Madison Avenue lawyer who's handling her affairs. He's 'investigating certain improprieties,' she says."

"Huh! She'd better straighten out her own improprieties first."

"Well, I don't pay too much attention to all the capitalist talk," Linda says, adding casually, "I've become a Marxist, did I tell you?"

"No! Well, stranger things have happened in this family. I once marched in a children's strike on the Lower East Side."

"Hmm," Linda says, crushing her lemon slice to a pulp with the tip of her teaspoon at the bottom of the cup. "It was interesting what you had to say about sex, Gee-Gee. Even at your age."

"Yes," Essie winks. "Even at my age, Linda."

"Interesting." She continues to worry and poke at what remains of her lemon slice. "And it would be interesting to know what would have happened to his family if Great-Grandpa hadn't made all that money."

"That's the sixty-four-thousand-dollar question!" Essie whoops.

*   *   *

Interesting. Yes. "It's just that I'm *weary* of them, Charles," she had said to him several years ago. "It's not that I don't love my children, but I'm weary of them coming back to me, again and again, demanding this or that. I wanted nice children—not *dependents*. Why haven't they learned to take care of themselves, to have responsibilities? Why haven't they learned that? Was there just too much money?"

"Josh learned it."

"I admit I tried to raise him differently. No bodyguards. No nannies. I guess I thought the others had examples of strong, independent, responsible people all around them. You, me, Jake—even Daisy. No one was more independent than Daisy! I guess I made a lot of wrong assumptions."

It was the year that Joan had married Richard McAllister and, with him, was trying to get her newspaper started, and had succeeded in extracting $250,000 out of Essie for that project, even though it was less than half the figure Joan wanted. Looking back, after this latest debacle, Essie has decided that she should have given her nothing.

In the years following Prince's death, Jake had begun taking long trips to distant places. The 1920s had been the years of the company's most vigorous expansion, and much of this travel had been in connection with that, though Essie suspected that much of it was also a kind of miserable self-exile. Often he didn't tell her of the imminence of these trips, or their duration, though Charles was always careful to keep her informed of her husband's whereabouts. At some point in their lives, though Essie could not tell you precisely where, there had been an almost-audible *snap!* in their married existence, and Essie no longer cared that they now led essentially separate lives, and she would hear with equanimity that her husband was in the Far East, in Tokyo, where he would be dining with young Emperor Hirohito, or that he was in Belgium, where he would confer with the king about a new plant there, or that he was in Hawaii, battling with American Factors, Inc., and threatening to build his own steamship line when there was some question as to whether Matson Navigation would agree to ship goods to the Islands which would compete with another Big Five enterprise—American Factors' Liberty House department store—

or that Eaton & Cromwell had sold 50,000 refrigerators in the year 1926, as opposed to 27,000 the year before. Sometimes it was necessary for Charles to accompany him on these travels. At other times, the always-obliging Daisy was his escort. For some reason—his odd sense of propriety, perhaps—he never requested that both Charles and Daisy join his entourage at the same time, though there were times when both Essie and Daisy were invited to join him. For such trips, Daisy's role was that of "close family friend."

Daisy's position in the Auerbach household was by now so secure that her companionship was no longer a subject for discussion within the family—though, outside of it, who knew? At home, she was simply Aunt Daisy. On the passenger lists of the ships on which she traveled with Jake, Daisy was always listed as "Private Secretary," and had her own stateroom, though she no longer performed any secretarial chores. Though she frequently spent weekends at The Bluff, even when Jake was away, where she had her own suite of rooms, she had also been provided with a comfortable apartment at 1430 Lake Shore Drive. "Appearances" were thereby observed. Were there also other women? Who knew? There were whispers to that effect. Obviously, this was something Essie and Daisy never discussed and, ah, the power of money to suppress gossip and malicious talk! In some ways, Essie had begun to see hers as a household like that of a Chinese aristocrat, in which Daisy Stevens was Number One Concubine, with all the privileges thereunto entailed. If there were numbers Two or Three or even more they did not intrude. The charm of Daisy—perhaps that was what kept Jake attracted to her—was that she never lost her temper, never complained, never made demands. As for Essie, she was simply, officially, Mrs. Jacob Auerbach, Number One Wife, patroness of the arts, with all the privileges thereunto entailed. It was an arrangement that worked. What more can be said?

And, needless to say, Essie came to welcome the times when Daisy was chosen as her husband's companion on his travels. It made her meetings with Charles easier to arrange.

It was in this period, too—the years between 1924 and 1929—that Jake Auerbach began expanding his personal scale of living. Perhaps because The Bluff evoked bitter memories, there were now additional residences required—a small, *pied-à-terre* apartment in New York at the new Hotel Pierre, a big house at Seagirt, on the New Jersey shore, not far from where his parents had once had a place at Elberon (he preferred Seagirt to Elberon, because Elberon was already being called "the Jewish Newport"), and a large camp, with many outbuildings, on Saranac Lake in the Adirondacks, where he liked to spend the month of August. Unless there was a special reason for her to be at his side as hostess, a command performance—a dinner for a head of state, or a visit from a celebrity such as Horace Dodge, Charles Lindbergh, or Mr. and Mrs. Douglas Fairbanks—Essie herself spent little time at these places. While her husband preferred to banish Prince's memory from The Bluff, she preferred to keep it alive in her walks through her gardens, though the idea of replacing him had not yet occurred to her.

"Weary of them," she had repeated to him that afternoon after completing the financial paperwork with Joan. "I thought the point of children was to take care of you in your old age. Not to have to keep taking care of them until they're middle-aged and older. Dependents. You're lucky you never had children, Charles."

What was the year Joan started the *Express*? Nineteen seventy-one or seventy-two. Essie could look it up.

"You made me independent, Essie."

"Oh, well. That was long ago."

They had been in her bedroom at The Bluff, she remembers, and it was a late autumn afternoon. Outside, the surface of the swimming pool was scattered with fallen leaves. Emboldened by the fact that Jake was traveling in Germany, where he had gone to appraise the deteriorating political situation and to decide what its effects might be on Eaton's; that Joan was honeymooning in Arizona with her second husband, who would become Karen's father; that Babette was off for her freshman year at Smith; and that Mogie was visiting his grandmother Auerbach in New York—emboldened by these circumstances, they had not bothered to meet at the Palmer House apartment. Instead, he had come to The Bluff, and Essie remembers that it was a Sunday. Essie was giving him a back-rub, which he liked because he said it relaxed him and because, that afternoon, she had thought that he did not look well. Suddenly, beneath her fingers, she felt the muscles of his shoulders begin to twitch and quiver. She turned his body to face her. "Are you all right, Charles?"

His face was pale, and his forehead was beaded with perspiration.

"I'm all right. . . . It's just . . ."

She covered his forehead with her hand. "I think you have a fever," she said, even though his skin was strangely cold to the touch.

"No . . . no. . ." But now his hands were shaking violently, and he seemed to be having trouble speaking. His jaw was clenched, and the chords on his neck stood out, his mouth stretched in a terrible grimace.

"Charles, I think we should call a doctor!"

"No . . . Medicine . . . in jacket pocket . . . flask. . . ."

She rushed to the closet where his jacket hung, and found a silver flask in his left-hand pocket. She quickly opened it, returned to him, and held it to his lips. He took a few sips, then lay back against the pillows. His eyes closed, she saw his face relax, and his mouth softened into a smile. "That's it," he whispered. "That's it. . . ." There was a faint medicinal odor in the air that Essie had noticed at hospitals.

"What *is* it, Charles?" she asked.

"Something I take for nerves," he said. "That's all."

"You never told me you suffered from nerves."

"Close the curtains, Essie."

Mystified, she did as he asked—went to the windows and drew the curtains. Then she returned to his bedside. His eyes were open now, and he was smiling, and in the semidarkness his color seemed to be returning to normal.

"Ah, I feel so good now," he said softly. "So good."

"Please tell me what's the matter." She picked up the open flask and sniffed it. The smell, rather like ether, was very strong, and she felt suddenly dizzy.

"No—don't sniff," he said in the same dreamy voice, and reached for the flask. "Here, put the lid back on." She handed him the cap, and watched as he screwed it on.

"Charles," she said, "please tell me what this is."

"Phenanthrene sulfate," he said, "for nerves."

"But why do you need it?"

"Ah, Essie," he said in that same sleepy voice. "Essie, Essie, Essie. I love you so. I love you more than all the world. I need it because sometimes I'm frightened. Shall I tell you all my secrets? Yes, I think perhaps it's time."

"Please do."

"So many lies. I don't want to lie to you anymore. I didn't know that I'd end up loving you so—that's the only reason. Will you forgive me?"

"Of course," she said. "But tell me."

"Do you love me too?"

"Charles, you know that," she said.

"Then you shall know the truth," he said, settling his head back against the pillows and staring up, still smiling, at the ceiling, "and the truth shall make you free—make *us* free. You see, when I met you on the train, I had no way of knowing we'd end up in love."

"Just tell me," she said.

"To begin with, my parents. Haven't you noticed I never mention them, that they didn't come to my wedding when I married Cecilia? They're not suburban Boston. I grew up on a farm in the western part of Connecticut, near Torrington. My parents were ignorant farm people, but I always had big ideas. At seventeen, I ran away from home. . . ."

"But—Harvard."

"I never went to Harvard, though of course I'd've liked to. Never went to the Wharton Business School. I went to Detroit, first, and worked on the assembly line at the Ford plant in Dearborn. That's where I learned something about mass production—but I wasn't satisfied there. So I went to New York, and worked for a while at Macy's, as a stock boy. That wasn't getting me anywhere either, but at least I could buy decent clothes at a discount and think my big ideas and have my big dreams, and that's where I learned a bit about retailing and merchandising. Then a friend said to me, 'You'll never get anywhere in New York without a college education. You've got to have a college education to be a success in New York.' And then he told me about Chicago, that it was a young city getting bigger every day. That's where the future is, he said, and in Chicago they don't ask questions. In Chicago, nobody gives a damn about your past or where you went to school or your family connections. In Chicago, they'll believe whatever you decide to tell them. And so I scraped together all the money I'd been able to save, put on my best suit, and bought a ticket on a train going to Chicago. And met you."

"And the calling card . . . the address on Lake Shore Drive . . ."

"Ah," he said, "you remember the calling card. That was a little luxury in which I indulged myself. But the only things that were correct on that card were my name and the telephone number I gave you—the rooming house where I'd arranged to stay."

In the darkened bedroom, sitting on the bed beside him, Essie said nothing, thinking: Why have my own children been afraid to tell the truth to me?

"And you brought me to Jake Auerbach." He laughed. "At first, with the story I'd decided to tell, I didn't know whether I could pull it off. But now, fourteen, fifteen years later, I guess you could say I've pulled it off."

"Yes," she said.

"Do you forgive me?"

"Of course," she said quickly. "I understand ambition."

"But it's been a nervy ride, ever since that train," he said, hunching himself up on his elbows on the pillows and looking straight at her. "A few years ago, a friend, a druggist, said, 'Try this—it'll relax you. It'll take the tension away.' It did. It does. Phenanthrene sulfate. But the only trouble is—"

"Yes. What is it?"

He laughed again, uneasily. "I try not to take it unless I—but the trouble is sometimes I need to, and the longer this damn Prohibition lasts—well, it's becoming harder and harder to get." His smile faded, and he was staring at her intently, worriedly. "Am I an addict, Essie?" he asked her. "Am I?"

And so, in the weeks and months that followed, whenever one of the seizures of craving came, with the cold sweats and the violent trembling, she would circle his body with her arms, clutching him tightly against her, whispering over and over to him, "Make one more minute last until two. Make two more minutes last till five. Make five minutes last fifteen. Let fifteen minutes last an hour. Let an hour last a day . . . a day a year. . . ."

Until he would finally cry out, "Now! *Please!*" And she would fetch the silver flask for him.

"Now what's that damned brother of yours trying to pull?" Jake had shouted at her. It was the winter of 1927 and 1928, and Arthur Litton had reappeared in Chicago.

Essie, seated on a sofa in the large solarium, said, "I have no idea."

"He's claiming that he and I signed a private buy-back agreement, allowing him to buy back into the company when profits reached a certain figure."

"Well, did you?"

"Certainly not."

"Then you've nothing to be upset about."

"Damnit, it was Daisy's job to keep him as far away from me as possible."

Though she did not smile, it amused her to hear that this was his description of "Daisy's job." "Daisy's in Ohio, visiting her parents," she said.

"I know where Daisy is!" he said. "But the minute she turns her back, your brother shows up like a bad penny. He's a crook and a liar, and he's not getting anything from me." He turned on his heel and stalked out of the room.

"Why was Papa yelling at you?" she heard Mogie's small voice ask. She had not seen him curled in a chair in the corner of the room with a coloring book.

"It's just grown-up business," she said. "Don't let it worry you."

"Do you have a brother, Mama?"

"I told you it was grown-up talk, and sometimes when grown-ups talk they say things they don't mean. Besides, it's not nice to eavesdrop, is it?"

"This document is an obvious forgery," Charles said, handing it back to him. "If I were you, Jake, I'd have no further communication with him whatsoever. We'll turn the whole matter over to our lawyers, and let them deal with it. He'll discover that extortion is a very serious charge."

But of course Abe Litsky—or Arthur Litton, however one prefers to think of him—had other strings to his bow, other arrows in his quiver.

"Please see me, Essie," he said to her on the telephone. "For old times' sake. After all, you're my only sister."

"Jake doesn't want me to."

"Do you do *everything* that Jake tells you?"

"No, as a matter of fact, I don't."

"Then see me, Essie. There's so much we need to talk about. It's been ten years. I'm your family, Essie. Even if there've been differences, a family has got to stick together somehow."

"Well—"

"Let me come by. Besides, I have some news of Mama."

"Jake mustn't know."

"He won't find out from me, Essie—you know that."

"You mustn't come here. I'll meet you tomorrow at the Palmer House. Two o'clock. We have an apartment there. Meet me there. It's apartment seven-B."

"It's a date," he said. "Thank you, Essie. Thank you, *bubeleh*."

Twenty-four

"This is my last-ditch effort to get you to say you'll come to the dedication of the building, Mother," Josh is saying to her. It is June, and they are sitting at one of the umbrella tables on Essie's wide terrace overlooking the city. Nearby, the men from Woodruff and Jones are pruning the boxwood hedges and setting out geraniums and petunias and marigolds in window boxes. In one corner, the big old flowering plum tree in its concrete planter spreads its branches like a tent set up for weddings, and Essie is thinking how becoming the early summer sunlight is to Josh's full, handsome head of graying hair, which has just the right amount of curl to it.

"Hm?" she says.

"Now, Mother. You heard me. You know perfectly well what I came here to talk about."

"Oh, yes. The building. Well, that's still a long way off, isn't it?"

"Yes, but we need to know now, Mother. Programs have to be printed. Invitations have to be sent out. A lot of important people are involved in this. There's a chance that the Vice-President will be coming."

"The Vice-President of the United States?"

"Yes."

"You know, I can't remember who the Vice-President of the United States is," she says. "Edith Wilson said a kind thing to me once. Of course your father was just trying to get war contracts, and did get them, but President Wilson didn't know that."

"Mother, please try to stick to the subject."

"Anyway, if you have all these important people coming, why do you need me?"

"Well, you're—you're a kind of a symbol, Mother. Of the company."

"I was afraid you'd say that. I don't like being a symbol. What am I besides being the oldest living person who remembers Jake Auerbach?"

"A sense of continuity—"

"Bah. Humbug. *You're* the continuity, if you ask me."

"All the generations of the family together. Four of them."

"Our last get-together was a lulu. Remember that?"

"Is that what's bothering you? That was months ago."

"There'd be another fight, I know it. I'm too old to fight."

"We can hardly have a fight sitting on a stage in front of half of Chicago, Mother. With television cameras, and—"

"Those too? Oh, no, no. I don't want to, Josh."

"Please, Mother."

"You'll want me to make a speech, won't you."

"Not a speech. Just a few words. A greeting. Something remembering Dad."

"Is the building to be a memorial to him?"

"In some ways, yes. The employees tend to think of it that way. His bust will be in the lobby, as the founder."

Essie laughs. "But he *wasn't* the founder! There was your uncle Abe. And everybody seems to have forgotten about poor old Mr. Eaton and Mr. Cromwell."

"But he's thought of that way."

"If you ask me, none of this makes any sense. A memorial. I detest memorials. Have I told you that I don't want a funeral? And no memorial services, either. I just want to be planted in the ground, as quietly and quickly as possible. Of course all that's in my will."

"There are other reasons why I want you to be there, Mother."

"Why? What are they?"

"Call them public-relations reasons if you like."

"Explain them to me, please."

"Well, you know—over the years there have been stories,

rumors that you and he didn't get along. That you and he led almost completely separate lives."

"True enough. Almost completely toward the end."

"But if you were there, on the stage, to say a few kind words about him—"

"And tell a few lies?"

"And there are stories, too, that for all his philanthropies, he was something of a monster and a despot—"

"Which he was. Money did that to him. Money does that to some people. To weak people. I know. I saw it happen."

"But he also had his kind and tender side."

"Ha. So, they say, did Adolf Hitler."

"That's a cheap shot, Mother. Surely you loved him when you first married him."

"Oh, yes. That's the trouble." Her eyes suddenly well up, and the moisture dims her vision. "Don't you understand? I married a totally different man. And then he changed, and he changed because I helped him."

"Then do it for the man you married. After all, Mother, he's dead now. There's nothing he can do to hurt you now. Can't you forgive the dead? I've always been of the opinion that while it may be hard to forgive the living, the dead should be forgiven. Doesn't the Talmud say that?"

"Who knows? I've forgotten what I ever knew about what the Talmud says. You should have asked my father that. He had some interesting theories on forgiveness. So. You want a memorial. A memorial to my dead love. Will it be bronze?"

"What?"

"The bust. In the lobby. Will it be bronze?"

"I think so, yes."

"Good. Appropriate material. A mixture of copper and tin, and sometimes other elements. Zinc and phosphorus. They wanted me to bronze your first baby shoes, but I wouldn't let them. But I do have a lock of your hair from your first haircut. Did you know that?"

"No, I didn't, Mother."

"I wonder where it is. Mary would know."

"So may I please have a decision, Mother? Yes or no? If it's no, I'll be terribly disappointed, but I'll promise never to pester you about this again."

"I don't want to disappoint you, Josh," she says. She hesitates, then, closing her eyes, says suddenly, "Suppose I say yes—on one condition."

"What's that?"

"That you ask Daisy Stevens, too."

He frowns. "Now, Mother. Why would you want her?"

"As an old family friend. If this is to be a memorial to Jake, then I think that Daisy ought to be invited."

"She's just the kind of person we *don't* want to be there."

"We? Who's we?"

"All of us. Look—you know there were those rumors about him, too—that there were other women—"

"Well, there were! And she was one of them. An important one."

"And you expect us to put her up there on the platform with the rest of us? To advertise the fact that—"

"Suddenly you're going all plural on me, Joshua. First, it was what *you* wanted. Now it's what a whole bunch of people want. Which is it?"

"Let me put it this way, Mother. I don't want my father's mistress at the dedication of *our* building."

"But if it's to be all lies anyway, then why not? If people saw her sitting up there on the platform, right beside me, they'd think to themselves, 'Why, those old stories couldn't possibly be true! Just see how friendly those two old ladies are.' Wouldn't that be what they'd think? That's public relations, if you ask me."

"Of course if she has a shred of good taste she won't come."

"I don't know whether she'll come or whether she won't. You're right—she probably won't. All I'm asking is that she get an invitation."

Shaking his head, he says, "Well, I guess that's not too much to ask. You drive a hard bargain, Mother."

"The same invitation that the high mucky-mucks will get. The same as the Vice-President, whoever he is."

"But if she decides to come—"

"We cross that bridge when we come to it. Do we have a deal, Joshua?"

He lets out a long sigh. Sitting back in the garden chair, he stretches his long legs, hooks his thumbs in the belt-loops of his trousers and stares glumly at the tips of his brown loafers. "Okay," he says at last, "we have a deal."

Abe Litsky is dead and, gone with him, is the alter ego he created for himself whom he had named Arthur Litton.

He was Arthur Litton that afternoon in the apartment on the seventh floor of the Palmer House when Mrs. Jacob Auerbach's visitor was announced from downstairs. But he was still Abe Litsky to her when she opened the door for him and let him in, in 1928, and though it had been more than ten years since she had seen him he seemed not to have aged at all. He still had the same youthful, wiry build, the same boyish, slightly lopsided, but nonetheless engaging smile—except that he was not smiling now.

"I've thought about this a long time, Essie," he was saying, looking straight into her eyes. "And it simply isn't fair. What's more, I'm sure *you* know it isn't fair. Who found out about Eaton and Cromwell in the first place? I did. Who came up first with half the money they wanted? I did. Who brought Jake into it, in the beginning, with the cash you were able to come up with? It was me. If it hadn't been for me, your husband wouldn't be where he is today, would he? He'd never have *heard* of Eaton and Cromwell, if it hadn't been for me. He'd still be running a second-rate clothing store for Sol Rosenthal if it hadn't been for me."

"I know all this, Abe," she said.

"So, I got into a little trouble with the New York cops years ago. *Years* ago. To save his stinking hide and reputation, Jake Auerbach wants to buy me out. He uses threats. If I don't take the price he offers, he'll put the New York cops on my trail. That's threats, Essie. That's blackmail, and I admit I was scared. He had me. He forced me out. But I'm not scared now. That case against me in New York was dropped years ago, and I'm not in any trouble now. I want back in. I want the share of the company that would rightfully have been mine. I want what's fair."

"I understand, Abe, but—"

"Now Mr. High-and-Mighty won't even talk to me on the

phone! Is that fair, after what I did for him? Is that fair in your book, Essie?"

"Fair or not, you've come to the wrong person," she said. "I have absolutely no influence with him."

"All I got out of it was a stinking million and a half bucks. But when I got Jake started in this company I owned twenty-five percent of it! Just think of that! And do you know what that same company is worth right now? Between two and three *hundred* million! Now that you've gotton so fancy, maybe you won't like my language, but Essie, I've been screwed."

"I'm sorry, Abe."

"I want my share."

"I'm sorry. That's all I can say."

He sat forward in his chair, hitched up his trouser legs, and reached in his jacket pocket for a cigar. "Mind if I smoke?"

"No."

Lighting his cigar, he glanced at her sidewise and said, "What do you hear from old Daisy Stevens?"

"Daisy's in Ohio for the summer, visiting her parents."

"Ah," he said, pulling on the cigar. "That so? Kind of a *long* summer visit, isn't it? Almost six months? You know, old Jake has me to thank for that one, too, though that's another favor I did him that he's managed to forget. Or maybe you didn't know that. I passed old Daisy along to him."

"I didn't know. But I don't really care."

"Daisy's done all right, too, or so it looks."

"Jake is—generous to her," Essie said.

"Yeah, it looks like everybody's done all right in this. Except me. Daisy's done all right, Jake's done all right, Charlie-boy's done all right. You've done all right. Everybody but yours truly. Doesn't seem quite right, does it?" He paused. "Sorry about your kid."

"What?"

"Prince. Read about it in the paper. Gun accident. Terrible thing."

"Oh . . . yes."

He crossed his legs and appeared to be studying the cigar. "So old Daisy's in Ohio, visiting her folks," he said. "Well, as a matter of fact I knew that. Ohio's where I just came from.

Columbus. Where her folks live. In fact, I popped in on her while I was there, just to say hello."

"Did you," she said.

"Yeah, she's doing fine," he said. "But I suppose she didn't tell you the real reason for her little trip."

"Reason?"

"She went to give birth to Jake's kid."

She stared at him. "You're lying," she said.

"I figured you might say that," he said. He was smiling the familiar half-smile now. "But would your baby brother lie to you?" He reached in his trousers pocket and withdrew a wallet. "So, I thought to bring along a little of what you might call proof. I managed to take a little snapshot of Daisy and her kid with my little Kodak. Thought you might like to have a look at it." He withdrew a photograph from the wallet and offered it to Essie. She reached for it, and saw that her hand was trembling.

"There she is, the nursing mother, with the blessed event itself. Real cute kid, too. Little girl. She named it Jennifer—honor of Jake Auerbach, I suppose."

Looking at the photograph of Daisy with the baby at her breast, Essie's first impulse was to tear it into pieces and scatter the pieces into a fire, as Jake had done with all the photographs of Prince, so that there could never be any remaining evidence of his existence on the earth.

Still smiling, Abe said, "You can keep that if you like. I've got lots of other prints."

"No, thank you." She placed the photograph, face down, on the table in front of her. "Why does Jacob have to be the father? The father could be anyone."

He shaped the end of his cigar against an ashtray. "Well, now, that's not likely, is it? I know Daisy. She's a one-man woman. Oh, there may've been more than one man in her life, but never more than one at a time. That's Daisy."

Staring at the back of the photograph, she said, "Does Jake know?"

He spread his hands. "Now how would I know that? Jake won't talk to me. I know he wanted her to get rid of the kid, gave her the money to have it done. But when she got to Ohio, she changed her mind, decided to have the kid. I know her folks have offered to raise it. That's about all I know."

"I see," she whispered.

"So," he said, speaking with his cigar clenched between his teeth, "what do we make of this development? What would the good board of directors and stockholders of Eaton and Cromwell make of this if it got out?"

"Daisy is our friend," Essie said. "She'd never let anything like this happen to us."

"There's not a hell of a lot Daisy can do about it at this point, is there? The kid's been born. We have the facts. Besides, there's a little business matter between Daisy and I that hasn't been settled. She got to be quite the little gambler when she was with me back in Reno years ago. A few little I.O.U.'s that haven't been paid. They'd amount to quite a bit, with interest, if I called them in. Would you like to see some of your friend Daisy's I.O.U.'s?"

"No!"

"Then there's another little important point, Essie, which I ask you to consider. What would your own nice little kiddies feel if they knew about this? Think they'd be a little—upset? Hurt, maybe? I maybe think so. I read in the papers where your Babette is having what they call a coming-out party this year. Could be rough on her. What would her friends say? And your youngest—only ten, isn't he? What do you call him— Moogie?"

"Mogie."

"Facing up to a thing like that could be rough on a kid of ten. Little kid of ten who worships his father. The publicity from it. His little schoolmates—they'd never let him forget it, Essie, oh, they'd tease the pants off him. Make his life miserable. You know how kids are. Wouldn't want to do anything that would hurt a little kid of only ten. It could scar him for life, a thing like that. Joan—well, she's older and been married twice already. She probably wouldn't give a damn. But a little kid of ten. And he's your only son now, remember that. You wouldn't want to have happen to him what happened to Princey, would you? A gun accident. That's what the papers called it. But you and I know different—"

"Stop it," she said. "Stop it!"

"One good threat deserves another, don't you think? Don't forget that I got threatened once. All I want to do is settle the score. Do unto others what others done unto me." He smiled. "The golden rule."

Suddenly she was in a rage more towering than any she had ever known. Her fury had a color. It was crimson, the color of blood, and if she had had Hans's service revolver strapped to her shoulder, she would have reached for it instantly and murdered her brother on the spot, and watched his gore spill anonymously across the hotel carpet. She leaped to her feet, rushed to the sitting-room window, and leaned against the ledge, gripping the sill with her fingers, thinking she was angry enough to plunge through the glass and hurl herself down onto the avenue below, feeling the taste and odor of her own vomit rising in the back of her throat. I must not feel self-pity, she told herself. I shall not scream out for mercy. There shall be no tears. He will pay for this and be found hanged on a tree, as it was written in the Book of the Chronicles before the king. "What do you want?" she said. "Just tell me what you want."

"I figure a rich lady in your position—you've got to have some bank accounts here and there. Jake's not that kind of husband, that shorts his wife. He wants his wife to look right and have nice things, her own money to spend, no strings. He may have his faults, but he's a good Jewish husband. I figure you and I can work out some sort of little arrangement. All I want, you see, is my fair share. Take your time thinking about what my fair share might be. A monthly check, maybe. We can work out the details later, when you've pulled yourself together over this."

"Money," she said scornfully. "Only money. You pitiful creature. You miserable, contemptible bastard. Bastard."

"You might say the same about the little girl in the picture," said Abe.

"All right," she said. "All right! We'll work something out. Now get out of here. But first—"

"Anything you say."

"All right," she said. "But if there's something you're going to get out of me, then there's something I'm going to get out of you, you bastard."

"What's that, *bubeleh?*"

She turned to face him, and felt the strength surging back into her with a charge of feeling. "They say you're in the liquor business. There's something we need that's becoming difficult to get. You can get it for us."

"Booze? Any kind. I've got the connections, *bubeleh*."

"No. It's called phenanthrene sulfate. It's a drug."

He laughed now. "Now, why would you want that? For yourself? That's kind of a heavy-duty item, Essie. For Jake? Not for Jake."

"Never mind who I want it for!"

"Or is it for old Charlie-boy?"

She felt her face redden. "I'm not going to tell you!"

"Oh," he said. "So that's it. Old Charlie-boy needs a little pick-me-up, does he? I might have known. Well, that stuff's really not my line, but I pretty much know how to get ahold of it. Across the street, as they say. So old Charlie-boy needs his little pick-me-ups. Very interesting."

"Shut up. You heard what I said. Get that for us, and I'll see that you get your filthy money."

"*Regular* money, okay, *bubeleh*? Monthly money—and don't be stingy, *bubeleh*. I like nice things, just like you." He rose from his chair and, with his cigar still clenched between his teeth, moved toward her where she stood, her back braced against the window ledge. "Remember, all I want is my fair share," he said. "What I got cheated out of. I don't *need* money. I *want* it, because I want justice." He reached out and put his hands hard on her shoulders, smiling at her with that crooked smile. "You're my only sister, after all," he said. "So no hard feelings, all right? We always looked out for each other. So you'll look out for me, and I'll look out for you. Just like always. Remember when it was you and I against the world? Remember when we used to cuddle against each other in that little bed to keep each other warm on winter nights on Norfolk Street? Remember?"

"Don't touch me," she said, struggling against his hold. "Get out of here. I don't ever want to see your face again. Get out of here before I scream for help."

His smile faded. Still holding her shoulders, staring hard into her face, he said, "Just one thing, Essie. Go and see our mama. Soon. She's very sick. She's going to die."

Twenty-five

In her dream, it is her bust, her bosom that is being admired, dimly in a hand-held mirror or in a shadowy windowpane, and yet the setting is some large public space, a great concourse filled with people, who are pausing, quite calmly, to examine her firm breasts and pale nipples. All around her is a white sea of marble across which people come and go. What is she doing here, naked and unashamed? A soft chipping, hammering sound alerts her, and she realizes what is happening. She is being turned into a bronze sculpture, and her living body is the mold. Little by little, the warm metal is rising around her, hardening, encasing her feet, ankles, legs and knees. Soon it will cover her entire body, but a terrible mistake is being made because it is not a statue of her that is wanted, it is of Jake, and far across the wide corridor she can see his statue now. But his statue is finished, standing imperiously in the Douglas Chandor pose, and his body is already entombed inside bronze. Even though there is something that she desperately wants to tell him, it is too late because he can no longer hear or see or speak to her. His eyes are dead hollows. Workmen she cannot see, meanwhile, are rapidly moving upward on her body with their molten metal, which hardens the instant it touches her skin. Her hips, navel and breasts are now covered, and she cannot move because her feet are rooted in a marble base. She tries to cry out because they think that she is dead, but she is quite alive, and once the poured metal reaches her mouth and nose and eyes she will be blind and suffocated. She tries to cry out, but no sounds come, and with that her mouth is plastered closed with bitter-tasting metal. The chipping, hammering sounds continue, and she realizes that the setting is not some indoor concourse at all, but out of doors, in Union Square, where she and Jake are to be placed, in bronze, facing each other across the park. Then her eyes are sealed shut, and she can no longer see. They must spare her ears, she thinks, because there is some last, important message that Jake, from inside his bronze casing, is trying to convey to her. She has just one last breath left, and she must cry out through her own bronze shell. They are shaking her now, as though to test the hardness of the metal, rocking her back and forth on the stone pedestal. Her scream will not come. She awakens, opens her eyes, and Charles is with her, gently shaking her shoulder. "You were having a bad dream," he says, and she realizes that the chipping, hammering sounds were the branches of the plum tree on her terrace rattling against her windows in a summer storm.

It had been a shock to see her mother's shrunken body looking terribly small as it lay in the center of the narrow bed in the bedroom of the house on Norfolk Street, her head propped up on a single pillow, the room much smaller and darker than she had remembered it. "Mama, why didn't you write and tell me that you were sick?" she said. "What is it?"

"It's nothing. The doctor says something is eating at my stomach, but what do doctors know? I'll be better in a few days."

Lifting a bottle of pills from the stand beside the bed, Essie said, "Is this your medicine?"

"Yes. Some of it."

"Have you been taking it, Mama?"

"When I think of it. It doesn't help. What helps is rest. Mrs. Potamkin is taking care of the store for me till I get better. In a few more days, I'll be able to go back downstairs. Wait and see."

"What's the doctor's name, Mama? There's no name on this prescription."

"Who knows? The visiting nurse comes. She brings it."

"Has the doctor seen you, Mama?"

"I think so. Yes, he came once. I'm all right. Rest is all I need."

"I want you to take your medicine, Mama. Here. It says every four hours. When was the last time you took some of these green pills?"

"I don't want medicine. When I take that medicine it gives me bad dreams. I don't like that medicine."

"Are you in pain, Mama?"

"Just my stomach, a little, where it hurts. Don't worry. I'll be all right."

"How long have you been like this, Mama?"

"I don't remember. Not too long. Mrs. Potamkin knows." Suddenly her mother, with some difficulty, raised herself on her wasted elbows against the pillow and looked hard at Essie. Then she lay back, smiled, and said, "Ha, I thought so!"

"Thought what, Mama?"

"You're going to have another baby, aren't you. I can see it in your eyes."

"No, Mama."

"Oh, yes. I can see it. You're going to have another baby. There's something in a daughter's eyes that a mother can always see when she gets that way."

"Well, Mama, I'm not."

"Don't deny it. My mother saw it in my eyes when I was going to have you. She saw it even before I knew for sure. It's something only the mother can see in the eyes of her own daughter—another life coming.

"I'm sorry, Mama, but it's not true."

Her mother closed her eyes. Still smiling, she said, "Ah, that will be nice for you. Another baby. I always wanted just one more, for my old age."

In the kitchen, her father, as always, sat with his books.

"Papa, I must speak to you," she said.

At first he said nothing. Then, without looking up, he said, "Who is this speaking? Who is this rich woman who has come into my house without an invitation?"

"I'm your daughter, Papa!"

"I have no daughter. My daughter is dead."

"She needs to be moved to a hospital, Papa. I'll take care of everything."

"Who is this?" he repeated. "Who is this stranger in my house who is telling me what needs to be done with my wife?"

"Papa, I insist!"

For the first time he looked up at her. "Who is this insisting?" he demanded. "Who is this rich woman in a fur coat, the fur of innocent animals which must be killed to clothe her? Look at her! What is that on her arm? A *wristwatch?* A wristwatch made of Tiffany diamonds. Do you know what day this is? This is the Sabbath. Do you know or care that you profane the Sabbath of the Jews in your furs and diamonds? Who is this, I ask myself? My wife and I have lived happily in this house for more than thirty years without ever asking advice or being told what we must do by strangers."

"Oh, Papa, *please!*"

"My wife and I do not ask outsiders for their visits or their help or their opinions. We fear God and His commandments. That is our way. Only God tell us what to do. We do not seek out the Christian Samaritans. We reject women like you who come to interfere with our lives. We did not ask you here. We do not wish you here. We do not wish you to come back. We ask that you go away and leave us alone and never come back."

His eyes returned to his books.

She gave him one last weary and despairing look, then gathered up her gloves and bag, let herself out the door, and made her way slowly down the narrow flights of stairs. "Mrs. Potamkin," she said when she reached the shop, "is there anything you can do?"

"With him—*nothing!* He will not speak to me because I keep the shop open on the Sabbath—for the Italians, and the *schwartzes*. Esther, you would not believe how this neighborhood has changed."

"For my mother, then."

The older woman shook her head sadly. "It is the cancer," she said. "There is nothing to be done. We must just wait for God to choose the time."

For several days she has been working on the short speech which she has been asked to give at the dedication of the new building in December, and which Charles and Josh have written for her, trying to memorize the words, rehearsing in front of the mirror in her dressing room with the typewritten sheet of paper in front of her and then, standing in the center of the library, with Mary Farrell seated in front of her, holding the script.

"'My husband, Jacob Auerbach, was a pious man,'" she recites to the seated Mary. "'He believed in the principle of *zedakah*, which is Talmudic . . .'"

"'. . . in the Talmudic principle of *zedakah*,'" Mary corrects, "though your way sounds just as good."

"'. . . in the Talmudic principle of *zedakah* which, in the Jewish religion, means something more than charity. It stands for righteousness. But my husband also had other faiths . . .'"

"'But my husband also had *great respect* for other faiths.'"

"Oh, dear. My memory has gone, Mary. I'll never learn this."

"Yes, you will, Mrs. A. There's plenty of time. Now let's start over from the beginning. . . ."

But the trouble is (she was thinking, gazing into her reflection in the glass in her bedroom at The Bluff, studying her eyes) that. The trouble is that. You are thirty-seven years old, not too old, not too young. For three weeks you have been trying to pretend that nothing is the matter, trying not to think about, trying to put out of your mind the thing that you think the trouble is. But now it will not go away. You have given no thought to this possibility, but now it is a possibility, and you must decide what you are going to do about this possibility. Because the trouble is that your mother, with her Old World intuition, may be right. For three weeks, you have dismissed it. Now you must face it, Esther Auerbach, and think hard.

Let us consider the choices. For instance, it could be something else altogether. You could see Doctor Ornstein and have him tell you what it is for sure. But do you entirely trust Doctor Ornstein? He is Jake's doctor as well. How can you be certain he will not say something to Jake, or are you ready to tell Doctor Ornstein that this is not Jake's child, and then proceed to the next step, whatever the next step may be? Do you know any other doctors well enough to trust? No, you do not. There are abortions. Women have them all the time, including a number of your friends. You have the money for it. You could say, casually, to one of your friends, "Give me the name of that doctor who—" Who. Daisy, of all your friends, would probably know best, but do you even know her well enough to trust her to keep this kind of secret? You do not know, because you have never tried. Nor do you trust Doctor Ornstein, and you can already hear him saying, "Essie, I think we must make Jake a part of any decision as crucial as this one." "But Doctor Ornstein, this is not Jake's child. We have not slept together since nineteen twenty-three." "I see."

So. You go to another city. You use another name. You have the money. You make the connections. You find the name of someone who. Who. Who will do it, of course. Of course, it is not quite that easy, you being who you are. You are Mrs. Jacob Auerbach, wife of the Chief Executive Officer of one of the largest retailing firms in the world, your picture is in the papers often. You pay with cash, but people have a way of finding out, and you do not need another blackmailer. How do you explain this journey to another city to your husband? That is perhaps the easiest part. Any lie will do. Of course there could be an accident, something could go wrong, a dirty knife and there will be no need for lying after that.

You could tell Charles what the trouble is. But what would that knowledge do to Charles? Could Charles accept this knowledge and continue to work with Jake as closely as they do? Charles and Jake need each other more than any two men you know. You also need Charles, and Charles needs you. And there is of course Cecilia. Divorce. Do you say to Charles, "Charles, I am going to divorce Jake and have your baby. I want you to divorce Cecilia, and marry me." That, of course, would be the end of Charles's career with the company where he has invested so many years. "But we will strike out on our own, Charles, build a new life for ourselves in another city. Yes, we may be getting a little old for that, but we can try. We won't care what Chicago says, the pregnant wife of the Chief Executive running off with the Executive Vice-President—the scandal, the stories in the papers . . ." But you do. Charles does. You have a ten-year-old son. You have a daughter who plans to make her debut, her formal bow into Chicago society, this autumn. No, you will lose Charles this way, my dear. And of course Jake. And the children. No, you do not tell Charles. Charles, forgive me. Us.

Or anyone else.

The only secret that is ever kept a secret is a secret that is never told. The only person you can truly trust is you.

And so the only solution to the problem, the only choice, is the one that is as simple as the conception of life itself. And you must do it, must force yourself to do it, and do it quickly, even though you are not sure whether it can be done, or exactly how to do it, it must be done.

She tapped lightly on her husband's bedroom door, and heard him call out, "Come in!"

He was sitting up in bed, propped up by many down pillows, a heavy man of forty-four who, with the thick mustache he had worn for the last seven or eight years, looked older—his dark hair graying and thinning on the top. He was wearing white cotton pajamas and a blue silk robe and half-spectacles, and spread out on the coverlet in front of him were many file-folders and loose sheets of paper. The room smelled of his pipe smoke and the cologne from his bath, and he looked startled, as she had expected he might, to see her.

"I thought it was the butler with my hot milk and fruit," he said. "Where are my hot milk and fruit?"

"I'll get it for you," she said.

"No, no," he said, reaching for the enunciator button by his telephone. "You've got to stop running errands for the servants, Essie. What do you think we have servants for? The butler, what's-his-name, is supposed to come in here every night at nine, bring my milk and fruit, and close the curtains."

"Well, at least I can do that part," she said easily, and moved to the windows and drew the heavy curtains closed."

"What can I do for you, Essie?" he asked a little crossly. "No Opera Guild tonight?"

"No," she said, returning from the windows. "And I was feeling a little—well, lonely. And I thought maybe you and I could talk. It's been a long time." She sat on the corner of his big bed.

He shifted his feet uneasily under the blankets. "Lonely?

With all you have to do? Why don't you find Daisy and have a game of Patience?"

"Daisy's in Ohio with her family, remember?" Did he really care so little for any of them, she wondered, that he had forgotten where Daisy was?

"Oh, yes. Forgot. And I thought you were in New York."

"I came back on the overnight this morning."

"Ah. Good trip?"

"Yes."

"Shopping, I suppose."

"Yes."

There was another tap on the door, and the butler, whose name was Yoshida that year, appeared with a goblet of milk, with an apple, an orange, a banana in a Meissen bowl, a white folded napkin and a fruit knife and fork, all on a silver tray. He padded on slippered feet across the room and placed the tray on the nightstand by Jacob Auerbach's bed.

"I've closed the curtains, Yoshida," Essie murmured. "But you should remember that Mr. Auerbach likes his milk and fruit, and the curtains closed, precisely at nine."

Yoshida bowed and, just as quietly, padded out of the room again.

"That was good, Essie," her husband said. "Got to keep reminding them. Keep them on their toes." He reached for his fruit knife and began to slice his apple.

"So can we talk a little, Jake?" she asked him.

"Certainly. What about?"

She was wearing a silver kimono with a silver sash and a white maribou collar, and with one hand she drew the collar a little closer about her shoulders. "I was thinking, coming back from New York," she began. "So many memories. I was thinking of Union Square, where we used to meet, and of my school, when you taught there. And of the pictures I used to draw of you—remember?—when you thought I was taking notes."

With his hand, he made a new arrangement of the papers in front of him on the coverlet. "If you've just come in here to reminisce, Essie—" he began.

"No. Wait. Let me finish. It was because I went to see my

mother, and the car drove me through Union Square. Yesterday. She's very ill, Jake. And she won't go to a hospital."

"Well, I'm certainly sorry to hear that," he said. "Of course for the life of me I've never been able to understand your mother. How many times have we offered to help her out? How many times have we invited her to come here? She won't be budged."

"No. She won't leave Norfolk Street. She'll die in Norfolk Street."

He cleared his throat. "Well, now—"

"But that's not what I wanted to talk about," she said. "It was more that I realized, coming back through Union Square, what a long distance we've come, Jake. You and I. What a terribly long distance—from there to here. From Mr. Levy's shop, and the egg creams. We've moved into a completely different world from that one, and it seems so short a time. We've been married twenty-one years."

"But—"

"Wait," she said, holding up her hand. "Hush. Let me finish. When I met you, I thought you were the handsomest man I'd ever seen, did you know that? It's true. Just the handsomest! And I always knew you'd be successful. But you've been more successful than anyone—surely I—ever dreamed, Jake. I mean, it's just extraordinary the success you've been. Who would have dreamed all this success? Did you?"

"Hard work is the answer."

"But surely some kind of vision, too. You must have had some special kind of vision."

"Well, yes, perhaps."

"Extraordinary. And yet, in the process, Jake, we've grown apart."

His voice had a guarded tone. "Well, perhaps that was inevitable. Separate interests. My business—"

"Oh, I don't fault you for that at all, Jake," she said. "No one could have had your success without complete devotion to your business—no one. I'm so enormously proud of you. I could just burst with pride, but—"

"But what?"

"But I just wanted you to know that I still have feelings for you."

"Feelings?"

"Yes. For all that our lives have changed, I haven't changed. Do you remember when you kissed me that first night you walked me home through Hester Street? You're that same man, for all your success, for all your fame. I'd like to be kissed that way again. Just once."

Once again, his feet shifted under the blankets. "What are you driving at, Essie?" he said.

"Jake," she said, reaching out to touch his knee beneath the covers. "Now don't interrupt, because this is the most important thing. I know you don't like to talk about little Prince, we both loved him so, and after what happened everything changed between us, between you and me. But what I want to say, what I've wanted to say to you for the longest time, is that I blame myself for what happened. For much of it, anyway."

"Nonsense, it was that damned—"

"Hush. Listen to me. I was too busy—building this house, decorating it, too busy watching and trying to adjust—that's it, adjust—to your enormous success. I was simply awed by it all, Jake, and so overwhelmed with what was happening to my *own* life, and yours, that I didn't give Prince the time I should have as a mother. Though he had everything in the world I thought he wanted, there was so much more that *I* could have given him, but didn't. I know better now. I would have done it all so much differently if I'd known then what I know now. And so I want another chance, Jake. I want to try it again. I'll be so different this time, Jake, I promise. Even with Mogie I didn't know what I know now. I want to be a mother again, Jake, but a different one this time—"

"Essie, are you saying—"

"I want to be a mother again, Jake—it's not too late! I want to give you a splendid son, the kind of son you deserve. I want you to make love to me, so that I can try to give you one more splendid son."

Slowly, he reached out and covered her hand with his.

She was weeping now. "Don't you see? I want to fill up your life again and mine. I want to fill that empty place in my heart, and in yours. I want to fill that empty bedroom. I want to replace my little Prince! Please let me replace my little Prince. Please let me try!" She fell forward across his knees and, with her cheek pressed tight against his chest, repeated, "Please let me try." His hand moved up her arm to the back of her neck.

"Essie," he said softly, "I had no idea—"

Later, when it was over, and she lay beside him on the big bed, in the darkened bedroom with tears still standing at the corners of her eyes, she said to herself: There. It is done. You have done it. You are what your father said you were, the Whore of Babylon.

Twenty-six

JOAN Auerbach and Cecilia Wilmont had, interestingly enough, become good friends, even though there was a difference in their ages of nearly eighteen years, and the two women often had lunch together at Eddy's, a popular speakeasy in the Loop where both were known. Cecilia used Joan as a kind of channel for information about the senior Auerbachs, of whom she saw little. Cecilia had long been aware that Essie Auerbach didn't like her, and she would happily admit—though not to Joan—that the feeling was mutual, thank you. Cecilia Wilmont also made no secret of the fact that she felt that her own husband's brilliance was responsible for Jake Auerbach's great fortune. And she also resented the fact that, though her husband was paid a handsome salary and though she and Charles lived in great comfort on the North Shore, Charles had hardly become a multi-millionaire like Jacob Auerbach. Through Joan, Cecilia was able to enjoy her resentment vicariously.

Joan, at twenty, had just married Horace Schofield, whom she had met in Palm Beach at a dance at the Everglades Club. They had danced to "Sweet Sue—Just You," and Horace had admired her legs. They had gone to bed together that night, and been married the next morning by a Florida justice of the peace who asked no questions. The fact that he had asked no questions created certain difficulties at the time, since Joan's divorce from Jean-Claude de Lucy was not yet final, and it had cost her family a certain amount of money to straighten everything out with Mr. de Lucy, who threatened to sue his wife on bigamy charges. Joan's father had also been distressed when he read in the newspapers that his new son-in-law was "a Palm Beach socialist." Joan explained that this was a misprint, and should have read "Palm Beach socialite." Of course all this was long ago in what Joan sometimes referred to as "my Flaming Youth Period." You had to admit that, when you looked at photographs of Joan in those days, she was a striking, haughty beauty.

Today, she and Cecilia were sitting at their regular table, sipping gin rickeys, prior to what would typically be a very light lunch, and Cecilia was saying, "You never really drink a drink, do you, Joan? You just sort of play with it with your straw. Here I'm ready for another, and your glass is still full."

"I can't seem to get used to the taste of alcohol," Joan said. "Mother can toss off three martinis just like that, and not feel a thing. Not me."

"Really . . ."

It was a delicate subject, Joan knew, because Cecilia had a certain reputation in Chicago for drinking a bit too much on occasion, and making a fool of herself at parties. "Speaking of Mother," Joan said, "are you ready for some perfectly revolting news?"

"What's that?" said Cecilia, all ears.

"She's gotten herself, as they say, in an interesting condition."

"Really!"

"*Enceinte*. I think it's disgusting."

"Really? Why?"

"Don't you think she's a little *old* to be having another baby?"

"How old is she?"

"Thirty-seven. And how can I possibly relate to a baby brother or sister that much younger than myself, who'll be spoiled rotten, you know that."

"Yes . . ."

"And suppose Horace and I decide to have a child. I'll have a baby brother or a sister just about the same age as my own child. It's embarrassing."

"I see what you mean," Cecilia said.

"I think older people ought to use a little more—restraint."

Cecilia's fresh drink had arrived. "Of course, I don't really have to worry about that," she said. "My husband's not really interested in sex."

"Really, Cecilia?"

"Minimally. For a while I wondered if he was—you know, one of those. But then I decided that it's just because all his energy goes into business." She sighed and sipped her drink. "How's Horace in that department?" she asked. "I must say when I saw him in his tights at the Souters' masquerade party, he looked awfully—well hung."

Joan giggled. "He likes to tie me up," she said.

"Really?" Cecilia said, leaning forward eagerly. "Is that *fun*, Joan?"

Joan extracted a cigarette from her gold case and lighted it with a gold lighter that matched. She inhaled, blew out a thin stream of smoke, then put her head back, shook her short bobbed hair, and smiled mysteriously. "'Nuff said," she said at last.

Of course it was not until several years later, after Joan's daughter Karen was born, that Horace Schofield accidentally tied his wife up too tightly in that California hotel room, and there were screams, and blood, and the police came, and the ambulance, and there was all that unpleasant business in the newspapers, and Horace tried—but all that was long ago, and ancient history. If you read about it then, you wouldn't want to hear about it here.

It was not from Essie, but from his wife, that Charles heard the news, which was not the way she had planned for him to hear it, but then she had developed no clear plan for how to tell him, or what to say, or when.

"There's a question I could ask you," he said quietly. "Unless you'd rather that I didn't ask it."

She thought about this for a moment. "I think I'd rather you didn't ask," she said finally.

"Very well. I won't," he said. "Ever."

"I'll just tell you that Jake suspects nothing."

He nodded.

"And he never will."

"Yes."

"Will this affect the way you feel about me, Charles?"

"Everything that happens to you affects the way I feel. I can't help that. It always has. It always will. Nothing ever happened before I met you. Cecilia was supposed to drive you out of my thoughts. It didn't work. Nothing worked. This won't do it either."

"I'm glad."

"I think we should never speak of this again."

"Never. To anyone."

"Never. Not to each other. Not to anyone."

"Ever."

The years go by, pulling their threads of memory behind them like the ripples from a hand drawn through clear water. Look, there is a deer drinking water from the lake, no it is two deer, a doe and her fawn, do you see them, darling? I love the lake in August, the smell of the pines. We should come here in winter, where we would have the lake quite to ourselves, and where the nights are so cold that the pockets of frozen sap in the pines explode with the sound of gunfire, at forty below, here in the Adirondacks. This house has no heat, but we could use log fires. For water, we could melt blocks of ice from the lake. Will we ever do it? Probably not. How far is it to Saratoga? Not far, twenty miles as the crow flies, we could go to the races there. No, I'm afraid I'd run into my brother; he plays the horses. I feel freer here. Why do we feel free? Because Jake is dead, and Cecilia is dead. Shall we see what they've packed for us for sandwiches? Are we getting old? I think this will be my last summer here, this place is just too big to keep up. Is that a bird calling? No, I think it is a tree frog, calling its mate. There—I hear it again.

She had named the baby Joshua, and as soon as he was old enough to understand she explained to him that he had his own book in the Bible, and she read to him from it: "As I was with Moses, so I will be with thee: I will not fail thee, nor forsake thee. . . . Be strong and of good courage; be not afraid, neither be thou dismayed: for the Lord thy God is with thee whithersoever thou goest. . . . And it came to pass, when the people heard the sound of the trumpet, and the people shouted with a great shout, that the wall fell down flat, so that the people went up into the city. . . . His fame was noised throughout all the country. . . ."

In a curious way, with this child, she felt that she was returning to the traditions of her own father. Not to the relentless unforgiveness of his later years, but to the discipline and faith she remembered in him when she was a child, when he took her on his knee and read to her from the Book of Esther. These were the disciplines and traditions which it now seemed important to honor. Once she had been willing to cast them all aside, but now, with this child, they seemed to be coming back, and she found herself telling her new son all the stories her father had told her—about Josh's great-grandfather, the blacksmith, and the great-grandmother who had owned the horse, about the hard times for the Jews in the days of the czars. She even, from time to time, began to entertain the odd, surprising notion that it might be nice if Josh decided to become a rabbi. It was an irony.

And Jake, too, with this son, seemed to want to come back to her, and to his family. She would listen to him talking to Joshua, explaining the stars, naming the constellations, explaining the movements of the planets around the sun, the moon around the earth, the galaxy of which the Milky Way was the outer rim, the universe. Perhaps it was because he was getting older, and felt at last secure in his wealth and position, relaxed into what he had become, that he wanted to return to all of them and grow closer to this son than he had been to the other children. She would listen to him explain to Joshua what caused the tides in the ocean, and what made the lightning streak across the sky, and how this created the thunderclap that followed, and how, by counting the seconds between the flash and the thunder, you could roughly judge the number of miles between yourself and the center of the storm, and thus tell whether it was approaching or receding. "Perhaps you've heard that if an electric light bulb is not screwed tightly into its socket, or if an electric plug is not plugged into every outlet in the house, the electricity will leak out into the room, like lightning," she heard him telling Josh. "This is not true. . . ." The words had a familiar ring. She had read or heard all this somewhere before, and then, with a little start, she remembered his lecture, years ago, in her school on Our Friend, Electricity.

"I'm going to Paris in June," he had said to her. "Will you come with me?"

"Will Daisy be going too?"

"Not on this trip, no."

The year was 1932, and Josh was four. What would later be known as the Great Depression was settling in, hard, and there were breadlines in the streets of cities. Essie knew that Eaton & Cromwell's stock had suffered along with others, and that the company had negotiated a number of very large loans from banks which were still unpaid, but the hard financial times had not seemed to affect Jake Auerbach's style of living. "We're lucky we deal in basic consumer goods," he would say. "Even in the worst of times, people still need warm coats, they need shoes, underwear, soap—the basic things." Also, earlier that spring, the Lindbergh baby had been kidnapped. A huge ransom had been demanded, and paid, but the child had not been returned and, two months later, its body would be found near the family's New Jersey estate. Among the Auerbachs and their friends who also had small children, there had been much worried talk, but between Jake and Essie there had been no mention of bodyguards.

"If I go, I think we should take Josh with us," she had said.

"I agree," he had said.

Then he had told her the purpose of the trip. He was to be presented with the French Legion d'Honneur.

"Will you wear your emeralds for the ceremony, Essie?"

"If you like."

Extraordinary! This new attentiveness to her. It had begun to express itself in other ways as well. He would knock at her door, and ask to come in. He would sit on her bed and ask to make love to her. Love! Sometimes, while he stood looking lonely and almost disconsolate in her doorway, she would say to him, "No, Jake, no—please, I'm too tired tonight. Please, I'm sorry." But there were other times when she could not force herself to be so cruel. Was this a part of her punishment? To have to accept unwanted love? Was this how justice was meted out? Was this her retribution? If so, she decided, she must accept it. "I love you," he would sometimes whisper. But

I don't love you, she would think. I haven't loved you for a long time. I can even put a date on it, I think. I think it was the day when Prince . . . went away . . . and you turned his life into a bonfire at The Bluff.

But I don't hate you, either. Who are you, Jacob Auerbach, Legion of Honor wearer, friend of electricity? The simple answer came: my husband. The man I asked to marry me. And somehow, just as she had managed to do it once, accidentally, inadvertently, she had managed to make this husband fall in love with her all over again. Extraordinary! So strange! It was another irony, another riddle. Was that what life was in the end—a conundrum? A question, or a puzzle, to which only a conjectural answer can be made?

Some specifics:

"You're going to be gone a long time," Charles had said to her.

"Only six weeks," she said.

"We can't turn the clock back, can we," he said, and she had studied his face, wondering what he meant, because it was not like him to speak in clichés.

"Do you mean you have regrets?" she had asked him finally.

"No. But it's so funny. His new dependency on you. When did it start?"

"I think you know that answer."

"But how do I feel about it? Am I jealous? Is that it? I have absolutely no right to be."

"And I don't want you to be."

"Or am I jealous because, as he grows more dependent on you, he depends less on me? Or is it because he can have you whenever he wants, but you and I have to meet in secret? All I can say is that, at times, my feelings are very complicated, Essie. Sometimes I think it's I who should be in Silver Hill, and not Cecilia."

"Complicated," she repeated. She smoothed his brow with the palm of her hand. "It's complicated for me, too," she said. "Difficult. All *I* can say is that if it weren't for you it would be just—unbearable. No, that's too strong a word. Empty. Dust in the mouth."

"For me also." Then suddenly, "It's just that I can't bear the thought of him touching you!"

She lied to him. *"He doesn't touch me!"*
He turned his eyes away.

Jake had developed another curious interest—genealogy.
He had begun constructing the Rosenthal family tree, writing
to distant relatives in the Rhenish Palatinate, full of questions,
gathering as much information as he could find about the
Rosenthal antecedents. On that trip to Europe in the summer of
1932, they had also visited Germany, where Jake had uncovered long-lost cousins and where they visited cemeteries
and copied inscriptions from headstones.

"Why don't you do the same for the Auerbachs?" she asked
him.

"The Auerbachs were small potatoes," he told her. "But the
Rosenthals are a distinguished family. Mayer Rothschild the
First was a second cousin of one of my great-grandfathers."

Strange to think, of course, that many of those newfound
cousins Jake Auerbach had discovered in the early 1930s
would later perish in places like Auschwitz and Buchenwald.
By the time it became clear that Hitler's attacks upon the Jews,
which at first had been only verbal, amounted to more than a
temporary political aberration—and Jake was offering to send
money to help members of his family to escape—it was too
late. But still the family tree grew, and it was all, Essie sensed,
somehow for Josh's benefit.

"Where should we send him to boarding school?" he had
asked her.

Again, astonishing! He had never consulted her about
schools for the other children. "The boys have always gone to
Lawrenceville," she had said to him.

"But for Josh—we might think of something different."

"Well, what if you and I were to take him around to various
schools, and let him make up his own mind?" she said.

"Excellent idea. We'll tour him around." And he added,
"This summer. Together."

"But Jake, he's only eight!"

"Can't get him registered too soon. Besides, he's bright for
an eight-year-old."

And so the three of them, in a series of chauffeur-driven

cars, had toured Eastern boys' schools, and Josh had selected the George School in Pennsylvania, a school which, as it turned out, was operated by the Society of Friends. Josh had chosen it because he liked the big trees.

"I never felt that Lawrenceville really welcomed Jewish boys," Essie said.

"Neither did I," said Jake.

"Am I a Jew?" Josh had asked his father.

"Well, in a sense, I suppose yes," Jake had replied. This would have been in the winter of 1940, when Josh was twelve, and home for the Christmas holidays after his first semester at the George School. There was some anti-Semitism there, it seemed, even among the Quakers and the Brotherly Love.

"Why don't people like us?"

"The fact is," Jake said carefully, "that *some* Christians don't like *some* Jews. Some Christians feel that some Jewish people like ourselves, who are well-to-do, have too much money. They are envious. They don't appreciate what men like myself have done for the less fortunate. You're too young to remember it, Josh, but there was one day in late October of nineteen twenty-nine—it was called Black Thursday—when I had the experience of seeing my personal fortune reduced by exactly one hundred million dollars. Think of that. And do you know why that was? It was because when the stock market crashed I personally wired every Eaton and Cromwell branch manager to say that I would personally guarantee the brokerage account of any Eaton employee who was in trouble. That day cost me—personally—a hundred million dollars, but it was one of the happiest days of my life."

Yes, Essie thought, smiling, remembering Black Thursday as she worked on a flight of needlepoint geese for a pillow-cover, it may well have been, but what Jake has neglected to mention was that the grand gesture made in October of 1929 was only performed after a large press conference had been called to announce it, along with the great philanthropist's belief in the future of America under Herbert Hoover.

"If that can't be called Christian philanthropy, then I don't know what it is," Jake continued. "You see, there is really very little difference between the Christian and the Jewish religions.

In some ways, they are identical. The Jewish religion, however, is much more ancient. Christ Himself was a Jew, and Christianity springs directly from ancient Jewish teachings and beliefs. That is why you must be proud to be a Jew. The only difference between Judaism and Christianity is that the Jews do not accept the divinity of Christ. To the Jews, Christ was not the Messiah. The Messiah is still to come, the Jews believe. So one way to think of Judaism is simply as a kind of Christianity without Christ."

It was Lily Auerbach's definition of Judaism, of course, slightly altered.

"So simply ignore people who say they don't like the Jews, Josh. They're simply jealous of Jews like us who are well off, and they want to take away our money. So, incidentally, does Mr. Roosevelt—along with wanting to get America involved in Europe's war."

Jake, she knew, was more than a little ambivalent about the prospect of America getting into the war. On the one hand, he took an isolationist stance, and supported people like Charles Lindbergh and the America First Committee. But on the other hand, he knew that Eaton & Cromwell had prospered enormously during the first war, and had every reason to believe that the company would do even better during another one.

Then, a year later, came Pearl Harbor, and America was in the war, and organizations like America First collapsed of their own weight. Secretly, of course, Essie was pleased that Josh was too young to enter the service and that, with luck, he would never have to fight. Mogie, at twenty-three, was just the right age and, to give him credit, he immediately tried to enlist—he had always been fascinated with soldiers and war games. But the chronic ulcers which had been troubling him since his early teens caused him to be rejected. Instead, he secured a position with the O.S.S. in Washington, where he refused to reveal what his actual duties were, though he implied that they were very secret and important.

As had been expected, too, with America in the war, and with government contracts for uniforms and other war materiel, the profits of Eaton & Cromwell began to climb slowly and steadily to heights even beyond those of the 1920s. It was in 1942 that Jake Auerbach announced that, for business reasons, the family's principal residence would become New York, and that he had purchased the large floor-through apartment at 720 Park Avenue. "We'll keep The Bluff as an extra summer place," he said. "I don't suppose we really need it, but this is a poor time to sell."

She and Jake had toured the huge empty rooms together.

"You'll need a good decorator," he said. Mr. Duveen was gone.

"I don't think so," Essie said. "I've learned a thing or two over the years, and I think I'd like to do this one myself."

"Whatever you say."

There were times when Essie wondered how Daisy was managing to raise her daughter. The girl would be about a year older than Josh, growing up, and it could not be easy for a young girl growing up in a small Ohio suburb, knowing that she was illegitimate. Or perhaps not knowing that, but certainly not knowing anything about her father. Did her schoolmates tease her—make her life miserable? How did Daisy handle it all? Daisy, on the other hand, though not an intellectual, was a resourceful woman, and Essie assumed that Daisy arranged for her daughter's life somehow. Daisy made periodic visits back to Ohio, and during these visits Essie supposed that Daisy somehow handled things. All this, of course, was something she and Daisy did not talk about. It would be years before Essie had the answers to any of her questions.

In the summer of 1942, while the world anxiously read reports of the Battle of Stalingrad, while Essie Auerbach toiled in Chicago for the Red Cross, and while whatever workmen and artisans who could be rounded up in wartime toiled with at least the basic refurbishment of the New York apartment, the four played bridge one evening at The Bluff—Jake and Essie, Charles and Daisy. Cecilia Wilmont was always in and out of sanatoriums now, and in four more years she would become a permanent resident of the Riggs Institute in Connecticut, where she would die in 1962. And so they had become a regular bridge foursome, and played about once a month.

They had, as usual, cut for partners, and Jake had drawn Daisy that evening which, Essie knew, displeased him, since Daisy was the least accomplished player of the four, and Jake only enjoyed the game when it was played for extremely high stakes—ten cents a point.

The contract was for four spades, and the hand was Daisy's to play, and Charles had doubled. Jake, frowning, lay down his cards.

"Very pretty, partner," Daisy said, and passed her hand across the table for him to inspect.

He fanned out Daisy's cards, and his frown grew deeper. He returned her hand to her without a word.

The play began, and Essie was immediately apprehensive. She herself had considered doubling. Under the table, she reached out to touch her husband's knee, which he withdrew.

The play continued, and Daisy said, "Oh, dear—where did *that* come from?" when Essie played her jack of trump.

"From Essie's *hand,*" said Jake.

"Oh, dear. . . ."

And when it was over, Jake said, "Down two. Doubled," and wrote the score on the "They" side of the scoresheet.

"I'm sorry, partner—I miscounted trump."

"Let's see—my deal, your make," Essie said brightly, picking up the cards and dealing them as rapidly as possible. Collecting her cards, she said quickly, "Pass."

"One no-trump," said Jake on her left.

"Pass," said Charles.

"Two no-trump," said Daisy.

"Pass . . ."

"Three no-trump," said Jake, and placed his hand face-down on the table.

"Pass . . ."

"Pass . . ."

"Pass . . ."

"Well, thank goodness you can play this hand, Jake," Daisy said, "and I can be dummy," and she began to lay out her hand, face up, on the table.

"Dummy," Jake said, "is a good word for you."

There was a little silence at the table, as Daisy continued to lay down her cards, in their suit order and value sequence, her fingernails clicking against the polished surface of the cards. Then she said quietly, "Excuse me, I'm going to powder my nose," and rose and left the table.

For a moment, the others studied their cards intently. Then Essie said, "Jake, that wasn't very nice. I wish you wouldn't speak to her that way."

Jake said nothing, merely stared at his cards.

"It's only a game. Isn't it supposed to be fun?"

Then, in a low even voice, Jake said, "She isn't moving with us to New York."

"What do you mean?"

"Exactly what I said. She isn't moving with us to New York."

"But what are you going to *do* with her?"

"Do? Nothing. Dismiss her. She hasn't earned her salary in years."

"But Jake, you can't *do* that! You just can't!"

"Why can't I? Why should I support dead wood?"

"Oh, Jake, you can't—after all these years! It's been almost twenty-five years, Jake!"

"I'm aware of that."

"After twenty-five years, you can't just—just *dump* a person like that. It's too cruel—it's—"

"I'll give her enough to tide her over until she finds something else."

"You can't, Jake. Jake, I won't let you. Jake, she's my friend, *too!*"

"What difference does that make?"

"You're moving me to a new city, where I'm going to have to make all new friends. I want Daisy with me in New York— as my friend. You'll have Charles with you, you'll have all your other executives, but what about me?"

"You'll make new friends."

"No! I want to keep Daisy!"

Charles spoke up for the first time. In a quiet voice, he said, "None of this is any of my business, Jake, but I'll tell you this—you're spoiling our bridge game. May I make a suggestion?"

"What's that?"

"Go find her, and tell her you're sorry. Apologize. And let's try to get through the rest of the evening on a pleasant key."

"But—"

"Please, Jake—do as Charles says. We can discuss all this later."

"Well . . ."

"Do it. Go find her. Tell her you're sorry."

"Well, all right," Jake muttered, and got up from the table and walked out of the room.

When he was gone, Essie and Charles put down their unplayed hands and stared at each other in dismay.

"Did you—" Essie began.

"No, I had no idea he was thinking of this," he said.

"He can't—"

"You've got to stop him, Essie."

"Help me."

"We need Daisy, to protect what we've got."

"Protect?"

"To protect what you and I have, Essie."

She would have asked him to explain what he meant, but with the sound of her husband's footsteps approaching across the hall outside the card room she said nothing.

"She'll be down in a minute," Jake said, sitting down at the table again.

"Jake, you owe her too much to treat her this way," Essie said. "You owe her too much."

He gave her a veiled look, and then gazed down at the red baize surface of the card table. There was no reply.

"I agree with Essie," Charles said quickly. "You owe her too much," and now Jake gave Charles the same look.

"I have an excellent idea," Essie said. "Why not let Daisy have the little apartment at the Pierre? We're certainly not going to need that any longer. Let that be Daisy's!"

"Well, we'll see—"

"You owe her that much, at least—"

But at that moment Daisy had reappeared at the doorway, smiling cheerfully, though her face had a pink, scrubbed look that suggested she had been crying. "My goodness, partner," she said, looking down at the unplayed hands on the table, "haven't you even started to *play* yet? Where's our three no-trump?"

And Essie's suggestion was the one that was taken, and the

apartment at the Pierre became Daisy's when they all made the move to New York at the end of that year.

Mrs. Schiff was a very old lady now, but she had been the first of the Old Guard New York group to pay Essie a call—or "pass a call," as Mrs. S. put it—at the new apartment on Park Avenue. She had brought a pair of heavy silver serving spoons, wrapped in tissue paper, as a housewarming gift. "Family pieces," she explained. "The children have been through all my silver, and put their names on everything. But I managed to tuck these two pieces away and saved them for you. They're good, German silver." Then, braced on a pair of walking sticks, she surveyed the apartment. "Very nice," she pronounced.

"It's far from done," Essie said. "There's a lot more that I want to do. I feel a little guilty, of course, decorating a big apartment like this what with the wartime shortages." She led the older woman into the library, and seated her in front of the fire.

Mrs. Schiff gazed up at the Chandor portrait over the mantel, which Jake had sat for three years earlier. "Jacob," she said. "He's gained weight."

"Yes, I'm afraid so. Tea? Or sherry?"

"Sherry, please."

Essie rang for the butler.

"Well, welcome back to New York," Mrs. Schiff said when she had her glass.

"Thank you, Mrs. Schiff. Of course I'm a little nervous."

"Nervous? Why?"

"Well, it was easy enough to get established in Chicago, where everybody is new-rich anyway. Nobody there gives a fig what your maiden name was. But in New York—isn't it old family names that count? And an old family name is something I don't have."

"Your reputation precedes you," Mrs. Schiff said. "The Opera Guild. The Red Cross. There's just one woman you need to know. Eleanor Belmont. She's interested in all the things you are. I'll bring her around and introduce you. She'll have you on one of her committees before you can say Jack-be-nimble."

"That's very kind of you."

"And the holiday season's coming up. Give a party. A big party. I'll give you all the names of who to ask. They'll all come. Out of curiosity. You'll be the hit of New York before you can say Jack-be-nimble."

And so that was how the tradition of the Auerbachs' annual Christmas party was carried from Chicago to New York, with the big Norway spruce tree, the stepladder and the toasts, with Mr. Lewisohn who always wanted to sing the *Lieder*, with Mrs. Warburg who was hard of hearing—always had been—and Mrs. Loeb, who invariably got lost in the kitchen on her way to the ladies' room. It was a tradition that would last for more than twenty years.

"What did you mean when you said that Daisy was our protection?" she asked him. They met, now, in his maisonette apartment on East Ninetieth Street, which had its own entrance from the street, and where Charles's one manservant was discreet.

"Don't you know? Can't you guess?"

"No. I don't know what you mean at all."

"Well, if you don't know, and can't guess, then I don't want to tell you. Someday, perhaps."

"Please tell me."

"Someday."

Now, increasingly, their fourth for bridge was Joshua, whom Jake much preferred as a partner, since Josh had become a clever and aggressive player. When Josh was home on his holidays from school, Jake usually saw to it that there was time for a few good evenings at the bridge table. Essie remembers, in particular, one April evening in 1944 when Josh was in New York for his spring break.

"Dad and Uncle Charles," Josh said while the cards were being dealt, "there's something I've been thinking about."

"What's that, Josh?" Jake asked.

"Have you been reading about this new bill in Congress— this bill for the G.I.s when they come home from the war?"

"I'm vaguely aware of it, yes."

"It's going to offer G.I.s mortgages to build new homes, with only four percent interest and no down payments."

"So?"

"So what do you suppose those G.I.s are going to do with that money? It seems to me that if *I* were a G.I. coming home from a war—well, the first thing I'd want to do, I guess, is marry the girl I left behind, and start having children. The next thing I'd want is a nice house in the country, where I can raise my kids."

"That makes sense."

"I think this means there's going to be a lot of building—not in the cities, but out in the suburbs. And I think that means the suburbs are going to kind of—explode. And I think all those people aren't going to want to go into the city to shop. There're going to have to be a lot more suburban stores."

"Yes, that sounds logical."

Essie noticed that Charles was staring intently at her son, the traces of a smile about his lips.

"I guess what I'm saying is that Eaton and Cromwell ought to get in on the ground floor of this. And start building stores— real stores, where people can buy off the counter, not just mail-order—but not in the cities. In the suburbs."

"Well, of course we had plans to expand into direct retail selling back in the nineteen twenties," Jake said. "But then the Depression came along, and everything had to be tabled, and then the war—"

"But the key is the suburbs," Josh repeated.

"I think," Charles said, "that the kid has just come up with a brilliant idea."

"Well, it's certainly something to think about," Jake said.

And it was not six months later that Essie turned to the business section of the New York *Times* and read:

EATON & CROMWELL ANNOUNCES BOLD NEW POSTWAR EXPANSION PLANS

Eaton & Cromwell, the mail-order giant, has today announced plans for expansion which will mark the company's first venture into direct consumer retailing. The announcement was made by Jacob Auerbach, president and chief executive officer of the company. . . .

As she read on, a queasy feeling began to develop in her stomach.

A series of Eaton retail outlets . . .

Betting on the growth of the suburban market . . .

As Auerbach conceives the bold move . . .

"Returning G.I.s will first want to marry the girls they left behind," Mr. Auerbach said in a press conference held in his New York offices. "These young couples will be eager to start their families. . . ."

"Homes in the suburbs . . . trees and green lawns, good schools for their children. . . .The suburbs will beckon. . . .The future of the suburbs . . . the growth of the suburban shopping center, on the model of one of the very first of these built in Kansas City in 19 . . ."

"The G.I. Bill will make it possible . . . low-interest home mortgages . . . no down payments . . ."

Mr. Auerbach stressed . . .

Mr. Auerbach spoke enthusiastically . . .

Citing research statistics, Mr. Auerbach said . . .

Further studies show, Auerbach added . . .

It is possible to predict, said Auerbach . . .

Looking ahead Auerbach foresees . . .

Essie put down the paper, and removed her reading glasses. They've stolen his idea, she thought. Just stolen it.

Then, a little wearily, she put her glasses on her nose again, picked up the paper once more, and, skipping through the long story, came to the end.

". . . and the most exciting part of the plans," Mr. Auerbach said, "is that the pivotal idea came not from myself, nor from any officer or employee of our company, but from my son Joshua, who is just sixteen years old."

Essie leaped to her feet, the newspaper crushed to her bo-

som, and ran to the window. What did she expect to see? Only
the facades of buildings across the street. Whom did she expect
to hail? The towers of the Queensborough Bridge? Is it possible, she thinks—is it just possible—that in this one good child
she has managed somehow to capture all the best qualities of
both Jake and Charles? And none of their worst? Is it possible?

Twenty-seven

As Jake grew older, he seemed to grow calmer, less impatient, particularly with this son. Mogie had become a moody, difficult young man, something of a loner. After the war, he had come home from Washington, full of international secrets which he would not reveal, though he often spoke intimately of the world leaders he had worked for—"Franklin" Roosevelt, "Harry" Truman, "Joe" Stalin, "Charlie" de Gaulle, "Hap," and "Ike," and "Doug" and "Dickie," as though he had been on a first-name basis with them all, and perhaps he had. He had not married, nor did he show much interest in the opposite sex as far as Essie could see (she did not know, of course, about the collection of photographs he kept in a locked file drawer, in a folder simply marked "M," for Masturbation). He had moved back into his parents' apartment on Park Avenue, where he spent much of his time in his room, listening to his records of classical music, reading his art books, and writing scraps of sentences and bits of verse in his Italianate script. Though he had been offered a position at Eaton & Cromwell, he had shown no interest in joining the company. He continued to see his analyst three times a week.

Josh was much more open and outgoing. The trips and tours of factories and warehouses that had always been promised to Prince, but had never been forthcoming, now took place for Josh. It is as though, Essie thought, Jake realizes that he himself made some mistakes in the past. Whenever it was possible, he took Josh to visit the construction sites of the new suburban stores that were rising across the country, and he had already begun to talk of Josh eventually taking over the company when the time came.

"Wherever we go, he keeps telling everybody that all this was my idea," Josh said to his mother. "It was more like—just a suggestion."

"Well, let's hope it works," Essie said. "If it doesn't, there'll be hell to pay."

"What do you mean?"

"If this suburban move pays off, you'll get all the credit. If it doesn't, you'll get all the blame."

"Golly, I hadn't thought of that."

But of course it had paid off and, by 1950, Essie could read with equanimity, in an article about the "Fortune 500" companies, that her husband's was the tenth largest in the land, and that Jacob Auerbach's personal fortune was estimated at six hundred million dollars. Where did they get such figures? Essie wondered. They probably just made them up. Someone—was it Jake himself?—had once said to her, "Any man who knows how rich he is isn't very rich." But there was no question that Jake was very rich.

"Eisenhower is my type of President," he had said to her. It was not long after Josh had graduated from Princeton, and the same year that Jacob Auerbach himself had been given an honorary degree, a Doctorate of Humane Letters, from the same university. That summer, Josh had formally joined Eaton's, where he had worked for the past four summers at various jobs, wanting to learn the business, as he put it, from the bottom up.

"We're lucky to be rid of Roosevelt and Truman, who wanted to sell us down the river to the Russians," Jake said. "What do you think, Essie? Now that the Eisenhowers have invited us to dinner at the White House, what if I were to call Ike and say that I'd like to bring Josh along?"

"Is that *done*, Jake? With an invitation to the White House?"

"Who the hell cares if it's been done or not? That's no reason why I can't do it."

"Mogie knows Eisenhower quite well, I think."

"But Mogie didn't get an invitation. I'm going to get one for Josh. It would be a hell of an experience for the boy. Besides, if Ike wants me to dinner, it's obvious he wants something out of me. If he wants something from me, I can ask a favor of him."

"Then do it, Jake," she said.

"Will you wear your emeralds, Essie?"

"If you like."

"I've always loved you in your emeralds. . . ."

"Cecilia's dead."

"Ah, Charles. I'm sorry."

But she was unprepared for his stricken look of grief, the tears that seemed to stand in his eyes.

"You did everything you could for her," she said. "She had the best care in the world."

"It's not that."

Then what was it? "I should think that there'd be a sense of release. From the burden—the drinking. In and out of hospitals all the time. What she put you through. Poor Cecilia. I say that even though I found her the most impossible woman—" But suddenly she knew that she should not go on. He was staring at her, not angrily, but almost incomprehendingly, as though she had failed to grasp some essential ingredient in Charles's relationship with Cecilia, and now all at once she knew what it was. Josh had put his finger on it years ago, but Essie had not really thought of it since. But Josh had been right.

"Charles," she said quietly, "I'm sorry. You know, we're very much alike. I know I'll weep when Jake goes."

"Yes," he said. "And so will I."

She came and sat beside him, and cradled his head in her arms, the way her mother had done when she was a little girl and needed comforting.

It had been in the early 1950s, and Cecilia had been briefly home from one of her sanatoriums. Josh and his pretty Katie Coughlin, whom he had known since her days at Smith, had just announced their engagement, and Cecilia had wanted to give a small dinner for them all at the house on Ninetieth Street.

"Is she really up to it, Charles?" Essie had asked him.

"I don't know, but she wants to do it, and we've got to let her try."

The evening had begun pleasantly enough, but, during the cocktail hour—though Cecilia did not appear to be drinking—she became increasingly agitated and distracted, and suddenly she ran out of the room and up the stairs. There was the sound of a door slamming.

In the awkward little silence that followed, Charles whispered instructions to his butler. The dinner table was quickly reset, Cecilia's place and chair were removed, and the others sat down at the table and proceeded as though the hostess were still there. She did not reappear.

After dinner, there were cheerful toasts to the young couple, and the evening ended with singing around the piano.

Driving home with Jake and Essie, Josh and his fiancée sat on the jump seats facing them, and Josh said, "Isn't it funny how Uncle Charles changes when she's not around? He becomes the life of the party."

"It's tragic," Essie said.

"Oh, I don't know," Josh said. "I think he needs a sick Cecilia."

"Why on earth do you say that?"

"She gives him independence. That's what Uncle Charles is all about. If she were a nice, normal corporate wife, she'd tie him down. Charles Wilmont is essentially a loner."

"Parlor psychologist," Katie said. "Then why did he marry her?"

"Because he knew she was a woman who would leave him alone."

"But surely he didn't bargain for *this*," Essie said.

"Intuitively, I bet he did. I've watched him at the office. There are two sides to Charles Wilmont. One is a nice, easygoing, jolly, considerate fellow. But there's also a dark side—a very private side, that he doesn't let many people see."

Well, Essie thought, that much was true.

"He doesn't want to make any deep commitments."

"Well," Jake said, "he's certainly committed to our company."

"Sure, but a company is a company. It's not a human being."

"You're making Charles sound like a very cold person," Essie said.

"Not at all. After all, don't the most decent people always have something to hide? Isn't that better than somebody who just lets everything about himself just spill out all over the place? I'll take a person with secrets over a person with *no* secrets any day. More interesting."

"Do you have secrets, Josh?" Katie asked him.

"Of course!" he laughed.

"Well, I just think that Cecilia is a tragic case," Essie said, "and that Charles handles it as best he can, like a true gentleman."

"And—funny thing. I never noticed until tonight at dinner. Uncle Charles is left-handed."

"Like you," Katie said.

And so, she thought now, it was true, Cecilia had meant something to him after all. He was, after all, a man who needed props, buttresses, and Cecilia had been one of his. So was Jake. So was Josh. So was she. Was he, then, so different from herself? Jake was one of her props, as was Charles, as was Josh, as was Daisy. How could she have been so insensitive? With Cecilia's death, one of Charles's props had simply been knocked away.

Props. When they begin to go, one by one, that is when you know that you are growing old.

Doctor Ornstein had come to her in the library of the apartment where she sat waiting, and said to her, "He's going fast. I think you'd better come." This was in the winter of 1965. Jake Auerbach was eighty-one.

"Call the children," she said to Mary Farrell. And then, "Phone Daisy Stevens and tell her to come." The king is dying, she thought. At Edward VII's deathbed, Alexandra had sent for Mrs. Keppel. Journeys end in lovers meeting.

She had been the first at his bedside in the big, semidarkened bedroom where the private nurses hovered and whispered and rechecked the levels of serums in their syringes. He seemed huge in the bed, too huge to be dying, his eyes closed, his breathing hard. Essie sat beside his bed and covered his hand with hers. In about ten minutes, Daisy arrived from Sixty-first Street, and whispered the news that Joan and Mogie and Josh were on their way. Babette was in Florida, and had been telephoned. At the sound of Daisy's voice, Jake opened his eyes, and when he saw her there he waved her away, whispering, "No . . . no. I want to see Essie alone." With a little sob, Daisy turned and walked quickly out of the room.

Not knowing what to do next, Essie said, "I'm here, Jake," and bent and kissed his forehead.

He said something she could not understand.

"What?" she said putting her ear to his lips.

"Tell me the secret."

"What secret, Jake?"

"The money. Where did you get it? Not in a sweepstakes."

She laughed a little wildly. She had almost forgotten about that, it was all so long ago. "No," she said. "Not in a sweepstakes. It was my mother's savings."

"Your . . . mother's . . . savings," he repeated. He frowned and closed his eyes. "Hard to believe."

And so he had died, it seemed, not knowing whether she had told him the truth or not.

"It's true, Jake," she told him, while a nurse, with a large stopwatch in her hand, checked his wrist for a pulse. "I swear to God to you it's true!"

But he did not answer her.

And the next morning, in all the newspapers, there were the front-page headlines—a full-page obituary in the *New York Times*—the great Jacob Auerbach was dead. Essie has saved all the clippings. They are filed away in Mary's files. Essie could show them to you, if you like.

Joan Auerbach's marriage to Richard McAllister was a quiet ceremony, attended only by Joan's daughter Karen, and performed by a Justice of the Peace at City Hall. Richard McAllister was described as "a journalist and writer for liberal causes," and, within weeks after that, Joan announced her plans to start up a new afternoon daily newspaper in New York. She had not yet received her full inheritance but, in anticipation of it, she had been able to secure several large loans from banks. Babette, too, had invested some money in Joan's project, and so had Essie, who had decided that Joan needed more than men and marriages to keep her occupied and out of trouble.

"New York needs a bright, young, informed and liberal voice to balance the stuffy, self-important and generally conservative *Times*," she told a news conference which she had called, as the new publisher of the New York *Express*, with Richard McAllister, its new editor.

"How do you justify a liberal, or generally left-wing political stance with your own family's conservative tradition, Mrs. McAllister?" a reporter asked her. "Your father was one of America's great capitalists, was he not?"

"Incidentally, on the masthead I will be identified as Joan Auerbach," Joan said. "To emphasize that the *Express* will be much more than a Mom and Pop operation."

There was laughter, and then Joan continued with her answer to the question.

This is what the newspapers printed:

"While it is true," said Mrs. McAllister, who will use the "professional" name of Joan Auerbach, "that my late father achieved great wealth in his lifetime, and was a longtime supporter of Republican causes, it should not be assumed that I have spent my entire life surrounded by luxury. On the contrary. When my younger sister and I were growing up, we were dirt poor. I had no toys whatever, and I went to school in rags and tattered garments. Our house was little more than a hovel. It had no heat, and I was often starved for food as well as affection, since Mother was far too busy keeping house and caring for a husband and growing family to give any attention to the needs of a little girl. In those days, our father worked in a menial position in a store owned by some cousins in New York. Quite often, there was not enough money to put bread on the table, much less to pay for a new pair of shoes for a little girl who had outgrown her old ones. Even in the dead of winter I went about barefoot. To earn a few pennies of spending money, my sister and I set up a small stand at a streetcorner to sell fruit juices. I did not own a pretty dress until I was sixteen. It is hard for my

two younger brothers, who were born after my father
started on his road to great success, to imagine how different my early life was from theirs. But I am perhaps
fortunate to have seen the other side of the coin, and to
know what it was like to be poor. I can champion the
underdog because I *was* the underdog, and have experienced poverty—abject, grinding poverty."

"Jake must be spinning in his grave," Essie said to Josh
when he read the story aloud to her.

"You're feathering your paddle, Essie," Charles said to her.
"We're going around in circles." They had gone together to the
Adirondacks that summer, and planned to spend the month of
August there, just the two of them. It would turn out to be the
last time they would spend there, and the following year Essie
would put the place on the market.

"Is that the story of our lives, Charles? Going around in
circles?"

"If you'll just paddle, Essie," he called back to her from the
front of the canoe. "Just paddle, and we'll go straight."

"So now you're the new president of Eaton's," she said.
"How does it feel?"

"I'm just holding it in stewardship for Josh. Next year, I'm
going to ask them to bump me upstairs—board chairman, or
something. Something mostly honorary."

"Is Josh ready for it, Charles?"

"That kid's been ready since he was thirteen. He's married
to the company now."

"Well, he's married to Katie, and their son."

"I mean married to it the way I've been married to it all these
years."

"Married? And not to—" She left the question unfinished,
and they paddled in silence again across the smooth water.

"Shall we have our picnic in the little cove where we saw the
deer?"

"Yes, that would be nice."

"You're feathering again," he warned her.

"I should have sat in front, and let you sit in back." Then she
said, "We could get married now, you know."

He rested his paddle across his knees, turned and looked back at her. "Do you think so?"

"Well, we could. We're both free now."

"Don't you think we're a little too old for that?"

"Oh, people get married at our age," she said. "Look at Averell Harriman."

"Hmm," he said. "But wouldn't your children—wouldn't they object?"

"We're free to do what we want, aren't we? Without consulting them?"

"No. They'd worry about their inheritance. There'd be a lot of unpleasantness."

"But you and I certainly aren't going to have more children, for goodness sake! Why should they worry?"

They were floating now, not far from shore, both paddles idle.

"But suppose you were to die first," he said, "and decide to leave everything to me. And then suppose I decided to leave everything to a cat hospital. That's what they'd worry about."

"That's silly, Charles!"

"Still, it would be the first thing that would come into their minds."

"Well, I don't care. I still think it would be nice."

"What would be nice?"

"To be married to you."

"I see," he said.

"There's nothing standing between us now—not Jake, not Cecilia. Not even Daisy, to protect us—whatever it was you meant by that."

"Don't you know, Essie?"

"No, unless you meant that Jake—knew?"

"Yes."

"*Did he, Charles?*"

"Yes. Knew. Or at least suspected. I'm quite sure of it. He must have. But Daisy was his Achilles' heel, the chink in his armor. As long as I knew about Daisy, as long as Daisy stayed in the picture, there was nothing that Jake Auerbach could do to touch me. He couldn't touch me, or do anything about us. Daisy was always my ace in the hole, my little bargaining chip."

She was looking at him, now, with dismay, at a man she felt she knew too well. "Do you mean to say that that was all it was for you—just keeping your job?"

"It was more than a job, Essie. It was a career. It was my life."

"And in order to have me—*and* your career—you—"

"I admit I wanted both. Why wouldn't I? Can't you understand?"

"I understand one thing," she cried to him across the length of the canoe. "I understand that I've been *used*—used for more than thirty years! Used as another little stepping-stone in your career! Right from the beginning, Charles Wilmont, because where would you be if it hadn't been for me? Who brought you to Jake in the first place? Where would Jake be, for that matter, if it hadn't been for me—but most of all, where would *you* be? Who sat with you—for three years—trying to break that—habit of yours? Who kept your bloody little secrets for you? Who helped you keep your cake and eat it too? Was that all I was for? And now that you've got both—me, and your career, you say no to me!"

"You're being hysterical, Essie."

"Oh, I see exactly what's happened," she said. "You've turned out to be exactly like Jake Auerbach. That's what you've turned into. That's who you're married to—not the company, but Jake! Jake had his cake and ate it too—your mentor, the man whose shoes you've filled!"

He turned completely in his seat to face her, the paddle still across his knees. "Essie, don't ever say such a thing to me!" he said.

"It's true! I see it in your face, and I can hear it in your voice. It's Jake!"

He raised his paddle. "Essie, I warn you," he said.

"Are you going to strike me with that? Jake hit me once. Is it going to be your turn now?" She stood up in the canoe and lunged toward him, and he also rose, the paddle held across his chest toward her off. "*Sit down!*" he shouted and, with that, the canoe overturned.

"Oh, help me!" she screamed. "I can't swim!"

Near her, she heard his voice say calmly. "Just put your feet down, Essie. The water's only about three feet deep." And then, "Come on. Help me pull this thing to shore."

When they had waded ashore, and pulled the overturned canoe up onto a strip of sandy beach in the cove, and stood, panting for breath, on the beach, looking at each other—two people in their seventies, in dripping wet clothes—they both began to laugh. They were still laughing after Charles had waded back out into the lake to rescue the floating paddles, and had righted the canoe again.

"Look at us. . . ."

"We'd better get out of these clothes. We'll both get pneumonia."

"Thank goodness it's a warm day. We can dry our clothes in the sun—on those rocks there."

"Our picnic's at the bottom of the lake."

"The fish will enjoy it."

"Caviar sandwiches?" They were still laughing.

When they had stripped off their clothes and had arranged them on the rocks to dry, and lay down in the sun on the beach near the water's edge, Essie let herself look across shyly at his naked body. Yes, they had both grown old, but with half-closed eyes she could still see the well-muscled body of a much younger man, in clear outline, and with one hand she reached out and ran her fingertips through his chest hairs. "I'm sorry," she said. "I didn't mean any of those things I said, Charles. You're your own man, and always were. There's only so much you can give me. I don't want more."

"Are you sure?"

"You've given me so much. I shouldn't have brought up marriage."

"There's another thing," he began, speaking slowly. "It's not just how your children would take it. You mentioned my so-called secret past. If you and I got married now, that would be bound to come out. Don't forget we're both pretty well known now, you and I. A wedding—if we were to get married—there'd be publicity. Reporters—they'd dig around. Harvard. Business school. They'd find out none of that was true. You wouldn't want that to happen, would you, Essie? That was really what I was thinking. That would just embarrass us both—and Josh, and the others. I've lived most of my life with my little secrets. I'd like to be buried with them now, if I can."

"I understand." But I understand much more than that, she thought. What made me feel I had to put him to the test at this point? Only to find that Charles is Charles.

He leaned toward her on his elbow and, with his free hand, drew a series of circles in the sand. "But that doesn't mean that it wouldn't be nice to be married to you, Essie. Let me put it more formally. Will you marry me?"

"No! Why should we marry when we have it all anyway?"

He sighed, leaned back.

"Do you remember that night? At The Bluff? Joan's party?" she asked him.

"Of course I remember!"

"Here we are again."

He turned to her. "Do you still love me?"

She smiled. "Always."

He was stroking her breast now, supple and pendulous, the tender nipples, the soft places of her flesh, and he—rounded, smooth, feathery as corn silk, still cool, shrunken and moist from the lake water—was in her hand. "Forgive me," he said, "but I'm not the randy fellow I once was."

"Oh, yes, you are," she whispered, and then, as their stroking became more determined and her breath began to come a little fast, she said, "Look. It's like a garden here, isn't it. This lake is our garden, and you are the tall birch tree growing up by the shore. Here. Let me water it with my lips. Think of nothing. Move a little here. Here, by this soft grassy spot. No pebbles. I will make a garden of my body. What did the girls in Delancey Street say? They could make gardens of their bodies, even in the shadows of the tenements, even in winter . . . my knees are like mountains. Let me taste your tree in its grassy place again."

After a time, he lay back again. "No use. Too old."

"No! Try that. Yes, let me try that. What did those girls say? I pretended not to listen, but I did anyway. Put your hand there, let me do the rest. There, you see? Oh, Charles, come to me in my garden. See, there it is, like a tree. Don't move for a moment, darling. Just lie still in my garden. There is a golden thing growing—yes, oh, oh, yes, do that. Is it warm there? Are . . . is . . . oh, yes . . . oh, my love. I do, did, can, will. Have done, do. *Do!*"

Afterward, they had fallen asleep and when they woke the sun was low over the trees and their clothes were stiff and dry on the rocks. A loon was calling.

"We'd better get back."

Then why, after that, when they were paddling back across the smooth lake in the righted canoe on a perfect summer evening, had she suddenly felt tears come? "What do I have, Charles?" she asked him. "Why am I crying?"

"What's wrong, Essie?"

"I have everything, don't I? Children . . . grandchildren . . . beautiful houses . . . beautiful things . . . all the money in the world . . . you . . ."

"What is it?"

How could she tell him that she felt as though she had flown out of her body, and was weeping for all lost things from some other past: Mama, Papa, Prince, Jake's old self.

"Here, let me do the paddling. You're feathering again. What's *wrong*, Essie?"

"No . . . no. . . ." He would never understand, not in a lifetime of explaining it. And she had wept all the way across the lake, sobbing uncontrollably, leaving him to pilot the canoe alone. And when they came to the landing, she had scrambled awkwardly, still weeping, up onto the dock, and had hurried down its length and up the path, into the big log house and up the stairs to her bedroom and flung herself onto the bed. He had followed her up and sat beside her on the bed, rubbing her shoulders. "Essie, please tell me what's the matter," he kept repeating.

"No . . . no. . . ."

"Please. Was it me, Essie?"

"No . . . don't you understand? I'm afraid. I'm afraid to die."

"You're not dying, Essie!"

"I'm old . . . we're old . . . where did everything go?"

"You're not old, Essie. We still have everything."

"No . . . no. . . ." Still she could not stop. She had continued to weep, noisily, like a child, for what seemed like hours

while he sat there with her in the darkness—wept until her
pillow was as drenched with tears as her dress had been that
afternoon from the lake, until there were no tears left, weeping
for nothing at all.

At least that was the way she remembered it.

It may not have been that way at all.

You know.

Twenty-eight

Now Essie and Josh are seated in the wide backseat of the limousine, and Mary Farrell sits on one of the jump seats facing them, a briefcase on her lap. The car moves slowly through the uptown traffic on the East River Drive, toward the Triborough Bridge and LaGuardia Airport. A light snow is falling, and Essie adjusts the soft fur robe across her knees.

"Do you have your little speech down pat?" Josh asks her.

"As pat as it'll ever be. At least Mary thinks so."

"You'll be fine," Mary assures her. "Besides, you'll have the words right on the podium in front you, Mrs. A, if you should happen to lose your place. Which you won't."

"Ha! Don't be so sure. Let me look at it again, Mary."

Mary removes the sheet of paper, neatly typewritten, triplespaced, from her briefcase, and hands it to her.

"'My husband, Jacob Auerbach, was a pious man . . .'" she begins. "Oh, but he wasn't, Josh! That's the trouble with all this. He wasn't the least bit pious, and you know it."

Josh touches her gloved hand. "That's just what's called a lead-in, Mother. To get to the Talmudic part, which we all like so much. He was interested in history, which is the point."

"Was he? I don't seem to recall this interest in history, unless it was trying to get one of his great-grandfathers related to the Rothschilds. Now tell me again who's going to be there."

"Mayor Byrne, Chuck Percy, Vice-President Bush . . ."

"I mean family."

"Everybody. Except Babette and Joe. Oh, and Linda. Linda

383

can't get the time off from her job. And Babette says she won't be under the same roof with Joan."

"Why not?"

"She's suing Joan, Mother—remember? For pirating her trust. So under the circumstances—"

"And what's Joan doing about that?"

"Well, she's hired Roy Cohn as her lawyer. Need I say more?"

The car has moved out of the heavy traffic now, and moves smoothly up the curved access ramp to the bridge.

"So who does that leave?"

"Mogie and Christina, Joan, Karen and Daryl. . . ."

"Daryl?"

"Karen's new husband, Mother, remember? You were at the reception."

"Of course I remember. Now don't try to rattle me, Joshie. I'm nervous enough as it is. What about Daisy?"

"Daisy says she'd rather not be at the speakers' table. But she'll be in the audience. She'll also be coming to your little cocktail party tonight at the hotel."

"Cocktail party? What cocktail party?"

"Mother," he says patiently, "I went over all this with you last week. Just a small cocktail party, in your suite at the Ritz. You don't have to do anything, the hotel will handle it all. It's just for the family. And—of course—Daisy."

"Of course. Well, I'm glad she's coming to that."

"Then, the plan is for you to have a quiet Room Service dinner in your room. You can invite anyone you want to join you. But I'd suggest early to bed, so you can be fully rested for tomorrow."

"Charles," she says.

"Hmm?"

"I think I'll ask Charles to dine with me. He's coming, isn't he?"

"Of course. We're all meeting at the plane."

Essie looks out through the blue-tinted glass at the passing shapes of the city, as Manhattan gives way to the less prepossessing aspects of Queens. "What must people think of us?" she says.

"Who, Mother?"

"People. Watching us drive by like this. Like royalty." And then, "Chicago. It used to take a full day or a full night to get there on the train. Now it takes—what?"

"Less than an hour, Mother. And with the time change, we'll actually get there a few minutes before we left."

"I'd forgotten about the time change," she says.

"So you get an extra hour of sleep tonight."

"Yes."

"Would you like to go out to see The Bluff tomorrow? We can fit it into the schedule, if you'd like."

"No. Definitely not. Whatever they've done to it, I don't want to see."

"Very nice housing, actually. It's called Lake Bluff Estates."

"Well, nice housing or not, I don't want to see it."

"You were wise to sell it when you did. In today's market—"

"Wise? I just wanted to stay in New York."

"But still—"

They ride in silence for a while, and Essie studies the typewritten words on the sheet of paper in front of her in the fading afternoon light. "Of course this is temporary," she says.

"What's that, Mother?"

"*This,*" she says, shaking the cane that rests against the seat beside her. "Didn't I tell you? I tripped on the rug in the library. But it's just a mild sprain. Nothing broken."

"I know, and remember what I told you, Mother. I think you should replace that Aubusson with a good wall-to-wall carpet. The Aubusson tends to bunch up. It's dangerous."

"And get rid of my Aubusson? Never." She looks out the window. "Now where are we?"

"Coming into LaGuardia. The jet's parked in the Eastern Shuttle terminal, and the driver will take us right to the plane."

"I never met him."

"Who?"

"Mayor LaGuardia."

Mary Farrell shifts her position in the jump seat. "Now, there's nothing at all to worry about, Mrs. A," she says.

The car turns through a gate in a hurricane fence marked NO ADMITTANCE, moves slowly across the tarmac, and comes to a stop in front of the Eaton & Cromwell jet. The chauffeur hops out, moves quickly around the car, opens the door on Essie's side and offers her his arm. "This is only temporary," she explains, showing him the cane. Nonetheless, he holds her elbow firmly as he helps her out of the car. Then Josh is at her other elbow, and they move slowly toward the short flight of steps leading up into the plane. At the top of the steps, a young man in a white mess jacket stands at attention. "Mother, this may be a little slippery, because of the snow," Josh warns her.

"I'll be fine."

"And this is our steward, Jim Ulrich," he says.

"Mrs. Auerbach, welcome aboard." Jim Ulrich is all youthful smiles, and his fine brown hair is blowing in the wind. "Here, give me your hand. . . ."

"This is only temporary," she says again, indicating the cane. And then, sharply, "Mary—have you got my speech?"

"Right here, Mrs. A," Mary says, patting the briefcase.

"Good! Don't lose that!"

Mary, who has many other Xeroxed copies of the speech in the briefcase and in various other pockets of her luggage as well, says nothing.

Helped aboard the plane, Essie sees the various members of her family rise from their seats to welcome her. There is Katie, Josh's wife, and there is young Josh; there is Karen and What's-his-name, her new husband, and there are Joan, Mogie, and Christina, and there indeed is Charles. Essie waves them all a distracted greeting. The interior of the plane is like no other she has ever seen—more like a small lounge on an ocean liner than an aircraft. It is all done in blue and gold which, of course, are the Eaton & Cromwell company colors, and instead of ordinary airplane seats there are a series of swivel club chairs and sofas in blue leather, each with a coffee table in front of it. On each table, there is a white telephone. In the front of the cabin is a bar, with barstools, and over this hangs a large television screen. The entire cabin is carpeted with thick gold carpet. "I want to sit in the back," Essie says.

"You'll get a better view from up front, Mrs. A."

"No. Whenever I read about a plane crash, it's always the stewardesses sitting in the back who get saved. Everybody else gets killed."

"Wherever you like, Mrs. A," Mary says, and they head toward the curved blue leather sofa that wraps around the tail end of the jet.

"When do we leave, Josh?"

"As soon as you're settled, Mother."

"Can I get you something from the bar?" Jim Ulrich asks her.

"Yes!" Essie says, perhaps too loudly. "A martini. Gin. Very dry. On the rocks."

The door of the plane is closed and, beside her, Mary Farrell helps Essie extricate the seat belt from the tufts of the blue sofa, and helps fasten it about her middle. "Let's keep your coat on till the plane warms up a bit," Mary says. The plane begins its taxi toward the runway and, over the loudspeaker, the pilot's voice is saying, "Ladies and gentlemen, welcome aboard Eaton and Cromwell's flight to Chicago. There are a few facts you might like to know about our aircraft and our flight today. We are flying a Gulfstream Three, one of the newest, fastest . . ." Essie realizes that she has to go to the bathroom, and she whispers to Mary Farrell. Mary takes Essie's hand and says, "Can you wait a minute or two until we're in the air?" But it is too late and, throwing Mary an agonized look, Essie feels the warm water gathering in her underthings, her dress, and in the folds of the lining of her mink coat. "Ssh," Mary whispers. "Pay no attention. No one will notice. We'll take care of it later."

The twenty-eighth-floor suite at the Ritz-Carlton Hotel is certainly very nice, and Josh, who has overseen the arrangements, certainly appears to have thought of everything. The sitting room and dining room are filled with flowers. Though Essie has never been personally fond of florists' "arrangements," preferring simpler treatments with just two or three blooms, there are bowls of spiky gladioli interspersed with calla lilies, anthuriums, rosebuds and baby's breath, dramatically framed by tall ti leaves. Bowls of salted nuts and Godiva chocolates have been placed about on tables, along with two baskets of fresh fruit and cheeses, with appropriate napkins and silverware. A full bar has been set up, and bottles of iced champagne are chilling in silver coolers. The kitchen refrigerator has been stocked with orange juice and sweet rolls, and Josh has even thought to provide her with a small stack of dollar bills, in a silver money clip, to be used as tips for maids and waiters. Essie has bathed and changed, and her laundry, including the mink coat, has been sent out for cleaning—with a discreet explanation from Mary of the problem, and with the promise that everything will be returned first thing in the morning. Now it is six o'clock, and a waiter has arrived with a large trayful of hors d'oeuvres—smoked salmon, caviar, stuffed artichoke bottoms, little Vienna sausages in a chafing dish—and soon the others, who are all staying in the hotel, will be gathering, and Mary is lighting the candles. "We've asked for three waiters," Mary says. "One to tend bar, and two to pass. I think that's everything, Mrs. A. If you need anything, my room is right across the hall. I've written the number on the note pad by your bed. Just pick up the phone."

"Thank you, Mary. As always, you're a godsend."

"I hope it's a lovely evening, Mrs. A."

"Well, it couldn't be worse than last Christmas, could it? Goodness, it's almost Christmas again."

"Good night, Mrs. A. . . ."

The first to arrive are Mogie and Christina—Mogie in black tie, and Christina in a red chiffon evening dress—and they are quickly followed by Joan, Josh, Charles, and the others.

"Golly, Mrs. Auerbach, what a beautiful apartment!" exclaims Daryl Carter—for that is the name of Karen's young husband, Essie remembers it now—"It's one of the most beautiful I think I've ever seen!" Mr. Carter still tends, Essie thinks, to be somewhat overawed by Auerbach purchasing power. But that, perhaps, will pass with time.

"Well, it's a little hotelish and impersonal, but I'm only going to be here overnight."

He takes her by the elbow and steers her to a corner of the big sitting room. "A quick word with you," he says in a low voice. "I want you to watch my Karen tonight. We've been going to A.A. meetings together."

"A.A.? What's that?"

"Alcoholics Anonymous. We go together."

"Are *you* an alcoholic?"

"No, but I've finally gotten Karen to admit she has a problem. I go to the meetings with her for support."

"Very nice of you, I must say."

Leaning close to her ear, he says, "She's been sober for two weeks, and so tonight may be a little rough on her. Her first cocktail party. But I think you're going to be proud of her."

"I think this is all a very promising development," Essie says.

"Just wanted you to know. I know how really concerned you've been about her."

Essie wants to tell him that, on the contrary, she has long since passed the point of being concerned about, or even surprised by, the behavior of any of her children or grandchildren. She lets this thought pass through her mind, and out again, and simply says, "I'm glad."

A waiter moves among them, passing drinks, and everybody seems to be expounding on how fit Charles looks. Well, he does look fit, but Essie permits herself a jealous thought: Why has no one remarked on how fit *she* looks? Essie moves back into the room again and says, "I'm afraid I was a little nervous and rattled on the plane, and I didn't really get a chance to talk to any of you. But anyway, I'm glad you're here." She lifts her glass. "Cheers. *L'chayim*. And Merry Christmas."

"Hear, hear," several voices say, and there is the sound of glasses clinking.

"Here's to Mother," Josh says. "And thanks for coming."

"Hear, hear . . ."

"Golly," says Daryl Carter, who is still hovering close to her. "Just think—the tallest building in the world!"

"I think we'll all be pretty proud and impressed by what we see tomorrow," Josh says.

More drinks come, and hors d'oeuvres are passed, and the candlelit room fills with chatter.

"Mother Auerbach, are you ready for some exciting news?" a woman's voice calls out. Mother Auerbach, Essie thinks? But surely she cannot be here. Essie distinctly remembers going to Lily's funeral. It was years ago. Then she realizes that the woman speaking is Christina, and that Christina is addressing her. "News? What news?" she asks.

Christina Auerbach swirls the skirt of her dress with one foot, tosses her blond hair, and raises her glass high. "Mogie and I are going to have a baby!" she cries. "The O.B. says the end of March. You're going to have another grandchild, Mother Auerbach. Is that *super?*"

"Well. Congratulations," Essie says.

Christina winks broadly at her husband. "Lord knows we tried hard enough, didn't we, honey?" she says.

Essie glances at Mogie for a reaction to what—or so it seems to Essie—is not an entirely appropriate remark. But Mogie's face is beaming, pleased as punch.

Joan, who has seemed somewhat subdued up to this point, now sits forward in her chair and, with a little smile, says, "That's lovely, Tina. And now I have some pretty exciting news of my own."

Christina, looking somewhat crestfallen at having been so quickly upstaged, says, "Oh? What's that, Joanie?"

"I'm going to make a movie."

"*Really?* You mean produce—"

"No," Joan says, still smiling in the direction of her left elbow. "Not produce. Act. Star in, actually."

"Oh, Joanie, how *fabulous!* How did that happen?"

"Isn't it funny? For years, people used to tell me I looked exactly like Gene Tierney. And now they want me to do this movie."

"But *how?*"

"Roy. He set it up for me. He has all these Hollywood contacts."

"Who is Roy?" Essie asks.

"Roy Cohn. My lawyer."

Essie thinks: clever Mr. Cohn, to come up with some new project for Joan, who has always needed a project of some sort, to divert her boundless nervous energy from her legal problems into something that probably has not much to do with anything, but will give her something to dine out on for a while. Still, there is something about Joan's announcement, and the manner in which it is being delivered, which gives Essie a slightly uneasy feeling.

"Well, tell us *more*, Joanie!"

"It's a made-for-television movie about the Kennedys. I play

Rose Kennedy—as a younger woman, of course. When Roy heard about the part, he decided I'd be perfect for it. He asked me if I'd do it, and I thought—why not? My divorce from Richard will be final in three more weeks, and I'll be free as a breeze."

"That's just *fabulous*, Joanie! When do you start?"

"We're just waiting for the contracts. Once they're inked in, we'll have a deal."

"Oh, Joanie, that is scrumptious news," Christina says. "Can we come on the set and watch you? I've always wanted to see a movie being made."

"Well," Joan says carefully, "I may insist on a closed set. My first acting experience, after all. . . ."

Essie has been counting heads. Someone is missing. "Where is Daisy?" she asks.

"She telephoned," Josh says. "She'll be a little late. Her plane was delayed because of New York weather, but she'll be here."

"Oh, good."

"Joanie, I just think that this is the most exciting news," Christina says again. "I'm so happy for you—it's much more exciting than having a little old baby. Any woman can do that."

Christina, believe it or not, is rising in Essie's estimation. Real joy over another's good fortune is something one doesn't encounter often these days, and it is altogether pleasant to behold. Essie only hopes that Joan appreciates this. Christina may not be a particularly bright woman, but at least she is a good-hearted one. For a good heart, a woman deserves high marks.

". . . I just want to quickly go over the seating tomorrow at the speaker's table," Josh is saying to her. "On your left will be Uncle Charles, and on your right will be a fellow I want you to be par*ti*cularly nice to—one of our most important suppliers, Ekiel Matoff."

"Who?"

"Ekiel Matoff—head of the Matoff Shoe Company. He makes all our men's and women's footwear."

Essie's head feels as though there are cobwebs growing in it, and she reaches for another martini from a passing tray. Could it be possible that there were two men in the world named Ekiel Matoff, and both in the shoe business besides? No, she thinks, it could not be possible, he must be the same. So much, then, for her long-ago vision of Ekiel Matoff as a victim of the Old World who would never enter the new. So much for looking for symbols in anyone, or in anything.

"He's sort of Mr. Shoes, U.S.A.," Josh says. "Kind of a curmudgeonly type, like a lot of self-made men, but don't worry. Under the gruff exterior he's a nice old guy. You'll like him."

"I think I met him once, years ago," she says at last, thinking: I am dreaming, and this is a dream.

"The podium and the mike will only be one chair away from where you'll be sitting. So when it's your turn, and when I introduce you, all you'll have to do is stand, step behind Uncle Charles's chair, and you'll be at the mike. A copy of your speech will have been placed on the podium ahead of time."

"Josh, sit down beside me for a minute," Essie says, patting the seat beside her. "I'm worried about Joan. What's this movie business she's talking about, anyway?"

"Just one of Joan's schemes," he says, sitting down. "Pie in the sky."

"*Another* pie in the sky! I'm positive of it. Just like her newspaper. Nothing will come of it—you know that. But the trouble with Joan's pies in the sky is that they always cost her money. This movie thing—wait and see. Before it's over, they'll be asking her to invest in it, and another pile of money will go down the drain."

"That does seem to be Joan's pattern, Mother."

"Please don't let it happen again." She leans close to him and whispers urgently, "Joshie, I want you to promise me something. You know Joan as well as I, but she's still my daughter and I don't want to think of her going bankrupt or starving in the streets, with all her money spent on Hollywood lawyers. When I'm gone, will you promise to take care of Joan for me? Will you promise to take care of the money Joan will get from me? I want Joan to be comfortable, I want her to be well off as she has every right to be. But she needs to be *controlled*, Josh. Will you be that control when I'm gone?"

"Don't talk like that, Mother."

"But I must. It's important. I'm going to be ninety, Josh. Joan's money must be controlled. She must be put on an allowance, or something. When I'm gone, there'll be only you to do it. Promise you will."

"Joan isn't going to like that very much, Mother."

"I don't care a fig whether she likes it or not! It's got to be done. Otherwise, it'll all go—" she waves her hand "—to Hollywood."

"All right, Mother. I promise."

"What are you two whispering about?" The voice is Mogie's, and he is standing in front of them in his dinner jacket, smiling slightly, drink in hand. "Family secrets?"

"No!" Essie says impatiently. "It's no secret at all." The martinis have given her courage, and she raises her voice so that the whole room can hear. They want her to give a speech, she thinks. Very well, she will give them a speech. "Josh and I were talking about Joan," she says, and her eyes find her daughter across the room. "Joan," she says, "we're all delighted with this movie thing of yours, as Christina has said. But your father used to talk a lot about a company's 'track record,' and I was simply saying to Josh—and I will gladly remind you—that in business as well as matrimony your track record stinks!"

"Mother!"

"And so I was saying to Josh that I do not want to see my daughter going bankrupt or starving in the streets. And I was saying to Josh that I do not wish to go to my grave without knowing that Joan will always be comfortably taken care of."

"Joan doesn't need you to take care of her," Mogie says.

"Shut up, Mogie!" Joan shouts. "We all expect to be taken care of, don't we? Let her finish what she has to say."

"And I was saying to Josh that since I do not want my daughter starving in the streets, it will be necessary to appoint someone to manage her money for her after I'm gone. To manage whatever sums she inherits from me. To handle the purse strings. And I have asked Josh to take on that assignment from me, and he has given me his promise to do so. Since you're all family, this pertains to all of you. There. That's all I have to say to you this evening, before God and this company."

"Josh!" Joan cries. "Josh, Josh, Josh! It's always Josh, isn't it, Mother? Well, I won't stand for this. I'll sue. I'll—"

"You won't sue," Essie says loudly, "because it's my will. And you are all witnesses to my will, every Jack Stout of you! There," she says, pausing for effect. "As I believe Huey Long once said, 'I guess that will show the yellow-bellied sapsuckers where the bear sits in the buckwheat patch!'" In the silence that follows, Essie sees, out of the corner of her eye, Karen moving quietly toward the bar. "*Karen!*" she warns. "Remember Alcoholics Anonymous!" Karen sits down hard on the nearest chair, head lowered, shoulders hunched, twisting her rings.

"Mother, I think you're drunk," Joan says.

"Think what you will, said hard-hearted Jill."

"Well, there's one more thing I'd like to know, while we're on the subject of Josh—" Joan begins.

And it is at this precise moment that Daisy Stevens St. George chooses to open the door to the suite, and step into the sitting room, a little breathless, in fur scarves. "Oh, dear," she says after a moment, looking about at the others. And then, "I think I've picked a bad moment—"

"Nonsense," Essie says. "We were just thrashing things out, as usual. Come right in—you know everybody here. You're family, too. Joan just told me I was drunk, and maybe I am. Waiter, fix Mrs. St. George a drink, and while you're at it, I'll have another myself. Welcome to the family, Daisy. And now Joan says she has a question she wants to ask."

"Oh, dear," Daisy says again, sitting down, still in her scarves.

There is another silence, and then Mogie says, "You've put us all in a listening modality, Mother, with that little speech."

"What does that mean? Psychobabble. You always were a damned fool, Mogie."

Mogie is still smiling, but it is an unpleasant smile now, and his eyes are like slits, and Essie briefly wonders—as she occasionally has in the past—whether he is "on" something. The smile reminds her, too, of the terrible temper tantrums of his youth, when even Miss Kroger claimed she could not control him, and when that first alienist, who specialized in troubled children, Dr. Von Mark, was consulted and suggested a military school—advice which was not, though perhaps it should have been, followed.

As she watches him, the smile fades. Leaning back against a writing table, he says, "I'll ignore the personal insult, Mother. It's just that we all think you're being terribly unfair to Joan."

"Fair or not, it's what I want," Essie says. "Give the little lady anything she asks for, as the fellow says. Thank you," she says to the waiter, accepting her drink.

Turning to Daisy, Mogie says, "Perhaps you'd like a little synopsis of the scenario thus far, Aunt Daisy."

"Oh, dear. I don't think—"

"Mother has just announced her intention of turning over Joan's entire financial affairs to Josh. He's to be in complete control of her. Of course it's always been Josh this, Josh that, see what Josh says—just as Joan points out. And if it were *me* Mother was trying to zap, I wouldn't be the least surprised. Nobody ever asks *me* for an opinion. Nobody ever asks *me* for the time of day, even though my sperm has managed to fertilize an egg cell that will bring another Auerbach into the world, which is more than anybody else has managed to do recently. But it isn't me—Mother's target is Joan. She's going to see to it that she runs Joan's life even after she's gone. And she's chosen to hit Joan at a particularly vulnerable moment of her life. Her husband's left her, she's had to fold her paper—pretty inhuman, don't you think?"

"Mogie, for Christ's sake!" Josh says.

"Mother is planning to leave Joan absolutely powerless in Josh's iron grip. She'll have no more free will at all. She'll be reduced to a puppet, with Josh pulling the strings!"

With that, Joan leaps to her feet. "Well, we'll just *see* how powerless, how much of a puppet I'm going to be!" she cries. She turns to the waiters. "Gentlemen," she says, "I'm going to have to ask you to leave the room. We are about to have a private family discussion."

"Joan, this is my suite. My party."

Daisy reaches for her gloves and bag. "Really, I must—"

"Everybody stay where you are," Joan says, as though she were holding up a bank. "Do as I say," she says to the waiters who, exchanging anxious looks, hurry into the kitchen and disappear behind the swinging door.

"What I have to say won't take a minute, Mother. But if I'm going to spend the rest of my life under my kid brother's thumb, I think I have a right to know something. And what I want to know, Mother, is who Josh Auerbach's real father is."

"What are you talking about?"

"You heard what I said."

"Joan, you're quite crazy."

Mogie closes his eyes. Phase Three is beginning perfectly.

"But that's what I want to know! He doesn't look like any of us—anybody can see that. He doesn't look like Papa. He has blue eyes—"

Essie stiffens slightly in her chair. The new drink, somehow, is not having its desired effect. She stares at Joan.

Daisy now stands up quickly, gathering her fur scarves around her. "I really think I must go," she says. "I'm sorry—"

"No, stay," Essie says softly. "Joan, please tell us what you're talking about."

"I'm saying that I don't think our Papa was Josh's father, and I'm saying that I think I know who Josh's father is."

Essie closes her eyes. "Say what you have to say, Joan," she says.

"It was Uncle Abe, wasn't it? It was an incestuous rape, wasn't it? Josh's father was your own brother."

Suddenly Essie has a fit of giggles, which threatens to expand into a fit of hiccups. Tears stream from her eyes and, through her laughter, she gasps, "Oh . . . oh . . . oh, Joan . . . you silly woman! Abe . . . rape . . . oh, my goodness me . . . oh, my Lord in Kansas. . . . Somebody get me a glass of water. . . ."

"All right, Mogie," Joan says. "Tell them what you know."

Mogie opens his eyes wide. "What *I* know, Joan?"

"Yes. About incest, rape—Mendel—Uncle Abe."

"What in the world are you talking about?" Mogie asks.

Joan's fingers fly to her lips. "This was all your idea, Mogie! You said it! That day at the Pierre . . ."

"Really, Joan, what a preposterous suggestion. I never said anything like that."

"How they looked alike, how they both—"

"It's not all that uncommon for someone to look like his uncle, Joan. But I certainly never implied—"

"Mogie, you lying little fart! *You know you did!* At the Pierre!"

"I haven't been at the Pierre in ages," Mogie says. "Joan, I think you're hallucinating. Obviously your recent bad luck has unhinged you. Yes, I think Mother's right. Your affairs should be placed in someone else's hands. Mother, I apologize for what I said."

"Mogie, you shit!" She starts toward him, hands outstretched as though to tear him apart. Christina rushes between them, and there is a brief scuffle between the two women, and the room seems to fill with cries and shouts.

"Quite crazy," Mogie says over the confusion. "Shall we call the hotel doctor?" He moves toward the telephone.

Suddenly Joan stands still. She turns to Essie. "Then why was Uncle Abe being paid off all these years, Mother?" she asks.

Essie blinks, and the giggles and hiccups stop simultaneously. "What?" she says.

"You heard me. Why the payoff?"

"How do you know about that?"

"And that's not all I know, Mother. Ten thousand dollars a month. Not exactly chicken feed. Checks to Arthur Litton— Uncle Abe—a known criminal. Going back to nineteen twenty-eight, the year that Josh was born. Coincidence? Not bloody likely, Mother."

"Get Mary Farrell for me," Essie whispers.

"Never mind her. Just tell us what that was *for*, Mother. If it wasn't to keep him quiet—then what?"

"I don't feel well. . . ."

"Just tell us the truth, Mother."

"It was—it was a private matter between Abe and me. It had nothing to do with Josh. It was—to protect, or so I thought, you children, all of us, from some—unpleasantness. Sometimes I wonder if it was worth it. That's all it was. It had nothing to do with Josh, or any of my children."

"Then who was Josh's father?" Joan demands.

Josh, who has said nothing during any of this, but has simply kept his steady, half-amused gaze on all of them, crosses his long legs, sits back in his armchair, steeples his fingers and says in an even voice, "Lay off it, Joan. You're making a horse's ass of yourself. I'll tell you who my father is, if you want to know."

"*Who?*"

Slowly, Josh turns his head toward Charles and smiles and Charles, in turn, lowers his eyes, then raises them to meet Josh's, and he returns the smile. Somehow, some filial gesture seems demanded now—an embrace, a kiss, even a handshake might be called for, but no such dramatic element is supplied, just the exchange of little smiles. The silence at last is broken by a woman's loud sobbing. It is Christina, and suddenly Essie's heart goes out to this forlorn, confused, benighted child.

"Is it true, Mother?" Joan asks.

"How long have you known, Josh?" Essie asks him.

"Sometimes it seems as though I've always known it. A feeling—since I was a little kid, that Uncle Charles was more of a father to me than my own father. Then, a while back, some anonymous friend"—his eyes travel briefly to Mogie—"and I'm pretty sure I know who that anonymous friend was— sent me a silly poem in the mail. With it were two photographs—an old one of Charles, and a more recent one of me. Then I was sure. And it made me feel—"

"Yes, Joshua," Essie says urgently. "Tell me how it made you feel."

He spread his hands. "It made me feel—happy. Pleased with myself. Special. And pleased for you, Mother, and proud of your spunk. And proud to have two parents who loved each other, which the others didn't have. I guess that sums it up. It made me feel happy and proud. So," he says, "now that we've had what seems to be our annual Christmas family row, I suggest that we all go back to our rooms and get some rest before the dedication tomorrow."

"Just a minute!" Joan cries. "If Josh isn't Papa's son, there's no legal reason in the world why he's entitled to a penny of Papa's money. Mogie, we can break the trust! Get me Roy Cohn on the phone right now!"

"Now just *you* wait a minute, Missy," Essie says sharply, feeling the strength which had felt so completely sapped out of her moments ago come surging back. "Before you go calling your Mr. Cohn, you might consider another little matter which has a bearing on this situation. There happens to be a woman named Jennifer Thorpe who lives in Columbus, Ohio, who also might like to know that she is entitled to a share of Jacob Auerbach's estate. Jennifer Thorpe has two children, and at least one grandchild. That's four more people by my count. If you try to cut Josh out of his trust, you can very easily find yourself with four more heirs you hadn't reckoned on—all with perfectly legal claims on your father's estate. Am I right, Daisy?"

Daisy sighs. "You know I came here with certain misgivings," she says. "My position in this family has always been a little—peculiar. I'm a part of it, and yet not a part. But I came for Essie's sake, because she asked me to come. . . ."

"Continue, please," Essie says.

"Well, you all know I was Jake's mistress," she says. "I've always hated that word, but there doesn't seem to be any other. He didn't want me to have the child, and was very angry with me for disobeying him. But I did, and it's true, as Essie says, that Jenny is Jakes daughter. My parents raised her. She was raised as Jenny Jackson—my little conceit. She never suspected she was illegitimate. I told everyone that my husband, her father, had been killed in a car crash before she was born. But Jake's name is on the birth certificate—I had to put someone's name as the father. Of course I've never told Jenny who her father was. And, in fact, Jenny now has four grandchildren, not just one."

"So, so I now count *seven* more heirs with claims for shares of Jake Auerbach's estate," Essie says. "Seven—is my arithmetic correct? Seven people—all perfectly entitled to sue for whatever they think they can get. Oh, won't that be *fun*, Joan? Just think what fun the newspapers will have with all of you when this can of worms gets opened up. Think what fun your Mr. Roy Cohn will have with this—and all the lawyers. Why, I wouldn't be surprised if it cost you all so much in legal fees before you're finished that there wouldn't be a red cent left for any of you! And *that,* come to think of it, might not be such a bad idea!"

Joan turns to Daisy. "Would you ever do such a thing, Daisy?" she asks.

Daisy shifts in her chair. "I admit it would be difficult," she says carefully. "It would be painful—to drag the skeleton out of the closet after all these years—for Jenny, for her children, her grandchildren. . . ."

"You see? I knew it. You wouldn't dare!"

"Now, wait a minute, Joan," Daisy says. "I didn't say I wouldn't dare. I would dare. I would indeed dare."

"You wouldn't dare let all these—horrors come out!"

"Oh, yes I would," Daisy says. "If Essie asked me to—yes, I would."

In the little silence that follows, Joan turns sharply away from her.

"You always were a conniving bitch, weren't you, Daisy," Mogie says.

Daisy's eyes travel to him. "Mogie, I pity you," she says.

Now Essie reaches for the cane beside her chair and slowly rises to her feet. With the assistance of the cane, she tries to reach her full stature, and she is suddenly proud to remember that she had her hair done that morning in New York, that she is wearing the green hostess gown by Charles James which the Metropolitan Museum has asked to have for its costume collection, and that she is wearing her emeralds which, of course, are very fine. "Now," she says, "Joan, you can tell the waiters to come out and clean up. My party's over. There isn't going to be any more bloodshed. You can all go." She turns to Josh. "Joshua," she says, "Charles and I are having our dinner sent up. Would you like to join us?"

He stands up. "Well, I think I've had just about all the emotion I can take for one evening," he says. "I'm going to turn in. But thank you, anyway." He moves quickly toward her, takes her elbows, and kisses her on both cheeks. "Good night, Mother. See you tomorrow."

Essie turns to Daisy with a little sigh. "Thank you, my dear."

Later, when they are alone together, Charles says to her, "Good job, old girl. I was rooting for you all the way. But I didn't need to."

"Charles, can I make it through another day?"

The huge white Travertine lobby of the new Eaton Tower has been turned into an auditorium of sorts, and some fifteen hundred chairs have been set up to accommodate the guests at the dedication ceremony—many of whom are dignitaries, but many of whom are ordinary, curious citizens come to witness the unofficial unveiling of the tallest building in the world, excited by the fact that it is in Chicago, not New York, that in sheer height it outstrips the World Trade Center, the Empire State Building, the Chrysler Building. It also may be, Essie thinks, the ugliest building in the world. At least all this whiteness, starkness, massiveness is not to her taste. The lobby itself is unrelieved by any touch of color, though Josh has told her that eventually there will be paintings on the walls, potted trees and flowers, more sculpture. She has paused, on her way in, to pay her respects to the bronze bust of her late husband, larger than life, which has been placed between the two main banks of elevators addressing a tall wall of sheer glass and a large, parklike plaza just beyond. The speakers' table, draped in white linen, is flanked by many large poinsettia plants in tubs wrapped in green foil, and is surmounted by a large formal flower arrangement of red anthuriums and green leaves—Christmas colors.

"Ekiel Matoff," she says to the elderly gentleman seated on her right, "do you remember me?"

He leans toward her lips, cupping his left ear with one hand, and she realizes that he is hard of hearing.

"Do you remember me?"

"I knew your late husband well," he says. "Fine man. And Eaton's always paid its bills. More than I can say with some retailers I've dealt with in my time."

"If you don't remember me, don't tell me. I don't want to know."

"Yes, fine day for this. Snow's held off. Quite a turnout."

Now Josh is speaking, and she hears his amplified words echoing throughout the marble lobby. "This building was not intended as a memorial to Jacob Auerbach," he is saying. "Nor was it intended as a piece of corporate puffery, nor as a kind of symbol to please our many thousands of stockholders. In fact, if this building is to be a symbol of anything, I would like to believe that it is a symbol of the dedication and devotion of the hundreds of thousands of loyal employees of Eaton and Cromwell who have served us over the years. . . ."

Loyal employees, Essie thinks, who were paid as little as five dollars a week, not even enough for carfare, so little that it was said that the assembly-line girls had to turn to prostitution to make ends meet.

"Our profit-sharing plan, revolutionary at the time . . ."

But what caused that revolution, Jake? Fear of more bad press. Fear of bad public relations.

"Jacob Auerbach's vision . . ."

But was it Jake's vision? Or was it Charles's? Or was it perhaps her own in some way? Of course it was.

"If Jacob Auerbach were here today, I know he would not only be personally proud of this new building, but would also want to say a personal word of thanks to each and every Eaton employee, from the lowliest mailroom clerk to our present Board Chairman, here on my right, Charles Wilmont. . . ."

But would he? I doubt it, Essie thinks. But how can she honestly fault Josh for what he is saying? It is only business rhetoric, the business rhetoric all these people have come to hear. He is, *au fond*, a businessman, not a poet or a rabbi. They were all businessmen—her blacksmith grandfather in Russia, her mother, Jake's mother and his uncles, Jake himself, and now her son. One cannot quarrel with what is in one's genes, and she did not marry a rabbi or a rabbi's son.

"Envisioning the rapid growth of suburban shopping malls . . .

"The dramatic decision to move from strictly mail-order to a chain of retail outlets . . .

"But of course Jacob Auerbach cannot be with us today to share our pride and our gratitude to one and all . . . but I am especially happy to present to you today the woman who shared his life for fifty-eight years, his widow, my mother, Esther Auerbach."

Was it fifty-eight years? Yes, Josh is right, it was. Think of it! Then she suddenly realizes that she has just been introduced, that she is expected to do something, that it is her turn to speak, that Josh is smiling and beckoning to her from the speaker's lectern, that there is applause, that she is expected to rise now. Had Josh warned her that it would be like this—so sudden? She reaches for her cane, but it slides from her grasp and falls to the floor. Deftly, on her left, Charles reaches down for it, retrieves it, and places it firmly in her left hand. In the same gesture, he squeezes her hand and whispers, "Good luck."

Slowly, Essie rises, using both the cane and Ekiel Matoff's shoulder for support, and makes her way with some difficulty—the passageway behind the chairs across the platform is rather narrow—to the lectern, and the microphone that rises from among the anthuriums. She grips the edge of the lectern, and, leaning into the microphone, says, "This is only temporary," and holds up the cane.

There is a ripple of polite laughter from the audience, but what astonishes Essie the most is the sound of her own voice coming booming and echoing back to her from every side of the big room. They have not warned her about that, either!

She knows now, too, that every word of her carefully memorized and rehearsed speech has flown out of her head completely. On the lectern, squarely in front of her, where they had promised it would be, sits Mary's neatly triple-spaced typing, but the floodlights—they have not warned her about the floodlights—are shining so brightly in her eyes that she cannot see the words. The sheet of paper is a white, blinding blank. Essie has often addressed meetings of the Opera Guild, where there were lights and a microphone, but there were never such angry, glaring lights as these, and there were never these thundering echoes from walls of bare marble and glass. She turns the sheet of paper this way and that, but the words refuse to come into focus. Still, she must say something. Clearing her throat she begins, "My husband was not Jake Auerbach. . . ."

There is a titter or two, and some coughing, from the audience.

"No, that's not right," she says. In the audience, now, she searches for Mary Farrell's face, or for Daisy's, or for any face that will seem familiar or reassuring, but she can find no one. In the distance, coming from somewhere—the street perhaps—she can hear the faint sounds of Christmas caroling, voices singing, "O little town . . ."

"O little town," she repeats into the microphone. "When I

first came to Chicago, in nineteen-o-seven, it was a little town. . . ." On her right side, she feels Charles reach out and touch her arm and, on her left, she feels Josh's hand. "My husband and I watched it grow. And now we have this big building. . . . Oh, dear," she says. "I had what I was going to say all memorized. When I was a girl, I was good at memorizing." From the audience, there is more coughing.

"Talmud," she hears Josh whisper to her.

"Talmud," she repeats, and the word "Talmud!" comes pounding back at her from the walls and ceiling. Perhaps, she thinks, if I speak more quickly, I can get the words out like lightning before the thunder, and so she begins again, "But it wasn't the Talmud, it was this: *Der shtrom fun menshenz maysim bayt zikh imer—nemstu dem rikhtigen, firt er tsu glik; hostu farzen—der ganster veg fun leben vet zikh durkh umglik un durkh flakhkeyt shlepen. . . ."*

There are whispers, now, and rustlings of programs, and the sounds of people shifting uncomfortably in their seats.

"But that's not the Talmud. That's Mr. Shakespeare— 'There is a tide in the affairs of men, / Which, taken at the flood, leads on to fortune; / Omitted, all the voyage of their life / Is bound in shallows and in miseries.' But my point is that my husband, who was Jacob Auerbach, became a very rich man— the tide taken at the flood. But the Talmud says that a poor man is more blessed than a rich man. And so I say—look around you—who is more miserable—the rich man or the poor? Those who expect the most often receive the least, and those who expect the least often receive the most. That's from the Talmud, too. My father taught me that, and what are the lessons we remember longest? Aren't they the ones we learned when we were young and new?

"But what is the connection between these?—my random thoughts and memories. What is the lesson to be learned from this new building?" And suddenly there is new confidence— the Shakespeare lines came back so easily!—and now she knows exactly what she would like to say. "To me," she says, "the lesson is very clear. It is the importance of remembering the difference between what is temporary—" She holds up the cane. "—and what is permanent. This new building, this great new building, looks very permanent today, and yet we all know it will not last forever. Experience tells us that. Today, it is the tallest building in the world but, before we know it, someone will come along and build a taller one, and then a taller one than that, and so on throughout the rest of time. This building is not dedicated to the memory of my husband, and perhaps that's just as well, because not even memory is permanent. In a thousand years, who will remember the name of Jacob Auerbach, and who will remember that I stood here once and spoke a few thoughts to you?

"What, then, is permanent? What will last? I believe that only love is permanent, cannot be torn down, cannot be forgotten. Love is the glue of generations, the cement of civilization, the span between life and death. To me, love must be the salvation of nations, the only cornerstone on which any future can endure. That is what must be built in our hearts, taller and stronger and more durable than any mere skyscraper, for love will defy any structure of stone and steel and glass and outlive any plunderer or any war. Love is the staff"—she lifts the cane once more—"we lean on, upon which we erect and dedicate the skyscrapers of our lives, taller and taller, on and on, through our children and theirs. Think of it! What a mighty symbol! Love is what God is. In the end, it's all we have."

She stops. The applause begins, quietly at first, perhaps because they are not certain that she has finished, and then its volume grows, filling the room. In front of her, she sees one woman in the audience rise to her feet, still clapping, and presently there is another standing, and then another, and suddenly the whole room is on its feet, and the sound of the applause is deafening. "Well," she says into the microphone over the thundering of the applause, "that is what I believe. Thank you." And now Charles and Josh, on either side of her, his father and their son, rise to assist her back to her seat. She waves them off, she can make it on her own, and still the noisy clapping does not stop.

At O'Hare Field, it is snowing, and some commercial flights have been delayed, but the weather is not expected to daunt the Eaton & Cromwell executive flight of its Gulfstream-3, which is equipped with some of the most sophisticated navigational equipment in the world.

"I suppose you're all cross with me for forgetting my speech," Essie says.

"Are you *kidding*, Mother?" Josh says. "You were magnificent! I just haven't been able to find the words to say it. It was better than anything I could have written for you. You got a standing ovation—didn't you notice that?"

"You knocked 'em dead, Mrs. A."

"Well, they did seem to like the last part," Essie says.

"There wasn't a dry eye in the house."

"Well, is my jet ready? I want to go home."

"It's ready whenever you are, Mrs. A."

It is hard to believe that she has asked that question—Is my jet ready? It is preposterous. My jet. Still, it is the way one comes, and the way one goes. And of course she is ready to go. "Let's go," she says, first to Josh, then to Charles. "So then let's go." They board the plane, and soon they are in the air again.

"Ladies and gentlemen, welcome aboard. . . . There are a few facts you might like to know about our aircraft. . . ."

Beside her, Mary Farrell whispers, "Here comes trouble, Mrs. A." Joan, in a fitted black Dior suit and a glittering pin by Kenneth Jay Lane, is moving down the aisle toward them. She perches on the arm of the double sofa into which Essie and Mary Farrell are strapped.

"That was a lovely speech, Mother."

"Well, thank you, Joan. I'm glad you liked it."

"It was addressed to me, wasn't it." She puts it as a statement, not a question.

"Well, no—not exactly. But if you choose to take it personally, you may."

"I felt it was addressed to me." Joan is silent for a moment, then she says, "I'm sorry about last night, Mother. I really am."

"Oh, that's all right. We're family, and it was a moment of—well, high anxiety, shall we say, for all of us."

"It's just that—with Richard gone, with the paper gone, I've been so terribly lonely." The Gulfstream bounces, slightly, on a pocket of air, and Joan's shoulders are tipped briefly against her mother's.

"Shouldn't you have your seat-belt fastened, Joan?"

"No, no. . . ."

And then, "Lonely?"

"Yes. It's been harder on me than I think you know. Harder than I've let show. And I'm not getting any younger, Mother."

"Well, neither are any of us, and perhaps that's a blessing. Lord knows, I wouldn't want to be young again. Not even your age again."

The Gulfstream bumps again, then seems to seek, and find, smoother air.

"Lonely," Essie repeats. "Perhaps you could spend more time with Karen, Joan."

"No. Karen has her own new life now."

"Or Linda. Your only grandchild. My only great-grandchild. I worry about Linda sometimes. That she's growing up—too cynical."

"No. Linda doesn't like me much. The generation gap."

"Or," Essie begins somewhat tentatively, "if you could make your peace somehow with Mogie and Josh. Bury the hatchet. That would make me very happy." And make your peace with yourself, she might have added, but does not. Or your peace with me.

There is no immediate reply. Then Joan says, "Are you happy, Mother?"

"Happy?" Essie laughs. "My own mother used to say, 'Show me a woman in this life who's happy, and I'll show you a woman without a brain.' Well. Happy? Yes, I suppose I'm happy enough. I've raised four children—five, if one counts— watched them grow—" She breaks off.

"But when I was growing up, you were never there."

"Never there? Never *where?* I've never understood that argument, Joan, of yours. When you were little, I was there— around the clock! You seem to resent the younger children because they grew up with more *things*. But if you ask me, it was the younger ones who got short-changed. I was so busy helping your father be successful that there never seemed to be enough time—"

"It was as though, when I was about nine or ten, you began to disappear. Perhaps those are the years when a daughter needs a mother most."

"Well, yes. Perhaps. Perhaps you have a point." Of course I

could say the same thing about you, she thinks. Where were you when Karen was nine or ten? Getting married and married and married. But Essie does not say these things. Instead, she says, "But Babette never seems to have felt that way. Or at least she never said as much to me."

"But Babette has no brains, Mother. I'm sorry, but you know that's true as well as I. I, believe it or not, have brains. And feelings."

"Oh, yes. I know." Perched on the arm of the sofa, Joan's thin body seems to sway slightly. "You know," Essie says quickly, "if you're lonely, Joan, you could always come and live with me. Lord knows I don't need or use half the acreage of that big apartment. I could convert the upper floor, yes, and we could—" Once more, Essie can't believe what she is saying. It is something that has been farthest from her thoughts until just now. "After all, we're flesh and blood," she says. There is more to say. The words won't come.

"Yes, but—" Joan laughs softly. "Oh, no, Mother. That would never work."

"Convert the upper floor—just for you. It has its own elevator entrance—"

"No, no. It would *never* work. We'd be at each other's throat in a matter of days—hours—you know that."

"Would we *have* to be? We could—"

"No, no. Live with you paying the maintenance? Live on your money? No, never."

"It could be treated as *our* money, Joan."

"No, I'm not a charity case *yet*, Mother, and I'm not ready for Josh's little handouts, either. You *see?* Here we are already—arguing about money again."

"Always."

A silence. Mary Farrell turns a page of her airport paperback, *Fodor's Guide to Modern Greece*.

"But still—" Joan begins.

"Do you think—?"

"If—No, no. Oh, Mother, Mother."

"Why—"

"Yes, why? What's the point?"

"I'd try."

"But no."

"Well, then—"

"Anyway," Joan says. Then her hand reaches out quickly for her mother's hand, covers it, and pats it gently, and for a moment it seems as though years of recriminations and hard feelings are about to be wiped away in this small gesture. "Anyway," Joan says again.

"You're sure?"

"Oh, yes."

Their hands separate, and Mary, concentrating on her book, turns another page.

"That's a pretty pin you're wearing, Joan."

"Thanks. Another Kenny Lane."

"Women don't wear real stones out anymore."

"No." Joan stands up. She touches her hair. Her eyes are very bright. "The seat-belt light's gone on," she says. "We must be getting near New York. I'd better get back."

"Yes."

Joan moves slowly up the aisle. Mary closes her book. "Mrs. A?"

Essie closes her eyes. Happiness. Loneliness. Well, I did what I could do, and the rest is rainbows, dreams. On cold nights on Norfolk Street, we used to huddle against each other to keep each other warm, but that was before our friend, electricity. And there was Mr. Levy's place with the good egg creams, and there was Union Square in the springtime by the fountain. And there was Prince with his pony at The Bluff, dressed in a new white suit from Best's, but no, he does not have the pony yet, but is rolling a hoop on a sidewalk of Grand Boulevard, or is it Elberon. Papa is at the kitchen table with his books. His voice is harsh: "Can fire and water be together? Neither can godliness and Mammon." And yet there is something in the steadfastness of his faith, a zealousness so pure that it seems carved into his face, that shines in his eyes, that Essie almost envies and wishes she could share, even a little bit of it, for herself. It is so confusing. There is a combustion of children. Jake is a shadow by her side, carrying her books through Hester Street. He will not go away. He follows her down among the paths of trillium, arbutus, maidenhair fern, lady's-slipper and lily-of-the-valley in her wildflower garden, his purposeful footsteps crunching on the tanbark trails. He will not free her, even when she is free. Where shall we spend the winter, my darling, now that we're both free? The Adirondacks? We should have to melt ice from the lake for drinking water, and heat the house with log fires, and cuddle against each other at night for warmth. Do you still love me? Always. Shall we have our picnic here, in the little cove where we saw the deer? Yes.

The young steward, Jim Ulrich, whispers to Mary Farrell. "Is the old lady all right? Is she okay?"

"She's just fine," Mary Farrell says. And, always attentive to order and detail, she places Mrs. A's cool hand gently back into the lap from which it has fallen. Jim Ulrich still looks uncertain but, with that protective, secretarial, and proprietary smile, Mary Farrell reassures him. "She's fine," she repeats. "She's just fine."

"We are being vectored into what is called the Liberty holding pattern," the captain's voice says. "So-called, because our focus is the Statue of Liberty. Below, on your left, is Ellis Island, where so many immigrants arrived in the nineteenth century. . . ."

Outside, the night has cleared. The city glitters like the towers of fairyland, but Mary Farrell does not look out or down, and instead fixes her eyes blindly on Fodor's depiction of the Attic hills. Oh, get us home, she thinks, just get us home.

Epilogue

ESTHER L. AUERBACH
1892–1982
In Memoriam

Because our mother requested specifically in her will that she be given neither a funeral nor any sort of memorial service, we, her children, have each elected to write a short tribute or memory of Mother, which we hope will be shared by our own children, grandchildren, and other members of our family. The result is this small memorial pamphlet, privately printed for distribution to family and close friends. We think it is interesting to note that, when these three short pieces were collated, each of us managed to focus on a different aspect of Mother's character and personality, but perhaps this was inevitable in trying to sum up, in mere words, a complex and many-faceted human being such as Esther Auerbach.

> *Joan Auerbach*
> *Babette Auerbach Stern*
> *Martin R. "Mogie" Auerbach*

JOAN:

It is very difficult for me to write of Mother because, for the rest of my life, I will have to live with the knowledge that, the night before her sudden death, she and I exchanged angry words. It doesn't matter any longer what those words were, or what we were angry about, but the fact that those words were spoken at all I shall forever regret. If a day of my life could be erased from history, that day would be it for me but, unfortunately, it cannot be. At least at the very end Mother and I had a wonderful heart-to-heart talk and were able to make our peace. This comforts me considerably.

I must also face the knowledge that, as far as the rest of the family is concerned, the single most memorable fact about my mother's and my relationship will always be that she and I did not get on. And, to be honest with myself, I must admit that this was true. I regret this, too, and in the months since her death I have struggled to figure out the reasons why it was true.

My brothers and sister used occasionally to say, or suggest, that I was jealous of Mother, and of course jealousy is not a pretty emotion to accept or admit to. But since this is being written to my brothers and sisters too, as well as to my daughter and granddaughter, I would like, if I can, to disclaim jealousy. In many ways, looking back, it seems to me, at least, that I had no cause for jealousy. In many ways, my own life was a happier one than Mother's. Her early years, growing up in New York, which she talked little about, cannot have been easy ones. And our father, when he became successful, cannot have been the easiest man to live with. Yet she lived with him for more than fifty years, and I do not ever remember hearing her complain. She had pride, and she had guts.

No, the real reason why my relationship with Mother was stormy, to say the least, was that she and I were so much alike. I was always *testing* Mother's love—to see to what extremes of behavior I could go, and still have her love. Mother, I think, liked to test people too, for the same reasons. Sometimes it was a subtle form of testing, but it was still there.

But in the end I suspect that Mother's and my habit of testing the strengths of each other's love may have done me some good. I'll mention only one incident. I went to Mother once, wanting to borrow a fairly sizable amount of money. She refused me. Naturally, that made me very angry at the time, and made me eager to do something that would equally anger and disappoint her. That was the way our battles went—what a psychiatrist would call the "dynamic" of our relationship.

In the end, of course, it turned out that it was a good thing that Mother refused me that money. It forced me to go out and do something on my own. I didn't enjoy it much, but perhaps I learned something from doing a thing I did not enjoy. I grew up a little.

Mother taught me not to be lazy, just as she herself was not a lazy woman. In the contest between us, in our lifelong competition with each other, perhaps we both benefited. The only thing I am sure of, though, is that I adored my mother. But I am not sure that she ever knew it.

BABETTE:

What I remember most about Mother was her gaiety and sense of fun, the wonderful energy she threw into giving parties at The Bluff, our home outside Chicago, her love of extravagance and the Grand Gesture. She loved jewelry, for example, and I recall so vividly her wearing, with great flair, the expensive Cartier emeralds which she passed on to me, and which I have had reset in more modern settings. Concerning the emeralds, one anecdote will say it all. Coming home one night from a party at someplace or other, Mother simply slipped off the necklace and earrings and dropped them in one of the chairs in the drawing room. The next morning one of her maids brought them up to Mother's room. She'd found them under the cushion when she plumped up the chair!

That was typically Mother. Devil-may-care!

MOGIE:

As the third-born, and first male, sibling, my early life was, needless to say, dominated by older women—Mother, and my two sisters. Learning to deal with this was, of course, a problem for me.

In order to cope with my fright of the *anima,* as Jung would describe it, I developed a strong and vigorous pursuit of the *animus,* and the intellectuality of scholarship (art, history, literature, and music) became my sublimation. I started to collect, and objects became my obsession. I have, for example, my collection of war games and tin soldiers which, I believe, will handily put the lie to the mythic assumption that in being dominated one cannot dominate. I learned to love and savor the effect of finally being able to control my destiny. Once, I remember my mother asking me why I had decided to collect and write about "things." I asked her, "What things?" She referred to my soldiers. I replied that this focus was simply my attempt to enrich and enlarge my ability to feel adequate; to show my newly discovered options; to have a hypothetical erection, and that through hypothesis comes apotheosis. She was deeply impressed.

Even though females ruled my life, I had no clear idea of the female psyche. Mother, of course, was of a generation which shunned discussions of the "facts of life," and, being a very Victorian woman, not to say a prude, Mother was also of that prim upbringing which, in its proper and straitlaced way, would have been shocked by the writings of Freud, *et al*. But it is clear to me that my cognitive development from infancy onward, my classificatory thinking and transitive inference under the *perceived control* of emasculatory females, can only have been direct result of Mother's own male-dominance.* Though I never knew my maternal grandfather, his influence ruled her life. Similarly, our father, in Mother's eyes, was a classic, God-like Father Figure. He could do no wrong! How natural that she should redirect her male-dominated life to dominance of me! Fortunately for me, of course, when it became clear to me that the matriarchy in which I grew up, and the Puritan repressions which I inherited from Mother were leaving deep psychic scars, Mother saw to it that I received the needed therapy. And the happy result is my beautiful wife, Christina, and our beautiful baby daughter, Artemis Esther Auerbach, named in Mother's memory.

EATON & CROMWELL, INC.
Executive Offices

February 4, 1983

Mrs. Joan A. McAllister
161 East 68th Street
New York, N.Y. 10021

Mrs. Joseph Klein
1089 South Ocean Boulevard
Palm Beach, Florida 33480

Mr. Martin R. Auerbach
4 Beekman Place
New York, N.Y. 10022

---

*See Gold, Irving L., M.D., "Maternal Influences Affecting Latent Ego Lacunae in Sexually Dysfunctioning Males." *Journal of Nervous and Mental Diseases*, 1973, 35, 639–652.

Dear Joan, Babette and Mogie:

Thank you for sending me a copy of the booklet which you prepared in Mother's memory. I read it with interest.

As you know, I declined to participate in this project, not out of any lack of love or respect for Mother, but because I was opposed to the booklet as an idea, and felt that a collection of views of Mother was somehow unfair to her, could not do her justice and that, finally, Mother deserved her privacy—and deserved to leave us with her mystery intact.

Each of you has tried to explain Mother, and I respect your sentiments. But in the end it was the unexplained about her that I treasure most and will carry about with me throughout my life. There are answers to questions about her, in other words, that I do not want to know, explanations about her that I do not want to have.

For instance, one fact about Mother came to light here only recently. In the process of going through old company records, I discovered that in the early days of Eaton & Cromwell Mother made an important financial contribution to the company. This fact has been overlooked in various corporate histories which the company has put out, but it seems that, without Mother's help, Jacob Auerbach might not have been able to get his enterprise off the ground—might not even have become involved with it. What was her role? I don't know, and I don't wish to know, beyond knowing that she chose never to mention it to any of us. Why did she keep this secret? Was it modesty? Or was it the Talmudic tradition which decrees that twice blessed is he who gives in secret? These are more mysteries which I would prefer left unsolved, because if Mother wished to keep a secret from us she would have had a reason.

Then there was the mystery of our oldest brother, Jacob Auerbach, Jr., who was called Prince, who died young, several years before I was born. Mother never spoke of him and, because I knew that Prince was Mother's secret, I never asked about him.

Prince's journey on this earth created a mystery about myself which, again, I do not want explained. Joan has said that it seemed to her at times as though she and I had two different sets of parents. My feelings about myself and Mother was that I had two separate selves—my own, and that of Prince, whose spiritual guardian I somehow was.

Somehow I had the impression from Mother that my mission was to replace Prince in her heart—that I was needed also to care for Prince, to see that he did the right thing, to see that he never got into trouble, and so on. Where did these feelings come from? I don't—and don't want to—know.

And so, throughout Mother's long life, this was what I tried to do. While she was trying to raise us children as best she could, this was what I tried to do to help her. Why I tried, I don't know. I don't want to know. Whether I succeeded, I don't know. Perhaps I did, perhaps I didn't. But it's not a bad mission—trying to replace a loved one you never knew in the heart of someone you love, but will never really know—if you ask me.

Love,
Josh

More Bestsellers from Berkley
The books you've been hearing about and want to read

Bestselling Books for Today's Reader